THE COLONIAL TEXTS SERIES

English Department, University College
Australian Defence Force Academy, Canberra

CTS 1

THE COLONIAL TEXTS SERIES

EDITORIAL COMMITTEE

Harry Heseltine (GENERAL EDITOR)
Paul Eggert
Joy Hooton

English Department, University College
Australian Defence Force Academy
Canberra

Colonial Texts Series

A WOMAN'S FRIENDSHIP

ADA CAMBRIDGE

EDITED BY
ELIZABETH MORRISON

Published by
University of New South Wales Press
Sydney Australia 2052

© Elizabeth Morrison 1988
First published in 1989
Reprinted 1995

National Library of Australia
Cataloguing-in-Publication entry:

Cambridge, Ada, 1844 – 1926.
A woman's friendship

ISBN 0 86840 163 3

I. Morrison, Elizabeth, 1936 – , II. Australian Defence
Force Academy, Dept of English. III. Title
(Series: Colonial Texts Series).

A825'.1

Available in North America through:
ISBS Inc
Portland, Oregon 97213-3644
Tel (503) 287 3093
Fax: (503) 280 8832

Available in Singapore, Malaysia and Brunei through:
Publishers Marketing Services
Singapore 1232
Tel (65) 256 5166
Fax (65) 253 0008

Contents

List of Illustrations:

General Editor's Foreword

The Colonial Texts Series is aimed at providing reliable texts of works of nineteenth century Australian literature which have been out of print or difficult of access through most of the present century. The selection of titles is deliberately slanted towards fiction—novels and collections of short stories—because the length of such work has militated even more than in the case of verse against its re-publication in whole or in part, in anthologies, representative selections or any other form.

The Editorial Committee believes that the provision of such texts will serve important intellectual and cultural purposes by allowing literary critics and historians to recover acquaintance with a range of artistic achievement which has been largely obscured for a hundred years or more. Literary merit aside, the significance of the titles chosen for publication derives from their power to represent to the late twentieth century a fuller and richer understanding of Australia's colonial culture than would otherwise come into its possession. The Colonial Texts Series may be expected to illuminate many aspects of Australia's nineteenth century experience hitherto only little explored: the nature of popular taste, the incidence and importance of serial fiction; the matrix of influences in which Australia's colonial writers were formed and grew up; the milieu which sustained, tolerated, or rejected them.

In short, while the Colonial Texts Series should enhance

understanding of Australia's literary culture as it developed from the middle years of the nineteenth century to Federation, the chosen works will certainly permit a fuller acquaintance with an era in the history of Australian fiction which has for the most part been interpreted in the light of far too small a body of texts.

In order to promote these aims the editors of individual volumes in the Series provide Introductions which outline relevant biographical, historical and critical contexts—a task to which many of the detailed explanatory notes placed after the main text, also contribute. To the extent that manuscript and archival resources permit it to be done, a composition and production history of the text is also provided.

The success of the Series, however, hinges upon the provision of *reliable* texts. Astonishingly few of even the major writers in Australia's literary tradition have been accorded full and accurate scholarly editions of their work, carried through according to the best current theory and practice. With the Colonial Texts Series—the first series of critical editions of Australian literature—it is hoped that the corner has at last been turned.

In line with usual practice the effort is made, for each title, to locate for collation all printed editions of the text produced in the author's lifetime—as well as any extant manuscript material. The policy of the Colonial Texts Series with regard to the selection of copy-text, and the presentation of variant states of composition will be less familiar. Some of the works will be found to exist in only one state with authorial involvement (a first edition usually), but where there exists more than one state of the text in which the author had a hand the Editorial Committee has decided against presenting the traditional eclectic text, determining instead to present a nearly unemended copy-text based on the earliest complete state of the text which is extant. (In practice, it is unlikely that many holograph manuscripts will present themselves; however, newspaper or magazine serialisations may provide a copy-text for some editions.) Thus the internal relationships of the words and punctuation of the copy-text, witnessing a single stage or phase of engagement of the author with the developing work, will be respected. The textual apparatus, which will appear at the foot of the reading page, will record all of the changes for which the author is deemed to have been responsible as the work moved from one state of the text to the next.

Thus the text of a literary work in a Colonial Texts Series edition may be considered as a combination of the copy-text and apparatus, for alterations the responsibility of scribes, typesetters, publishers, and others (and variant readings first occurring in posthumous editions) will not normally be printed there. Before distinctions between authorial and non-authorial variants are made each editor will have compiled a complete bibliographical record of the textual transmission of the work in hand. While much of that compilation will not appear anywhere in the edition, a full historical collation will nevertheless be lodged in the Library of the Australian Defence Force Academy, and will be available for inspection. In accordance with the aim of presenting a copy-text which reproduces as closely as possible the earliest complete state of the text, the punctuation, spelling and style of the copy-text will not normally be regularised; and where a serialisation provides copy-text care will be taken to indicate the manner in which instalments were printed and presented.

A new departure for the editing of fiction, the editorial approach of the Colonial Texts Series is, necessarily, a (calculated) experiment. While there is no intention to apply the approach where textual problems peculiar to a particular work strongly counsel its modification, editors will be testing its usefulness and the limits of its applicability while simultaneously making the contribution to an understanding of Australia's colonial culture which it is the Series' primary aim to achieve.[*]

---

[*] For the background and evolution of the editorial principles adopted for the Colonial Texts Series, and the computer software employed, see: Peter Shillingsburg *Scholarly Editing in the Computer Age: Lectures in Theory and Practice*, Occasional Paper No.3, English Department, Faculty of Military Studies, Duntroon, 1984— republished as *Scholarly Editing in the Computer Age* University of Georgia Press, 1987; Paul Eggert 'Ideological Innocence: Editing in Australia', *Meridian* Vol 5 1986 pp 175-81.

Acknowledgements

I would like to record my gratitude to those who, in various ways, have assisted in the preparation of this edition. It could not have come into being without the archivists and librarians who helped me locate relevant materials and arranged access to them; thanks especially to Jennifer Broomhead and Shirley Humphries at the Mitchell Library, where I consulted the Angus & Robertson correspondence, the papers of Bertram Stevens and Ethel Turner, and the manuscript of 'The Good Old Times'; to Tony Marshall and the Australian Manuscripts Collection staff at the La Trobe Library, where I consulted the papers of W. P. Evans, W. P. Hurst, the Lothian Publishing Company, Percival Serle, the Syme Family and Henry Gyles Turner; to Deirdre Wilmott and the State Library of Victoria Newspaper Room staff, who met my frequent and complicated requests with patience and promptness; and also to Professor Dame Leonie Kramer for allowing me to consult *Australasian* and *Sydney Mail* index files at the Department of English, University of Sydney. Grateful acknowledgement is made to Mr K. S. Cross for permission to reproduce 'The Reform Club' and quote from unpublished letters of his grandmother, Ada Cambridge.

I am enormously grateful to Margaret McNally for her skilful and efficient word processing of drafts and preparation of camera-ready copy. Thanks are due also to Colleen Claudius, Mary Lou Maroney and Trish Middleton for typing and secretarial support and to Paul Ballard and Jenny Crook for preparing the maps.

To Patricia Barton, for generously sharing her scholarship, I am particularly indebted; I should also like to thank Marion Amies, Elizabeth Lawson and Elaine Zinkhan for providing scholarly information to fill gaps in my research. And finally I would like to express my appreciation to the CTS Editorial Committee—Harry Heseltine, Paul Eggert and Joy Hooton—for valuable guidance and encouragement, and to thank the staff of the Department of English at University College, Australian Defence Force Academy for their hospitality and friendly interest in my work.

Editor's Introduction

Preliminary Note

MEASURES

Imperial measures are used in the text and, for consistency and to avoid anachronisms, in the Editor's Introduction. The approximate metric equivalents for the inch, foot, yard and mile are, respectively, 2.5 centimetres, 30.5 centimetres, 0.9 metres, 1.6 kilometres.

CURRENCY

The unit of currency in Victoria and other Australasian colonies in the late nineteenth century was the pound (£), divided into twenty shillings (s) each of twelve pence (d). Gold sovereigns were minted in Melbourne from 1872, while silver and bronze coinage of lesser denomination was obtained from England.

BIBLIOGRAPHICAL STYLE FOR CITING NOVELS

When a work as published in a newspaper or periodical is referred to, the title is enclosed in single quotation marks, for example, 'A Woman's Friendship', 'A Black Sheep'. When a work as published in book form is referred to, the title is italicised, for example, *A Marked Man*, *Path and Goal*.

Editor's Introduction

An analytical portrayal of social and sexual relationships, *A Woman's Friendship* makes ironic comment on a section of Australian colonial society and the roles which women were assuming for themselves within it. Re-publication of the novel now may help to reinstate its author, Ada Cambridge, to the position she once held as a leading novelist of late nineteenth century Australia. It is one of her 'lost' works, published originally through the standard outlet for resident Australian authors of the 1870s and 1880s, the colonial newspaper press, and unrecorded in bibliographies and literary histories.[1]

'A Woman's Friendship' was serialised in the *Age*, a Melbourne daily with a huge circulation, in weekly instalments from Saturday 31 August to Saturday 26 October 1889. One year earlier the Centennial International Exhibition, which looms large in the novel, had been in full swing in Melbourne. At that time the *Age* had been running Cambridge's 'A Black Sheep', the work which was to be published in book form by the London firm of William Heinemann as *A Marked Man* in 1890, bringing the author international fame.[2]

Written and published on the eve of this turning point in her career, *A Woman's Friendship* amply demonstrates the considerable development of Cambridge's literary talent, gives insights into her distinctive use of irony[3] and provides powerful

THE AGE, SATURDAY, AUGUST 31, 1889.

FOOTBALL GOSSIP.

(BY FOLLOWER IN THE LEADER.)

That the atmosphere of Victorian football has been cloudy during the past week or two can hardly be denied, and I am not by any means certain that the mist has quite lifted yet. There is a very strong probability of a crisis being at hand, and the outcome is war from being an agreeable certainty. It may, indeed, very soon become a question as to whether Victorian football will continue to be supported by those who have made it and rightly appreciate it as a manly British pastime, or by an entirely different class of people who devote their time and attention to the game merely because it is "good business." With every desire to avoid sensationalism I warn those who really care for the game that the time is probably at hand when they may be called upon to re-establish the fair fame of Victorian football by the adoption of strong measures, or leave it to the tender mercies of unworthy sponsors. The proceedings of the past couple of weeks have set folks thinking, and have given undeniable rise to some doubt in the public mind as to whether this same game of football which has evoked for years past the enthusiastic, almost frantic, acclamations of admiring thousands is quite the national and noble institution which they

THE DECAY OF RURAL MERRIMENT.

[ST. JAMES'S GAZETTE.]

It has been said by a well known authority that the rustics of East Anglia are losing their capacity for laughter, and this has been supposed to indicate a growing distaste for innocent mirth in the English peasantry. The disappearance of rural sports may be thought to tell in the same direction. For there are very few left. Some have drifted into history, and are interesting only to the antiquary. The average rustic has perhaps read in his school books about a maypole, but he is as little able to imagine the nature of it as he is in his mind to picture the Battle of Waterloo; of single stick he hardly knows more than he does of the quintain. Every athletic curate is aware that it is almost as easy to get together an adult Bible class as it is to form a parish cricket club. Football, which was originally an essentially village game, is played in the old style—a rougher Rugby Union—only in outlandish places, such as Kirkwall, where the Up-the-gates and Down-the-gates on Christmas Day still struggle as valiantly as they struggled all over Great Britain in the good old times. But the Orkneys are behind the world, and there are parts of them where they say that crinolines are just coming into vogue.

The disappearance of the old games—the end of which has been apparent since the time of Sir

A WOMAN'S FRIENDSHIP.

BY A. C.

CHAPTER I. THE REFORM CLUB.

If it was not publicly distinguished, it was, at any rate, select. It consisted of three members. There was talk at one time of admitting a fourth, but the ballot went against him. Three was the full number.

The quantity might be small, but the quality left nothing to be desired. However inferior to other clubs in its political and social status, in the matter of intelligence and culture it was second to none. Other clubs—the very best of other clubs—are more or less mixed, resembling the proverbial chain with the weak link; but this club was of equal excellence all through, and its excellence was of a very high order. Three more refined and enlightened people than the three members of which it was composed—certainly three such persons in one group—it would be hard to find in these colonies. They were two women and one man and the women were the founders; they were practically the committee also. And Mrs. Clive was president.

She was the wife of a newspaper editor — not an editor who had to be in evidence to modify what has long been the dominant view of her place in Australian literary history as a minor Anglo-Australian writer of romantic novels and interesting poetry, marginal to the Australian literary tradition.

Born in England in 1844, Cambridge had lived in Australia since 1870. Married to George Cross, an Anglican clergyman, she was known personally as Ada Cross. To the readers of her novels in newspapers she was usually 'A. C.'; later, for her books, she reverted to consistent use of her maiden name. It is thus, as Ada Cambridge, that posterity knows her.

'Up the Murray' was her first published novel—it was serialised in the *Australasian*, a Melbourne weekly, in 1875; 'A Woman's Friendship' was her sixteenth; and *The Making of Rachel Rowe* (Cassell, 1914) her last. In all there were twenty-eight novels, together with short stories, essays, and volumes of poetry and of autobiography.[4] Cambridge died in Melbourne in 1926, aged eighty-one.

Novels in Newspapers

An essential context for 'A Woman's Friendship', the Australian newspaper fiction of the 1870s and 1880s has been, by and large, passed over by literary historians and critics. This has hindered consideration of the important part played by the colonial newspaper press in the development of the Australian novel, particularly when the serialising of fiction became widespread in the seventies and eighties. Novels about Australia by visitors, such as Anthony Trollope, and by colonials who went to live in Europe, such as Rosa Praed and 'Tasma' (Jessie Couvreur), were published in London. But those by novelists living and writing in Australia did not readily receive publication overseas. At the same time, local facilities for book publishing were very limited and unsatisfactory.[5]

While Australian literary magazines also serialised novels, drawbacks for aspiring professional authors were uncertain payment and limited circulation.[6] Writers turned more readily to newspapers. Metropolitan weeklies, some dailies (usually on Saturdays), and many suburban and country papers ran serials and, occasionally, whole 'tales'.[7] Most papers made arrangements for regular receipt of imported copy, often through a local or overseas syndicating agency. The copy came from Britain and the United States. Almost without exception, the British novels were by currently popular authors and about to be released as books in London. Whether to foster Australian literature, to cater to reader interest or to offset difficulties in the procurement of overseas copy, some newspapers also published local writing. The journalist Richard Twopeny noted of the *Australasian* that 'Occasionally a colonial work is chosen, and the proprietors do a great deal of service in bringing out really promising authors'.[8] Randolph Bedford however, freelancing as a journalist in 1889, found that 'big papers that could pay were as mean as a Mile End Road pawnbroker'.[9] In fact, about twenty percent of the serial fiction published in Melbourne newspapers of the 1880s was of local authorship.[10]

By the nineties what the journalist and critic James Smith in 1878 called the 'Grub-street condition' of local literature was gone.[11] Some Australian journalists continued to try their hand at creative writing, and some Australian papers published a great deal of short fiction. Metropolitan papers continued to serialise (though many country and suburban ones stopped doing so), but less and less did they feature primary publication of Australian novels. Local book publishing outlets were developing and, in addition, some local authors were snapped up by new and expanding London publishing houses. In 1890 Ada Cambridge began her association with Heinemann, and Rolf Boldrewood continued an arrangement made with Macmillan in 1889.

In 1903 Clara Cheeseman wrote of the Grub Street condition as a thing of the past: 'It is to the old newspapers we must go if we want to see the beginning of colonial fiction...[T]here are in the dusty files of these and other journals many stories of colonial life which have never struggled out of the papers into book form'.[12] As far as Ada Cambridge is concerned there are nine novels which appeared solely in newspapers: they are part of a still largely unexamined archive, the size of which can only be guessed at until a complete indexing of colonial newspapers is carried out.

A survey of Melbourne metropolitan newspapers of the 1880s hints at the richness: during this decade three dailies and four weeklies published a total of one hundred works by overseas authors and twenty-seven by resident colonial writers.[13] The imported novels include several with Australian themes, among them Rosa Praed's 'Miss Jacobsen's Chance' and Tasma's 'The Pipers of Piper's Hill'.[14] The local novels were contributed by eighteen authors: Cambridge wrote nine, David Falk two, and the other novelists one each. Some of these authors, such as Rolf Boldrewood and Mary Gaunt, are today recognized writers of the colonial period; some, such as Harold W. H. Stephen, N. W. Swan and Thorpe Talbot, are little more than names; most are now unknown. In this company Cambridge was the local star but, in the Melbourne press of the eighties, she no longer had the stage 'very much to [her]self', as she claimed had been the case when she began to write novels for the *Australasian* in 1874.[15]

When the *Age* began to serialise 'A Woman's Friendship'

in August 1889, over one hundred of the two hundred or so newspapers and magazines then being published in Melbourne and country towns throughout Victoria were providing serial fiction for their readers. Thirty-two different novels were appearing, several of which came out in more than one newspaper as part of syndicated supplements of additional general and light reading matter.[16]

In this 'slice' of the Victorian press, imported novels, as usual, preponderate. Twenty-four are from Britain and America. Most of the works by British authors (Walter Besant, William Black, Hall Caine, W. E. Norris, Dora Russell and others) were serialised in the major Melbourne papers and released in London as books within a year. In contrast, most of the American works were serialised in smaller suburban and country papers, and seem not to have been published at all in book form, although their authors (Sylvanus Cobb Jr., Eliza Dupuy, Harriet Lewis, Alfred Rochefort, Hero Strong and others) were prolific writers of novels which were.[17]

Juxtaposed with this Anglo-American material were some eight works by local authors. Three of these novels are set in the Melbourne and Victoria of their contemporary readers: 'A Woman's Friendship' in the *Age*; 'The Accusing Scar', J. J. Utting's story of murder and detection, in the *Evening Standard*; 'Eve's Sacrifice', by 'Katrine' in the *Australian Journal*. Four novels contribute to the construction of a colourful past for the colony: Boldrewood's 'Nevermore' in the *Centennial Magazine*, Falk's 'The Recidiviste' in the *Leader*, Robert Ross Haverfield's 'Scattered Leaves: A Romance of Old Bendigo' in the *Bendigo Advertiser* (a provincial daily) and 'W. H. H. F.'s' 'Harold Everleigh: An Anglo-Australian Story' in the *Tarnagulla and Llanelly Courier* (a small country weekly). One novel is exotic in setting: Aubrey Haine's 'Kidnapped', which appeared in the *Brunswick and Coburg Medium* (a small suburban weekly).[18]

These works were simultaneously, through the newspaper and magazine press of Victoria, presenting images of present and past life of the colony—familiar elements of Australian literature and history such as ex-convicts, gold-mining, bushranging, outback heat, drought and bushfire. At the same time a strong English connection was maintained, in that many characters are shown in and arriving from England, and some returning. The sample of newspaper fiction comprises five colonial romances, a murder mystery of the type usually associated with Fergus Hume (whose *The Mystery of a Hansom Cab* was published in 1886) and an island adventure story of the kind popularised by Louis Becke in the *Bulletin* in the 1890s. 'A Woman's Friendship', with its qualities of humorous detachment and fine analysis, is less readily assignable to a genre, but is no less a product of its time.

Five of the newspaper novels in this group of eight were not published in book form. In 1889 C. T. Clarke observed, with some complacency, that the best of novels in newspapers would get themselves published as books.[19] The present edition bears testimony to the fact that this did not always happen at the time.

Ada Cambridge and Literary History

'A Woman's Friendship' has been overlooked because it was published only in a newspaper, because Ada Cambridge was not in vogue during the reign of literary nationalism which has dominated cultural thought until recently (and thus she was not a subject for intensive bibliographical research) and because she left comparatively little personal documentation which could have facilitated such research.

Novels published solely in newspapers have lain outside the cultural structure within which 'literature' has been created: a structure which comprises not only composition, publication in print, and reading, but which includes also evaluation, advertising and stocklisting by publishers and booksellers, reviewing in the media which influence literary opinion, depositing in libraries, and listing in their bibliographies and catalogues. The documents produced by these processes have provided the bank of information for literary bibliographers and researchers to draw on.

Newspapers in nineteenth century England adopted the practice of serialising novels to attract more readers and increase sales (and therefore advertising revenue) at a time of press expansion—more and bigger papers for an increased readership.[20] And authors, to maximise their income, sold serial rights which were additional to and separate from those for publication in book form. The newspaper was not seen, *per se*, as literary publisher. Australian newspapers began to serialise for precisely the same reason: a serial helped sell a paper.[21] When novels by Australian authors were published solely in Australian newspapers, however, there was no mechanism operating to flag them automatically and set in train the process of their evaluation and transmission. Documentation of their existence was a matter of accident.

By her own account, 'Up the Murray' brought Ada Cambridge 'flattering notice' in 1875, and a 'passport to those dignified homes' of the 'intellectually-cultivated class of the colony';[22] no definite traces of this acclaim however, nor pointers to the persons who gave it, have been found. It is conceivable , but unverifiable, that it was she whom James Smith praised in an issue of the *Melbourne Review* in 1878: '[W]e have in our midst gentlemen—and at least one lady—who can write in a far different style to that of the "Penny Dreadfuls", but who find it almost impossible to gain the public ear, except perhaps through the medium of a weekly newspaper'.[23]

Her second newspaper novel, 'The Captain's Charge', was submitted to the *Sydney Mail* in a competition for a prize of £100, and subsequently shortlisted and praised in that paper in March 1879 as 'quite equal to the tales published in magazines', but its author was not named in this announcement (though the actual instalments which began to appear in July did carry her name— uncharacteristically as Ada Cross, not A. C.).[24] The first clear reference to her as a newspaper novelist is a passing one, in a review of her book *A Mere Chance* (Bentley 1882): 'By far the best of this class of novels [set in Melbourne] is that published in the columns of the *Australasian* by the lady who calls herself Ada Cambridge'.[25] This mention may be the first clue which led to some of her novels in that newspaper, but none in any other, being noted in E. Morris Miller's bibliography, *Australian Literature*.

Cambridge's documented fame as an Australian author is readily traced from 1890, beginning with favourable reviews of *A Marked Man* and, soon after, *The Three Miss Kings* (1891) and *Not All in Vain* (1892).[26] Entry in Mennell's biographical dictionary of 'eminent colonists' and high praise from fellow-novelist Rolf Boldrewood (T. A. Browne) in an address to the Australasian Association for the Advancement of Science elevated her literary status in 1892,[27] and evaluation in the literary tracts of Byrne, Turner and Sutherland, and Patchett Martin later in the nineties, confirmed this position.[28] Meanwhile, approving comment had been continuing in the literary columns of Melbourne and Sydney newspapers.[29] John Barnes, in 1964, saw the reputation which she had in her own day as 'quite undeserved now',[30] repeating a literary valuation first made around the turn of the century but which has come to be re-examined in recent years.

The popular colonial writing of Ada Cambridge, Rolf Boldrewood and a host of other authors began, in the 1890s, to be displaced by the activity of a group of writers centred in the Sydney *Bulletin* (founded in 1880). This group's concern to foster a distinctively 'Australian' (rather than Anglo-Australian) literature reflected the movement towards federation of the colonies, which culminated in the establishment of the Commonwealth of Australia in 1901.[31]

The nationalist literary tradition in the making postulated the Australian locked in an uneven struggle for survival with an unyielding environment, the harshness of which disallowed or eliminated nice distinctions of class (egalitarianism), was alleviated by sharing of the condition (mateship), and was glamourised by stories of endurance and achievement against odds.[32] The legend so created was predominantly non-urban and masculine.

Writing which did not fit this mould was rigorously excluded, and the novels of Ada Cambridge were no exception. In 1901 A. G. Stephens, literary editor of the *Bulletin*, drew the boundaries with the ambiguous comment: 'She does not claim recognition as an Australian writer';[33] and in 1905 a very young Vance Palmer, in his first published article, disqualified her as 'an Englishwoman who writes agreeable novels with Australia for background', but whose books 'make no pretence to being literature'.[34]

Long after they were first published, these and similar opinions continued to influence literary valuations. In the 1900s Cambridge's contribution as poet was acknowledged and she was represented in anthologies of Australian poetry, but her fiction—the novels still appearing and the earlier ones which had been so acclaimed—seems no longer to have been of prime interest in the dominant literary and publishing circles. The enthusiast for Australian literature Henry Gyles Turner, writing in 1909 to an American bibliophile James Carleton Young, said that Mrs Cross and Rolf Boldrewood were the most representative of Australian fiction writers, and he said he deplored the 'repulsive realism' of much *Bulletin* writing. But he was speaking for a generation being superseded, and himself called his point of view 'conservative'.[35]

Public recognition of Ada Cambridge as a woman writer continued to be accorded by women during her lifetime, and for about twenty years afterwards.[36] The Lyceum Club of Melbourne made her an honorary life member in 1921, and in 1945 Kate Baker, friend to writers, campaigned successfully for a plaque in memory of the author to be erected in Williamstown where Cambridge had lived from 1893 to 1911.

Australian literary histories from mid-century on, however, provide a predominantly male view of Cambridge as a gifted but insignificant writer, a polite, class-bound lady novelist who was not really 'Australian'.[37] Later feminist critics, however, starting with Anne Summers in 'The Self Denied' (1973),[38] have begun to draw attention to her as a woman writer who has been unfairly neglected, and there have been some less partisan attempts to examine her actual literary contribution rather than to demonstrate either the limitations or the neglect of a *woman* writer: Jill Roe, in 1972, discussed Cambridge and the 'New Australian Woman', with particular reference to the early serialised novels, and noted the increasing firmness with which they are placed in colonial society; Beilby and Hadgraft, in 1979, discussed several of the later novels in detail.[39] But, in general, neither detractors nor supporters have made sufficient examination of Cambridge's writing or her life, with discussion usually confined to two collections of poetry (*Unspoken Thoughts* and *The Hand in the Dark*) and four or five novels of the early nineties, with mention of her domestic concerns as a clergyman's wife and of a personal 'crisis' in 1887.

Ada Cambridge did not assist the survival of her literary reputation when she destroyed her collection of manuscripts before leaving for England, 'not dreaming that it could have any interest for anybody'. With 'no storage for superfluities', a drawerful of press-cuttings went also—into the fire, 'a cruel sacrifice'.[40] Thus, although she had always, she said, 'provided for accidents with a duplicate [MS]',[41] had been a collector of memorabilia, had kept a diary[42] and corresponded widely, there is no sizeable personal archive of the years to 1912, the major part of her writing life. The autograph manuscript of 'A Woman's Friendship' was presumably destroyed; no textual state other than its publication in the *Age* has been discovered.

Apart from her published reminiscences, *Thirty Years in Australia* and *The Retrospect*, which in any case give few details of her writing,[43] sources of information about her are comparatively scanty. Bedridden in her last years, she kept at hand a 'strong box' with documented evidence of the copyright of her works, and manuscripts of some unpublished late writings, mostly what she called 'bits and scraps', intended for a sequel to the two autobiographical volumes.[44] These were donated by her grandson, Mr K.S. Cross, to the Fryer Library, University of Queensland, in 1973.

Some of her letters do survive, preserved with the personal papers of her correspondents (Ethel Turner, Henry Gyles Turner, Bertram Stevens and others) and in publishers' archives. Her many letters to Melbourne bookseller and publisher George Robertson, written from 1920 to 1925, and copies of his replies form part of the Angus and Robertson archive in the Mitchell Library, in Sydney.[45] The correspondence yields a great deal of information about her relations with publishers and agents, and her views of her own work, but little about 'A Woman's Friendship'. There is, together with a letter of 22 October 1924, a typed list of publications which the author says she 'came across' in an old note-book. It is not a complete record, but does include 'A Woman's Friendship', and appears to be the only surviving mention of the title outside the columns of the *Age*. [46]

The Angus and Robertson archive also contains a typescript entitled 'The Good Old Times', which Cambridge sent to the firm in January 1921 to be considered for publication, after having written to them on 30 December 1920 about 'a little volume of short stories, wh. I have not hitherto offered, in present form, elsewhere'. On 10 February George Robertson replied, declining to publish but offering to purchase the document for £10 and to have a fresh copy typed for the author. Cambridge accepted and, accordingly, a cheque and a retyped copy were despatched to her with a letter of 9 March 1921.[47] This retyped copy is now in the Fryer Library. The original typescript is annotated in pencil: 'Unpublished at 9.3.21'; otherwise it is undated. The author's letter of 17 January 1921 implies that the work was prepared in late 1920 (when she was seventy-six). It is a collection of six short stories, one of which, 'The Reform Club', is obviously based on 'A Woman's Friendship'.[48] Less than one third the length of the novel, and greatly altered in text, theme and tone (see below) it is a weak effort. The author was old and unwell, and herself aware of its limitations; referring to the collection, she confided to Robertson, 'It was not what I could have made of it if I had the physical powers of only a year or two ago'; on its rejection she commented, 'I was so conscious of its inadequacy that I was in two minds about sending it'.[49] 'The Reform Club' is reproduced as an appendix to this volume—its first appearance in print.

Life and Literary Career

Many accounts of Cambridge's life epitomise it in terms of crisis and denial. This interpretation, expounded by A. G. Stephens in 1926, sees the 'great crisis' of her life as coming in 1887, following a breakdown in her health and then hospitalisation the previous year, and her husband's dismay at the publication of her outspoken poems, *Unspoken Thoughts,* in early 1887. Stephens claimed that she withdrew the volume from publication immediately (which is not correct),[50] made a visit to Sydney, found peace, atoned for the shock she had given George Cross, 'strangled her dreams, silenced her mind and conformed'.[51] As this view has it, she did her duty and thereby was diminished both as person and artist, and failed to realise her potential.

However, examination of the available evidence suggests a talented and active market professional who organised her life to write while not forgoing her domestic commitments, and who utilised available publishing outlets to best advantage over a period of thirty-five years of very concentrated writing in Australia. There is no cogent support for the 'crisis of 1887' theory as described by Stephens. It would appear, rather, that this was the beginning of a period of health and happiness, and that the turbulent and often terrible times were earlier, during the ten years from 1874 to 1883, in the author's thirties.

Ada Cross made a strong impression on those who knew

her. She was short and, until quite elderly, dark-haired. Photographs from early to late middle age show an oval face, hair drawn neatly if severely back, big, wide-set eyes and a gaze which is steady, serene and reflective. Descriptions and recollections by people who knew her suggest a powerful and generous personality. The contemporary novelist, David Falk, wrote a sonnet to her, published in the *Centennial Magazine* in 1890, describing her 'great and ardent nature, strong, intense, and real'; Jennings Carmichael spoke of her 'loving friendship'; Mary Grant Bruce (who had been a member of the Writers' Club in the 1900s when Cambridge was President) wrote of 'a revered leader'; and Mary Gilmore recalled her as 'a mighty among pygmies', and 'I think the greatest woman in personality...I ever met'.[52]

An unnamed friend from the 1900s was quoted, in the *Argus* obituary of 23 July 1926, as saying that Ada Cambridge was 'captain of her soul', and indeed a most striking characteristic which presents itself through her published autobiographies and articles is an assertion of independence—the antithesis of conformity. Though she made friends easily with people in many walks of life, she usually held herself aloof from social groups. Early in her married life she, by her own account, abandoned the regular duties expected of a clergyman's wife,[53] and began seriously to question the conventions and tenets of organised Christian religion—evident in her novel 'The Three Miss Kings', and more so in 'A Black Sheep' (*A Marked Man*) and her poetry. The apartness and questioning seem to have developed into an existential aloneness. In her late sixties, in articles for the American magazine, *Atlantic Monthly*, she expressed her religious unorthodoxy, her lack of belief in an afterlife, and her sense of a deep, solitary spirituality—'this quiet chamber of the mind'.[54] She recalled 'defending the soul's sanctuary' against the well-meant ministrations of a clergyman when she was thought to be dying in 1886, and saw herself as (recalling Wordsworth) 'Voyaging strange seas of thought, alone'.[55]

Ada Cambridge's career as a published author runs from 1865, with *Hymns on the Litany*, to 1922, with her article, 'Nightfall' in *Atlantic Monthly*.[56] Novels constitute her most voluminous contribution to literature, and almost all were written while she lived in Victoria. She came to regard herself as belonging more to Australia than England, though acknowledging a 'chronic nostalgia' for the country in which she spent her first twenty-five years.[57]

Her novel production has two phases: the first, from 1875 to 1891, when the colonial newspaper press was her chief publisher; the second, a sustained and successful connection with London book publishers from 1890 to 1914. The overlap period, 1890 to 1891, was a transitional stage, when Heinemann published *A Marked Man* and *The Three Miss Kings,* and 'Not All in Vain' and 'The Charm that Works' came out in the *Australasian.*

The seven novels published as books from 1890 to 1896 were all related to earlier newspaper novels, whether as scarcely changed versions, partial or complete revisions or, in the case of *Fidelis,* a sequel. With *Materfamilias* (1898) she broke new ground, and from then until 1907 produced seven substantial novels. This continuous flow was then interrupted by a visit to England in 1908, and only one more novel was published after this, *The Making of Rachel Rowe* (1914), when the author had gone back to live in England.

Driven to write and armed both with literary talent and confidence from the modest success of her early attempts at authorship in England, Ada Cambridge in Australia sought and found a range of publishing outlets, both local and overseas. Though in old age she was to deprecate her entrepreneurial abilities ('being...such a duffer at business'),[58] her performance contradicts this disavowal. Her approaches to the editor of the *Australasian* in 1874 demonstrate forthright practicality in the discussion of the conditions of her offer and the invitation of response.[59] Though she cast widely after publishing media, she almost always narrowed her choices to those most profitable.[60]

Thus she favoured the newspaper press when it was, in the colonies, the dominant mode of publication of locally written novels; she negotiated successfully with the London publisher William Heinemann when he was launching his first list and Australian newspapers were giving up the practice of original publication of Australian novels. Then she moved fairly quickly from direct negotiation with Heinemann, notwithstanding his telegraphic protests, to the use of a London literary agent, A. P. Watt, recommended to Cambridge and Rolf Boldrewood by Rudyard Kipling,[61] probably during his brief visit to Melbourne in 1891. (Boldrewood did not follow the advice and remained with Macmillan.) In turn, in 1897 Cambridge was extolling to a young Ethel Turner the advantages of having Watt place her manuscripts.[62] Even Heinemann, for whom agents were anathema, was later to admit their usefulness for authors resident overseas.[63] Cambridge also found it convenient to 'have nothing to bother about—only to send home MSS as fast as I could write, sign agreements, and bank the money'.[64] According to the Melbourne *Punch* in 1897 she was earning £1000 a year.[65] Her correspondence reveals that there is no doubt that it was she who managed her literary property, keeping track and control of the copyrights to the very last.[66]

A myth that she helped create was that she was not

seriously involved in writing, that she wrote novels at odd moments and to 'buy pretty things' for her babies.[67] A quite different emphasis is revealed in private correspondence. To Ethel Turner in 1896 she complained of being 'frustrated by the many domestic & other affairs which are always warring against literary interests' and she commented to George Robertson in 1924, with realistic resignation, that 'book-making was but a side-line in the life of a female jack-of-all-trades'.[68] As far as she was able, Cambridge gave priority to her writing. She engaged ample domestic help throughout the 1870s and 1880s; the income from her writing enabled servants and governesses to be employed more easily than would have been the case on a clergyman's stipend alone.[69]

As material for her novels, Cambridge seems to have seized every opportunity to snatch at and store up experiences which she would draw on again and again. She turned to creative account the circumstances of her first twenty-three years in Australia as not only colonial exile but also isolated country dweller and woman with responsibilities to husband and children.

As her autobiographies reveal, she brought to Australia memories from England—of her protected childhood in Norfolk, part of a large family; of her annual visits to an aunt in London to do the rounds of galleries and museums; and of her adult years in Cambridgeshire. In 1870, in the cathedral town of Ely, she married George Cross, a young curate who intended to go to the Australian colonies. She also brought her memories of shipboard life during the three month voyage out that same year. Most of her novels introduce, in some manner, this England which she knew. Only *The Making of Rachel Rowe* was written with the benefit of return journeys to her country of birth—in 1908 for six months, and from 1912 for five years. (It was against her wishes that she returned there to live,[70] and she came back to Australia in 1917, after the death of her husband.)

In Australia, from 1870 to 1893 there were clerical postings to six Victorian country towns.[71] Ada Cambridge wrote for publication almost from the start of her life in the colony;[72] and in 1874 she began in earnest to write a novel for newspaper publication. The task she set herself was, at first, formidable: to write an insider's view of colonial society, based on brief glimpses as an outsider, and with no developed expertise as a novelist. Hitherto, she had produced hymns, poems, devotional tales and fictional sketches. It was some years and some novels before she could accomplish this task competently. 'Up the Murray', and several of the works which followed, convey more about the conventions of the English romantic novel than they do about any aspects of Australian society. 'Missed in the Crowd', her seventh

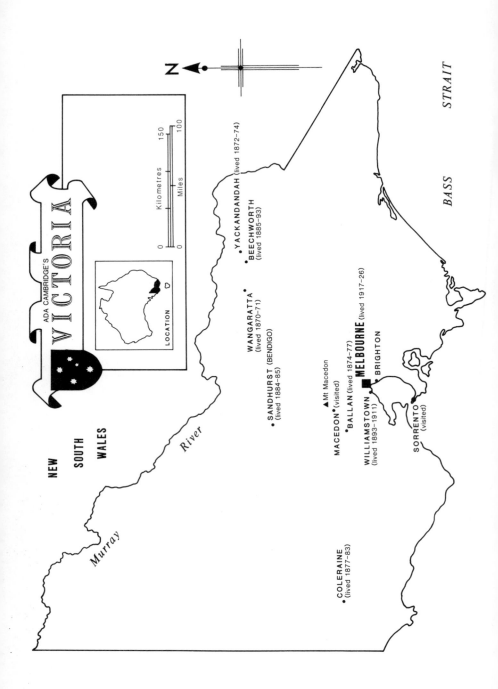

ADA CAMBRIDGE'S
VICTORIA

NEW
SOUTH
WALES

Murray

River

COLERAINE
(lived 1877–83)

SANDHURST (BENDIGO)
(lived 1884–85)

WANGARATTA
(lived 1870–71)

YACKANDANDAH (lived 1872–74)

BEECHWORTH
(lived 1885–93)

▲ Mt Macedon

MACEDON (visited)

BALLAN (lived 1874–77)

MELBOURNE (lived 1917–26)

WILLIAMSTOWN
(lived 1893–1911)

BRIGHTON

SORRENTO
(visited)

BASS

STRAIT

LOCATION

Kilometres

Miles

150

100

0

0

serialised novel (*Australasian*, 1881-82), marks an advance towards understanding and mastery of local material. Its country town, Deloraine, is identifiably based on Cambridge's experience of Coleraine, and its Melbourne is recognizably that of the 1880 Exhibition, which is made part of the setting. In the next few years the newspaper versions of some of her most polished and popular works came out, notably the romantic 'The Three Miss Kings' (1883), which again makes use of the 1880 Exhibition as rendezvous for its characters; and the ironic 'A Little Minx' (1885), with its sharp characterising of country town small-mindedness and feminine wilfulness.

The contrasts in Cambridge's life from 1874 to 1883 seem bizarre. In July 1874, when she had two young children and was living in the town of Yackandandah, she was firmly pulling out of parochial obligations.[73] She offered to write 'an Australian story' for the *Australasian*.[74] Between the initial letter to the editor and her submission of the first instalment came the death of her one year old daughter from whooping cough, and a move to another parish to get away from 'agonising visions of what had been'.[75] In the two years following, at Ballan, also a small place and without a railway but twenty miles by coach from the provincial city of Ballarat, she became a district celebrity, being lionised after 'Up the Murray' came out in the *Australasian*. And her son died from scarlet fever, leaving her childless for two weeks until she gave birth to another daughter.

Some months later the family moved to Coleraine in the far Western District of Victoria. George Cross had this post for seven years, during which time Cambridge produced eight novels. She also spent a considerable time away, with extended visits to Melbourne at the time of the 1880 Exhibition. Her reputation as author gave her, it seems, *entrée* to houses of the rich and famous not only in Melbourne but also in the Macedon district some forty miles away, where the elite had their country retreats. On one tour lasting some months she took her youngest child and her maid. It was, she later claimed, 'perhaps the gayest period' of her life.[76]

Coleraine was isolated enough: it was 236 miles from Melbourne and twenty-two miles by coach from Hamilton, the nearest railway station. The parsonage was lonelier still: a farmhouse six miles from the town. There Cambridge gave birth to two more children, one arriving during a terrifying bushfire. There also, it appears, she suffered a miscarriage which left gynaecological problems to plague her until hospitalisation and surgery in 1886.[77]

In *Thirty Years in Australia* she wrote of her 'brooding solitude' and 'broken health' at Coleraine, and her insistence on leaving.[78] The misery of the years there contrasts with the gaiety of the times when she escaped, and is perhaps explained in part by the delayed compound effects of the emotional arousal of giving birth together with the trauma of suffering child deaths. The contrasts in her life are reproduced in her novels of this time. This period saw, with 'The Three Miss Kings', the perfecting of the lightly ironic romantic novel, and, with 'Across the Grain' (1882), the beginning of work which conveys a gloomier view of the human condition.

The short stay in the city of Sandhurst (from 1891 called Bendigo) seems to have marked a return to a more stable manner of living. Cambridge continued to write, although she found this very hard in the cramped conditions of a terrace house. She delighted in having for the first time in Australia a good library at hand, and enjoyed some anonymous liberty strolling the streets at night with the children's governess as companion.

Her move to Beechworth (in northeastern Victoria not far from Yackandandah, but a much larger town) came in 1885. It was the start of a settled phase which was to last for eight years, until her husband's final posting to the Melbourne suburb of Williamstown in 1893.

Apart from preparing her poems for *Unspoken Thoughts*, Cambridge seems not to have written for publication for most of 1886, the year of her hospitalisation and convalescence, nor in the first part of 1887. The publishing gap synchronises with the period of the 'great crisis' of which A. G. Stephens wrote, and it may have been some sort of watershed—a period of reflection commencing with the regaining of health and vigour.

From 1887 to 1889 there was a new flowering of her talent, stimulated and nourished by three weeks in Sydney in July 1887 (where she mixed with writers and artists and was herself a celebrity), by delight in her surroundings at Beechworth, and by frequent visits to Melbourne for the Exhibition in 1888. In the middle of 1887 (whether before or after going to Sydney is not clear) she collaborated with James Smith and Andrew Semple to produce part of the text for the *Picturesque Atlas of Australasia* edited by Andrew Garran.[79] Her hand is clearly to be discerned in the accounts of Macedon and Beechworth and her glowing description of the latter exceeds the requirements of documentary prose and bespeaks great pleasure in her surroundings. Drawing on her Sydney experiences, she wrote 'A Black Sheep' and contributed short pieces to the *Australian Journal* and the *Centennial Magazine*, and an extraordinary novella or Christmas tale to the *Illustrated Australian News* of December 1887. This last, 'The Perversity of Human Nature', has, like 'A Little Minx', sardonic and summary treatment of human relations and misfortunes, and shows the author experimenting with conventions of the novel and with ironic modes.

Cambridge received the unusually high sum of £197 from the *Age* for the serial rights of 'A Black Sheep'.[80] (Randolph Bedford recalled that 'the big Australian dailies bought their serials from London, paying £10 or so for the rights of a serial running into sixty to one hundred thousand words'.)[81] This payment, she later noted, enabled her to make the two hundred mile train journey from Beechworth to Melbourne frequently to visit the Exhibition; and her pleasure in it, especially her joy in the music and art it offered, provided material for 'A Woman's Friendship' written the following year.

Looking back a decade later she saw the Exhibition differently: it was the climax of a boom when 'we were rich and dishonest and mercenary and vulgar' with the end not far off; 'the best thing that ever happened to Melbourne Society, as I have known it, was the snuffing out of the lights of that feast, the coming of that cold daylight to the revellers'.[82] Certainly another phase in her own life was to begin. From 1890 she directed her attention away from her press connections in Sydney and Melbourne and towards her London publishers. Though she was to experience more personal tragedy (the death of a son and suicide of a son-in-law)[83] her life was more ordered, and would remain so until her return visit to England in 1908 began the disruption and uprooting which marked the last eighteen years of her life.

Ada Cambridge surmounted many obstacles in maintaining her literary career during her first twenty or so years in Australia. She had not received literary guidance in her formative years as novelist, and her immediate family and friends do not seem ever to have shared her literary preoccupations. Old and crippled, but mentally in command, she wrote to George Robertson in 1924 from the 'rest home' to which she had gone after living with her son for some years, asking Robertson to keep a guard over her 'literary remains'. With a bitter realism she commented on the value, to her family, of her literary creations: 'I have no one belonging to me to whom they would be anything but waste paper'.[84]

A Woman's Friendship

A Woman's Friendship presents an interlude of six months in the lives of two women (married) and one man (a widower). Husbands are in the background. It takes place during, and is given artistic shape and unity by, the Melbourne Centennial International Exhibition of August 1888 to January 1889. The blossoming and wilting of relationships are identified with the seasonal span from early spring to oppressive summer, and further symbolised by the Melbourne land boom which reached a peak in late 1888, then began to decline—the start of the 'bust'.

The interlude is presented almost entirely from the viewpoint of the women, and mostly that of the younger one, Patty Kinnaird. The eponymous friendship could be Margaret Clive's for Seaton Macdonald or Patty, or Patty's for Macdonald or Margaret; it could be the abstract notion or the women's relations with their husbands, or it could be all of these. But it is Patty's friendship—or infatuation—with Macdonald which is the focus: a centrepoint for exploring the psychological and social dimensions of sexuality, power and class in a precisely located milieu.

The setting would have been instantly recognizable to readers of the *Age* in 1889. Wherever they lived in Victoria they would have been aware of the huge growth in size and importance of the metropolis, and of the recent Exhibition. In 1885 the visiting journalist, George Augustus Sala, dubbed the capital 'Marvellous Melbourne', and the term stuck. From the seventies professional writers—Marcus Clarke, Richard Twopeny, Alexander Sutherland, and others—had described and celebrated the city.[85] Its landmarks became known as much through literary image as personal encounter, and Cambridge was drawing both on her own experience of Melbourne and on contemporary images of it in writings of the time.

As documentary of the Melbourne of 1888, *A Woman's Friendship* is impeccable. In particular, its description of the layout and offerings at the Exhibition tallies with accounts in newspapers and in the *Official Record of the Centennial International Exhibition*.[86] While there is some similarity with the Melbourne presented in 'The Pipers of Piper's Hill' (*Australasian*, 1888)—for example, the importance of Collins Street—most of Tasma's local references carry no particular significance, and it is impossible to date the setting with precision.[87] Tasma's novel suggests, though it does not depict in detail, a broad and familiar backdrop; *A Woman's Friendship*, on the other hand, offers a sketch map of paths recognized by its characters (because socially significant to them) through terrain which is mostly unfamiliar (and unimportant) to them. Every marker carries special meaning, and one may date the action as it proceeds, almost to the day.

The world of the novel is an amalgam of the separate worlds of the two couples and the third man. The key elements of each, appropriate to and indicative of social status as defined by property and occupation, are identified: residences, work and clubs. Raymond Clive is editor, not proprietor, of a newspaper and is member of a journalists' club; the couple live in a modest rented cottage in a prosperous and smart district. Edward Kinnaird owns a sheep property and visits Melbourne's most exclusive club; he and his wife take rooms at the leading abode for country visitors. Seaton Macdonald, one-time barrister, has several country properties, and when in Melbourne stays at the same exclusive club. The territory is marked out by the men; the women have a smaller domain within it. A temporary extension or addition is the Exhibition, free to all. Within its vast acreage the women select a very small, but to them supremely important, part as their ground—the picture galleries and concert hall. They pay but token and passing attention to 'wool, and grain and buggies' (p 53) and none at all, it would seem, to the industrial and technological exhibits which in fact constituted the largest part. A further extension of their sphere is provided by the excursion, sanctioned by husbands, to Macdonald's property, Yarrock.

The action is initiated when Margaret and Patty have, despite differences in background, become friends on a two-day sea voyage from Sydney to Melbourne, and the Exhibition provides a further meeting ground for them. The action is complicated when Margaret (who had met Macdonald through the freemasonry of press circles) effects the introduction of her two friends to each other; it transpires that Patty's husband is, like Macdonald, propertied, belongs to the Melbourne Club[88] and was educated at Melbourne Grammar.[89] The niceties of Melburnian class distinctions come into play and the social advantage Patty gains thereby lays the basis for her ensuing *rapprochement* with the man; later they will explore together some private territory, an activity which, while not explicitly forbidden, has no public sanction.

The two female characters differ not only in background but also in appearance and behaviour. Though without the bloom of youth (being in their thirties), they are not unattractive. Margaret, the journalist's wife, is tall and dark, with some grace of movement; her clothes are unfashionably simple to the point of being dowdy. Patty, the squatter's wife, is short, quite pretty and dresses with respectable smartness. Margaret, who would like to see herself as intellectual and refined, is opinionated and a little eccentric, while Patty, who sees herself as interesting and lovable, is pleasant enough, but frivolous.

The women are presented responding to the most exciting event in years and also, for a time, turning their attention to the reformist aims of the strong but minority women's movement. Like the earlier Exhibition of 1880, that of 1888 brought a treasure chest of art and music to a young colonial society unused to this kind of cultural plenty. *A Woman's Friendship* shows these two earnest and rather simple women trying to make something of it—Margaret with her scraps of knowledge and opinion retained from her London girlhood, Patty uncultivated but eager. Discussing what were in fact the most talked about and popular exhibits, they flounder as they attempt to express and explain their responses. Margaret, while urging sincerity, praises what she thinks ought to be good, and Patty, with embarrassing candour, states what she does and does not like, and why. Their reactions to Holman Hunt's 'Scapegoat' echo the controversy which the painting actually aroused: it was reported at the time that there were 'few paintings...which, at first view, excited more mingled feelings of surprise, bewilderment and attraction'.[90] Through their disjointed discussions it becomes clear that judging what is good art is a problem for both. Another problem, which they cannot begin to solve, is how to reconcile expenditure (personal and public) on works of art with the claims of the deserving poor for material assistance. For all her proclaimed social conscience Margaret hankers after a Norman Shaw house,[91] and Patty has a taste for diamonds. Though the Exhibition expands the horizons of these fictional women, as it must have done for thousands in reality, they are not sure what to make of the masterpieces from distant Europe, and in no way do they become assured connoisseurs.

Margaret and Patty, in establishing their 'club', are shown to be involving themselves in women's issues of the day. In 1888, organisations in Victoria (and in other colonies) were actively promoting the moral role of women of setting an example in the conduct of their lives in the interests of social improvement. The central aim of the Victorian Women's Suffrage Society, established in 1884, was the securing of the vote for women. While this was seen as the key to change, reformist aims also encompassed matters of dress, diet, exercise and, more controversially, changes to the marriage and divorce laws. Ada Cambridge's characters are expressing well-publicized views of the Victorian group on the 'Woman Question', generally.[92]

Margaret, in style of dressing, household management and enthusiasm for the franchise question, is the leader of the two. Her choice of simple, homemade clothes, however, may be governed by her limited means as much as by her enlightened notions; in any case she looks rather drab. Her household arrangements are frugal, but not at the expense of comfort, particularly that of her husband. She cannot sustain the interest of her friend in pursuing the cause of electoral reform, and is unable to extend her influence any further.

Patty at first takes up her older friend's enthusiasms with almost religious fervour, but soon returns to her accustomed behaviour. Though giving some thought to Margaret's views on fashion, she continues to dress for the admiration of men. She is not persuaded to effect changes in the running of her household where she sees herself as indispensable—although her husband seems able to manage for a time without her. And her interest in the franchise drops away as her interest in Macdonald strengthens.

Margaret initiates their attempts to ignore class barriers. Her insistence on cheap seats at concerts and theatre, and on second class railway travel, is in keeping with her democratic attitude to household help (which Patty would not countenance for her own kitchen), and possibly also with her purse. Patty is acutely embarrassed by the disdain which these activities attract.

The novel subtly mocks the reformist ideals, not *per se* but as held by the two female characters, showing Margaret out of touch and Patty class-bound. The capabilities of each, as wives of journalist and squatter respectively, lie in the sphere of household management. They only dabble in culture and make abortive attempts to aid the women's movement, without actually joining it (their 'club' is exclusive). The novel's cynicism about the power and desire of women of the time to assert their independence and influence social change, if a realistic view, cannot have been welcomed by the Melbourne campaigners for the rights of women: the Women's Suffrage Bill was introduced into the Victorian Parliament on 4 September 1889, four days after the first instalment of the novel but, failing to gain sufficient support, was withdrawn on 20 November, four weeks after the serial finished.

The novel also mocks Margaret's high-minded assertions about women's loyalty to each other, and comradeship between women and men. The claims are belied by her clear sexual attraction to Macdonald—she felt 'the subtle something that is like wine in women's veins' (p 71)—and by her jealousy of the growing attachment between him and Patty. Both women seek to extend what is offered within their marriages by their respectable, good-humoured, utterly dependable husbands. As an attractive man enters their lives, the cultural and reformist pursuits tend to give way to the more powerful attraction of sexual dalliance.

Beginning with Helen Fitzgerald in 'Missed in the Crowd' (1881-82), who wanted 'room to live fully and freely' and 'a fair chance to work out the kind of life that we are by nature fitted for',[93] Cambridge created characters, female and male, who resisted what they saw as the confines of 'loveless' and even of conventional marriage.[94] What was sought, though not always gained, was permanent romantic union with a soul-mate. The difference between these earlier novels and *A Woman's Friendship* is that Patty's attraction is to a womaniser, not a soul-mate. The opportunity being offered is adultery, not marriage. Her rejection is based on fear of consequences rather than a high moral stand or abatement of desire, and the whole experience becomes an ultimately chastening exercise in self-knowledge.

The core of *A Woman's Friendship* is exposure of the sham

of the 'purely intellectual friendship' (p 57) and what underlies it—increasing sexual competition between the two women who are married for the attentions of the man who is not, and the jealousy of one which develops while the groundwork for an affair is being laid by the other. The high point of sexual possibilities is reached in an idyllic setting, but the actual consummation is averted; later, in more domestic surroundings, the woman attempts to fit herself back into the role of loving wife. The effect of this forced suppression of sexuality is, for a time, disoriented misery until after the devastating news of the engagement of the man leads her to reconcile herself dutifully to her marital and domestic lot.

A Woman's Friendship demonstrates the subtlety of Ada Cambridge's writing craft; the short story based on it, 'The Reform Club', written about thirty years later in the author's seventies, does not. This story was intended, along with five other 'little tales' in the collection 'The Good Old Times', to represent 'gentle and mannerly life' in 'times of peace and plenty, of security and contentment';[95] its tone of fond nostalgia is a poor replacement for the delicate but pervasive irony of the earlier work.

About one third of the length of *A Woman's Friendship*, it re-uses about one quarter of its text (sometimes reproducing intact, often rephrasing) to tell a similar story in which the main characters of the novel are present and key settings, the Exhibition Buildings and Yarrock, are preserved. Significant scenes at the Clives' East Melbourne house and the Kinnairds' Coffee Palace rooms are, however, omitted, as is the crucial episode of the novel—the escapade of Patty and Macdonald to the mountain summit. In effect 'The Reform Club' is a different work, presenting a more trivial affair of petty jealousies and coldness, with scarcely a hint of improprieties. Much of the introduced text is weak, and the final sentence, which alters the ending, particularly feeble.

The later work lacks almost all of the finely crafted linguistic patterning running through *A Woman's Friendship*. The characters in the novel have a language of their own to convey and sustain the enthusiastic innocence of their perceptions of themselves as 'charming' and their surroundings as 'delicious', set apart from 'common' persons and behaviour. The threesome relationship is 'a purely intellectual friendship'; the twosome which later develops is legitimated as that of 'brother and sister'. When the sexual possibilities are manifest both glosses disappear; the words no longer serve, and in due course the story comes to a 'common' end.

Delicately suggestive imagery sustains this exploration of sexuality: the roses which Macdonald gives to the women—Patty's 'a "dream" of beauty' (p 77), Margaret's half-blown; the equestrian activities and language of Patty and Macdonald both masking and conveying a mating ritual; and the insect tableau which Patty studies in that moment of truth on the mountain, 'far from the madding crowd' (p 98). She watches a spider, a quivering dragon-fly and a cockchafer beetle with horns; she sees, perhaps, a seducer, the prey and a cuckolded husband. Thus, in the mind, she loses her innocence.

A Woman's Friendship examines the 'proper sphere and business' (p 115) of wives, focussing on the phenomenon of female extra-marital sexual attraction. Its characters act within a framework of conventions and expectations erected by and for the social class with which they would identify: it is they who are class-bound—and not necessarily the author who creates and exposes them. Cambridge portrays a society in formation, at a certain point in history; what women of the future will be is a matter, in *A Woman's Friendship*, only for speculation: Margaret Clive sees that 'Other women will have their chance' (p 48), and Patty wonders how it might be one hundred years hence. Cambridge herself had already theoretically expanded the opportunities of the rising generation of women, through Sue Delavel in 'A Black Sheep', and would do so again in many of the novels to follow.

With the ironic realism of *A Woman's Friendship* Cambridge takes a view which disentangles sexuality, love and marriage, and in a sense paves the way for new directions in her fiction: the extended ironical portrayal of family relationships in the later domestic sagas *Materfamilias* (1898) and *A Happy Marriage* (1906); the examination of distorted and restrained sexuality in *Not All in Vain* (1892) and *Path and Goal* (1900); and the study of various paths to female fulfilment in *The Devastators* (1901) and *The Eternal Feminine* (1907).[96]

Cambridge depicts the characters and setting of *A Woman's Friendship* with a sureness of touch which testifies both to her development as a writer and to her familiarity with the milieu which she reproduces. She could draw on her recent experience of the 1888 Exhibition and also her memories of the earlier one and her literary treatment of it. Her recollections of her visits in the early eighties to country houses in the Macedon district would have helped her construct the fictional Yarrock. Perhaps in the character of Patty Kinnaird there is even a suggestion of the thirty-four year old Ada Cross from the country visiting the 1880 Exhibition, and in Margaret Clive a trace of the thirty-seven year old at Macedon in 1883. Possibly there were real-life models for the fictional men: in 1880s Victoria there were newspapermen and politicians who gave support through the press, parliament and public activities to the women's movement: George Higinbotham, Charles Edwin Jones, and William Maloney, for example.[97] Whatever the autobiographical and biographical elements, the novel creates its own historical narrative, demonstrating the reputation for 'finished workmanship' she once had, and of which she was so proud.[98]

While *A Woman's Friendship*, rescued and re-published, displays Cambridge's virtuosity as novelist and demonstrates that she was not always constrained by the 'strait-jacket of the romance plot',[99] it also enlarges our knowledge of a body of Australian literature which warrants more scrutiny—the novels in newspapers of the late nineteenth century. Cambridge wrote 'A Woman's Friendship' (and fourteen novels before it) in the first instance for readers of Australian newspapers, and in it she depicted contemporary colonial society, focussing on its codes and standards of behaviour. The society was of course an offshoot from England, and this is reflected in the novel. But at the end a clear distinction is made between *here* and *there*: to Patty and Edward Kinnaird, 'home' is up the country and England is the 'outer darkness' (p 120) to which Seaton Macdonald and his new bride vanish.

The works of Ada Cambridge, and of other colonial writers whose roots were in England but who were making a life for themselves in Australia, bear the marks of both worlds. For twenty years or so in a colonial culture lacking well developed literary traditions, institutions and formations of its own, Cambridge nourished her 'creating self' on the one hand through personal and professional links with the colonial press and, on the other, through procuring and perusing the literary products of the culture she had left.[100] By 1889 she had been associated with colonial newspapers for eighteen years, and was well known in press circles, especially in Melbourne. As social commentary, *A Woman's Friendship* is part of the journalistic and literary representation of Melbourne and Victoria. At the same time, as a novel, it bears the influence of the prolific reading of English and American literature which she kept up, supplied with material by friends, mechanics' institutes, libraries and bookshops.[101]

The novel's strongest discernible affinity is with the works of George Meredith—possibly her favourite novelist. Meredith's novels, in particular *The Egoist* (first published in 1879 and again in the 1885 Chapman and Hall collected cheap edition),[102] probably influenced Cambridge's development from sentimentalism in the early novels to ironic realism in *A Woman's Friendship*. The 'Comic Spirit' sketched in the 'Prelude' to *The Egoist* could as well describe the spirit of Cambridge's novel;[103] the conceited pompous Sir Willoughby Patterne could have inspired the creation of Macdonald, the dissembling womaniser; and if *A Woman's Friendship* has a moral then it must be contained in Dr Middleton's advice: ' "Plain sense upon the marriage question is my demand upon man and woman, for the stopping of many a tragedy".'[104]

There are also some striking parallels in theme and content with Henry James' *The Bostonians*, published in 1886 and reviewed in the *Australasian* in October of the same year. James depicts fashionable Boston, the friendship of Olive Chancellor and Verena Tarrant, the fanatical enthusiasm of the former for female suffrage and the abandonment of the cause by the latter in favour of union with her suitor, Basil Ransom.[105]

A Woman's Friendship displays the constraints of class and gender operating in a segment of Melburnian society of the late 1880s, epitomised in Macdonald's use of the phrase 'a free country' and the articulation by each of the women of the particular 'bondage' in which they see and place themselves.[106] As such, Cambridge's novel is part of a long Australian literary tradition which extends beyond radical nationalism. It may be seen as one variation on the 'entrapment' theme formulated by Graeme Turner in *National Fictions* (1986). The condition of entrapment, which Turner sees as central to the narratives of Australian novels and films, is 'the fixing of social horizons and personal possibilities in the imprisoning concepts of race', convict institutions, gender, and capitalist systems as well as physical surroundings.[107] *A Woman's Friendship*, in reproducing a more complex and hierarchical society than allowed by the myth of democratic mateship, is a telling reflection of social processes in late nineteenth century Australia.

Reception

'A Woman's Friendship' was not amongst Cambridge's five newspaper novels which were published in book form in the 1890s.[108] These were chosen, presumably, on the basis of favourable reception locally and estimated market appeal in Britain; they were not all her own favourites.[109] A romantic love interest, sometimes passionate and always linked to marriage as the proper state for its expression, figures large in all. With the exception of 'Missed in the Crowd', those which were left in the papers were short (between 45,000 and 60,000 words). Their shortness could have inhibited, but would not have precluded, publication in book form. 'A Woman's Friendship' would not have been difficult to market as a book in the nineties, when the standard three-decker novel (which ranged in length from about 120,000-200,000 words) was giving way to a variety of formats. *A Little Minx* (about 60,000 words) is not very much longer than 'A Woman's Friendship' (about 47,000 words), and *A Humble Enterprise*, while expanded from the newspaper version, 'The Charm that Works', is of similar length (about 48,000 words). Cambridge did not need or want to put all of the newspaper novels into books. The prime reason for leaving 'A Woman's Friendship' alone was probably its limited popularity: the work could have been seen as too localised and, lacking a satisfactorily romantic story-line, too austere for the British novel-reading market; and estimation of appeal throughout the Australasian colonies may have been gauged from an actual mixed reception by Victorian readers in 1889.

The instalments of 'A Woman's Friendship' in the *Age* would have had a huge *potential* readership, for in 1889 over 81,000 copies of each issue of the paper were being circulated to households and persons throughout Victoria.[110] This circulation was four times larger than that of the *Australasian* (though more confined to Victoria), and one of the largest in the British Empire outside London. With a population of a little over 1,100,000, there was one copy of the *Age* to every fourteen inhabitants of the Colony. Almost everyone would have had the *chance* to read the novel. Would they have taken it, and would they have liked what they got?

They would have found it very different from the English and Scottish novels of romance, mystery and adventure which the *Age* usually serialised, and a marked contrast to the serial running before 'A Woman's Friendship'—Mary Elizabeth Braddon's melodramatic 'The Day Will Come'. (Her 'Whose Was the Hand?', cast in the same mould, was to come straight after Cambridge's novel: Braddon was prolific and popular.)[111] And readers who remembered the passion and imaginative sweep of Cambridge's 'A Black Sheep' in the *Age* a year earlier might have been disappointed and perhaps discomfited to find not an exciting fictional world to escape to, but a somewhat cynical, gently mocking reflection of themselves. As a reminder of the Exhibition now months past, it is hard to say whether it would have read as yesterday's stale news or have brought back agreeable memories. News of the day was of unprecedented labour unrest in London. The start of a strike of dock workers which would bring the unloading and departure of colonial ships to a halt was the dominant item in the Victorian press for most of September.

Whatever the various reactions of members of the reading public that of David Syme, proprietor and chief editor of the *Age*, was unequivocal according to a memorandum copied in his Letter Book:

> This tale is the dullest & stupidest Mrs Cross ever penned & had it not been extensively advertised beforehand I shd have paid the money for it & kept it out of the paper altogether.

Syme also found it, in parts, 'indecent' to the extent that his sub-editors 'roared over' one scene which he, by his own account, excised because it 'wd have been no laughing matter had it appeared'.[112] Hilarity does not seem consistent with dullness, and the fact that newspapermen found something amusing (which would also have been bad for the *Age*) suggests that there may have been incidents and observations which could have been taken to refer to actual persons, or their wives, in the world of the press and, perhaps, of politics. The intriguing 'excision' and other possible tamperings by Syme with the text, are discussed further below. There may have been allusions which, if not actually libellous, might have been embarrassing. Cambridge appears to have protested by letter to Syme's nephew, Joseph Cowen Syme (with whom publication had been arranged), when the altered version appeared. David Syme was adamant about his editorial rights. Cambridge had an intense dislike of having her 'copy touched' but the damage was done by the time she would have seen it.[113]

Apart from Syme's remark, there is no record of reaction to 'A Woman's Friendship'. However, in local contemporary writing on the 'Woman Question', allusions to the novel may be conjectured. From the mid-1880s the Victorian newspaper and magazine press from time to time included leaders, reports, and articles on the subject, some in support, some derisive. Looking at items which appeared while the novel was being serialised and soon after there are some which might have been influenced by it.

One such is an article by M. L. Manning on 'Women's Clubs' in the November issue of the *Centennial Magazine*. Referring to these institutions as the 'latest and most marked innovation', the author describes the ancient (Roman) history of clubs in general and the modern spread of clubs for women in particular, showing how Australia ' "far from the madding crowd" ' is slowly following the example of London.[114] It is tempting to think that the 'reform club' of 'A Woman's Friendship' was at least a partial inspiration to Manning to discuss the topic.

Editing the Text

Publishing in book form this novel which was serialised in a newspaper one hundred years ago has required the resolution of several editorial problems: assessing the extent of agreement between the text as published in the newspaper and the author's wishes; determining what, if any, changes to make to the text; considering whether it is necessary to attempt to compensate for any loss in the conversion from newspaper to book format; and deciding which references and allusions which would have been understood by contemporary readers need explanation now.

As no manuscript or setting copy survives, the alterations

David Syme effected and the reasons they were made can only be conjectured at—by making inferences from the Syme memoranda, by scrutinising the newspaper text, and by drawing on information about newspaper practices of the time and on the scanty available evidence of the author's compositional habits.[115] Whether or not Cambridge submitted 'A Woman's Friendship' complete or in portions,[116] Syme's interference was probably to the second instalment (Chapters III and IV). The first 'Mrs Cross' memorandum, dated 10 September, three days after this instalment appeared, was occasioned by a letter of protest about the changes from the author.

Syme's changes would have been made either to the setting copy or to the proofs, following which (if the latter were the case—and what evidence there is suggest it was[117]) the required changes to the type formes would have been made. Accounts of *Age* practices point to copy for a given issue being set in a single shift preceding printing (there is no evidence to suggest advance setting). Assuming that David Syme, the chief editor, looked at the handset proofs of a Saturday issue which included one instalment of 'A Woman's Friendship', he could have decided upon alterations in accordance with the normal exercise of editorial prerogative in the newspaper world. The proofs would then have been sent to a sub-editor to prepare the 'revises' which would then be sent to the stereotypers for making the moulds used for the actual printing. The whole process was carried out at high speed. Copy was divided amongst the compositors late on Friday afternoon and some parcels of papers would have been ready for despatch on the first country train at 3.40 a.m. on the Saturday.[118]

The dating of the first two memoranda (10 and 12 September), considered together with the fact that the second instalment (published on the 7th) is one of the shortest of the nine and the fourth chapter the shortest of the eighteen, strongly suggests that this instalment was the subject of the interference. It introduces the three male characters to the readers and consists of conversations amongst various of the five persons at the Exhibition and at the Coffee Palace. There is no obvious break to indicate the censor's pencil, and looking for physical evidence of typographical changes is problematic. The text of an instalment occupied at the most not quite four full columns of an eight column page. Removal of a chunk of matter from the serial could be compensated for by the addition of readily available 'fillers' somewhere else on the page. Removal of a word or two within a line might be made good by extra spaces evenly distributed, and so a possible clue to such deletions could be the presence of abnormally generous spacing. But this method of detection is so hypothetical that it should first be tested to see if the effect of known changes is discernible before being used with any confidence; and in this case there are none. (Nor need compression of textual matter indicate additions to the text; it could be compensation for additions to matter elsewhere on the page, external to the serial.) The nature of the changes has then to remain a mystery, with the present editor inclinated to believe that, before Syme's interference, Raymond Clive had some resemblance to a real editor and Seaton Macdonald to a real man about town.

In the newspaper text there are over thirty minor errors which this edition treats as inconsistent with publishing practices of the period (missing or misplaced inverted commas and apostrophes, and words obviously misspelled). It is reasonable to assume that many of the errors were introduced by compositors working at speed and were overlooked at the proof-reading stage. Spelling and punctuation of Cambridge's surviving letters from 1874 to 1925 are correct and consistent, even though her handwriting deteriorated as her arthritis worsened and her sight failed towards the end of her life. As noted earlier she was proud of her 'finished workmanship' and abhorred interference to her work. Other authors may have required the service to authors offered by the Centennial Publishing Co. which advertised help in the preparation of manuscripts for serial and book publication.[119] It is reasonably safe to assume that she did not, and that she delivered clean copy for typesetting.

The newspaper text also contains many inconsistencies of spelling, hyphenation and capitalisation unlikely, for the same reasons, to have occurred in the manuscript. It would be simple to ascribe these to a variety of compositorial styles and practices: over the two month period that 'A Woman's Friendship' was serialised many compositors would have had a hand in setting parts of the text. This explanation *alone* is put in doubt by the fact that inconsistencies in this novel and in other serials run in the *Age* in 1889 tend to occur more often than in its leaders, news items and advertisements. For instance, in the latter items, figures commonly represent numerals; in the serials there is a mixture of words and figures. And 'Situations' advertisements always call for 'house maid' while in the novel this word is rendered as 'house maid', 'housemaid' and 'house-/maid'. While it *may* be the case that serial fiction was not as closely proof-read as other material in the newspaper, it is more likely, given the extremely limited time available for proofing, that inconsistencies were the outcome of disagreement between practices of the *Age* and those of the author. A compositor would have had to decide, for each particular case where authorial practice differed from his understanding of house-style, whether to leave or to alter. The result would most likely have been a mixture of authorial and house-styles, moderated by the professional predilections (and alertness, on night shift) of a number of compositors. Thus more of the texture of the setting copy provided by the author could have made its way into the published version than would have been the case with book publication.

The version—which Ada Cambridge and tens if not hundreds of thousands of readers saw in print—was, nevertheless, not that which she submitted: it had been altered by inadvertent, uncorrected compositorial error, modified by inconsistently applied house-styling and censored by the chief editor. Syme had no intention of replying to Cambridge's letter of protest ('I know too much of authors to undertake to do anything of the kind').[120] Perhaps it was this experience with the *Age* which caused her to take back to the *Australasian* her final two newspaper novels in 1890 and 1891. Ironically she had earlier moved to the *Age* with 'A Black Sheep' when a new editor at the *Australasian* had wanted to make alterations to it.[121]

There is no way of restoring the material taken out by Syme nor, given the absence of all pre-publication states, of presenting a text which records the compositional development of the novel by systematically removing alterations attendant on the production processes. But it is possible for the editor to intervene to remove identifiable errors (instanced above) and to preserve inconsistencies (which are, conjecturally, a combination of authorial practice and house-style, and reflect historically possible forms). The text as first published is thus left in its virtual integrity. While neither the newspaper editor nor the author would have sanctioned errors, both would have taken for granted the imposition by the publisher of a house-style. Editorial judgment is exercised in discriminating between the historically acceptable and the unacceptable in deciding what constitutes 'error', but the standards of the 1980s are not taken to be relevant. The edited text is intended to reflect the originally published version as 'the product of the social event'.[122]

Thus there has been no attempt to regularise, whether according to a guess at the manuscript, an estimate of majority practice in the *Age*, or a contemporary publisher's house-style (for example, that of Heinemann, publisher from 1890 to 1893 of four novels by Cambridge). All such approaches would take the work further from its historical actualisation and all would involve conjecture. The aim is to re-present 'A Woman's Friendship' as the *Age* made it public, with the elimination of what are deemed to be introduced errors, but with the retention of inconsistencies which are assumed to be a mixture of authorial forms and house-style—the (lucky) product of inadequate guidance for the typesetting of literary works.

Thus, minimal changes have been made to the inscriptions. They have all been recorded in the List of Editor's Emendations on page 176 (except for those few silent alterations referred to in the Note on the Text, page 2; for emendations to the text of 'The Reform Club' see the note which precedes it).

Conversion from newspaper serial to single volume form entails the loss of the instalment factor and of the journalistic context. 'A Woman's Friendship' as published in the *Age* has two inner divisions—instalments and chapters. Each two-chapter instalment could be argued to have a narrative unity, with an interplay between the headings to the chapters which is both verbal (as in the sixth number, which covers the start of the break-up of the friendship *à trois*: 'The First Hour' and 'The First Tear') and conceptual (as in the eighth number which is the climax of the affair of Patty and Macdonald, when the twosome is revealed as neither ' "A Purely Intellectual Friendship" ', nor 'Brother and Sister'). Accordingly, a Table of Instalments follows the Note on the Text, page headings from the *Age* showing date of instalment have been provided (in square brackets, at the start of each one) and the '*(To be continued.)*' statement from the newspaper printing has been reproduced at the end of instalments one to eight.

An illustration of part of the first instalment as it appeared on 31 August 1889 on page 13 of the *Age* has been included (p xiv) to convey its appearance in the context of general reading matter provided in the Saturday paper, and also to display the columnar format. Conversion from the narrower format of the column to book page entails decisions about the preservation or elimination of end-of-line hyphenations: where a decision has had to be made between two historically acceptable forms, and there is no clear majority practice within the text to follow, the decisions have been recorded in the List of Editor's Emendations.

'A Woman's Friendship', written for readers in Victoria in 1889, includes many topical references and allusions, which may not be apparent to readers of today, particularly to those not familiar with the city of Melbourne. Notes to explain these have been provided where important to an understanding of the text. The maps on pages xxvi and 122 provide guidance to the Victoria and Melbourne of 'A Woman's Friendship' as its readers would have recognized them.

Notes

1   Other unrecorded novels known to the editor are: 'The
    Captain's Charge' *Sydney Mail* 1879; 'A Girl's Ideal' *Age*
    1881-82; 'The Perversity of Human Nature' *Illustrated
    Australian News* 1887. See Bibliographical Note pp 170-5 for
    further discussion.

2   The favourable reception of *A Marked Man* from 1890 is
    discussed by Debra Adelaide on pp vii-viii of her Introduction
    to the Pandora edn (London 1987). London reviews included
    those in the *Athenaeum* (20 September 1890) and the *Spectator*
    (27 December). The first Australian edn (Petherick Melbourne
    Sydney and Adelaide 1891) was acclaimed in the *Australasian
    Critic* (Vol 1 No 7 April 1891 pp 158-9). See also note 26.

3   Cambridge's use of irony has puzzled some critics. Eg: 'The
    problem [of understanding her attitude to class and behaviour]
    is further complicated by her irony, a device that is quite
    frequent in her writing. The difficulty is that sometimes one is
    not sure if it is present' (Raymond Beilby and Cecil Hadgraft
    Ada Cambridge, Tasma and Rosa Praed Oxford UP Melbourne
    1979 p 7); and 'They [Cambridge, Tasma and Praed] were
    bound, however, by the conventions of polite female fiction
    and were, perhaps, more satirical than we know' (Geoffrey Serle
    The Creative Spirit in Australia Heinemann Australia
    Richmond Vic 1987 p 37; 1st edn 1973 under title *From
    Deserts the Prophets Come*).

4   See Bibliographical Note pp 170-5.

5   James Smith 'Colonial Literature and the Colonial Press'
    Melbourne Review Vol 3 1878 pp 337-43; G B Barton 'The
    Status of Literature in New South Wales II: How the Publishers
    Look at it' *Centennial Magazine* Vol 2 No 2 September 1889
    pp 89-92; C T Clarke 'The Sorrows of Australian Authors: A
    Reply to Mr G. B. Barton' *Centennial Magazine* Vol 2 No 4
    November 1889 pp 300-5; Serle *The Creative Spirit* pp 57-8.

6   Discussed in Lurline Stuart 'Nineteenth-Century English and
    American Literary Periodicals and Their Australian
    Counterparts' *Bibliographical Society of Australia and New
    Zealand Bulletin* Vol 4 No 3 May 1980 pp 179-90.

7   Serialisation in newspapers is examined briefly in the
    following (which deal at more length with magazines): Pauline
    Kirk ' "Colonial Literature for Colonial Readers!" ' *Australian
    Literary Studies* Vol 5 No 2 October 1971 pp 133-45; Elizabeth
    Webby 'Before the *Bulletin*: Nineteenth Century Literary

Journalism' in *Cross Currents: Magazines and Newspapers in Australian Literature* ed Bruce Bennett Longman Cheshire Melbourne 1981 pp 3-34. Elizabeth Morrison 'Press Power and Popular Appeal: Serial Fiction and the *Age*, 1872-1899' *Media Information Australia* No 49 August 1988 pp 49-52 (based on her 'Newspaper and Novelists in Late Colonial Australia' MA Prelim Diss Monash U History Dept 1983) is a case study of one newspaper. The term 'tale' was frequently applied to novel and novella length works of fiction in newspapers (and 'sketch' rather than 'short story' to designate a short fictional work).

8   *Town Life in Australia* Stock London 1883 p 236.

9   *Naught to Thirty-Three* Melbourne UP Carlton Vic 1976 p 121. First published 1944.

10   This figure is based on the editor's research: see note 13.

11   Smith 'Colonial Literature' p 337.

12   'Colonials in Fiction' *New Zealand Illustrated Magazine* Vol 7 January 1903 p 274.

13   Based on the editor's current research, as yet unpublished—as is the survey of novels in Victorian newspapers and magazines in August 1889. Melbourne daily newspapers which regularly serialised novels were: the *Age*, the *Daily Telegraph* and, in 1889, the *Evening Standard*; weeklies were the *Australasian*, the *Leader*, the *Sun* (in 1889) and the *Weekly Times*.

14   Published also as books: *Miss Jacobsen's Chance* Bentley London 1886; *Uncle Piper of Piper's Hill* Trübner London 1889.

15   Ada Cambridge *Thirty Years in Australia* Methuen London 1903 [hereafter *Thirty Years*] p 122.

16   It is not possible to give an exact figure of the numbers of newspapers which provided serials because the supplements have not always been preserved with them.

17   Sources for checking publication in book form are: E Morris Miller *Australian Literature: A Bibliography to 1938, Extended to 1950* ed Frederick T Macartney Angus and Robertson [hereafter A & R] Sydney 1956; British Museum Dept of Printed Books *General Catalogue of Printed Books* London 1959-66; *The National Union Catalog: Pre-1956 Imprints* Mansell London 1968-80. The presence of unidentifiable American novels suggests that they were published in the U. S.

solely in newspapers and magazines, and that they were sold and syndicated by newspapers or press agencies in that country to newspapers or agencies in Victoria (and probably other Australasian colonies).

18   A ninth work, 'The Fratricide', a self-contained story but also a regular instalment of the 'Detective's Album' in the *Australian Journal*, has not been counted. These short crime stories by 'W. W.' or 'Waif Wander' (Mary Ellen Fortune) had been appearing in the 'Detective's Album' series for over 20 years.

19   Clarke 'The Sorrows of Australian Authors' p 305. The serials also published in book form are: Rolf Boldrewood (pseud of T A Browne) *Nevermore* Macmillan London 1892; Aubrey Haine (pseud of J H Dawe) *Vahiné* (serialised as 'Kidnapped') A Redfern Brunswick Vic 1885; David G Falk *Rick, or The Récidiviste* (serialised as 'The Recidiviste') Trischler London 1891.

20   Graham Pollard 'Novels in Newspapers' *Review of English Studies* Vol 18 1942 pp 72-85; Michael Turner 'Reading for the Masses' in *Book Selling and Book Buying* ed Richard G Landon American Library Association Chicago 1978 pp 52-72.

21   The selling power is clearly implied in Catherine Spence's own serial 'A Week in the Future' (*Centennial Magazine* 1889; in book form, Hale and Iremonger Sydney 1987): the futuristic newspapers 'confined themselves to their own department, and did not publish serial stories to induce a large circulation. If people wanted stories and poetry they had to buy them in books' (Vol 1 No 12 July 1889 p 900).

22   *Thirty Years* pp 132-6.

23   Smith 'Colonial Literature' pp 337-8. He collaborated with Cambridge some years later—see p xxviii.

24   *Sydney Mail* 8 March 1879 p 366. The competition was won by N W Swan, a journalist from Stawell, Victoria, for his 'Luke Mivers' Harvest' (forthcoming in the Colonial Texts Series).

25   'Editor's Library Table' *Melbourne Review* Vol 7 1892 p 225.

26   Many of the reviews in major British and American periodicals are listed in Janet Grimes and Diva Daims *Novels in English by Women 1891-1920: A Preliminary Checklist* Garland New York 1981. See also note 109.

27 Philip Mennell *The Dictionary of Australasian Biography* Hutchinson London 1892 pp 110-11; T A Browne (Rolf Boldrewood) 'Heralds of Australian Literature' *Report of the Fourth Meeting of the Australasian Association for the Advancement of Science, Hobart, 1892* Tasmania 1893 p 811.

28 Desmond Byrne *Australian Writers* Bentley London 1896 pp 131-58; Henry Gyles Turner and Alexander Sutherland *The Development of Australian Literature* G Robertson Melbourne 1898 pp 87-92; A Patchett Martin *The Beginnings of an Australian Literature* H Sotheran London 1898 p 28.

29 The *Age* and *Sydney Mail* in particular.

30 John Barnes 'Australian Fiction to 1920' in *The Literature of Australia* ed Geoffrey Dutton Penguin Ringwood Vic 1964 p 158 (p 173 in rev edn 1976).

31 For the contribution of the *Bulletin* to literary nationalism see William H Wilde Barry Andrews and Joy Hooton *The Oxford Companion to Australian Literature* Oxford UP Melbourne 1985 pp 123-5.

32 Examined most recently in Graeme Turner *National Fictions* (Allen & Unwin Sydney 1986); successive editions of Russel Ward's *The Australian Legend* (1st edn 1958) have continued to popularise the tradition.

33 *A. G. Stephens: Selected Writings* ed Leon Cantrell A & R Sydney 1978 p 84. (Stephens' article 'Australian Literature I' was originally published in the *Commonwealth* in 1901.)

34 *The Writer in Australia* ed John Barnes Oxford UP Melbourne 1969 p 170. (Palmer's article 'An Australian National Art' was originally published in *Steele Rudd's Magazine* in January 1905.)

35 Copy of letter 12 November 1909 MS 8062 Henry Gyles Turner Papers La Trobe Collection, State Library of Victoria.

36 Eg: the anonymous item 'Women in Literature: Popular Novelist, Ada Cambridge' in the regular feature 'Women's World' *Herald* (Melbourne) 20 February 1912 p 3; Eve's Daughter [pseud] 'Australian Women Poets' *Aussie* 15 December 1922 pp 65-6; Georgia Rivers 'Early Women Writers of Victoria' in *Centenary Gift Book* ed Frances Fraser and Nettie Palmer Robertson and Mullens for the Women's Centenary Council Melbourne 1934 pp 93-4; Winifred Birkett 'Some Pioneer Australian Women Writers' in *The Peaceful Army* Women's Executive Committee of the Advisory Council

of Australia's 150th Anniversary Celebrations Sydney 1938 pp 109-24; Kate Baker 'A Williamstown Novelist: Ada Cambridge (1843[sic]-1926)' *Williamstown Chronicle* 1 June 1945 p 1.

37   Eg: Colin Roderick *The Australian Novel* Brooks Sydney 1945 pp 66-8; Barnes 'Australian Fiction to 1920' pp 158-9 1964; John K Ewers *Creative Writing in Australia* 5th edn (rev) Georgian House Melbourne 1966 pp 14-15; Serle *From Deserts the Prophets Come* p 37; Adrian Mitchell 'Fiction' in *The Oxford History of Australian Literature* ed Leonie Kramer Oxford UP Melbourne 1981 pp 66-8; and *cf* disparagement expressed by Miles Franklin in *Laughter Not for a Cage* A & R Sydney 1956 p 84.

38   *Refractory Girl* No 2 Autumn 1973 pp 4-11; the most extended feminist treatment is Susan Sheridan's 'Ada Cambridge and the Female Literary Tradition' in *Nellie Melba, Ginger Meggs and Friends* eds Susan Dermody John Docker and Drusilla Modjeska (Kibble Books Malmsbury Vic 1982 pp 162-75).

39   Jill Roe ' "The Scope of Women's Thought is Necessarily Less" ' *Australian Literary Studies* Vol 5 No 4 October 1972 pp 388-403; Beilby and Hadgraft *Ada Cambridge, Tasma and Rosa Praed*. H M Green's extended discussion of Cambridge in *A History of Australian Literature* (A & R Sydney 1961 pp 244-52) chiefly concerns *A Marked Man*.

40   Letters to George Robertson 12 February 1921 and 25 December 1924 A & R Correspondence ML MSS 314/20 Mitchell Library, State Library of New South Wales.

41   Letter to A & R 30 December 1920 *ibid*.

42   Evident from many references to it in *Thirty Years*.

43   *Thirty Years* deals with the years 1870-1902, *The Retrospect* (Stanley Paul London 1912) with her visit to England in 1908 and her childhood and growing up, as she revisits places she knew in her early years.

44   Eve's Daughter [pseud] 'Australian Women Poets' pp 65-6.

45   ML MSS 314/20; *Dear Robertson* (ed A W Barker A & R Sydney 1982) includes a selection of this correspondence between Cambridge and Robertson.

46   But *cf* pp xxxviii-xxxix and note 112.

47   The A & R Correspondence includes 4 letters from Cambridge to Robertson (30 December 1920; 17 January, 12 February, 15

March 1921) and his 3 replies (12 January, 10 February, 9 March 1921) concerning the transaction.

48 ML C842 The Good Old Times. Some Episodes. By Ada Cambridge. Author of 'A Marked Man', 'Thirty Years in Australia', etc. Typescript 64pp Mitchell Library. 'The Reform Club' (pp 41-64) bears, in the author's handwriting, 161 cancellations (an average of 6.4 per page) and 13 added readings. While the cancellations are heavily overscored and, frequently, almost or totally illegible, the great majority appear to be mistyped words or phrases recognized as such in the course of typing and followed by the words or phrases typed correctly (the handwritten cancellations being made later). A small number appear to represent shortenings of the text. All but one of the added readings are single words—either inadvertent omissions being supplied, or substitutions for cancelled text. The one lengthy cancellation (9 lines) is replaced by the one added reading longer than one word: 'not there—only a housemaid emptying slops' (p 154 line 45, below).

49 Letters to George Robertson 17 January and 12 February 1921 A & R Correspondence.

50 Sue Thomas 'Ada Cambridge's "Unspoken Thoughts" ' *Notes & Furphies* No 18 April 1987 pp 9-10; Patricia Barton 'Re-Opening the Case of Ada Cambridge' *Australian Literary Studies* Vol 13 No 2 October 1987 pp 201-9.

51 'Ada Cambridge: A Remarkable Woman' *Sydney Morning Herald* 31 July 1926 p 9; this obituary contains other errors.

52 David G Falk 'To A. C.' *Centennial Magazine* Vol 2 No 6 January 1890 p 450; 'Some Australian Women' *Illustrated Sydney News* 11 April 1891 p 14; *Woman's World* August 1926 p 495; *Letters of Mary Gilmore* Melbourne UP Carlton Vic 1980 pp 138, 296.

53 *Thirty Years* pp 89-90.

54 'The Retrospect' *Atlantic Monthly* Vol 103 January 1909 p 130.

55 'The Lonely Seas' *Atlantic Monthly* Vol 108 July 1911 p 95. *The Prelude* of William Wordsworth (1770-1850) reads 'Voyaging through strange seas of thought, alone' (Bk iii l 63); first published in 1850, posthumously.

56 Vol 130 August 1922 pp 231-4. *Hymns on the Litany* (J H & J Parker Oxford and London 1865) is her first published book;

however the 'Women in Literature' item in the *Herald* (20 February 1912) mentions that Cambridge won £10 for a competitive essay at seventeen, and 'Eve's Daughter' in *Aussie* (15 December 1922) states that Cambridge's first published work was a hymn in a church magazine and that she had won prizes of £10 and £5 for competitive 'tales'. Both reports were probably based on interviews with the author.

57   *The Retrospect* p 11.

58   Letter to George Robertson 25 December 1924 A & R Correspondence (*Dear Robertson* p 134).

59   Letter 16 June 1874 MS 11242 W P Evans Papers La Trobe Collection, State Library of Victoria; Letters 15 and 23 December 1874 MS 169/1 W P Hurst Papers La Trobe Collection.

60   Except that she published *Unspoken Thoughts* and *The Hand in the Dark* at her own expense (Letters to A & R 25 June 1898 and George Robertson 12 February 1921 A & R Correspondence).

61   Letter to George Robertson 25 December 1924 A & R Correspondence (*Dear Robertson* p 134).

62   Letter 11 April 1897 ML MSS 667/12 Ethel Turner Papers Mitchell Library, State Library of New South Wales.

63   In an interview with William Archer, December 1901 (Archer *Real Conversations* Heinemann London 1904 p 196).

64   Letter to George Robertson 25 December 1924 A & R Correspondence (*Dear Robertson* p 134).

65   John Moroney *Anchorage of Faith: A Short History of Holy Trinity Parish Church Williamstown* [the Author Hawthorn Vic 1971] p 23.

66   Even in a letter of 29 May 1926, dictated to Percival Serle several weeks before her death when she could no longer read or write. MS 8486 Percival Serle Papers La Trobe Collection, State Library of Victoria.

67   *Thirty Years* p 45; *cf* 'Women in Literature' *Herald* p 3, and Eve's Daughter [pseud] 'Australian Women Poets' p 65.

. 68   Letter 7 August 1896 Ethel Turner Papers; Letter 22 October 1924 A & R Correspondence.

69   Extracting information from *Thirty Years*, D J Jordan has tabulated this domestic help as an Appendix to her thesis ('Ada Cambridge's Elaboration of Status' BA Hons U of Melbourne History Dept 1974) and shown it to be in excess of the norm for a clergyman's wife.

70   She wrote to Henry Gyles Turner on 12 January 1911 that returning to England was her husband's wish and 'I reconcile myself because I must' (Henry Gyles Turner Papers).

71   For the location of Wangaratta, Yackandandah, Ballan, Coleraine, Sandhurst and Beechworth and for all other geographic references see maps on pp xxvi and 122.

72   Her poems appeared in the *Sydney Mail* from February 1871 and fiction in the *Australasian* from 1872.

73   *Thirty Years* pp 89-90.

74   Letter 16 June 1874 Evans Papers.

75   *Thirty Years* p 131.

76   *Ibid* p 163.

77   Ill health is referred to several times in *Thirty Years* (eg pp 159-63), and the actual miscarriage and its continuing effects are clearly implied in 'The Lonely Seas' (1911). Bushfire and miscarriage are combined in 'Across the Grain' (1882).

78   *Thirty Years* p 162.

79   Picturesque Atlas Publishing Co Sydney Melbourne London & Springfield Mass '1886' but in fact first issued in parts 1886-88; (the part including the sections on Beechworth and Macedon, late 1887). In Volume II, which includes 'Towns of Victoria. By James Smith, Andrew Semple, and Ada Cross', Macedon is described on pp 283-4, and Beechworth on pp 308-10 where Cambridge includes reference to five feet of snow having fallen on 6 June 1887—also described in her 'Notes of an Australian Snowstorm' (*Age* 11 June 1887 p 13).

80   *Thirty Years* p 186.

81   *Naught to Thirty-Three* p 122.

82   *Thirty Years* p 188.

83 *Ibid* p 296; Letter to Bertram Stevens 29 May 1904 ML A2440 Bertram Stevens Papers Mitchell Library, State Library of New South Wales.

84 Letter 13 December 1924 A & R Correspondence.

85 *A Colonial City: High and Low Life: Selected Journalism of Marcus Clarke* ed L T Hergenhan U of Queensland Press St Lucia Qld 1972; R E N Twopeny 'A Walk Round Melbourne' in *Town Life in Australia* Stock London 1883 pp 1-18; Alexander Sutherland *Victoria and Its Metropolis* 2 vols McCarron Bird Melbourne 1888; Jill Roe 'Historiography in Melbourne in the Eighteen Seventies and Eighties' *Australian Literary Studies* Vol 4 No 2 October 1969 pp 130-8.

86 From 14 August 1888 the *Age* produced a series of weekly Exhibition Supplements which provided a detailed guide to the exhibits, and a comprehensive catalogue forms part of the *Official Record of the Centennial International Exhibition...Melbourne 1888-1889* (Sands & McDougall Melbourne 1890).

87 It may be the 1860s (*cf The Oxford Companion to Australian Literature* p 700).

88 See note 4 to Chapter IV.

89 See note 3 to Chapter III.

90 G S F 'The Scape-Goat' *Centennial Magazine* Vol 1 No 7 February 1889 pp 449-53; see also note 8 to Chapter II.

91 See note 2 to Chapter IV.

92 Farley Kelly 'The "Woman Question" in Melbourne 1880-1914' Ph D Monash U Faculty of Education 1982; Coral Lansbury 'The Feminine Frontier: Women's Suffrage and Economic Reality' *Meanjin* Vol 31 No 3 September 1972 pp 286-96. The 'Woman Question' is discussed extensively in *Dawn: A Journal for Australian Women* (Sydney Monthly from 15 May 1888) edited by Louisa Lawson. Lawson's Dawn Club, founded in May 1889 as an adjunct to the work of her journal, is also discussed in Brian Matthews *Louisa* (McPhee Gribble Fitzroy Vic 1987).

93 *Australasian* 22 October 1881 Supplement p 1.

94 Particularly, Constance Fleming in 'Across the Grain' (1882), Mrs Hallam in 'Against the Rules' (1885-86) and Richard Delavel in 'A Black Sheep' (1888-89).

95 Preface to 'The Good Old Times: Some Episodes' A & R Publishing MSS Mitchell Library.

96 *Cf* Patricia Barton 'Ada Cambridge: Creative Roles—Fact or Fiction?' in *Role Playing, Creativity, Therapy* ed Harry Heseltine English Dept University College Australian Defence Force Academy Canberra 1987 (Occasional Paper No 7) pp 33-46.

97 George Higinbotham (1826-92), journalist, politician and Chief Justice of Victoria, advocated the female franchise from the 1870s and was known as 'friend to women'; Charles Edwin Jones (1828-1903), notorious politician and journalist, advocated women's rights in his paper the *People's Tribune* (1883-86) and actively assisted the Victorian Women's Suffrage Society; William Robert Maloney (1854-1940) introduced the unsuccessful Women's Suffrage Bill in September 1889—see note 2 to Chapter VIII.

98 *Cf* 'my jealousy for my reputation for careful workmanship' (Letter to A & R 24 October 1906); [the quality of my books being] 'referred to by an English reviewer as "the graceful vigour of her finished workmanship"—a phrase I never forgot' (Letter to George Robertson 22 October 1924)); '[and being] so jealous for what a reviewer called my "finished workmanship"' (Letter to George Robertson 25 December 1924) A & R Correspondence.

99 Barnes 'Australian Fiction to 1920' p 159 (p 174 in rev edn 1976).

100 *Cf* Harry Heseltine on writers in colonial Australia: 'For the hundred years after 1788, our poets grappled with basically the same problem as that which tasked the writers of prose: how to realize the demands of the creating self in the kind of cultural vacuum to which they were condemned' (*The Uncertain Self* Oxford UP Melbourne 1986 p 9). For the importance of cultural formations (circles, movements, societies, 'schools' etc.) see: Raymond Williams *Culture* Fontana Glasgow 1981 pp 57-86.

101 Frequently mentioned in *Thirty Years* and to be inferred from literary allusions in her novels.

102 *Mullen's Monthly Circular* (Melbourne No 21 p 2) announced with pleasure in September 1885 the new Chapman and Hall cheap edition of the works of Meredith (1828-1909).

103 'Comedy is a game played to throw reflections upon social life, and it deals with human nature in the drawing-room of civilized men and women, where we have no dust of the struggling outer world...The Comic Spirit conceives a definite situation for a number of characters, and rejects all accessories in pursuit of them and their speech' (Penguin Harmondsworth 1968 p 33).

104 *Ibid* p 598; for Cambridge's admiration of Meredith see note 4 to Chapter VI.

105 'Literature: Some Recent Novels' (*Australasian* 2 October 1886 Supplement p 1) includes a lengthy description of *The Bostonians* and also of *Indian Summer* (by William D Howells), a novel with a similar plot, published in Edinburgh by Douglas; both are said to be available through Mullen's. Cambridge mentions James (1843-1916) in 'Missed in the Crowd' (1881-82) and 'Across the Grain' (1882). Given that Cambridge was participating in an international discourse on women's rights, the thematic parallels between *The Bostonians* and *A Woman's Friendship* (where, additionally, one of the Kinnairds' horses is called 'Henry James Junior') do not establish influence. However there are enough similarities to warrant further study.

106 '[Patty] "It is the most absolute bondage in the world" ' (p 13); '[Macdonald] "It's a free country, isn't it?" ' (p 23); '[Macdonald] "But you are in a free country now. Don't feel yourself in any sort of bondage, even to the cook"—[Margaret] "The cook is the one person we *must* bow to" ' (p 71).

107 P 51.

108 These were: 'A Black Sheep' as *A Marked Man* (1890); *The Three Miss Kings* (1891); *Not All in Vain* (1892); *A Little Minx* (1893); 'The Charm that Works' as *A Humble Enterprise* (1896). In addition, 'Mrs Carnegie's Husband' was rewritten to appear as *A Marriage Ceremony* (1894).

109 In letters to George Robertson (A & R Correspondence) she wrote ' "The Three Miss Kings"...has seemed the most widespread of all & the most popular though not with me' (16 December 1924); 'I never thought that book [*A Little Minx*] more than a slight sketch, but you see others did...& it...[is] one of the only two books the reviews of wh. I condensed & had printed' (25 December 1924). The printed record of condensed reviews is preserved in the Correspondence, following this letter: 20 reviews, mostly in English and Scottish publications (but including one in the *Toronto Mail*) have been culled.

110   Daily circulation of the *Age* was given as 81,149—an audited figure—in the issue of 6 November 1888 (p 4); on 1 February 1892, as 101,346. On market penetration see Morrison 'Press Power and Popular Appeal'. Circulation of the *Australasian* is recorded in 'Men Who Made the *Argus* and the *Australasian* 1846-1923' in Records, Minutes et al Australian Journalists' Association Victoria District (microfilm copy in U of Melbourne Archives).

111   For an annotated list of the 60 serials in the *Age* from 1872 (when this paper began the practice) to 1899 see: Morrison 'Newspaper and Novelists' pp 47-54.

112   The Syme Family Papers (MS 9751 La Trobe Collection State Library of Victoria) contain four documents clearly relating to the serial publication of 'A Woman's Friendship', although the novel is not mentioned by name. They are memoranda between David Syme and his nephew Joseph Cowen Syme; each is headed 'Mrs Cross': JCS to DS 10 and 16 September 1889 Box 1180/3; DS to JCS 12 and 16 September 1889—copies in Letter Book Box 1180/3. The sentence quoted is from David Syme's memorandum of 16 September. The 'younger Syme' as Cambridge later called J C Syme (Letter to George Robertson 25 December 1924 A & R Correspondence; *Dear Robertson* p 134) was in charge of much of the day to day running of the paper. The formality of written communication between the partners is explained by C E Sayers in terms of David Syme's autocratic aloofness and irritability and the increasingly strained relations between the two men (*David Syme: A Life* Cheshire Melbourne 1965).

113   In the same memorandum David Syme refers to 'Mrs Cross's letter where she says that it was agreed that "the work shd not be altered in any way" ' and continued: 'If such an agreement was made it is an unprecedented thing in this office'. See letter to George Robertson 25 December 1924 (A & R Correspondence; *Dear Robertson* p 134) for a description of two other occasions on which her copy was altered—she had perhaps forgotten the interference to 'A Woman's Friendship'.

114   Vol 2 No 4 November 1889 p 255. The October 1889 number of the *Australian Journal* carried a large advertisement for the bookseller E W Cole, but instead of his usual verses about the benefits of books to mankind there were six stanzas entitled 'Women and Books. Our Angel, Not Our Legislator' in which women were firmly placed in their domestic sphere—probably a tilt at the Suffrage Bill then before Parliament, but possibly also at Cambridge's novel. *Cf* the report in the *Coleraine Albion* (11 October 1889) of a meeting of the Coleraine Debating Club on 'Woman Suffrage'. One of the debaters

claimed that 'Women are great readers of newspapers', to which the 'Speaker', the Rev W J Gillespie, interjected: 'Especially of stories'. (He may have been recalling stories by the author who had once lived in his parish.)

115   Practices of the *Age* are described (anonymously) in 'A Popular Newspaper' (*Age* 25 September 1888 Exhibition Supplement p 2); printing practices generally, with some references to newspaper printing, are described in a series, 'The Progress of Printing', in the Exhibition Supplements for 11, 18, 25 September and 2 October 1888. Contemporary British manuals of printing practice contain chapters on newspaper work which confirm and amplify the above: eg Charles Thomas Jacobi *Printing: A Practical Treatise* G Bell London 1890; Joseph Gould *The Compositor's Guide and Pocket Book* Farrington London 1878. On the Syme memoranda, see note 113.

116   It was common practice for authors to supply their novels in instalments (*cf* Mary Hamer's study of Trollope, *Writing by Numbers* Cambridge UP Cambridge 1987). Serialisation of imported novels in the *Age* was often interrupted by late arrival of a mailboat, or by failure of the ship's mail to yield up the expected instalment (Morrison 'Newspaper and Novelists' pp 22-3). In a letter of 23 December 1874 Cambridge promised the editor of the *Australasian* that she would send 'the weekly portions [of 'Up the Murray'] as they are written' (W P Hurst Papers). On the other hand, David Falk submitted a whole manuscript to one or other Syme (implied in another memorandum by David Syme dated 12 September 1889 and headed 'Falk's Tale', this may have been Falk's 'The Recidiviste' running in the *Leader* contemporaneously with 'A Woman's Friendship').

117   To judge from the regular (and often acerbic) remarks and directives recorded in his Letter Books from 1871-96 (Syme Family Papers), David Syme made a practice of scanning each issue of the *Age* (either from proofs or printed copy).

118   'A Popular Newspaper' p 2. In 1889 the *Age* was set by hand. Printing was from lead plates cast from papier-mâché moulds in turn made from the type formes. This process of stereotyping enabled five machines to print simultaneously.

119   A widely advertised service (eg in the *Australian Typographical Journal* No 214 July 1888 p 895 and *Inglewood Star* 30 August 1889).

120   Memorandum of David Syme to Joseph Cowen Syme 16 September 1889 Syme Family Papers. The relative powerlessness of nineteenth century novelists when writing for

serial publication in magazines and newspapers and subjected to editorial censorship is described in N N Feltes *Modes of Production of Victorian Novels* (Chicago UP Chicago 1986); Feltes comments: 'The writer's work was produced in a journal within relations of production analagous to those prevailing in a textile mill' (p 63).

121 Letter to George Robertson 25 December 1924 A & R Correspondence (*Dear Robertson* p 134).

122 Peter Shillingsburg *Scholarly Editing in the Computer Age* English Dept Faculty of Military Studies U of New South Wales Duntroon 1984 (Occasional Paper No 3) p 32. Another edn University of Georgia Press Athens Ga 1986.

A WOMAN'S FRIENDSHIP

Note on the Text

This edition is based on the text of 'A Woman's Friendship' serialised in the *Age* newspaper in 1889 (see Table of Instalments on the following page). The copy-text has been transcribed from photoprint enlargements of microfilm copy of the newspaper and checked against hard copy in the State Library of Victoria.

The title-author statement which heads each of the nine instalments (see Illustration page xiv) is omitted. The '(*To be continued.*)' statement which concludes instalments [1] to [8] is retained, silently regularised to majority practice. (In two instances the full stop occurs outside the parenthesis.) Errors of spelling and punctuation are emended, and are enumerated in the List of Editor's Emendations on page 176; otherwise copy-text is followed precisely, and historically acceptable inconsistencies of spelling, capitalisation, hyphenation/word separation and punctuation are allowed to stand (see pp xli-xlii). Editorial decisions concerning four compound words which occur as end-of-line hyphenations in the *Age* printing are also recorded in the List of Editor's Emendations.

Table of Instalments

'A Woman's Friendship'
The *Age* (Melbourne) 1889

[THE AGE, SATURDAY, AUGUST 31, 1889.]

CHAPTER I.

– THE REFORM CLUB.

If it was not publicly distinguished, it was, at any rate, select. It consisted of three members. There was talk at one time of admitting a fourth, but the ballot went against him. Three was the full number.

The quantity might be small, but the quality left nothing to be desired. However inferior to other clubs in its political and social status, in the matter of intelligence and culture it was second to none. Other clubs—the very best of other clubs—are more or less mixed, resembling the proverbial chain with the weak link; but this club was of equal excellence all through, and its excellence was of a very high order. Three more refined and enlightened people than the three members of which it was composed—certainly three such persons in one group—it would be hard to find in these colonies. They were two women and one man, and the women were the founders; they were practically the committee also. And Mrs. Clive was president.

She was the wife of a newspaper editor—not an editor who had to be in bed all day and in his office all night (except on Wednesdays), but one who could breakfast and dine with his family, and otherwise perform the normal duties of a husband and father; for the *Rising Sun* was a weekly paper.[1] Many years ago she was a tall, dark-eyed, serious girl, acting as reader and companion to a rich and stingy old lady, and in her scanty leisure writing rather intense and

5

transcendental little essays for any periodical that would take them; and it was in the office of the *Rising Sun* (which had been rising for a good 10 years before that), while seeking editorial favor for her work, that she found favor for herself in the eyes of Raymond Clive, and was drawn into those relations which resulted in one of the happiest marriages ever perpetrated by two radically unsympathetic people. He was hard headed, practical, clear and calm minded, solid in every way; and she was all air and fire, a restless, craving, rebellious creature of ideals and dreams, hungering for better bread than is made of wheat, and, rather than eat that common food which is good enough for common folks, preferring to remain hungry; whereby it often happened that they seriously disagreed. But in the worst of their disagreements they never for a moment regretted the act that had made them one, and were as faithfully attached to each other as any husband and wife could be.

When the Reform Club was inaugurated they had been married for fourteen years, and the husband was grey and the wife was no longer young; she was nearer forty than thirty. But what of that? To those who are themselves old enough to be the best judges, thirty-seven is the age at which an attractive woman is in the zenith of her attractiveness, especially if her charms are of the intellectual order. Margaret Clive was very intellectual, and had never had the least hint that her woman's power was on the wane. Though her sympathies were wide, embracing every form of disreputable opinion, she was rather an exclusive person, shrinking from strangers and finding it difficult to make friends, so that her intimate circle was a small one; but to all within that circle she was as charming as she had ever been—a little amusing sometimes, but impressive always, with her passionate sincerity and seriousness, her impracticable aspirations and ideals, and her beautiful dark eyes that could shine and flash so splendidly. Technically she was a very handsome woman, with classically regular features and a graceful shape and carriage; but while her beauty was acknowledged, it weighed but little in the sum total of her attractions. I think it seldom does weigh anything like as much as people imagine.

There is, at any rate, one more potent charm, and she possessed it; so, in a still greater degree, did her beloved friend and club colleague, Mrs. Kinnaird. Mrs. Kinnaird had a rather large mouth, a rather prominent chin, and a slightly turned-up nose; and her warmest admirers, on whom she acted like a magnet upon steel, declared with one consent that she was a plain woman. "She has a plain face," they would say, with their conventional stupidity and contradictoriness; "there is not a good feature in it. But what a delicious face it is!" It was just the irregularity that was disapproved of which gave it its life and soul. One felt, in looking at her, that any straightening of that piquant profile would have tamed all the character out of it and made it insipid and commonplace. Nevertheless, because it was not straight, she was adjudged to be no beauty.

Neither was she clever, in what we may call the vulgar acceptation of that term. She had been brought up on a station and taught by a quite ordinary governess in the old ordinary style, and had experienced no instinctive thirst for better things until she came under Mrs. Clive's influence. She had a sweet voice and a delicate touch upon the piano, and sang simple songs to her husband of an evening in a manner which greatly impressed that easily pleased person, who could hardly tell one tune from another; and she had a pretty taste in the arrangement of flowers and of her clothes; and she had an undeniable talent for butter and cake making. But when one speaks of a clever woman one does not take into account such humble qualifications as these. Patricia Kinnaird was not conventionally clever any more than she was conventionally beautiful.

But she was that other and rarer and better thing—she was *interesting*. It is a subtle quality, very difficult to define, but we all know it when we see it; at any rate, we all *feel* it, with an up-springing alacrity of responsiveness which mere excellence of itself has no power to call forth. She was delightful to talk to; it was exhilarating to be in the same room with her; not a man could breathe the atmosphere of cheerful and intelligent sympathy which she diffused around her without feeling immediately cheered or soothed, as his case might be. The very dogs, which she soundly whipped when they misbehaved themselves—the very puppies, which had nothing but their shapeless puppy instinct, and no light of reason or ideas of self interest, to go by—fawned upon Patty Kinnaird and watched her every movement with yearning eyes of adoration, compelled by the nameless charm which subjugated their human brothers. As for Mr. Kinnaird, familiarly called Ted—a big, bluff, upstanding fellow, with as honest a face and as fine a seat on horseback as one would wish to see—the best of husbands, as she truly declared, in his dear, sweet, stupid way—he thought his little missus the pink of perfection in every respect, and would have knocked down any man who dared to hint to the contrary.

And these two remarkable and superior women came together and were bosom friends. Never, indeed, had there been such women friends, so loyal and faithful to each other, so mutually safe and sure, so utterly without suspicion or jealousy of one another, or any of the petty feelings that tradition associates with such a union. They looked upon themselves as a standing refutation of the cruellest slander cast upon their sex—the common assertion that

7

friendship between woman and woman is insincere and impermanent in the nature of things. Given the intelligence, high-mindedness and true-heartedness which were the equal heritage of both sexes, and two women were as capable of a noble and lasting friendship as two men, or as a woman and a man—or more. So they said, with absolute conviction; and did not their own case prove it? Their sympathies were not concerned with those trivial and shifting feminine interests to the prevalence of which insulting generalisations are due; they were based upon a deep belief in the large significance and responsibility of life, and in the duty and blessedness of mutual help between those who desire to live loftily and worthily in their difficult struggle towards the attainment of that end. Thus their friendship seemed built upon solid rock, and not upon the sand,[2] as usual; and it confidently defied the slow hostilities of time and the wildest caprices of the weather.

It was for their own sakes, in the first place, that they instituted the club, with its formulated rules and aims. They wanted to make their ideals as real as possible, to put their faith into practice, to use the strength afforded by their mutual support to the best advantage; and while one alone was comparatively vague and helpless, two together, standing shoulder to shoulder and keeping each other in courage and countenance, would be able, it was thought, to do great things. But when they took in the third member it was with the idea of communicating their strength to the world at large. A third implied an indefinite number; they had visions of a "movement," a beneficent propaganda, that should slowly but surely reform the whole vulgar system of society and be helping on the cause of human progress when they were in their graves.

The third member was as remarkable as themselves. He was not, as the thoughtless might suppose, one of the excellent and beloved husbands; he was not a brother, or even a cousin. The relationship was one of soul and sentiment only. I say *only,* but, of course, that relationship, in the estimation of his colleagues, was far more binding than any ties of blood. He was a tall, dark, well bred, highly cultured man of 37—the same age as Mrs. Clive and four years older than Mrs. Kinnaird—and would have been a mere boy to them but that his youth had been prematurely blighted by a domestic tragedy, and that he bore in his melancholy eyes and austere gravity of manner proof of the precocious soberness of character which was the result of his large experiences. There are some men who are always young; but Mr. Seaton Macdonald at 37 had the air of an elder who had outlived things (though it may be said that he had not really outlived them); and this, and the perfect taste of his deportment in the society of women, made it possible to admit his person as well as his opinions to the most exclusive club that ever called itself by that name.

They held their first full meeting at Mrs. Clive's house, which was an old-time cottage surviving amid the uniform white terraces of an East Melbourne street.[3] The second took place at the Imperial Coffee Palace,[4] where Mr. and Mrs. Kinnaird had taken rooms for several weeks in order to thoroughly "do" the Exhibition. After that—for the space of a month or so—the members assembled wherever and whenever they could do so conveniently,[5] more and more frequently as each week passed, and with ever-increasing profit and enjoyment; always, it must be understood, with the full knowledge and approval of Mr. Kinnaird and Mr. Clive. Thrice they met in the Public Library; once in the Botanic Gardens; twice in the University museum; four times they went down to Brighton and sat on the beach, and once they took the "Ozone" to Sorrento. But the regular rendezvous was, of course, the great building in Carlton gardens;[6] it was there they had an almost daily symposium, and all that seemed worth remembering of the summer was associated with it.

Apart from its great attractions, the music and the pictures, our Centennial Exhibition was a very good place in which to enjoy the society of your special friend, as must be well known to a great many of my readers. Few private premises licensed by Mrs. Grundy[7] could furnish such peaceful nooks and corners, such opportunities for comfortable retirement from observation, as were to be found by those who wanted to find them in that apparently public resort. You had but to pass through the turnstile into the fernery, and follow the left hand path to the end, and there you found a quiet bench out of everybody's way, a cool green bower all to yourself (or yourselves), with only twittering little birds to spy upon you—and they twittered so softly you could hardly hear them. Or you could go into the fisheries court, which was a very deserted place, and sit in a corner on a soft settee that had springs in both back and seat; and if a casual wanderer happened to see you he would not come anywhere within sound of your voice. When evening drew on, and the seals and the sea birds had grown sleepy and uninteresting, there would be great peace in a certain alley of the aquarium, and a darkness in which you could hold your companion's hand as he or she sat beside you, without fear of being discovered by the people passing through. Then there was the dome. At certain times in the day there were no sightseers up there; you could sit on the steps or lean upon the parapet, and breathe the lofty air, and take your bird's eye view of the far spreading city, undisturbed by strangers coming suddenly round the corner. In the grounds below there was the hollow tree— what tales that tree could tell if it could speak! There was the pretty, airy bamboo house, with its delicate scent of tobacco and its pleasant cane seats, where one could often sit as in one's own house, no one near but the invisible custodian in his little vestibule at the top of the stairs. There were Cook's rooms;[8] there were chairs behind the big carriages in the armament court; in short, the place fairly bristled with invitations to privacy and repose. Lovers, as a rule, monopolised these retreats,[9] but the unsentimental observer, throwing a furtive glance into them as he passed by, would often notice with amusement that three people had withdrawn themselves instead of two. It was the Reform Club holding its little meetings, and not a pair of sweethearts and a "gooseberry,"[10] as he vulgarly supposed. And perhaps there was nothing more curious and interesting in that place of interesting things than those three fairly young people of kindred spirit and mixed sex, who—honestly—had no sense of redundancy in their number.

CHAPTER II.

– HOW THE CLUB ORIGINATED.

In the early days of the Exhibition and of the friendship between Mrs. Kinnaird and Mrs. Clive, the British loan pictures were the absorbing interest[1] of the show to all cultivated and would-be cultivated persons. And on a certain sunless morning, when the light promised to be rather better than usual, our two ladies repaired to the gallery containing these treasures and studied them with a delicate enjoyment together.

Mrs. Clive was there first. She might have been seen at a very early hour (for she disliked crowds) moving slowly round the room, a tall woman, with a thin, refined, rapt face, and an air of natural dignity and distinction that enabled her to wear an unfashionable dress without degrading herself in the public eye. She had on a dark woollen gown that had a loose body with a mere apology for a waist, and a skirt without a scrap of bustle; and her bonnet, instead of soaring half a yard into the air, touched its highest point about 3 inches above her head. These articles of attire, which were obviously home made (because no dress maker or milliner could have been got to manufacture them for love or money), rendered her a somewhat conspicuous figure[2]—and she suffered terribly in feeling herself conspicuous; but the judgment on her was that she was eccentric, not that she was dowdy, because it was so evident that she was a lady in spite of her clothes.

She was standing in a corner, looking up at Leighton's

copper-colored Phryne,[3] when her friend, not knowing she was there, came tripping in. Mrs. Kinnaird was dressed in the correctest manner, not extravagantly in the fashion, but not in the least outside of it. The back draperies of her skirt hung from the universal cushion, and her smart little jacket "sat" to her charming figure in a manner that necessarily implied stays; while her hat was tall, with tall bows sticking up in front of it—all in the ungraceful and inartistic mode of the day, modified by individual good taste as far as possible. Her face was like a ray of morning sunshine, and her costume to the conventional eye left nothing to be desired; but Mrs. Clive looked her over with sad dissatisfaction, while bestowing on her a welcome of almost impassioned cordiality.

"My darling! Oh, how glad I am! I hurried down to the Coffee Palace directly after breakfast, hoping to catch you before you went out, and you were gone, and there was nothing written in the message book to show me where you had gone to."

"I was gone to your house, Margaret, to look for you," returned Mrs. Kinnaird, holding her friend's hand tightly in both her own. "Ted had an engagement to go and see some horses, and didn't know when he would be back, and I thought it would be such a chance for us to have a quiet morning with the pictures, all by ourselves."

"Yes, a beautiful chance. I am so glad we didn't miss it. We will make a day of it, Patty; we'll lunch here and go to the concert this afternoon. Shall we?"

Patty assented eagerly, and they proceeded to inspect the pictures in a mood of radiant satisfaction, beginning with the beautiful figure over their heads. Mrs. Kinnaird remarked that it was not a picture, but a statue,[4] and was quite sure that Phryne never had that complexion.

"Take her as a statue," Mrs. Clive replied. "How lovely she is! Oh, to think of the human body being made like that, and that we should know no better than to distort it so hideously as we do!"

"I suppose we do really know better," Mrs. Kinnaird suggested, "even while we do it."

"Yes, that is the worst of it. We are educated now—we can't plead ignorance. The most of us know that we are acting like barbarians who think it beautiful to tattoo themselves, and yet we do it all the same. It is a disgrace to us, in these days. It justifies the men in sneering at us. They are quite right to despise women."

"But it is a good deal the fault of the men, Margaret. A man can't bear to see a woman going outside the rules, even if she herself has the courage for it. He makes fun of our absurdities in dress, but if we look the least odd he is the first to take fright and to shrink from being seen in the street with us."

12

"But if enough of us—if just that number of us who know what is true in art and life—would only make up our minds to be sincere and natural, we should cease to look odd—it is the others who would look odd. And the men would side with us as soon as ever they saw we meant it."

"Ah, it is so easy to say all that! But no talking alters it, Margaret. It is the most absolute bondage in the world. We are tied hand and foot—we *can't* escape. One here and there—one like you—refuses to wear a bustle, and feels very uncomfortable because people stare but it makes no difference. It doesn't affect the mass."

"Oh, Patty, don't, *don't* allow yourself to think that!" Mrs. Clive implored, with an earnestness that made her intense eyes burn and glow. "It is the most paralysing thing—it simply *kills* you. Why, if everybody had that idea—that it was no good for him or her to try, because one can do so little by one's self—what sort of a world would it be? How would *anything* get done? All the great reforms begin with a few people—they begin with *one*—and who knows which one? The history of success is the history of minorities, John Morley says.[5] We never can tell how far our influence goes, but if even it went no further than we can see it, we are still bound to do our best. Don't let us make each other faint-hearted, Patty."

"*You* never make *me* so, Margaret," the little woman replied with fervor. "You always lift me up." But she felt she would have to make a considerable struggle on her own account before she would rise to the level of her friend's courage and conscientiousness; and, as she quite intended to make that struggle, being an aspiring little soul, she began to wonder whether it would quite spoil the set of her skirt if she took the pad out, and whether Teddy would notice the difference and make a fuss about it.

They had been sauntering slowly as they talked, looking at the Dying King, and the Fowler's Crag, and the Poor Man's Friend without remark, and passing over Gilbert's warriors and Frith's street procession with a mere surface-skimming glance; and now they sat down before that glorious landscape of Vicat Cole's, which, perhaps, of all the Exhibition pictures,[6] will be the most living and loving memory to those who were never tired of looking at it while they had the chance. Surely the man who painted it—if he could know—would count it the best part of the fame his work had achieved that to thousands of English folk on the other side of the world the thought of their native land, which many of them may never see again, will henceforth be the thought of those beautiful green woods and golden autumn fields—that all the power of British statesmanship has not done so much to weaken the tie between the home country and her colonies as he, by this one bit of canvas, has done to strengthen it.

"Oh," said Mrs. Clive, when she and her companion had gazed at it for some time, in a silence broken only by a sighing murmur of delight, "Oh, what wouldn't one give—if one had it to give—to be able to hang such a picture on one's own wall, to look at always! What an effect it would have on one's life—one's temper, one's imagination, one's casual inspirations! And yet see how it is—a dozen such, if one could suppose it possible there should be a dozen of anything so beautiful, have not the market value of one black and faded old master that never at the best of times had a spark of poetry in it. These men with money—these Governments that are forming national collections[7]—they will give a fortune for an old daub with a name to it, while hundreds of young artists, struggling to express the noblest spirit of their time, enlightened as those old painters never could have been, must struggle and starve or come down to vulgar *genre* and portrait painting for a living. Oh, what a world of shams it is!"

They went round the room until they reached the Turner pictures, which admirably served to illustrate this fervent lady's argument. "Look at that," she said, pointing to the least well preserved of the two, grey and dim as a rain washed sky. "There you see one of the gems of the collection, Patty. It is offered to the Government, dirt cheap, for £4000, which probably is much under its market value; and having been an early and inexperienced piece of work in the beginning, it is now a mere faded smudge, a little darker in some places than in others. But it is a genuine Turner, and that is sufficient. If every line were smudged out, so that you couldn't tell sea from rock or rock from sky, that would be sufficient. Now, Patty, if you were a rich woman, would *you* spend £4000—money that would mean life and comfort and *goodness* to scores of gutter children, who, wanting it, will die miserably or grow up thieves and prostitutes—*would* you spend all that on a genuine Turner from which Time had taken all the color and all the beauty that it ever had?"

"What a question!" cried Patty, with smiling indignation. "You know I shouldn't do anything so absurd."

"This old picture is like diamonds, and all those things that are conventionally precious and yet don't do you or anybody the least bit of good. Would you spend a lot of money on diamonds, Patty, if you were a rich woman?"

Mrs. Kinnaird winced for an inappreciable moment, but she thought of the gutter children and answered, conscientiously, that she hoped not.

"I hope not, too," said Mrs. Clive. "But I am sure you would not—you know better. Oh, Patty, do, *do* let you and me try

14

to follow conscience and not vulgar fashion—as far as we possibly, possibly can! Let us say what we think, dear, and do what we know, and not be afraid of being laughed at. Let us feel *ourselves* that we are not miserable sheep-like imitators—machine-made goods, as Raymond calls us—but individuals with souls and with responsibilities of our own. If we shake ourselves free, we may encourage others—at least we shall feel we have a right to our own self respect."

"Margaret," responded Patty, whose soul was uplifted by these eloquent words, "I do want to be sincere and true—as true as you are. Help me to be like you."

"We will help each other, darling," said Mrs. Clive.

They stood before the famous Wattses and Holman Hunts, and Mrs. Kinnaird, having been given to understand that these were pictures one was expected to kneel down before and worship, drew upon her newly augmented courage to the extent of saying plainly that she thought them horrid.[8]

"Not quite horrid, dear—you don't quite mean that," Mrs. Clive gently corrected, having been an art student and critic from her youth up; and when Patty had looked at "Hope" a little while, and had the allegory of "Love and Life" explained to her, she did modify her sweeping condemnation somewhat and admit that she was probably an ignoramus. "But if I am to speak my real mind, Margaret——"

"Darling, of course you must, fully—always."

"Well, do look at 'The Spirit of Christianity,' and those dreadful infants under her skirts! Look at their legs—the 'doublet of the flesh,' indeed! It is like the hide of a hippopotamus. And look at 'Mammon,' and those wisps of creatures under his feet. Call those young men and maidens! They are neuters—they have never had any life to be crushed—they are like things dead before they are born. And 'The Shadow of Death' "—moving a step or two—"it's just an old painted window—what you call 'conventionally treated,' I suppose, like flowers on an art wall paper. And 'The Scapegoat'— oh, Margaret, the Scapegoat! That moon is just a white wafer you might have stuck on with your thumb, and the rainbow is like the Book Arcade,[9] and neither of them is possible with those magenta mountains, and that green sky. I am not artistic, I know, but truth is truth, and if it comes to moons and rainbows, I have the faculty of observation like other folks."

Margaret looked with some mournfulness at these several features that were so irreverently exposed, for as a young girl in London, Watts and Holman Hunt had been a part of her religion. "Yes," she said, after a long pause and a long search for the beauty and meaning that had passed away, "Yes, Patty, truth is truth, and if

15

we cannot see it as we are asked to see it, we must not pretend we do. I used to think——however, the illusion is gone. I felt it the first day. Artists must judge artists; this is true for them, I suppose, but it is not true for us. Come on, and let us find something that is true for us."

They moved up and down the room for some time longer, continuing their study of the pictures and their earnest but ruthless criticism, and keeping up a running commentary of moral reflections which tended to bring them more and more to the position soon after fixed by the club rules. Then they went down stairs and had their lunch; then, after a little quiet saunter through the draughty avenues, which furnished so many sight-seers with bad colds to begin with, they repaired to that bower of bliss, the concert hall,[10] and sucked fresh inspiration into their souls.

Margaret Clive sat through what Patty secretly called the "heavy" numbers, a Wagner overture, and a movement from a Beethoven Symphony,[11] with clasped hands and solemn, fixed eyes, like a transfigured saint, evidently steeped in rapture too deep for words. Patty's little heart bounded to the measure of the "Yellow Jasmine" gavotte, and "The Last Sleep of the Virgin"[12] brought delicious tears to her eyes. "Margaret," she whispered, in one of the intervals, "may I say something?"

"What, my darling?"

"I don't like Wagner a bit, Margaret."

"Oh, *Patty!*"

"You know what you said upstairs, dear? It is true for many people, but it is not true for me. I must be honest and say what I really think, mustn't I?"

"Of course—*of course*. But you will come to it, Patty. No one can take in Wagner all at once. It will grow upon you by degrees, you'll see. When they play Wagner you should shut your eyes tightly—shut everything out—and not open them until it is over; and while the music goes on try to forget where you are, and *imagine things*. That helps you wonderfully."

They came out of the hall in the mood of devotees coming out of a church, and as they slowly drifted doorwards with the crowd they discussed a plan for going to the next choral concert together.

"The front seats will be 4s.," said Mrs. Clive, "and that is not such a good part of the house for hearing the music as the cheap places. Patty, as we are ladies, and neither of us too well off, shall we be superior enough not to mind sitting in the cheap seats, to save our money and hear the music better? Shall we come early and have tea here, and be warm in our cloaks and bonnets, and sit in the gallery?"

16

"Yes, if you like, Margaret," answered her friend, who had never been a second class person in her life, but saw at once what a beautiful chance this was for exercising moral courage; "if our husbands don't insist on coming too and making their own arrangements. Would Mr. Clive mind, if he knew?"

"Not in the least; he is very superior to human weakness of the vulgar sort. He'd just as soon take a back seat as not."

Patty was a little in doubt as to what Ted's view of the case might be, but he was so amiable, she said, that he would do anything anybody asked him.

"Very well," said Margaret; "it is a compact, then. We are going to make no vain shows any more, Patty, you and I. We will help each other to set an example. And this will be a very good beginning."

(To be continued.)

17

CHAPTER III.
– THE THIRD MEMBER.

Coming out of the concert room and mixing with the crowd under the dome, our two ladies met the potential third member, who had just entered the building. A decidedly distinguished looking person he was, as he passed quietly on his way through the bustle of moving figures, his tall head carried with the air of one to whom a position of social superiority is a matter of course, his melancholy face as impassive as a mask, his sober costume the perfection of tailoring and taste; and Patty, when her attention was called to him, was greatly struck with his appearance. She did not remember to have seen him before. Margaret, however, had known him for some time, and regarded him as her most interesting acquaintance.

"There is Mr. Seaton Macdonald," she said in a hurried undertone, while he was yet some distance off. "You don't know him, do you, Patty? But you must know him. He wrote that beautiful paper in last Saturday's *Sun* on *The Liberty of Woman*.[1] He is one of the few men who do us justice."

"What a handsome fellow!" murmured Mrs. Kinnaird.

"Oh, handsome—that's nothing," Mrs. Clive rejoined impatiently. "I never think of his looks. He's one of the most enlightened men I ever met. I have been wanting so much for you to know him—will he see us, I wonder? Ray met him at the Hamlet Club,[2] and liked his talk, and got him to write things for the paper—he is so very literary in his tastes—and brought him one day to see me. He often comes now; but he has been in the country for some weeks."——Her voice fell to a whisper; she bowed, and the gentleman lifted his hat, acknowledging her recognition with a smile that, though grave, was full of cordial friendliness. "Good afternoon, Mr. Macdonald. Have you just arrived? Let me introduce you to my friend—my great friend—Mrs. Kinnaird."

Mr. Macdonald bowed low, and received the usual impression of Patty's piquant and charming face. "Mrs. Edward Kinnaird?" he questioned gently, in a voice of singular refinement, and with a slow drawl that had a sound of affectation until one became accustomed to it.

"Edward—yes," Patty answered for herself, for she was too sure of her position in the estimation of the abstract man to be afraid of him in any shape. "My husband is the second son."

"I have the pleasure of an old acquaintance with him," said he; and, though he did not seem to move a muscle, somehow his face reflected the pleasant brightness of hers. "We were at school together."

"Were you? He was one of the doctor's old boys. Oh, I am sure I have heard him speak of you. But how is it I have never seen you before?" She smiled at him as if she had been seeing him all her life. "Have you been out of Australia since?"

"Yes, mostly. I went to Cambridge from the Grammar School.[3] Then I was a Temple barrister,[4] and then—well, I haven't been at home much, till lately."

Mrs. Clive looked at her companion from the corner of her eye; the look was as swift as a flash of lightning, and seemed to fall upon Patty's ear, but it had the effect of immediately diverting the conversation into other channels. Mrs. Kinnaird launched forth upon the subject of the Exhibition, and asked Mr. Macdonald if he didn't think that, apart from its music and pictures and electric lights, it was inferior to the Exhibition of 1880.[5] Mr. Macdonald said he had not seen the first one, but believed on Mrs. Clive's authority that it was much the better of the two in quality, though not in quantity. And they talked in this preliminary manner for a few minutes, while Margaret looked on with smiling satisfaction, glad to have brought them together and hoping they would become friends. Then a question arose as to what they were severally going to do.

"I telegraphed to Raymond before lunch, and asked him, if he did not see me at the office this afternoon, to meet me at 5 o'clock by the Bull," said Mrs. Clive, consulting her watch. Boehm's marble group of the bull and herdsman, in its first position under the dome,[6] was the popular point of rendezvous. "We have half an hour yet, Patty."

"I ought to be getting home," said Patty, "as I don't know when Ted will be back. But perhaps I can stay half an hour."

"Then what shall we do, love?—the pictures again?"

"I am dying for a cup of tea, Margaret."

"Let me get you some tea," said Mr. Macdonald, with less of his drawl than usual. "Come, Mrs. Clive, if you have been here all day you must be dying for tea, too."

"I am not the slave to tea that she is," said Margaret. But she submitted to the proposal, and he took them to the commissioners' dining room, where tea was to be had, fresh brewed, in little pots; and there they sat together in great peace and quietness round a nice white table and had a most interesting conversation.

"Mrs. Kinnaird and I," said Mrs. Clive, "at the moment we met you, were talking of going to the concert on Thursday night and sitting in the cheap seats. In fact, we have decided to do it. Because we agree that it is both vulgar and cowardly to spend more than is necessary or than we ought to afford, merely because we are afraid of losing caste with Mrs. Grundy—and especially as the music sounds much better in the gallery than in the front seats below. Don't you think we are right?"

She looked at Mr. Macdonald with a calm frankness that betokened a consciousness of established sympathy between them, and he looked at her with evidently friendly and admiring regard. Patty was ashamed to feel that she was capable of blushing at hearing the second class project divulged to a stranger.

"I think you are always right," he said; and he looked as he spoke at Patty's rosy countenance. "I don't know whether you are aware of it, Mrs. Kinnaird, but Mrs. Clive is certainly the most sincere and courageous woman—however, I must not say such things before her face. But you understand me?"

"*Quite,*" said Patty, with fond enthusiasm. "I am perfectly aware of what she is. I am in the position of the weak brother,[7] whom she is teaching by her example to grow strong——"

"The weak sister," he corrected. "*I* am the weak brother."

"And I am never with her for five minutes that I don't feel ever so much better—*higher,* you know."

"Nor I. Mrs. Clive, I want to go to the choral concert, too. May I join your party and sit in the cheap seats with you?"

"I don't know," she replied seriously. "You are a rich man——"

"And it is easier for a camel to go through the eye of a needle[8]—just so. I read your thought. And I should be a sort of defaulter if I did not pay the highest prices for everything. But I can get a front seat ticket and still sit in the gallery, can't I? And thus I shall enjoy the luxury of virtue without defrauding the

20

commissioners of their just rights—if you will only allow me."

"Oh, it will be no virtue in you. Everybody knows you. Nobody who sees *you* in the cheap seats will look down on you for being there."

"Is it necessary to the purpose that one should be looked down upon?"

He smiled his grave and distant smile, but she continued to regard him and the subject in question with profound gravity. "That's a very stupid question," she said, and as such she put it aside. "The purpose, ultimately, is to teach people not to look down on anybody—to accustom them to ideas and habits of honesty and good taste. But we must make a real thing of it, not a sham."

"I see. And I am disqualified?"

"Certainly. It would be play and pretence with you; with Mrs. Kinnaird and me it will be serious. We shall be pioneers in the proper sense. We shall have to suffer for our cause. However"—and she looked encouragingly at her friend—"the more we suffer the greater will have been our share in the work of human progress, Patty."

"Do you think there will be much to suffer?" inquired Mr. Macdonald, with his gentle drawl. "You have the true martyr spirit—I could go down on my knees before you in admiration of it; but the opportunities for its exercise are so terribly small and few in these days."

"It may seem so to *you*," she replied, with quick sarcasm, and a lifting of her head. "You may consider it a small thing, for instance, to take a railway journey in a second class carriage[9] with workpeople and Chinamen, and to have your friends who see you looking at you coldly, and porters treating you with familiarity or neglect—because *you* are so rich that nothing of that kind can touch you; but how do you think Mrs. Kinnaird would feel it?"

She still spoke without the least embarrassment, and would have regarded it as mere affectation to be otherwise than candid in the company of true and congenial souls; but her two companions, who did not yet know each other, felt the subject a little awkward.

"Mrs. Clive regards me as a criminal for being what she calls rich," Mr. Macdonald said to Mrs. Kinnaird, "though I have told her again and again that I can't help it. It is my misfortune and not my fault. I have done all I could to neglect my property, and it will continue to thrive in spite of me. When she drives me to despair with her reproaches, and I offer to give it away to charities, she turns round and abuses me for insulting the honest independence of my betters, and says I want to pose as a pious founder and a candidate for knighthood."

Margaret went on as if he had not spoken. "It is not alone

21

in a little thing like sitting in the gallery at the concert that we are going to show our determination to break through the bad habits of a bad state of society," she said calmly. "That is nothing. But to systematically defy the laws of caste on the railway will mean a great deal—as you would see if you would trouble yourself to think about it—but you seem in a flippant mood to-day. You know as well as I do that a lady would be simply insulted—not in words or deeds, but in the general regard of her class and the authorities—if, because she was strong enough not to mind a hard seat, and had no money to waste, she chose to travel for a pound instead of thirty shillings (and, Patty dear, that is just about the difference in your fare when you come up or down—a difference of half a sovereign, which you know you could spend in a thousand better ways). And yet you tell me that such an act of courage—true courage, I call it— is too small and paltry to deserve mention!"

"Oh, I don't—I don't indeed!" He held up his long hands, palm outwards, and looked at her appealingly. "It would imply the highest and noblest courage."

But though he said this, he was not cordial to the railway project. She saw it, and pounced upon him quite fiercely.

"I know what you are thinking of," she said. "I know why you look at Patty in that way. You are thinking you wouldn't like to see her boxed up with roughs and Chinamen, because she is a lady—just what all the *common* men would think."

He humbly confessed that he wouldn't like it, apologising for his commonness.

"And why not?" she demanded. "There are no more roughs in the second class than in the first, and, if there were, a lady would manage to smooth them; and Chinamen are human beings and as inoffensive as possible. Oh, don't *you* talk like that—you who *do* understand, even though you are rich. Don't discourage her with conventional platitudes about ladies being out of place when they are here or there where ladies don't usually go."

But Patty, kindled by contact with this fervent spirit, did not mean to be discouraged. "I shall never feel that I am out of place where you are, Margaret," she said, stretching her pretty hand across the table to touch that of her friend. "Where thou goest, I will go."[10]

"Darling!" ejaculated Mrs. Clive, almost with a lover's passion. "It shall be the test of the sincerity of our principles, that we don't show ourselves afraid to travel second class on the railway, or to sit in back seats at concerts."

"And what about the theatre?" Mr. Macdonald queried gently. "Stalls or gallery?"

"Stalls. Patty, we will go and see The Magistrate[11] to-morrow night, if you like, for three shillings apiece."

"Well, we could," said Patty. "For Ted is engaged to dine at the club[12] to-morrow night."

"Let us go, then. You must do all you can while you are in town, and Brough will amuse you, darling, if you haven't seen him in that part."

"I shall be there," said Mr. Macdonald, in a tone of determination.

"No, no," said Margaret; "we cannot have you—a rich man like you—turning all our reality into sham. You stay in the dress circle with your class."

But Patty looked at him wistfully. She thought sitting in the stalls would be much pleasanter if he sat there with them, and he read her thought plainly.

"What do you think, Mrs. Kinnaird? It's a free country, isn't it? And if I give Mrs. Clive the extra two shillings for—for the amelioration of the condition of the human race—"

"Don't, *don't* laugh at him, Patty," cried Margaret, in quick resentment of his tone, which was as grave as possible. "Don't you see that he is only mocking us—that he thinks us a pair of crack-brained idiots."

"That I think you a pair of—gracious heavens! But I suppose it is of no use protesting. I must bear it," said Mr. Macdonald plaintively.

"And I must go back to the dome," she cried, looking at her watch and finding herself five minutes late for her appointment. Whereupon they left their tea table abruptly, and the ladies drew on their gloves as they hurried through the gay avenues to the place of rendezvous; for, with all their modern notions, they were still quite conventionally punctilious in their regard for the convenience of their husbands, both of whom were waiting for them beside the Bull. At the Coalbrookdale corner an acquaintance of Mr. Macdonald's rudely arrested him for a minute or two, and gave Margaret an opportunity to deliver herself of a few words that evidently burned for utterance.

"You must not think he is always like this, Patty," she whispered rapidly, with an apologetic air. "I have never seen him so frivolous before. He is always serious and thoughtful with *me*—I suppose he doesn't feel sure of you just yet. You have no idea how earnest he is, really; and it is so strange, considering his circumstances. He was married to a dreadful woman of the world—you didn't know that when you began to question him. She was a fashionable animal merely, with no more intellect than a cunning animal, and she might have destroyed him—happily, she did not live long enough; and he has always had wealth, that greatest blight

23

and curse on all that is good in most people. And yet—and yet here he is, *one of us.* When you know him better, you will see how thoroughly he is one of us. To-day he is not doing himself justice a bit."

Patty stood looking at him with a serene, approving smile, as he politely struggled to shake off his inconvenient friend. "I think," she said, "that he is perfectly charming."

CHAPTER IV.

– THE PROCESS OF AMALGAMATION.

The editor of the *Rising Sun* was a little elderly man, with a shrewd, intellectual, leathery face and a rusty office costume, betokening as great a contempt for current fashions as did that of his wife, though he transgressed the law of custom in these matters from utter indifference, and she from religious principle. Edward Kinnaird was a fair-bearded, broad-shouldered young fellow, some inches over 6 feet, well dressed in grey tweed, and altogether good looking, on whom the eyes of his little missus, as he called her, rested with admiring affection—as his did on her. "Ah, Teddy, dear," she cried, "did you think you had lost me? Have you been looking for me long?"

"No," he answered, in a big, hearty voice. "I just called at Clive's office to hear where Mrs. Clive was—I knew you'd be off with her as soon as my back was turned." And he laughed at the frequent joke as if it were quite new and original, while he shook hands with the grave-faced lady who never would laugh with him. Patty was about to introduce her new friend to her husband, but discovered, to her surprise, that they were in the habit of consorting together at the club, and knew each other perfectly well. Ted had never told her of this, and he now accosted the interesting person as if he were but an ordinary man. "Hullo, Macdonald! Got back again? How are things looking your way?"

"Dry," said Macdonald.

"Yes. It's a bad look out, with summer coming on. But it is no use fretting—it won't rain any the sooner."

"I don't fret," drawled the other, with his melancholy, indifferent air.

"Oh, you can afford to despise the freaks of the weather, with about half a million at your back. But it's a serious matter for us poor devils to get two bad seasons running. I shall be dead broke if we have another big drought," said Mr. Kinnaird, with the utmost cheerfulness.

"That's how you men always talk," Mrs. Clive interposed, in a tone of mingled resignation and reproach. "What does it matter, after all, if you *do* lose your money? You have no suffering—you retain health and working powers, all that is necessary—it is perhaps better for you to lose money than to have it; droughts don't hurt *you*. Yet you think only of yourselves, and don't care a straw for the hundreds and thousands of wretched animals that slowly starve to death in unspeakable agonies——." She shuddered, and her dark eyes looked tragic.

"Oh, pardon me, Mrs. Clive—we do care, I assure you. But what's the use? We can't help them, poor brutes. When I see a heap of struggling skeletons trampling each other in the mud of a dry waterhole, upon my word, I feel bad—I do, indeed. But there it is, you see—if it won't rain I can't help it." He turned for relief from this romantic woman to her practical husband, who stood with a quiet smile upon his face beside her, and, remarking on the great increase of advertisements in the *Sun*,[1] hoped that some proportion of the golden harvest reached the pockets of his friend.

"No," said Mr. Clive, "it doesn't. I have no share in the concern, except as editor. I wish I had."

His wife interposed. "Why should you wish it, Raymond? We have enough. We don't want to be rich. We are not so *low*, I hope."

"Well, my dear, when you dream of a Norman Shaw house at Bedford Park,[2] and leisure for me in which to give all the powers of my great mind to the writing of great books, you dream of something that can't be realised without money."

"I know," she rejoined; and her thin face flushed quickly. "It is weak to want to be in England, and have an artistic surrounding, and to pick and choose one's work—I am ashamed of it. Even a Norman Shaw house may be a vulgar ideal," she added, in a tone that was almost solemn.

Mrs. Kinnaird did not know what a Norman Shaw house meant, but she recognised the sublime quality of her friend's high-mindedness. It seemed a sort of desecration to talk of land booms in her presence. The little woman made an effort to turn her Teddy's thoughts into nobler channels.

"You've made acquaintance with my wife, Macdonald? That's right. He and I were at school together, Pat. I say, have you anything on hand for to-night, Macdonald?"

Mr. Macdonald said he had nothing on hand.

"Then why not dine with us? Eh, Patty? They don't give you any wine at that place we're at; my wife likes that—there's no bar, you see, and no rowdy suppers to disturb her when she's alone, and when I'm there she thinks it good for me to live on effervescing waters. But we can go to some other place. Eh? Will you?"

Mr. Macdonald looked at Patty, who said, "Do," and he accepted the invitation. "But don't go away from your quarters," he begged her. "I don't care for wine, and I would rather dine with you in what you regard as your own house."

"Then come a little before 7. Floor number three—room twenty. Margaret, dear, is it any use asking you to come too—you and Mr. Clive?"

"No," said Margaret. "We have been all day together, darling; I must give myself to the children now."

They sauntered out of the Exhibition and parted at the gate, the two ladies having engaged to meet again on the morrow. The Clives took one tram,[3] the Kinnairds another, and Mr. Macdonald returned on foot to the fashionable club,[4] which was his Englishman's castle when he came to town. As he walked along, with his customary deliberate step and slightly haughty carriage, the interesting widower, who had all the advantages of youth in addition to the privileges of age, thought with much satisfaction of his newly acquired friend. Mrs. Clive, he said to himself, was always Mrs. Clive and unapproachable in her way, but Mrs. Edward Kinnaird was charming. There was no other word for her—she was simply and altogether charming—and he was extremely pleased with the prospect of cultivating her acquaintance.

The Kinnairds had two rooms in the Imperial Coffee Palace—a little bedroom, which was almost filled by the bed, and a little sitting room adjoining, both opening upon a balcony whereon the big man found space to stretch himself and liberty to smoke a quiet pipe when so disposed. The sitting room in its normal state was smart and prim, and not very comfortable, with its brand new, straight-backed, gorgeously upholstered furniture; but Patty had introduced a couple of softly cushioned homely wicker chairs, which altered its character entirely. Edward had also smuggled a little cabinet into one corner, a little cupboard with a lock and key, from the contents of which he derived some measure of compensation for enforced self-denial at the public table. Though he frequently inveigled his wife into the drawingroom close by, in the hope that she might be persuaded to sing before the assembled inmates of the house—which would have filled his otherwise modest soul with pride—he and she had much pleasure in the privacy of their little parlor, which, on this particular evening, with its bright fire and its pervading air of being lived in by people who knew how to make themselves comfortable, presented as cosy an appearance as any of the five hundred rooms under that roof could show.

Patty walked into it out of her bed chamber, looked around critically, altered the position of the chairs, and opened both French windows to counteract the fire; as it was impossible for her and Ted to dress at the same time, she had made her toilet early, and now talked to him through the open door while he made his. As he splashed and stumbled about in the inadequate space at his disposal, and roared questions and answers at her in his big voice, she put the finishing touches to her costume before the mirror in the overmantel, turning her head from side to side in a manner that would have sadly grieved Mrs. Clive could she have seen it. The soft curls on the little woman's forehead had had a fresh twist with the curling tongs—that vile instrument of imposture which Margaret had never condescended to touch with the tips of her pure fingers—and the black dress which had been selected as suitable for a dinner in a coffee palace restaurant left a wedge-shaped section of white bosom uncovered to passage draughts and publicity, and made open declaration of steel springs and horsehair cushion behind. Alas, alas! But such is the margin between theory and practice in the case of the very best of us.

They had a cheerful meal without the aid of wine, for the host was an invariably happy mortal and the guest was a person of tact and cleverness, who had seen a great deal of the world. Patty had an end seat at one of the small tables, with her companions on either side of her, and he would have been a dull man who had not enjoyed his dinner the better for sharing it with her. They led her into simple chatter about dogs and horses and to telling tales of Teddy's prowess as a whip and rider which showed her as proud of him as he was of her.

But when, having concluded their repast with coffee, they returned to the third floor together, she had an opportunity to improve her acquaintance with that part of Mr. Macdonald which she regarded as *her* part—hers and Margaret's. Ted invited him to light a pipe on the balcony, where it really wasn't cold, he declared, but quite a mild spring night; pointing out that Patty could talk to them through the window, and, moreover, that she was fond of the scent of tobacco. And it was then discovered that Mr. Macdonald did not smoke. He installed himself in one of the pillowed wicker chairs, and refused to move from the fireside. Ted, whose whole soul craved for its accustomed comfort, hung about the sitting room, and made efforts to be sociable that failed lamentably. And as soon as the conversation seemed able to sustain itself without him, he stole out on pretence of looking at the night, and the furtive scrape of a match was heard, and a pleasant perfume stole in from the balcony. A few minutes later, another man, whose room was near, went out to smoke; and presently Mr. Macdonald and Mrs. Kinnaird heard talk of land and syndicates, in which Ted seemed to become so absorbed as to forget all about his guest. The guest, for his part, forgot all about Ted.

(To be continued.)

CHAPTER V.
– AN EVENING AT THE C.P.

"Have you known Mrs. Clive long?" asked Mr. Macdonald.

"Only for a few months," said Patty, "though it feels like years. Have you?"

"No. I met her for the first time this winter. But, like you, I can't believe it."

"We were coming home from a visit to Ted's people in Sydney, and the Clives had just had one of the short trips they take together whenever Mr. Clive wants to blow office cobwebs away, and we both happened to come by sea and to take the same steamer. It was a wonderful piece of luck. We were so nearly coming by train. And the sea was quite calm, and Margaret and I sat on deck and talked the whole time. In those two days we got to know each other and found out how well we suited."

"Since I have known Mrs. Clive," said Mr. Macdonald, "I have been encouraged to feel that ideals may be realised sometimes. We are so kept down, as a rule, by the people who surround us— there is a sort of common consent that we are not to have ideals, don't you know?—as if we all understood that they mean nothing. We are so unoriginal—all going through life on the same poor, common road, like smiling images pushed from behind, as Stephenson says.[1] Now Mrs. Clive puts life into one. She makes one ashamed of being wooden—and of being pushed."

"Oh, yes!" Patty's quick warm voice broke in upon the

refined, deliberate drawl of her companion. This, she felt, was true sympathy, and all her innocent heart responded to it. "Oh, yes! What are only ideas and opinions with us *she* lives and practises. Don't you feel that? And how it stirs one to try and get up a little courage, too, and not be afraid of being laughed at. I never had any sense of the responsibilities of living till she taught me. I just ate and drank and slept and dressed and enjoyed myself like an unthinking animal. Now," she added pensively, "the sense of responsibility quite weighs on me. I never feel comfortable now. It is a great thing, Margaret says, to be made to feel uncomfortable—it is the first step. Ah me, if we could all be like her!"

"It isn't necessary to be *like* her altogether," he returned, with a long look at the piquant face that so strikingly illustrated the charm of variety; "only in her sincerity, and her lofty aims and her desire to be true in everything. She has her limitations, like the rest of us."

"I see none," said Patty. "To me she is a perfect woman."

"I'm glad to think she isn't *quite* that," he rejoined, with a laugh. "We couldn't do with wholly perfect people in this world."

"Perfect in *my* sense, then."

"And enough so for me. I would not have her different. Ever since I have known her I have thought better of all women for her sake. She has wholly revolutionised my ideas about her sex."

Patty looked at him quite lovingly, for Margaret's sake. "And did you think so badly of us before?" she inquired, with a charming wistfulness in her ever changing face.

The young man, with his deceitful air of old age, lifted his melancholy eyes and said gently, "You don't know what good reason I had to think badly of women before she cured me of it."

Patty did not like to say she did know, and sat silent, with pink cheeks and a throbbing heart. He went on, in a low tone of brotherly confidence, to explain.

"It is not a thing I ought to talk about—indeed, I don't talk about it—but I may tell *you;* you are like Mrs. Clive, and will understand. The woman who used to stand to me as the type of them all was—was—well, she was a degradation both to her own sex and mine."

He was again staring at the fire, with a face that seemed to be lined with care and pain, and it is needless to say that Patty's heart went out to him.

"Oh, I do feel for you!" she breathed in a sighing whisper. "Thank you so much for telling me—for trusting me. Margaret told me a little—not much—only just that; she was afraid I should say something to hurt you, if I didn't know. Oh, I am so sorry! I can feel for you all the more, as I have been so happy myself—so very,

very happy! We have never had a cloud between us."

They listened for a few minutes to the jolly voice of Ted on the balcony, declaring to his unknown friend that brokers were the very devil, and that any man with a head on his shoulders should know how to do his own buying and selling without their help; and then Mr. Macdonald told his hostess she was a fortunate woman indeed to be able to say that she was happy, in the condition of life that rendered so many wretched.

"As for me, I bore it somehow for seven years—I don't know how I did it. Then she ran away from me. Then she died."

"Don't talk about it," pleaded Patty, gently. "It only makes you miserable."

"It is a comfort to talk to you," he returned. "Of course I never open my lips to ordinary people."

"I am so glad you feel you *can* talk to me," said she.

"Now I am a lonely man," he went on, with a pathos that roused maternal solicitude in her. "I have been a widower for a year. I have no child—no home to call a home; and yet my experience of marriage is such that I shall never risk it again—never! I will be a free man henceforth, whatever happens."

"Oh, I hope not! You will find somebody some day—"

"No. I have done with all that. I don't want to find anybody. I shall be content to sit down with you and Mrs. Clive sometimes, for a quiet talk—to share your plans and interests, if you will let me. As she is always telling me, there is plenty of work for me to do to keep me from feeling lonely—"

The clock on the chimney piece chimed 10, and Ted came in with a deprecatory bustle, and Mr. Macdonald stirred in his chair as a guest who recognises that it is time to go. And Patty, rousing herself to greet her husband, felt that she had never spent a more interesting or profitable evening in her life—not even in Margaret's company.

"Let's have the little kettle, Pat.," said her husband, unlocking his cupboard in the corner with the air of a schoolboy who has a secret prog box[2] under his bed. And he proudly produced a bottle of fine old whisky and a couple of glasses, which he set upon the small table with a defiant thump.

"There! You see, if we do live in a coffee palace, we are not bigoted," he remarked, with a twinkle that was dreadfully like a wink in the corner of his eye. "And though you don't smoke, you can take your nip of whisky like a a proper Scotchman, I hope."

Mr. Macdonald said he could, which somehow was a relief to Patty. It brought him nearer to her level, though she did not drink whisky herself. She filled a tiny kettle from the water bottle and set it on the fire, and she brought out a diminutive sugar basin and a lemon, and with her own hands brewed the fragrant punch in a manner that showed her well accustomed to that business. It never tasted the same, Ted said, when she didn't mix it; and he gave her a kiss in return for the smoking tumbler she handed to him, and pulled her to a chair beside him, and sat with an arm around her waist.

They talked for another hour, and the land boom came on again. Ted said he thought he saw his way to making a fortune that would render him indifferent to droughts for the rest of his life, and his guest delicately warned him against the possibly too gorgeous prospect, with sundry morals drawn from his own experience, which went to show that he had the shrewd caution of his race in business matters. Patty took no part in this discussion, to which she listened without interest or comprehension, with an absent smile.

When at length Mr. Macdonald took his departure, she and Ted accompanied him along the corridors and down the great staircase, on the plea that they wanted a walk before going to bed; and they parted with him in the hall on the understanding that he and Mrs. Kinnaird would meet at Mrs. Clive's on the following evening.

"I don't at all like the idea of my wife sitting in the stalls," said Ted (having said it several times before), "though I don't mind where I go myself, of course; but Mrs. Clive, I know, is never happy if she isn't doing something that nobody else does, and Pat. is her sworn ally in everything."

"I am," said Patty firmly.

"However, if *you* are there to look after her, it'll be all right," said Ted cheerily. "It's a great relief to my mind, your undertaking to shepherd them, for I know Clive's too busy."

Patty looked at Mr. Macdonald with an intelligent smile, which his eyes acknowledged. And they bade each other good-night. Mr. Macdonald went out into the windy street and hailed a passing tram, which bore him to his club. Mrs. Kinnaird lingered a moment on her palatial doorstep and clasped her husband's arm, and leaned her cheek on his coat sleeve.

"Tired, old girl?" he queried, laying his big hand over her curly head.

"No, darling. I was only feeling how nice it is to have you," she answered, fondly. "Not to be like that poor fellow—with nobody."

"Well, I wouldn't change places with him," said Ted. "But, all the same, I don't think he's a subject for pity, by any means. He simply rolls in money."

"That's nothing."

"Oh, isn't it?" Ted laughed his jolly laugh, that echoed

33

through the vestibule as he led his wife across it to the lift corner.

"I am quite sure he doesn't care a straw about money," said she.

"Then there you're wrong. He's as 'cute[3] a man of business as ever you came across, and it would take an uncommonly smart chap to get the better of him, I can tell you."

"I daresay. That's quite another thing."

"And as for not having anybody, if there's one man more than another who's run after by all the people in the place, it's him."

"If they run after him, they don't get him," she returned, with a quick smile.

"They don't, much. He's a fastidious sort of fellow, who doesn't find ordinary folks good enough for him——"

"I can see that," she interposed.

"And he hates to be bored, even by fine company——"

"Yes."

"But he'd feel the difference if he was suddenly to find himself a person of no consequence—you bet! He likes to be run after, though he doesn't let himself be caught—he likes it as much as anybody, though he pretends he doesn't."

"Were you running after him when you asked him to dine with us, straight off, like that?" They had ascended the lift to their floor, and were slowly pacing the corridor towards their passage, she hanging on his arm.

"No. I saw you'd got him already, and I knew he'd like *you,* though he is so hard to please, and I thought you'd like his coming, because he's a friend of your dear Margaret's. However he came to take a fancy to *her* caps me," said Mr. Kinnaird, who was more honest than elegant in his manner of speech.

"You blind *mole!*" his wife retorted. "Why—why, anyone can see—*anyone,* with half an eye—that they are simply *made* for each other."

"Oh, come now—I say! Why, old Clive and her——"

"Yes, yes, I know. They are a most happy couple, of course. Margaret is devoted to him, and he's as good as gold—awfully clever, and all that; but there—there"—flourishing her little hand in the direction of Collins-street—"*there* goes the man who thoroughly understands her."

"Well, if he understands her—if he understands *Mrs. Clive,*" said Ted, "no doubt he finds her awfully interesting. She *is* interesting, I know; she's a charming woman, with no end of brains and culture, and so on; but——"

"Well?" said Patty, menacingly. "But what?"

"You'll have my head off if I say any more."

34

"Oh, go on. I like to see how stupid you *can* be when you really lay yourself out for it."

"Well, she's severe; now, isn't she? And she's not young—you can't say she's young. And she's dowdy—oh, she *is* dowdy, Pat.; don't you, for goodness' sake, go and copy the cut of her clothes, whatever else you do—and everybody who knows him says he is a fellow of such taste, don't you know?"

"He *is,*" said Patty, "to prefer her to a milliner's doll."

"You should have seen his wife, Pat. My word, she was a clipper.[4] Poor thing, she was a bit too fond of gaiety—however, she's dead. But *she* did credit to his taste, now, if you like. Carried herself like a Queen, with her head up, and dressed!—There wasn't a woman in Melbourne could hold a candle to her. All the fellows were after her."

"I dare say," said Patty, coldly. "Don't put any more coals on, Ted. It's bed time."

CHAPTER VI.

– MARGARET'S FAITH.

"I don't half like this theatre business," Ted continued to say (he had a dreadful habit of boring on at the same old subject after everybody else had done with it), hanging around her while she washed and curled and bonneted herself. "I'd as soon sit in the stalls myself, or up in the gallery, as anywhere else—it doesn't matter for a man; but ladies are different."

"Ladies are not so different as you suppose—at any rate, they are not going to be in future," she gaily replied. "And don't call us ladies, if you please—say *women*. That's the word we like. When we get the electoral franchise,[1] as we very soon shall, and have a hand in the making of the laws——"

"Oh—ah!" he interrupted, with his ignorant man's jeer. "Nice laws you'd make!"

"There will be a revolution in present habits and customs that will astonish you."

"That there will—you bet! But I say, Pat., joking apart, what will Macdonald think of this stalls business?"

"Oh, *he* understands," she replied promptly. *"He* knows why we do it."

"And why do you do it? For hang me if *I* can understand."

She attempted for the fifth or sixth time to make him understand, in terms such as Margaret would use, but there was not time, so she merely said that it was not right of poor people to pretend to be richer than they were.

"I tell you we are not poor," he maintained, with his amiable obstinacy. "In point of fact we're rich, for I'm as certain to make twenty or thirty thou.' within the next 12 months as I am to get my dinner to-night. Look here, Pat, on your very next birthday you shall have anything you like to choose out of any jeweller's shop—there."

She swept him aside, and bade him not be ridiculous if he could help it.

"But I mean it—honor bright, I do. You shall ruffle it with the best of them. Black velvet and diamonds—that's your style."

"It isn't my style a bit. I'm not imposing enough for black velvet."

"Satin then, or some Brussels lace out of the Exhibition—and diamonds"—

She stopped his mouth with a kiss, and told him he was a darling, but that, if he should happen to make money with his syndicate and things, he must find a better way of spending it than that.

"Oh, yes, Teddy," she urged earnestly. "We must do some good with it, dear—not throw it away on diamonds and rubbish of that sort."

"Rubbish!" he echoed, quite staggered. "Why, haven't I heard you say that if you'd only a few good diamonds—"

"Yes, yes, but that was a long time ago."

"No longer than the last Government House ball, my lady."

"I knew no better then. I do now. I don't care any more for diamonds, nor for balls either. What *have* I done with those gloves? Teddy, you've been to my drawer again—oh, here they are. The fact is, I should be ashamed to wear diamonds, Ted—I should feel it wicked. Diamonds—when so many poor creatures are starving! How Margaret would despise me!"

He burst into a great laugh. "Oh, that's it, is it? I thought Margaret was at the bottom of it. I'd like to try the experiment of giving Mrs. Margaret a diamond necklace for herself. She'd soon change her views, you'd see."

"That's all *you* know of her," said Patty, calmly. "She simply wouldn't touch it with a pair of tongs."

He laughed more loudly than ever, and Patty wouldn't condescend to remonstrance. She might talk for an hour, and he would never understand. Besides, she was ready (in all her best clothes) to go, and it was close upon 4 o'clock. "Well, good-bye," she said, kissing him.

"Oh, I'll go with you," he replied, "and carry your cloak." Which he did, with his usual devotedness. He carried her cloak to

Mrs. Clive's gate, and there bade her a tender farewell, begged her to take care of herself, promised to fetch her from the theatre when the play was over, and returned somewhat disconsolate to his club, to amuse himself as best he could till dinner time.

Amid streetsful of smart white terrace houses, Mrs. Clive's one-storied, shingle-roofed, antiquated detached cottage, in its rose bushy garden, was considered by most people to be conspicuously out of place. The old man who had built it in the old days, and still refused to pull it down or sell the land it stood on, was called bad names by these sticklers for architectural uniformity, and he and it regarded as cumberers of the ground that it was high time should be removed from the path of progress. But to Mrs. Clive her landlord was an enlightened person in a city full of barbarians, and her house an oasis of good taste in a desert of genteel vulgarity. Thus happily do we enjoy our several opinions in this free land.

It was early in September, and, though winter had lingered beyond its time, the little garden was sweet and gay. A lilac tree just coming into bloom, a clump of red-brown stocks, a bush of boronia, a bed of violets, exhaled the delicious breath of spring; and the flush of living color in red japonica and yellow jonquil and white feathers of spiræa, and in the fringe of wistaria hanging from the low eaves of the verandah, lit up this one only of all the front gardens in that section of the street. Within doors the house was still more unlike its neighbors. The aesthetic spirit had presided over all the arrangements, great and small, but its manifestations were not what we are accustomed to. No swathes of Liberty silk, no festoons of kalizoic muslin adorned that little drawingroom where Margaret received her friend with literally open arms.There was not a china plate anywhere, nor a Japanese fan—none of the familiar gimcracks.[2] She was above the frivolities of fashion in pretty things as in ugly ones; nothing was there for the mere sake of showing itself except the pictures, which were a singularly interesting collection. The dark floor was almost bare, the furniture of a capacious and substantial type not designed for the apartments of ladies, and leaving an unusual amount of space for moving about in, but everywhere color and form and harmoniousness had been studied. The delicate, austere simplicity of the whole was the quintessence of refinement.

Margaret, in a yellowish Greek-draped dress that beautifully adapted itself to her dark head and gentle majesty of movement, clasped her friend to her bosom, as we have said, and then fed her with tea and bread and butter, and then planted her in one of the large chairs by the fire. Divested of her bonnet and boa, Patty leaned back luxuriously, stretched her little feet on the fender, and said to her hostess, who was searching for a book in the well-filled shelves that made a dado round the room—"Shall we talk this afternoon, Margaret, instead of reading? I feel as if I wanted a talk most." One of their newly formed habits, anticipating the regulations of the club, was to read together when they met in Margaret's house. Margaret selected the books, and they read aloud in turn, discussing freely as they went along; and thereby Mrs. Clive helped the education of her friend up to her own high standard. Not that their reading was of the conventional educational character; it was wildly irregular and miscellaneous. Thoreau one day, Cotter Morison the next—always an author of revolutionary ideas,[3] but never an author who did not know his mind, or lacked the literary sense to properly express it. Fiction was not despised, though Mrs. Clive hardly associated it with amusement, and selected it with the utmost fastidiousness. Indeed, she was painfully susceptible to a novel of the right sort. She was a thoroughly modern woman, who would rarely look into a book that was more than 10 years old, but this latest vagary in fiction, the taste for crude ghosts and nursery marvels, she passionately resented, as an insult to the intelligence of grown up people, and (since so many failed to see it so) a discouragement to her dream of progress. George Meredith was her king of novel writers,[4] about the only one in whom she unreservedly delighted. Patty could not grasp George Meredith, just as she could not grasp Wagner, but Margaret was sure she would "come to it" in time. "It is only that you haven't got the taste of him yet—you haven't made a beginning," said the enthusiastic woman. "Once you have made a beginning, you will find all novels pale and wishy-washy by comparison. And, oh, Patty, no man in the world ever understood *us* as he does! No man ever wrote of women with such nobleness and delicacy and fine intuition. If only for that, he would stand first of all—for me."

But fiction and philosophy were alike laid aside to-day. A personal interest took precedence of all abstract subjects, and it was not Patty's interest only; they shared it equally between them. In a few minutes they were earnestly talking of it—or, we should say, of him. The one was asking scores of apparently trivial questions with an alert air of concentration, and the other answering them with a fullness and patience that neither would have manifested in an ordinary gossip about their neighbors.

"It is not at all unlikely that he will drop in this afternoon, after being away so long, and if he does I will ask him to stay. I don't mind *him*—he is not company; and he seems to feel more at home in this house than anywhere else," said Mrs. Clive, looking round her with a smile.

"I don't wonder," said her friend, with a faintly envious sigh.

39

"Did you read his paper in the *Sun*, Patty?"

"Yes, Margaret; twice. At first I did not take much notice. But I read it over again last night. It's lovely."

"Oh, it went to my heart," cried Margaret. "I wrote him a letter to tell him so when Ray brought home the literary supplement on Thursday morning. I wrote to him before breakfast. I wanted to encourage him. It is beautiful to see a man recognising the claims of women like that. He didn't use to be so clear about it—his bitter experience had clouded his mind and made him narrow and hopeless; but of late—well, I think it is since he has known me—you couldn't believe how he has broadened out."

"I can understand how you have taught him," breathed Patty softly. "I can see it in every word he says."

"Oh, the teaching has not been all on one side," said Margaret.

She leaned back in her big chair. The faint grey blue of the chintz that covered it made a good background for the rich darkness of her hair and her liquid eyes. With her face to the firelight, she looked beautiful in her tawny draperies, lying at rest in that flexible, curving pose, with the red glow flushing her all over; but when she turned to speak, and lost her artificial color in the cold light from the window, it struck her friend that she looked unusually thin and old.

"Patty," she said, after a brief silence, "there are people who say—almost *everybody* says—it is one of those horrible axioms which the world takes for granted—that a man and a woman cannot be close friends without danger of becoming more than friends. You know what I mean?"

Patty nodded.

"Oh, it does make me so *savage*," Margaret continued, a visible tremble running through her. "That it should be thought possible we can *all* be so low, so degraded as that!—that there are not *some* of us who have higher tastes and aims in life than—than—oh, I can't speak of it! It makes me sick. Patty, darling"—leaning forward and putting out her hands—"don't *you* believe that a man and woman—say a man like Mr. Macdonald and a woman like me—can be friends, intellectual, sympathetic, confidential friends, as a man and a man, or a woman and a woman, are, without thinking, without for a moment dreaming of—of *that?*"

Patty gathered all her mind together to face this momentous question; then she said stoutly, "Of course I do." She went over and sat on the arm of her friend's chair, and caressed the dark head that leaned itself on her breast. "Of course I do," she repeated. "But it is made very hard for us. People are always in such a hurry to misjudge."

40

"It doesn't really matter what 'people' say or think."

"No. But one would be afraid the man *himself* might misjudge."

"Oh, I am not speaking of common men. Of course they would misjudge, if one gave them the chance. But no woman who respected herself *would* give them a chance."

"I have only known common men," Mrs. Kinnaird confessed. "Dear, kind, good fellows—I like them—I have always liked men, even when they were common, and liked to know them well and be nice to them; but somehow one can never let one's self go, so to speak. They would make love at once—they would hold one cheap. There is always a line you know—with common men."

"Of *course* I know that. But it never ought to have been so, Patty. Men and women have been spoiled, have been simply *ruined*, as companions for each other. That shows it. Oh, what it *might* have been, but for the horrible ignorance and tyrannies that have corrupted us all, and turned innocent human nature into deceit and crime! But it will all be better some day. Slowly, as the mistakes were made, they will be rectified—slowly, but surely. We are at the turning point now. We are beginning to live a purer, honester, broader life; and the few of us who are able for it must lead the way for the others. We must set an example, Patty. You and I, my own darling, will show them how women may love and support and be loyal to each other, and he and I—he and both of us—will prove that men and women can be the comrades they were meant to be without forgetting the dignity of their sex."

Patty squeezed the dark head against her bosom. "You and I, at least," she said, "will do our part."

"And he his, I am sure. He is *not* one of the common ones, Patty. You will see that when you know him as well as I do. He has had great sorrows—they have chastened him. He will not marry again—all that is over for him; he cares nothing for women in the common man's way—"

She paused suddenly, for the door opened. One of her little daughters, a sad-eyed, lanky child in a loose smocked frock, entered softly and said, "Mr. Macdonald, mother." And Mr. Macdonald stepped in after her, grave, deliberate, with just the air of the man who has had great sorrows and been chastened by them. But there is no doubt that the settled melancholy of his mien lifted and lightened when he caught unexpected sight of Patty's charming, smiling face.

(To be continued.)

41

CHAPTER VII.
– "WE THREE."

"Oh, how glad I am!" Margaret exclaimed, rising. "This is just what I was wishing for!"

Mr. Macdonald pressed her hand with grave cordiality, and then turned to sun himself in Patty's smile. "Had ever unworthy mortal a more divine welcome?" he said, and his manner toned all extravagance out of the words. "I had primed myself with apologies for intruding on you twice in one day, Mrs. Clive, and with two or three of the best excuses I could find"—leisurely drawing some new magazines from the pocket of his overcoat.

"How good of you!" she cried, seizing them eagerly, and rapidly turning the leaves. "But it needn't be twice in one day. Make it once by taking off your coat and staying till it is time for the theatre. I won't say if you have nothing better to do, because I am quite sure you can have nothing better, but if you have no other engagement."

"If I had, I would break it without scruple," he said, promptly.

"Mrs. Kinnaird is with me, and we three"—this phrase, "we three," became very common with them after this—"can have a quiet hour to ourselves before tea. It is *tea,* you know—tea with the children—that I am asking you to, but I don't suppose your meals are a matter of such consequence to you as they are to men in general."

They were really of quite as much consequence to him as to men in general, but he said he was sure she would not do him so foul an injustice as to suppose that any such consideration could present itself in the present case. "Give me a crust of bread and your company—yours and Mrs. Kinnaird's—and you will leave me nothing to wish for," he declared, with his grave drawl.

"Then take off your coat and sit down. Dorothea"—to the little girl, who was nestling up to Patty—"take Mr. Macdonald's coat into the hall, and then go back to the schoolroom, love; you shall see Aunt Patty presently. And let us three draw round the fire and have a symposium."

How bright she was! Patty had never seen her so near to gaiety before. She pushed up the great, comfortable chairs, and poked the fire and swept the hearth, while Mr. Macdonald took his own coat into the hall, and, it was surmised, transferred a surreptitious card-board box from one of its pockets to Dorothea. Then "we three" grouped themselves in a half-circle, very close together, and held what was practically the first meeting of the club.

"You looked so happy," said Mr. Macdonald, warming his outspread palms, "when I first saw you, before you moved."

"We were," said Patty. "We always are when we are together."

"And you were so perfectly at rest. It was brutal to break in and disturb you."

"You did not disturb us," said Mrs. Clive. "And we are resting still." There was every indication of it in her satisfied pose. "Having also earned the right to rest, we are enjoying it thoroughly. Mrs. Kinnaird has been trotting about the Exhibition all day, and I—not being able to get her till this afternoon—have been cleaning windows."

Patty was rather disconcerted by this latter statement; Mr. Macdonald received it as a matter of course. "Cleaning windows must be hard work," he remarked. "Isn't it a little too hard for your strength?"

"Other women have to do it, who are no stronger than I. It is not so hard as scrubbing floors," said Margaret calmly, "and I like it much better. It is only the reaching that makes one ache afterwards. You see I don't keep the ordinary servants—only a very good governess, who wholly gives herself to the girls, and a lady help, with a charwoman once a week. The lady help is an excellent creature in many ways, but she is not educated to the point of liking to clean street windows in the day time. So I do it. It is an example for her, and for the children, whom I try to keep uncontaminated by any vulgarity of that sort. I had them both to help me for a little while. It was like one of their lessons."

"I wish I had been here to help you," Patty exclaimed, fervently.

"I think that sort of work should be done by men," said Mr. Macdonald. "It is not good for the physical woman to strain her back. We want to sort the occupations of the sexes, badly. There's one that is in the wrong place."

"What we really want is to be brought up to our original strength, by having the wholesome life that we have been deprived of for so many ages," began Margaret, thoughtfully. But Mr. Macdonald did not listen.

The joint authors of *The Liberty of Woman* and their ally found unqualified satisfaction in the new *Westminster,* which happened to contain Mona Caird's marriage paper,[1] the purport and fame of which was already vaguely known to them. On discovering that this treasure had fallen into their hands, Mrs. Clive thrilled with excitement and joy. "Read it—read it," she cried, thrusting the Review into Mr. Macdonald's hands. "Read it aloud to us that we may share it together. Oh, what a courageous woman, not to be afraid to stand up alone, in her own proper person, against the solid army of prejudices arrayed against her! She will hearten us, Patty."

Mr. Macdonald settled himself comfortably in his arm chair and cleared his throat. He was a charming reader, and from this time did all the reading for the club when it met together. The two ladies, on either side of the bright fire, leaned back luxuriously, and stretched their feet upon the fender. They were delightful listeners. At certain passages, if they did not interrupt the reader with impulsive comments, they looked across at each other with eloquent smiles and signs. When he read this sentence—"The difficulties of friendly intercourse between men and women are so great, and the false sentiments induced by our present system so many and so subtle, that it is the hardest thing in the world for either sex to learn the truth concerning the real thoughts and feelings of the other"— their eyes said "Did we not say so?" as plainly as eyes could speak; and the parable of the chained dog roused them to a brilliant glow of indignant comprehension. Mrs. Clive was in a seething passion of sympathy with the author all through, and led Patty along with her, showing her how to look at each point as it arose, amplifying and emphasising its significance and application; while Mr. Macdonald's personal circumstances, in addition to the contagious enthusiasm of his friend, disposed him to a like deep interest in the subject and its striking treatment. But he was imperturbably calm, as usual. "She'll be pelted with dead cats and rotten eggs for this, poor thing," he said, dropping into his tired drawl the moment he left off reading. And Margaret's fervent voice swept over his cold tones like a flame: "A poor thing do you call her? She is a greater woman than the

44

Queen on her throne!"

They talked so much over every paragraph that they did not get half through the article at that sitting, and in their talk they became very intimate together, sharing equally in the general stock of intellectual interest and sympathy. When the dusk fell, and they heard the little girls setting the tea table, and the step of the house master on the gravel outside, Mrs. Clive drew the magazine from the reader's hands, closed it and laid it on a book shelf near her.

"Let us keep the rest," she said, "till we three can meet again."

"Come both of you to afternoon tea with me to-morrow," said Patty; "we can finish it then."

The invited ones looked at each other and nodded. Mr. Clive entered the room.

"What, sitting in the dark, Madge? Who's here? Oh, Macdonald, glad to see you. And Mrs. Kinnaird, of course—she's like Una in the way she shines in a shady place."[2]

"Thank you, Mr. Clive," laughed Patty, as gaily as if this were just a world of pleasant men and well-treated women; "that's the very prettiest compliment I ever had in my life—and I've had a good many."

"That I'll be bound you have," he responded heartily, shaking her hand. He thought her a charming little person (there was no known individual of his sex who thought otherwise), though he did not agree with his wife that she had much in her—it was Margaret's transfiguring imagination that idealised her, he said; while as for poor Ted, Mr. Clive simply regarded him as an inoffensive fool. He said he reminded him of a Newfoundland pup. Margaret gave up her darling's husband without any hesitation; she also thought him a fool, and quite unworthy of the treasure he possessed; but she would not admit that any excellence of mind was lacking in the other case, except in the sense of being somewhat undeveloped—a thing Time and she would cure. When Raymond disparaged Mrs. Kinnaird in his blunt editorial way, Margaret contented herself with the remark that he didn't know Patty, and she did.

The two ladies went to Margaret's bedroom to make their little preparations for the evening meal—a family high tea, for which no one, of course, was allowed to "dress" in the conventional evening-toilet sense, though the mistress of the house required her daughters to recognize that working hours were over by an extra freshness and cleanliness of costume and person, which came to much the same thing. And as she poured water into the hand basin and laid out her delicate towels and brushes, Mrs. Clive expressed her delight in the discovery that her two dear friends got on so well

45

together.

"He has quite taken to you, Patty—I saw it at once—and I *am* so glad, darling! I thought he would—that he *must*—and yet I could not help feeling anxious. He is so fastidious and reserved, and so very, very few people suit him."

"Ah," said Patty, "he will never think so much of me as he does of you, Margaret."

"The more he thinks of you the better he will please me," Margaret answered. "There is no rivalry possible in *our* case, happily."

"No, indeed. Fancy you and me being jealous of each other!"

They both laughed, and then, passing as they crossed the room, exchanged a solemn kiss. "We leave all that to the poor creatures who don't know any better," said Mrs. Clive. Patty laughed still, but the smile faded quickly from her comrade's tragic eyes. "Oh," she cried, in her passion-thrilling voice, "think of the fine friendships, the noble enterprises, that have come to nothing all in a moment—like great ships that strike on little bits of sunken rock—cast away for some poor, trivial, conventional cause, mere petty jealousy, or vanity, or sham dignity—as if we had a thousand years to live and these priceless treasures were to be had every day— were not worth keeping when we did get them! Oh, Patty, I have seen it so often—I have suffered it myself more than once; but don't *don't* let you and me come to grief like that!"

"My dearest," cried Patty, clasping her, "how *could* we?"

"I don't see how we could," Margaret wistfully rejoined. "We are neither of us petty—we know the value of true friendship. But we must remember it is the sunken rocks, the wretched little things we don't see till we are on them—misunderstandings, as they are rightly called—that wreck us unawares, when we least expect it. We must love and trust each other in the largest, fullest sense— walk by faith, Patty, when we cannot walk by sight[3]—knowing in our hearts that neither of us would hurt the other if we knew it, and that we would not lose each other for the world."

She seemed to have a moment's prophetic misgiving that what had happened in ninety-nine cases might happen in the hundredth; but when her friend assured her again that it never could, her sanguine spirit re-asserted itself.

They returned to the drawingroom, where Mr. Clive sat by the fireside with Dorothea on his knee, talking practical politics— the politics of the *Rising Sun*—with Mr. Macdonald. In the diningroom the lady help and the bright eyed, active eldest daughter were putting finishing touches to the tea table, round which they all gathered in a few minutes, joined by a spectacled and white haired

46

German governess, who spoke either her own language or French to the inmates of the house for the children's benefit. The appointments of the table, though simple, were dainty, like everything that appertained to Margaret, but there was no luxury in the matter of food. Plain living and high thinking was the maxim of that household. A concession was made to the coarse appetites of men in the shape of a broiled beefsteak and bottled ale, but mother and daughters kept to a Lenten diet, disliking the former on principle, the latter from habit,[4] what Margaret shudderingly termed "flesh," as if to like it were a sort of cannibalism. Patty was still partial to a savory dish—she had not reached the point of feeling that anything impure or gross was involved in eating a dead body purveyed by the butcher—and as an accomplished bush cook it was difficult to reconcile herself to Margaret's ideal bill of fare; nevertheless, she made a substantial meal of bread and butter and strawberry jam, and greatly enjoyed the feast of reason that she simultaneously partook of.

The English language being allowed to everybody, and the children having been brought up at liberty to be as old as their young capacities permitted, the conversation was general, and ranged without restriction in all directions. The father talked politics to his children, and condescended to argue with them when they disagreed with his views; the mother did likewise. Eleanor Clive, aged 13, got up to remove soiled plates, including that of the lady help, who had her place at this patriarchal board, and, passing to and fro between table and dumb waiter, the child continued a hot discussion upon the Canadian-American question,[5] all the bearings of which she appeared to understand, in a manner that astounded Patty, to whom such matters were as mysterious as mathematical problems. Eleanor was constitutionally a cautious imperialist, and took that side of the argument, while her mother, three times her age, was as naturally a reckless and ardent separatist, a nationalist for Canada, as she was for Australia, not to speak of Ireland, in spite of the fact that a Norman Shaw house at Bedford Park was the castle of her dreams. Mr. Clive held the balance between them, rather inclining to favor Eleanor, while Mr. Macdonald always broke in at any moment when Margaret seemed in need of backing. By the end of the meal they had all grown very excited, especially Margaret, whose impassioned spirit was like an Æolian harp[6] in a high wind, and who was always wandering from the concrete to the abstract, whence it was so difficult to recall her. Half an hour after the time for rising from the table, and when the destiny of Canada was long disposed of, she was sitting behind the teapot, leaning upon her folded arms, her dark eyes ablaze, and all her delicate frame a tremble with emotion, pouring out her soul on the subject of human rights in general, in a manner that, Mr. Clive said, showed her capable of "giving points" to Mill.[7] Patty, thrilling sympathetically as she listened to the inspired oration, thought him a dreadfully hard-hearted husband when he got up in the middle of it, and made fun of the whole thing with a quotation from the Book of Ecclesiasticus— "As the climbing up of a sandy way is to the foot of the aged, so is a wife full of words to a quiet man."[8]

However, he explained that all he meant was that time was going on and it was his busy night at the office—that as the foot of the aged in the sandy way, so his foot was hindered by the compelling power of his wife's eloquence; and he kissed her with manifest tenderness before he left, by which time she, having her matronly dignity in the eyes of her household to consider, had quieted down and recovered her self-possession.

"What a leader you would make!" Mr. Macdonald said to her, when the club members returned to the drawingroom and stood together for a few idle minutes round the fire.

She looked up at him with eyes that showed gratitude for being appreciated and understood, and smiled silently. Patty remarked that Mrs. Clive *did* make a leader already.

"Ah, but a leader in some great, desperate cause—some sublime rebellion of a little people against a big," he drawled, in a tone that comforted the person referred to by its excessive seriousness.

"The causes are there, and waiting," she said quickly.

"But no Messiah appears."

"A woman cannot be a Messiah—not yet. When the time comes—oh, how slowly it comes!—I shall be in my grave. Other women will have their chance, not I—not you and I, Patty."

"Oh, we have some chance," said Patty, cheerfully. "It would be nice if we could be born again a hundred years hence, but, on the other hand, supposing we had been born a hundred years *back!* That *might* have happened to us, you know. And look at Mona Caird——"

"Have we time for a little more of the article?" Margaret interposed, with a swift look at the clock.

"I think not," replied Mr. Macdonald, consulting his own watch, as a man always does, that being the only infallible timekeeper, no matter how bad an article. "I was going to propose, as the night is fine, that we start rather early, and—having no evening dresses to spoil or catch cold in—walk to the theatre. Would you like that? Or will you have a cab?"

"Oh, no cab, certainly. The tram is our conveyance, if we need one. But I should like to walk very much, if Mrs. Kinnaird is not too tired."

Patty declared herself as fresh as possible, and delighted with the proposal; and they presently set forth.

CHAPTER VIII.

– THE CLUB ESTABLISHED.

The night was fine, though dark. The three friends had given themselves plenty of time, and paced the quiet streets leisurely, in tacit agreement that the longer they could make the road the better. Stoutly shod and comfortably clothed in gowns that had no tails to be held up, and furred coats buttoned to the chin, the ladies enjoyed the cold freshness of the air, and the exhilaration of pleasant exercise, in addition to the company of their congenial comrade, and the satisfying contemplation of the enterprise before them. By a common impulse of friendship they walked arm in arm, Mr. Macdonald in the middle; and they had much profitable converse as they went along.

"Oh, isn't it nice!" Margaret sighed happily, when they began to be jostled by the Bourke-street crowd.[1] "Don't you like to feel yourself amongst the toilers and strugglers, Patty—with them and of them—not fenced off with the ignoble herd who have no thought but for their own comfort and glorification?"

"Yes, dear," said Patty. But what she particularly liked just now was to be amongst them under Mr. Macdonald's wing.

"Of course that allusion to the ignoble herd was aimed at me," he pensively remarked. "It's just as if she blamed me for being born with a mole on the back of my neck."

"Oh, you can't help it," said Patty, soothingly.

"I really can't, you know. If I only had something to

struggle for, like them," nodding towards some rough men who spat upon the pavement with alarming recklessness, "I should naturally struggle—as they do."

"I'll give you something to struggle for," said Margaret. "Get yourself into Parliament next election, and then use your influence and money—well, the influence your money gives you—to get us the franchise."[2]

He said he was already thinking about it. And they reached the door of the theatre and proceeded for the first time in the experience of any of them to poke their way to the floor of the house.

Mr. Macdonald betrayed a certain anxiety as he looked about him. "You two ladies had better take end seats, and let me—"

"Barricade us against contact with the coat or gown of a shopkeeper."

Margaret caught him up quickly. "If you have any idea of that sort, I shall take Mrs. Kinnaird to the gallery at once. Patty, dear, you sit outside, because you are the shortest, and these detestable high hats won't screen everything from you. You sit in the middle, Mr. Macdonald, so that you can distribute yourself equally between us."

They thus arranged themselves on the chairs at the end of a midway row, and Margaret found herself beside a burly gentleman who smelt strongly of whisky and onions—odors that were abominable to her fastidious nose. But she said she was very comfortable, and could see beautifully. The full dressed people were sauntering by twos and threes into their circle overhead, and, as they settled themselves, drew forth their glasses and swept the house in that rude fashion which custom has made legitimate in polite society—the men to see if there were any pretty girls about, and the ladies to investigate the details of other ladies' costumes. As a rule the dress circle never thinks of casting its eyes downwards—the ground floor might be sheep or pigs for all the notice it takes of them; but Patty, looking upward from the corner of her eye, conscientiously struggling against the temptation to hope, or rather to prefer, that she might remain unobserved in her obscurity, saw two gentlemen in a box near the stage gazing smilingly towards her party, while leaning forward on their folded arms and talking with their heads together.

"Is there anyone here you know?" she whispered to her neighbor, who sat with his usual imperturbable gravity, apparently seeing nothing.

"Two or three," he whispered back.

She felt a little uncomfortable under the eyes of those two men, who presently levelled their glasses at her. "Please," she whispered, "talk to us both," which he immediately did. Margaret meanwhile sat back in her chair, neither seeing nor caring whether people observed her or not. And all through the evening the two men looked at them intently.

But when the play began Patty enjoyed herself so much that she forgot to think of them. She was naturally full of fun, and the star comedian's delicious humor, together with Mr. Macdonald's unsmiling comments upon it, so wrought upon her that she giggled like a person who had sat in the stalls all her life, and knew no better. Indeed, by the time the Magistrate was at the end of his troubles with his step-son, she was stifling hysterical peals of laughter with her handkerchief in her mouth, and sweeping tears from her eyes—to the great amusement of her confederate, who was himself as grave as a judge.

"Oh, I *am* so ashamed of myself!" she gasped, as she recovered from the crowning paroxysm, brought on merely by the magistrate calling his step-son a little beast. "What *will* Mrs. Clive think of me?"

"What do you think of her?" he inquired, passing the question on. "Don't you think she disgraces us with this levity?"

Mrs. Clive, though a little surprised at her beloved's conduct, looked round at her with an indulgent smile. She said Patty was always natural, and that it was a pleasure to see her enjoying herself.

Certainly Patty did enjoy herself thoroughly, and the same might be said of Mr. Macdonald, who was as much attracted by her as a platonic gentleman could be, and found their solitude in the alien crowd a most advantageous circumstance. Margaret was troubled by a misgiving that they did not take their enterprise seriously enough, and that the company of a rich man deprived it of its true significance; otherwise she too was happy. When they emerged into the vestibule at the conclusion of the play, Ted, catching sight of the three distinguished faces in the plebeian stream, was struck with the expression of satisfaction that pervaded them all. His "Well, how did you like it?" was a superfluous question.

"I only hope you've enjoyed your dinner half as much," said Patty, who was still bubbling with reminiscent merriment.

He tucked her hand under his arm, as if relieved to have rescued her, and the four passed into the now swarming street. They made their way to the *Sun* office,[3] where they delivered Mrs. Clive to her husband. Then Mr. Macdonald said good night, not being invited to go further, and the exciting day was at an end.

As she glided down Collins-street in a full tram, by her husband's side, Patty asked him whether he had anything particular to do on the following afternoon.

"Nothing that I can't put off if you want me," he replied.

"Because Margaret and Mr. Macdonald have promised to come for an hour or two to do some reading."

His face fell a little and he gave a discontented grunt. "Then I shall clear out," he said promptly. "You won't want *me.*"

"I always want you," she answered, slipping her hand under his ulstered arm.

"But Margaret doesn't. She'd only feel me in the way. I'll clear out to the club or somewhere."

"I thought you said you had something to do? You know it would only bore you, Teddy—you wouldn't enjoy it a bit."

"No, I shouldn't. If she's coming, I'll clear out."

He cleared out accordingly when the appointed hour came, and the club held a second successful meeting under his virtual roof. They finished the marriage paper and had a profound discussion over it; and—though Margaret thought it unnecessary, and a waste of precious time—Patty boiled the little kettle and made tea, and brought out delicate cakes and buttered scones. And Ted came home, expecting to find the coast clear, and it was time to be thinking of dinner before the trio separated.

They met again in the Exhibition next day. After a morning with her husband on the ground floor, looking at wool, and grain and buggies, and the landing of Captain Cook, and so on, and having comfortably lunched with him, Patty repaired to a given rendezvous in the Ladies' Court,[4] and there found her bosom friend in a state of shuddering indignation at the horrors exposed around her. "Oh, Patty," she cried—they were her first words of greeting——"look, *look* at these things! Isn't it awful?" She pointed to the bead work and the crochet work and the wax flower work and the Berlin wool and crewel work as at so many gory corpses. "Did you think such monstrosities had survived to these days? Oh, to think there are women, and so many of them, capable of such deeds——*still!*" Her voice was a wail of anguish. "Come away, darling——let us go upstairs and try to forget it."

They went to the German picture gallery,[5] and that consoled her. There were Müller Kurzwelly's Autumn Evening, and Winter Evening, and Gude's Seashore, and that most exquisite Douzette in the corner, to which one went back again and again, and quite a number of satisfying things. She said she wondered if if would be any use to pray that the good thought might be put into the heart of someone with money to buy the Moonlight Night on a Dutch Canal for the National Gallery, where poor folks could go and look at it in the Exhibitionless days to come; and she confessed to feeling the temptation to be covetous when she gazed at another little moonlight scene that fascinated her still more—a lonely, reedy mere and an old boat and a flight of wild ducks, that reminded her of the Norfolk Broads at night-time, the dear fen country in which she was born.[6] "I wonder who has bought it, Patty?" she sighed. "Whoever it is, I envy him. It is very wrong, I know, but I do."

They passed from the German gallery to the Victorian loan gallery,[7] and sat down before Leader's April Day, to talk and to gaze at that superlative picture and all the fine collection around it, and here, by no arrangement, and yet to nobody's surprise, Mr. Macdonald found them, and the three sat side by side and discussed modern art—the good paintings upstairs, and the bad fancy work below—with that sense of a common fellowship in taste and ideas, which was by this time matter of course, and no longer a charming novelty. Having thus refreshed themselves, they rose from their settee, and passed by a neighboring door into the gallery of the concert hall, where they realised yet more distinctly the closeness of their spiritual relationship. Patty found that Mr. Macdonald, as well as Margaret, was a Wagner worshipper in his undemonstrative way, and she was doubly assured of having it in her to become one also; at the first notes of the prelude to Lohengrin she shut her eyes tightly, and resolutely detached her mind from local concerns; and gradually the majesty of that romantic music was revealed to her— she began to feel its influence at last.

"I knew you would," said Margaret, who thrilled in response to it as violin strings to the bow. "Did I not say so, Patty?"

It is needless to chronicle the fact that they went to the choral concert together, when the charge for admission offered Mrs. Clive an opportunity to assert club principles. They also went to the Public Library to read Milton and Mary Wollstonecraft on *Marriage and the Rights of Woman*.[8] On a subsequent fine day they took the train to Brighton Beach, and sat in a group on the steps of the boat landing below the pier, while Mr. Macdonald recited Arnold and William Morris[9] to the accompaniment of the lapping water amongst the barnacled piles beside them. Later they spent a sunny afternoon discussing the development of socialism in the lake house at the Botanic Gardens; and again they found grateful privacy for talking over their thoughts on friendship in the deserted galleries of the University Museum. They met at the Exhibition almost daily, until they knew every nook and corner of it by heart. In short, they became conspicuous and notorious for their inseparableness, and only saved themselves from the tongue of scandal by never reducing their number to two. Poor Ted grumbled and felt a little neglected at first, but by-and-bye became so much absorbed in his own land booming transactions that he ceased to miss his companion at the hours when her more intellectual friends engaged her; he contented himself with getting her on his knee by their fireside at night and telling her how rich they were going to be some day.

By the middle of October, however, his pursuit of wealth had slackened somewhat—the financial prospect was contracting[10]—and he began to grow tired of the Exhibition and Melbourne life, and to long for his country home. He had left it before the shearing, to satisfy Patty's impatient desire to be with her bosom friend; now shearing was almost over, and he wanted to see how things were going on. His brother and partner, Jim, was at the head of affairs, and perfectly competent to manage them; but the bush-born man found plenty of excuses to explain the fact that he was homesick. He said he would just run up for a week or two before the races,[11] and he expected Patty, as a matter of course, to run up with him.

But Patty wanted to stay in town, and Margaret insisted upon it. She proposed that the rooms at the I.C.P., which was now inconveniently crowded, should be given up, and that Patty should be her guest till his return. This plan was carried out. And the loving husband and wife were separated for the first time in their married lives.

(To be continued.)

CHAPTER IX.
– TWO LETTERS.

"My Dearest, Darling Old Boy,—

"I hope you are not very lonely without me. Sometimes I feel very selfish not to have gone with you, but after all it is only for a week or two, and the time will soon pass. I hope Mary attends to you properly and gives you the things you like to eat, and doesn't put you off with cold meat and no sweets, as she will if you don't look after yourself better than Jim does when I am not at home, for he would be quite contented to have mutton chops and potatoes boiled till they were broken, and then bundled higgledy-piggledy into the tureen all the year round, and that is just the sort of easy way that ruins good servants, and Mary *can* cook when she is kept up to the mark. So, my dear boy, *do* assert yourself and give your orders for anything you fancy, and don't leave her to give you just anything that's the least trouble, while she spends her time flirting with Dan and Alec, which I expect is her chief occupation when there is only Jim to do for, who never sees what is just under his dear old nose unless it's something to do with sheep or horses. I hope my dear Bret Harte is all right. You had better ride him a little, hadn't you? He'll be so awfully wild and frisky by the time I get home. But be sure you tell Jim and Pat Murphy that nobody else is to get on his back *on any account* while I am away, for though you are far too heavy, still you will take care of him, and if the men are allowed to mount him they might knock him about as they do their own. I hope Mrs. Murphy attends to the bees properly, and that old Peter doesn't forget to water my flowers, but I am sure he won't, as I told him to do it regularly, and he'll do anything in the world that I tell him. Pat my dear old Rover and all the dogs for me, the darlings, I do hope the servants don't neglect them. You might bring one of Flo's prettiest puppies back with you for Eleanor and Dorothea. Give my love to Jim, and ask him *from me* to see that they are all fed every day. In this busy time he might forget if you don't remind him, and I can't trust Mary, who is always driving them out of her kitchen, poor dears, and shouting at them as if they were thieves, when there is not one of them that would meddle with a dish unless she actually set it down before them on the floor.

"I hope you have had a good clip, darling, and no trouble with the men. The weather has been splendid for shearing, at any rate, and I dare say we shall have rain before long. Mr. Macdonald says there is good grass still, though the crops are stunted. He has done shearing on two of his stations, and is just finishing at Yarrock,[1] where he lives, but for a cute man of business, as you say he is, he has been taking it very easily, leaving all the work to his managers, which Margaret does not think right of him, and she has been talking to him seriously. However he is going to Yarrock to-morrow—Mr. Clive says it is a beautiful place, and one of the finest country houses in the colony—and he is very anxious for Margaret and me to pay him a visit there. It is only a two hours' railway journey and a drive of about eight miles, and the weather is so beautiful, and Mr. Clive would come after us from Saturday to Monday, and a little trip into the country does do him so much good after the hard work of the office. You haven't any objection, have you, darling? Certainly there is no mistress at Yarrock, but then as there will be *two* of us, that doesn't matter. One lady alone couldn't go, of course (though Margaret says there oughtn't to be any such "of course" in the question), but both of us together, and Mr. Clive coming too—, and we shouldn't stay more than a few days. If you are *sure* you don't mind, we shall start on Thursday afternoon (I shall have time to get your answer before then), and I daresay we shall return with Mr. Clive on Monday. He (Mr. Macdonald) is not going to have anybody else, to spoil the harmony of the party, he says, since *you* are not here (I wish you were to join us, dear old boy). I am sure people must wonder to see us three so much together, for so few people, as Margaret says, understand what a purely intellectual friendship means. If we three were three women or three men it would be just the same. We don't remember what we are, we are so full of interest in other things. We have got some new books to read together, and we have some great plans for the future that we are going to draw up when we are quiet at Yarrock with no interruption—things Margaret wants Mr. Macdonald to do with some of the time and the money that he has so much more of than he wants for himself.

"How I do *wish* you liked Margaret more, Teddy, dear! But you don't *know* her, else you would. She doesn't seem to have *any* of the weaknesses and worldliness of common women. I never knew anybody so different from everybody else, and her house is just the same, and not a bit like the other houses you see. She calls it a republic, because all are equal, and no one does more manual work than another. The lady help is the real servant, and she seems to have been used to washing dishes and cleaning saucepans, which Margaret *does* hate, because she can't bear to touch dirty things, and her hands are always white because she is so careful, and she has all sorts of clever dodges for saving labor and messing. Her husband says it is using fine instruments for coarse work, and not true economy, for her to scrub and clean, and she says so it is, and agrees that the less refined sort of women should do the rough work, which is all they may be able for; but then, above all that, she says there is the crying necessity to reform the present system of housekeeping, with the servants on one side and the employers on the other, as if they were enemies instead of friends, and human brothers and sisters, and that is why she does it—to set an example. I am afraid it would be very dificult for me to do anything in that way at Warandara,[2] for I haven't the material she has, and we are always having people drop in, whereas no one comes here except by invitation (for Margaret keeps quite out of the regular visiting routine, of course), and only people of more or less their own sort. Still I see how right it is, and I feel as if I should like to do something. But what would Dan and Alec and the others think if I waited on them? And if I made an equal of Mary I am afraid she would be impudent, for she is a little inclined that way already, being so pretty, and the men always hanging about her. Here every member of the household is in harmony with the rest. Dear old Frau Bauer was Margaret's own governess years ago at home, and after she was a widow and poor Margaret sent for her for her own girls— just like her!—and the old thing makes beds and dusts of a morning before lesson hours as naturally as possible. I have been doing some cooking, and Mr. Clive has paid me no end of compliments. It is a pleasure to see how he enjoys nice things, and sometimes the girls do, too, but they are very whimsical, for they have never been accustomed to much variety, and Margaret eats as if she were a spirit rather than flesh, and doesn't seem to care for anything except milk, and you know what town milk is! Make Mary give you some fowls for dinner, and something besides mutton chops for breakfast. She won't trouble to dress brains and kidneys and things unless you tell

58

her, but there they are, and you may as well have them and be comfortable as not. "And will you, please darling, look on the top shelf of my wardrobe and find a piece of terra cotta cashmere, and also my grey hat with the gull's wing, which I want to have done up, and please send them to me the first chance you have. Mary will pack them. And take care of yourself, love, and don't be long, for I *do* miss you. It seems so strange not to have you to come to at the end of the day, and I don't like it at all. But it won't be for long. Good night dearest one. Your own loving

PATTY.

"P.S.—Let me know if you are *sure* you don't mind my going to Yarrock without you."

"Warandara, Wednesday.

"My dear old Pat.,—

"Of course I don't mind. If you and Mrs. Clive go together it's all right, and I hope you'll enjoy yourselves. Don't forget to take your songs, and do sing if he asks you. It's an awfully pretty place, but I haven't seen it since I was a boy. He keeps a butler and a swell housekeeper, and the wool shed and men's huts and yards and all that are miles away from the house. I daresay he'll give you a good time. Don't forget your old husband while you're gadding about. I feel like a fish out of water when I haven't got you alongside. However, don't you fret yourself about Mary. She bustles round in style, and gives me all the good things she can think of, and takes the best of care of me. She's got her hair done on top of her head, and the most fetching fringe in front. I've had to speak to Dan about being so much in her kitchen of a night.

"Bret Harte is lame and no one knows how he got so; but I've been doctoring him, and I think he'll be all right by the time you come home. Jim takes care of him. He's been riding Henry James Junior with a skirt, for he's growing a beauty now he's got his spring coat, with lots of fire but a temper like milk, and you shall have him if you like him. Jim says he'd suit you down to the ground, and I think so too, when we have tamed him a little more. Old Rover got a poisoned bait, you'll be sorry to hear, but the others are all right, and Mary says she's always stuffing them. Flo's pups are as fat as butter. I'll bring you the all-black one—he's the best of the lot.

"The garden is awfully pretty, with the roses coming out. The Banksia along the verandah is a picture. Old Peter is watering all the time, and the place is full of flowers, but the crops are only about a foot above the ground, and they ought to be twice as high by now. The wool was got in splendidly, and we sent the first drays to the station yesterday. I was there looking after it, and I took the chance to send Mrs. Clive a hamper of asparagus and green peas and a few of the first strawberries, also some butter and cream and some young fowls, which Mary dressed nicely so as to be no trouble. I hope you won't be gone before they get there.

"I have found the hat and the thingembob cashmere—at least, Mary says that's it—and I'm sending a man to the station with the parcel. I hope you are not going to wear such a beastly color. Don't you go and let Margaret make a guy of you, there's a dear girl. There's no one can beat you for taste when you're left to yourself. And as for your doing scrubbing and cleaning and waiting on Dan and Alec, just let me catch you at it, that's all. Margaret is a very superior woman, I know, but I think she's decidedly cracked, and I don't want her to make you so too. I like you best as you are, and don't want to see you a bit altered—improved you couldn't be.

"Jim sends his love. He was a good deal disappointed at your staying behind. They are all asking when you are coming back. I think by the time the races are over we shall have had enough of Melbourne, don't you? There's no place like home, where we can be always together, and I hope we shall be well enough off in future to take little trips whenever we feel to want a change. We'll go to Europe next year, if you like—if you think you can leave your Margaret for that long. Ask her, if you like, to bring her family and spend Christmas with us.

"I'm glad your new friends don't keep you from wanting me sometimes, old woman. You don't miss me more than I miss you, I'll bet. I'll be down again in 10 days or a fortnight, and we'll go back to the C.P., where I told them to keep our rooms for us. I couldn't stand staying with you at the Clives, and I'm sure if she asked me it would only be for politeness and to please you, so mind you don't encourage her to make any such plans. You be ready at the old shop when I come, and we'll tip that pretty house maid and have a jolly supper upstairs, and enjoy ourselves without anybody's interference. I want Jim to have a turn, but he won't go before Christmas, he says. I believe that's just because he won't run the risk of cutting your holidays short, though he *says* he don't care a straw for the Exhibition.

"Send me a line as often as you can to let me know you are all right. And take care of yourself, my dear old girl, and enjoy yourself all you can.

"Your loving husband,
"EDWARD KINNAIRD."
"P.S.—Be sure you don't forget to take your songs."

CHAPTER X.

– ON THE WAY TO YARROCK.

On Thursday morning Mrs. Kinnaird and Mrs. Clive were in the bedroom of the latter—a severely simple, carpetless, curtainless, but extremely dainty apartment—preparing for their visit to Yarrock. Mrs. Clive's portmanteau lay open on the polished floor, and some clothes of a less quaker like appearance than usual were spread upon bed and sofa. Patty was standing before a full length swing glass in the dressing table, wearing a strange straight garment of that color which Ted called beastly, over which Margaret was draping some rich looking muslin, gleaming with gold thread (it was, in fact, a finely textured Oriental window curtain), with an enthusiastic interest that betokened a genuine, if passing, sympathy with the ruling passion of her sex.

"There," she said, drawing back for a moment to take a comprehensive view. "If you could see those lovely folds, Patty, I don't think you would ever endure the hideous, bunched-up, meaningless jumble of a dress maker's dress again."

Of course it was quite easy for Patty to see them. She took up a hand mirror, turned her back to the long glass, and surveyed herself intently. They *were* lovely folds, certainly, lightly festooned from shoulder to shoulder and sweeping in free lines to the floor, the gold-veined pattern shining on the outer curves, a deep bloom of Eastern color filling the inner; but she saw at once that such classic robes were more becoming to a tall and willowy figure like

Margaret's than to one so short as hers. "It is a beautiful piece of stuff," she said timidly; "but doesn't it make me look a little broad across the back?"

"Of course it does. So it ought. Nature never meant us to have backs like the letter V. But I can drape it another way, if you like." She undid the fastenings at the shoulders, and gathered about a yard of the upper edge of the window curtain into a box pleat at the back of the neck, pinning it firmly under the frill of tawny lace that finished the top of the shapeless bodice, whence the full width of the muslin fell straight to the hem of the dull silk skirt. "Perhaps that's better for this kind of stuff. But you can't do your cashmere so—it's not wide enough, and you couldn't bear the weight pulling at your throat. Besides, it's more difficult to fix on without help, until you get used to it. There—how does that do?"

Patty looked at herself again, and thought it did much better; there was an endearing familiarity about a watteau pleat,[1] and to see her arms from shoulder to frilled elbow was to feel that something of a figure was restored to her. She turned slowly round to get a front view. The upper ends of the curtain crossing her chest were fastened above the shoulders with invisible button and loop, and the dependent superfluity was pulled through a silk girdle at the waist and drawn up and back with hidden safety pins at the side; in short, it was that modified Greek costume which those of us who are accustomed to it grow so tenderly attached to but find so impossible to describe to our friends who have not seen it. Margaret and Patty had manufactured the foundation robe, which is simplicity itself, and Margaret had produced the still simpler four yards of stuff for the outer drapery from her artistic stores, in order that Mrs. Kinnaird should have what her friend considered a suitable dinner dress for her visit to Yarrock. The result was beautiful and graceful as far as the dress was concerned, but Patty remained uneasily conscious that she was not tall enough for it. She contemplated the obliteration of her trim little waist, and wondered what Teddy *would* say if he could see her. She also wondered what Mr. Macdonald would think when he walked into his drawingroom thus fantastically attired. "Do you know if he has ever seen a Greek dress before?" she asked anxiously. "Of course he has," answered Margaret. "He has seen me in one. And he said it was lovely. He hates the conventional fashions, as he does all ugly things. When he has done his paper on 'Ideals,' he is going to write one on 'The Relation of Women's Clothes to their Moral and Intellectual Development.' "[2]

This reconciled Patty to her unfamiliar picturesqueness. When the gold-veined muslin was unbuttoned and unpinned, she folded it up like a shawl, and the straight-skirted silk robe on the top of it, and proudly carried them to her room to pack them. One of the many advantages of a Greek dress is that it takes up no space to speak of, and can stand any amount of squeezing; so, finding her portmanteau still gaping for more, she put in her best dinner gown—ugly though it might be. "In case of accidents," she said to herself, as she gathered its bulging masses together, and with difficulty patted them down.

Mr. Clive came home to lunch as usual, and parted with his wife and guest when it was time to return to the office. They would not allow him to see them off at the station, for reasons which he perfectly understood and did not attempt to question.

"Well, good-bye, my dear," he said. "All I ask is that when you undertake to take care of yourself you'll do it."

"Good-bye, dear Ray. Don't you see yourself what a bit of conventional nonsense it is for a busy man to leave his work to dangle about a railway station in attendance on grown women who are perfectly capable of buying tickets for themselves? If we were children it would be another matter. We shall see you on Saturday, love?"

"Yes, I'll be over on Saturday. Going second class, Madge?"

"Certainly we are."

"That's right. I do like to see people, when they say a thing, stick to it, no matter what it is."

She threw her arms round his neck in gratitude for this unlooked for encouragement, and he kissed her tenderly—Patty turning her head away, and missing her Teddy quite acutely for the moment. Then Mr. Clive departed, and the two ladies were left with still an hour before their train time.

"I know how you love your cup of tea, darling," said Margaret. "You shall have it before you go."

And they all had tea together, Frau Bauer and the lady help being called to drink a farewell cup, and the girls waiting upon them; and they exhorted each other as to their respective duties during the next few days until the cab came. Then Margaret embraced her family, Patty had a tender parting with Eleanor and Dorothea, and the two friends set forth on the interesting expedition which was to have more momentous results than they foresaw.

At Spencer-street,[3] while their portmanteaus were being labelled, Margaret purchased the two second-class tickets, Patty standing by with the dressing bags and wraps. An amiable porter came along, and recognised Patty's charming face—as even porters would, when they had seen it once or twice—and remembered to associate it with the open-handed gentleman who had hitherto been her travelling companion. "All right, ma'm, I'll put 'em in for ye," he said, having ascertained her train; and he caught up all the small traps and rushed away with them. When the ladies, having pocketed their change, passed through the wicket to the outer platform, they met him returning from a first class carriage with an air of deferential goodwill that they were conscious was misplaced. "The ladies' carriage was pretty full, ma'am, but I've found ye a comfortable one where ye'll be all to yourselves."

"Thank you," said Margaret. "But we are going second class." That porter's face and manner changed in an instant. He gave them a brief puzzled look, and then turned nonchalantly to drag the bags and wraps from the rack where he had placed them. He talked to the other porters, who passed by, but said nothing more to our two friends, though he finished the job he had undertaken on their behalf. Even when Patty, with rather pink cheeks, and unobserved by her more inflexible comrade, slipped a furtive shilling into his palm, there was no restoration of his former manner; he calmly pocketed it and walked off.

Margaret sat down in a corner next the platform with an expression akin to triumph. This was just what she had foreseen, and the proof that her enterprise had ample justification. "Sit here, darling," she said, pointing to the opposite seat. "Don't let us be afraid to show ourselves. Now, Patty, *look* at the sort of people who travel first class."

It was the usual miscellaneous assemblage, some evidently of their own social grade, but the majority as evidently below it— Government people with passes, girls who chaffed the porters, men who spat on the floor; whereas in their own compartment they had a beautifully neat old woman with a basket, a pale faced young one with a pathetic sick baby, and a modest and cleanly Chinaman—all serious and well mannered persons who paid their way, and would do nothing disgusting. Mrs. Clive was quite satisfied with her position and company, and Patty soon accustomed herself to it.

In a little while the former was in deep conversation with the pale young woman, at whose side she sat, listening with tears in her dark eyes to a sad history of a husband crippled by a mining accident and a child that could not have the remedies it needed for want of means to procure them; and it ended in her slipping into the narrator's hand a sum that would have bought several first class tickets. For Margaret had the sublimest faith in her fellow men and women, and an equally sublime contempt for all the orthodox fashions of dealing with poor folk. Patty nursed the sick baby, to relieve the weak arms that were weary with holding it. She had once had a baby of her own, the birth of which had nearly cost her her life, and only she and Teddy knew how she longed for another at all risks to herself; the old woman with the basket, smilingly remarking that it was easy to see the lady was a mother by the way she handled the present infant, was told the secret in a low voice, though Patty would not have thought of confiding it to a travelling companion of the ordinary type. The Chinaman was the first to leave the carriage, and they bade him a kindly good day, that he might feel not himself outside the pale of men and brothers. And, altogether, the first second class journey was a success.

As the train approached the small wayside station[4] which was the nearest point to Yarrock, Mrs. Clive straightened herself with a little gesture of pride, and Mrs. Kinnaird's heart began to beat a little faster. It is quite possible that both felt relieved to see that Mr. Macdonald only, and not his servants, was waiting on the platform. At the back of the station yard stood an imposing sort of brake,[5] to which four fine bay horses were harnessed, and it took the two grooms in attendance all their time to steady those animals while the engine remained upon the scene.

"I knew where to look for you," said Mr. Macdonald, as he opened the carriage door and handed them out, "I felt sure you would seize this opportunity to try the great experiment. Has it answered?"

"We don't look for answers in our time," said Margaret, whose face was almost radiant with the pleasure of this moment. "But we have had a most comfortable journey."

"And what a lovely evening," cried Patty, looking beyond the station sheds, and the store and public house behind them, to wooded ranges that were just coloring to the setting sun. "And you have brought a four-in-hand[6]—how delicious."

They had been separated for three long days, and they were confessedly happy in the prospect before them. The man in the grey Norfolk jacket and knickerbockers, and felt wide-awake of the country,[7] looked rather more handsome than in his town clothes, and much more alert and commanding; he was delighted to have secured a club meeting under his own roof, and showed it almost as plainly as his more demonstrative friends. Together they paced towards the waiting carriage, talking, smiling, feeling a new spring in their bodies, and, the train having passed on, a groom was sent back for the luggage. They turned to show him where they had left it, and saw the station master, with the tickets in his hand, gazing after them from the platform.

"He can't understand it," laughed Patty, "and why you take so much notice of us. I'm sure he is convinced there is something improper somewhere. He'll go in and tell his wife, and dreadful village scandals will ensue."

"We can stand that," said Margaret, smiling at her host, "if you can."

"Certainly I can," he returned promptly.

65

Patty walked round the horses with the deep interest of a bush-born woman who loves a horsey husband, and whose husband brags to all his friends that she knows a good thing when she sees it almost as well as he does. "What a splendid team!" she cried, with heartfelt enthusiasm; and she proceeded to criticise their points in the most discriminating manner. *"Wouldn't* Teddy like to have the driving of them! Are *you* a good whip?"—turning upon the owner with a business-like air.

"Is it permitted to a modest man to say 'yes'?" he drawled, smiling.

"It is not permitted to any of us to say 'no' if we mean 'yes,' " Margaret put in. Margaret, by the way, knew nothing about horses, and eyed the dancing bays with some misgiving.

"Get up, then," said Mr. Macdonald, "and you shall see for yourself."

Then there came the question how the ladies were to sit. Mrs. Clive suggested that they should both sit in the body of the vehicle, but Mrs. Kinnaird could not sacrifice the box seat behind a spanking four-in-hand in that way, and proposed they should sit by the driver one at a time—Mrs. Clive for half the distance and herself for the other half; which arrangement was entirely satisfactory to their host. So Margaret was hoisted to the place of honor and tucked up in an opossum rug, Patty was made comfortable just behind her friend, the grooms taking their places by the door; and with a great bound the four horses answered as one to the word of command and swept out of the station yard into the apparently roadless bush.

Margaret's inward nervousness kept her still and silent for some time, but Patty soon rose out of her enveloping furs, and, kneeling up on her seat, watched over her friend's shoulder the splendid paces of the team and the neat manœuvres of the coachman, and chattered to the latter in irrepressible exhilaration. Her patronising approval of his skill and style surprised and amused the elder lady, who was not accustomed to see her taking the lead. "Yes, you can drive," was her verdict, delivered with the air of a judge upon the bench. "You didn't look as if you could, somehow—in Melbourne. But I see you're an old hand. To describe a letter S between ruts and stumps, at the pace we're going, isn't such an easy thing as it appears, and Teddy couldn't have done it better."

"As you know so much about it," he returned, "perhaps you'd like to drive yourself?"

"I should like it above all things."

"Oh, pray don't!" cried Mrs. Clive, in genuine alarm.

"My dear Margaret," Patty remonstrated, "are you such a renegade to your principles as to say that a woman can't do what a man can do?"

"Yes—when it's a matter of physical strength and training, all of which is on one side."

"I have been used to it from a baby, Margaret, and my muscles are like steel. Of course I don't mean here, on a bush track where I don't know my way, but presently, when we come to the open road. I have often done it—and you'd see how I'd tool you along."

"Well, I'd rather be tooled along by Mr. Macdonald, if you've no objection."

"All right," assented Patty, with a sigh. "He'll let me try some other time, perhaps. Will you, Mr. Macdonald?"

"I'll have them put in for you to-morrow morning," he replied promptly, apparently forgetting that to-morrow morning was to be devoted to an important conference on the franchise question.

From a certain blacksmith's forge in a small hamlet on the way[8] a groom had to fetch some iron work, and they pulled up to wait for him. By this time the rosy blush on the ranges had died into a soft bloom of dark blue shadow, and the gorgeous west that had dazzled their eyes was a pale band of the tint of a yellow topaz, and the hush of night was in the air. They had left the bush for a country of fertile flats, full of farm fields where the crops were green, and of rich orchards and vineyards—a settled country that exhaled prosperity from every acre of it. "There's my boundary," said Mr. Macdonald, pointing to a gate which was presently to admit them to his wide domain. "We are about half way now."

"Then take my place, Patty," said Margaret, rising, "I know you are just pining for it. Only don't attempt to drive, *please,* dear."

"All right," said Patty, as she helped her friend to the lower seat, and eagerly scrambled to the box. "I can amuse myself criticising *his* driving."

"You make me so nervous," said Mr. Macdonald, "that I shall not do myself justice."

But he did do himself justice, of course, not being at all a nervous man, and being sharply spurred to rival Teddy's prowess, if possible. He swept through the trackless paddocks and their numerous gateways in a manner that gave Mrs. Clive the sensation described as having your heart in your mouth; but the little woman beside him looked on with calm approbation, and occasionally uttered a "well done" that he found singularly gratifying—considering how thoroughly he had outlived the petty vanities of youth. They were very much in their native element just now, and Margaret felt the least bit out of it. As she sat below them, rolled in furs (for the air was chilly), and pensively watching the oncoming of the darkness, the brightening of the little crescent moon in the duck-egg-colored sky, she caught scraps of the conversation which she was not near enough to join—"off shoulder," "near hind foot," and so on—and it made her feel a little isolated. However, the unwonted sensation did not last long. They presently entered a public road, and then, through a wide gateway, a noble avenue of English trees, all in spring leaf and blossom; which brought them at the end of half a mile to another gate, in a huge laurelled hedge enclosing acres of shrubbery, and velvet lawns, and flower beds, and gravelled paths as smooth as the dressed granite of the flights of steps between the terraces—a dream of a garden, as Patty said, sniffing the perfume of acacia and orange blossom as they passed through it in the dusk. And at last they drew up before the house—a spreading group of odd blocks, some of one story, some of two, added to each other from time to time, and all brought into harmony by the hand of wealth and taste, by the embrace of ivy and flowering creepers, by wide verandahs and intersecting conservatories connecting one with another—the notoriously "beautiful place" of that division of the colony,[9] by no means displaying its beauty to the worst advantage in the luminous, transparent twilight upon which its irregular outlines were drawn with the delicacy of an etching on blue paper. The wide hall door stood open, and in the effulgent aperture they saw a stout person in black satin and two men in quiet livery, the latter of whom came down the steps to receive the occupants of the brake, while one groom held the leaders' heads and the other shut the gate behind them.

Patty held her hand for the reins as the bays stopped dead together and shook their light harness and dropped their quivering noses earthward with a sigh of satisfaction; and, comrade fashion, Mr. Macdonald gave them to her. Then, springing from his perch, he went to the back of the carriage and lifted Mrs. Clive to the ground.

"I know you are shocked at these fellows," he whispered, indicating the butler and footman. "But it isn't my fault. They were old servants of my father's before I had them, and I can't turn them off. You won't be too hard on me for trying to make you comfortable?"

"Is it likely?" she responded, with a happy smile.

She was his earliest friend, and the first to receive his welcome to Yarrock.

(To be continued.)

CHAPTER XI.
– THE FIRST HOUR.

The guests were led into a great hall—a low but very large, irregular shaped room, covering the whole space of the original dwelling house, now merged like a seed potato in the cluster of buildings that had sprung from and grown around it; and Patty was comically reminded of her host's description of himself as having "no home to call a home," as she rapidly glanced from side to side. Walls, floor and ceiling were inlaid, panelled and embossed with New Zealand woods, light and dark, grey and yellow, dull and polished, with spaces for pictures and niches for china, and alcoves in which life sized statues could stand at ease without getting in the way of living people; and if our *nouveaux riches,* who make a point of artistic decoration, knew what that material was capable of in proper hands, we should have more beautiful houses for the money than we see now. The hall at Yarrock had dim and distant recesses (sometimes half-masked, like the passages, with Eastern hangings) that were found by the explorer to contain the very chair or sofa he desired. It displayed a charming big wide window, low and wide— the real old latticed window that suggests thatched roofs—with its lower sections opening outward like doors, and a deep, cushioned seat beneath it; and it showed the way to ferny bowers and palm roofed alleys of a conservatory that was no less a "dream" than the garden. And in the midst of all, glimmering on the wood carvings and the brass work of the lamps, deepening the soft bloom of

Persian carpets and Oriental *portières*,[1] a great log fire blazed on a capacious open hearth—the last touch of beauty and color that the genius of art and hospitality could give. Low arm chairs were drawn around it, and a tea table stood there; the silver and china twinkled in the ruddy flame light, and the little kettle spouted steam enticingly.

"Come now, and get warm," said the host with unusual animation, when the housekeeper, having been presented and talked to, retired with the servants, and the three friends were left together. "Who will make the tea? I am sure Mrs. Kinnaird must be 'dying,' as she calls it, for tea by this time."

"I was not conscious of wanting anything till I saw the teapot," said Patty, drawing off her gloves.

"Make it, darling," said Mrs. Clive. "I can't sit down in a place like this—at least, not yet."

She began to wander round the hall, with a rapt face, absorbed in her discoveries. This kind of thing might be all against her principles, but it appealed irresistibly to her weak side—to that part of her which longed for a Norman Shaw house at Bedford Park. "Who did it?" she asked, with a sighing intonation, regardless of invitations to refresh herself with tea.

"I did, mostly," said Mr. Macdonald.

"I thought so."

"Does that mean praise or blame?"

She did not answer, but continued to drift from place to place. He knew it did not mean blame, and he was very proud of his own good taste. With one eye he watched her passage from point to point; with the other he contemplated Patty's pretty curly head, gilded by the firelight, and her evident enjoyment of her cup of tea.

"How delicious it is!" she exclaimed, looking up at him as he stood, in the house master's attitude, warming his hands behind him.

"I was just thinking so," he replied.

"But you are not taking any?"

"Tea? I was not referring to that."

"To the general situation?"

"Yes."

"Thank you. It is very delightful to us, I assure you." Then she added quickly, "Do make Margaret come and have some."

He crossed the wide floor to the wide window, where Margaret stood at the moment, looking into the moony twilight. She turned her deep eyes on him when he delivered his message, and took not the slightest notice of it. "It *isn't* right," she broke out, under her breath, "that you should have all this to yourself!"

"Do you mean," he drawled gently, "that I ought to marry again?"

"Oh no, no! You know I don't mean that." She glanced round the room with a little yearning sigh. "If only beautiful surroundings were for *all*—and not just an idle few!"

"Don't call me idle any more," he pleaded. "You don't know how I feel it."

"I don't mean you, individually; you do what you can."

"And try to enjoy the things you like without worrying, won't you? Just for these few days? The honest truth is that I am very glad to be rich when I have you to entertain, however reprehensible it may be. I now feel the real value of my surroundings."

There was no apparent trace of flattery or trifling in his staid manner, or his quiet voice, or his long, grave face. And yet the subtle something that is like wine in women's veins quickened her pulse for the moment. He was a delightful man.

Patty stepped across the hall towards them, asking "What time dinner?"

"Eight," he said. "But you are in a free country now. Don't feel yourself in any sort of bondage, even to the cook."

"The cook is the one person we *must* bow to," she rejoined. "And Margaret, dear—if you won't have any tea—it is half-past 7."

The fat housekeeper appeared again, and took them to their rooms, where fires burned, and baths stood ready, and luxuries innumerable were prepared for them. Margaret's chamber was dimly rich and stately in its appointments—it had the air of a "best spare room;" Patty's apartment was light and gay with delicate chintz and lace and abundant *bric-à-brac*. The friends looked at each other's rooms before they began to dress.

"Isn't it a sweet, sweet place," sighed Patty, as soon as they were alone.

"Too sweet," Margaret answered, drawing her slender hand lovingly down the folds of the curtain that hung across her door. "This is South Kensington work,[2] Patty, and I believe I know the very hand that did it."

"Do you think his wife furnished——"

"No!"

"But I think she must have had some taste, Margaret."

"She probably expended it on your room; I am very sure she never touched *this*." Mrs. Clive looked round her with an almost exulting smile.

"You cannot compare them—they are so different," said Patty, vaguely divining her friend's thought. "And mine is exquisite in its way. And *so* comfortable! My wardrobe would hold all the clothes I have in the world twice over, and I have three sets of drawers beside. But I must go and dress, or I shall be late."

"I will come to you as soon as I am ready, darling, and fix you up."

"Thank you, dear," and Patty darted off.

Invisible maids had unpacked for them while they were having tea, and Mrs. Clive's only evening costume, which was already exciting much interest in the servants' hall, was spread upon the bed. In it she proceeded to array herself, when she had bathed and brushed and satisfied the passion for fresh linen that was her only personal extravagance; and no unprejudiced and cultured eye could have seen her when her toilet was completed without acknowledging that the Greek dress was fully as beautiful as she believed it. Her under-robe was of ripe-wheat-tinted satin, her outer drapery gauze of the same color, covered with a conventional embossed pattern of brown and golden sunflowers; and they "went" with her tall shape and dignified carriage, her fine, thin face and her coil of dark hair, in perfect harmony. Even the baggy waist did but make her graceful slenderness more graceful. She stood before a huge mirror, which was flanked by two silver branches having each a cluster of wax candles, and looked at herself in the peculiar light which is of all lights the most becoming; and, even as Mr. Macdonald had felt just now a little younger than usual, so did she. A question that seemed to have been long laid aside—whether she was a handsome woman or not—suddenly presented itself with fresh interest, when she saw herself framed like a picture on the wall of this artistic house. As a picture—any figure picture in the Exhibition—she studied her full length reflection, and in that idealising illumination, thrown up against the dim and rich background of the room, found herself young and beautiful to an extent that astonished her. Her faded skin bloomed like the fresh petals of a white rose, her eyes shone like stars, and the natural elegance of her shape, and the delicious color and taste of her apparel, held her gazing in impersonal admiration as at a fine painting that she had not seen before. She gazed until a small clock on the chimney struck 8 and she suddenly remembered Patty, when she flew in remorse and haste down the passage to her friend's room.

Patty was gone. Of course, she had not been able to await the promised help—she had managed to "fix" herself. But what was this? The terra cotta robe hung over the back of a chair; the gold veined window curtain was a tossed heap upon the bed. Had she not yet begun to dress? Had she, in despair at the lateness of the hour and the difficulties of the unfamiliar costume, abandoned the attempt? And why, in any case, had she gone to the drawing room without waiting for her sister guest? As Margaret asked herself these questions, with a vague sense of dissatisfaction, a smart housemaid appeared at another door of the deserted room. Mrs. Clive inquired, unnecessarily, whether Mrs. Kinnaird had gone.

"Yes, ma'am," said the maid, "just gone."

"Without dressing?"

"No, ma'am. Mrs. Kinnaird is dressed."

"Didn't she want—how did she manage?"

"I helped her[3] ma'am."

Then Margaret saw it all. Patty had smuggled one of her bustled and whaleboned dresses along with her Greek robes, and had relapsed at the last moment, and then taken flight, but no, that could not be possible! in order to escape expostulation or reproach. Mrs. Clive was conscious of a momentary disappointment, but she quickly shook it off. It was not want of courage or principle on her darling's part, she was resolutely assured, but simply want of time. She had not gone to Patty's aid, and Patty could not arrange a Greek dress by herself, and therefore, seeing the dinner hour draw on, had hastily thrust herself into the gown she was used to—the only thing she could do. But why a gown that laced up? Why had she brought such a gown, and without saying that she had brought it?

"How *can* I be so foolish?" Margaret thought angrily, as she swept down the passage to the hall. "As if the dear child mayn't please herself, and wear what she likes!"

The fact was that Patty's courage had failed at the vision of herself in the sack like under portion of her classic garb. She was small, and inclined to plumpness, though as yet her figure was one to be honestly proud of, as figures go in this present world; and she was convinced that a Greek dress did not suit her. "I can't carry it off like Margaret—I look podgy and unnatural," she thought, as she turned round and round before the glass while waiting for her friend. "The servants will smile behind my back, and *he* will think I look absurd—I know he will!"

There was a tap at the door, which she knew was not Margaret's tap, and she wildly tore off the terra cotta robe before replying to it.

"If you please, 'm," said the smart housemaid, "Mrs. Barton sent me to see if I could give you any assistance."

"Oh, thank you—thank you very much! If you would just help me to fasten my dress——"

Patty seized a skirt of black lace, twinkling with jet ornaments, and tossed it over her head; the band was quickly hooked, the satin bodice was put on, and the little woman felt herself again.

She rustled into the passage, shaking out her train behind her; and, lifting a heavy curtain, found herself in the hall. There stood Mr. Macdonald on the hearthrug, in evening dress, with his back to the fire, and, whatever might have been his passion for

73

classic raiment, and his abhorrence of the current mode, he certainly regarded her with eyes of admiration as she stepped towards him. She knew the look too well to make any mistake about it, and congratulated herself with fervor on having chosen to be modern, after all.

He led her to a deep chair, and put a stool under her feet. "I am not allowing them to ring the bell to-night," he said, "because I will not let Mrs. Clive feel that she is under any restraint while she is in this house. She will never get all the freedom she wants, but she shall have what is possible here. Simpson will call for the soup when she appears, but she is not to be bustled."

"I thought she was out," said Patty. "She is a punctual person, you know. She rings the bell at home when they are not all there at the right time. She may be waiting for the bell now." And she said to herself, "How devoted he is to her!—even to the extent of letting his dinner spoil!" It seemed to her that a man's devotion could go no further than that. But then, as Margaret had so often told her, he was not a common man.

"I quite forgot," she continued, "about our club meeting to-morrow morning when you said I might drive your horses." They called themselves "the club" nowadays, and spoke of their profounder discussions in this official manner.

"So did I," he replied. "But can't we do both?"

"I'm afraid not. Margaret doesn't like horses, I'm sure—she wouldn't trust herself—and I should not like to leave her alone."

"Oh, but you must not be disappointed—I know your heart is set on it. And I want you to have everything you can wish for while you are at Yarrock."

"Me, too!" she thought, with a little flutter of pleasure. She said aloud, "I can't leave Margaret to sit by herself."

"Can you get up early?" he asked her, after a moment's pause.

"Oh, yes! I am used to that. I get up to look after the fowls and the dairy when I am at home, always."

"Six o'clock?"

"Yes, if you like."

"Wouldn't you as soon have a ride around to look at the place?"

She quickly saw that he would prefer it, and also what a fuss and trouble it would be to get the four-in-hand out at that hour. So she said she would *love* a ride, but that she had no habit with her.

"That will be all right," he answered, lightly. "Mrs. Barton shall put one in your room."

"Do you keep a supply of habits on the premises?"

"My sister keeps one here to save the trouble of bringing it when she comes to see me. She is in England just now," he added, answering a whole string of questions that he saw in Patty's eyes, "and she comprises all my family. Well, what do you say? Will you be up at 6 o'clock if I order the horses? You are a good rider, I suppose. But I am sure you are?"

"I can ride anything you like to put me on," she proudly declared.

Margaret glided through the curtained archway at the end of the hall, and was half way across the floor before they saw her. She heard their voices, full of interest in the subject, whatever it was, and did not fail to note that they abruptly ceased talking as soon as she appeared.

CHAPTER XII.
– THE FIRST TEAR.

Patty could hardly sleep that night for thinking of the morning. She had her watch at the bedside, and began striking matches as early as 3 o'clock to see what time it was. At 5 she crept to the window to look at the weather. It was a dewy, silvery, delicate dawn, clear and still—everything that heart could wish. A little later she got up and dressed herself quietly; and her temporary maid stole in with tea, bread and butter—tea in a minute teapot, hot and fresh—which exhilarated her already joyous spirit and fortified her body against the rawness of the unsunned atmosphere. At 5.55 she tip-toed down the passage like a cautious burglar, and, entering the dim hall, found her host waiting for her.

"Good morning. Isn't it a delicious morning?"

"Lovely. The horses are ready, but I would not have them brought round, lest the noise should wake Mrs. Clive. Do you mind coming to the stable yard."

"No. I want to see the stables."

They spoke in whispers until they had let themselves out of a glass door into the garden, when they became mutually conscious of a pleasant sense of youthful liberty. The first rays of the morning were streaming along the level terraces and the vivid lawns that might have been so many bowling greens, and threw the shadow of their two figures before them as they walked. The cold, pure air brought whiffs of dewy fragrance from lilac bushes and

English hawthorn hedges and groves of densely flowering orange and lemon trees. The roses were a "dream" of beauty. Mr. Macdonald stopped to gather one, while she looked around with exclamations of rapture, and she pinned it under her chin.

"You are like a rose yourself," he said, as he watched her do it.

"Don't talk nonsense," she retorted, speaking as she would have done to any common man.

They had a considerable walk before they reached the stables, which, however, had electrical communication with the house to obviate the inconvenience of their distance from it. In the yard the horses, saddled and bridled, were being led up and down, arching their necks as they went, and breaking into a gentle, sidelong dance at intervals—a huge dappled grey like a field marshall's charger, and a dark chestnut with a black nose that was such a picture of equine shape and elegance as Patty had never seen before. She was overwhelmed with admiration and delight, and realised what it was to "roll in money" more clearly than she had done at any moment since her arrival at Yarrock.

"Now I warn you," said Mr. Macdonald gravely, "that that mare takes riding. There's not a scrap of vice in her, but she's got the spirit of fifty race horses when her blood is up."

The old head groom, whose darling she was, and who patted her satin neck and "whoa'd" persuasively as she sidled round and round him, recommended her in these terms:—"She's the mettledest little devil, mum, that ever dropped down from Heaven."

Patty laughed at this delightful description. She was thrilling with exultant anticipation from head to foot, as her host could see, critically watching her from under his drooping eyelids. "It has been the dream of my life," she said rapturously, "to ride a horse like that."

"You are sure you *can* ride her? A little devil from Heaven is not an every day affair, you know, and I don't want to have to answer to Kinnaird for breaking your neck."

"Put me up and see."

She took the reins and laid her hand on the pommel; upon which the mare began to dance and edge away and generally "play up" in a sportive fashion. "Quick!" called Patty, whose own quickness to seize the right moment was very reassuring to the anxious eyes that watched her, and in a twinkling she was in her seat, firm and square, with steadfast hands held down, evidently an accomplished horsewoman, and perfect mistress of the quivering animal beneath her, which now pranced about the yard backwards and sidewards, in every direction but the right, like a cat on hot bricks. The little figure was tossed in the air, like a thing on

77

springs, without shifting or bumping, swinging easily to each erratic motion without losing its poise for an instant. It was a pretty picture of grace and power, and it was a glorious moment for Patty when she heard the old groom say to his master, "My word! They're a pair—they are."

"You'll do," said Mr. Macdonald approvingly, and her bosom swelled with pride at his approval. "But keep her as quiet as you can. She'll be like a bird let out of a cage as soon as she's outside the gates. Don't let her fly away with you."

"All right. I think I'd better go first, before you mount, so as not to make a clatter."

She sailed out of the yard, holding the mare in check with one small, clenched hand, and with the other patting the arching neck as she leaned a little over it; and as soon as she saw space to ride in she broke into a sweeping canter, then into a wild gallop, and was out of sight in two minutes.

Mr. Macdonald, who was lengthening a stirrup, jammed the leather into the buckle, and mounted hastily to ride after her. "Redwing is too fresh," he shouted angrily; "she has not had half exercise enough."

"She has, sir," the old groom bawled in reply. "I've seen to it myself—twice a day, regular. But no exercising'll keep her down. Don't you be afeared for the lady, sir—she knows what she's about."

The great grey pounded out of the yard, and his rider started to race across the paddock, when he saw the chestnut mare returning to meet him, skimming the sunlit plain like a swallow, and bearing Patty as lightly as a feather is borne on a high wind. The little woman was wildly happy, her eyes danced, her cheeks were more roselike than ever.

"I couldn't help it," she panted, laughing. "I had to let her out. Oh, she *is* so delicious! May I jump her? *May* I? I know she must fly fences like a bird, and she *would* enjoy it so!"

"You would, you mean."

"Then may I? But I know I may. I'll try this one, and afterwards you may stop me, if you like."

She turned the mare's head towards a stout rail fence, about 4 feet high, and Mr. Macdonald was afraid to speak lest he should flurry her, for he saw that she meant to do it, and that Redwing, understanding the intention in a moment, was equally determined. And they did it to perfection, taking off at the right distance to an inch, sailing over as if on wings, and steadying to a joyous trot as soon as the flying hoofs touched turf again, horse and rider having one mind and impulse, as if they had been used to each other all their lives. Patty rode a little way, and, turning, jumped the fence again, with the same ease and judgment as before; and then Mr. Macdonald called her to him.

"It is beautiful," he said; "you are quite perfect. But please don't do it any more. It makes me nervous."

She laughed happily, contented to give up jumping now that she had shown him how she could jump. "Why don't you race her?" she demanded with enthusiasm, patting Redwing's neck to calm her excited nerves. "It is what she was born for. She would go over anything, if ridden properly, and her pace is magnificent."

"I don't care for racing," Mr. Macdonald answered. "It knocks them about so. And I like to keep an animal like this for lady visitors—in case I have any who are equal to riding her, which is not often the case. She has never had one like *you* on her back before."

"But you don't have lady visitors at Yarrock, do you?" Patty hastily exclaimed.

"It has been known to happen," he replied. And in fact it happened rather frequently—which was a circumstance that had never been before the club, and was undreamed of by his fellow members.

He and Patty had a charming ride, galloping side by side through the great paddocks and long grassed roads, walking and talking in narrow lanes and up and down stony hills, clattering through the streets of the little post town, which was only beginning to wake up, and where he roused a sleepy innkeeper to inquire about a parcel that should have come by the coach, and a curl-papered postmistress to transmit a telegram concerning it; and then, gently cantering home in the gorgeous sunshine of as perfect an October day as ever mocked the longings of a drought-stricken squatter. It was unnecessary for him to ask his companion whether she had enjoyed it.

"I never, *never* enjoyed a ride so much!" she recklessly assured him.

"We must have one every morning while you are here," he said.

They found Margaret sitting on the verandah in the sun, with a book on her lap, looking as if she also had been up for hours, and her pensive face was rather damping to their exuberant animal spirits. It said, as plainly as an expressive face could speak, "Why did you not tell me you were going to do this?"

Patty ran up to her and kissed her, and poured out her plausible excuses. "We didn't want you to be disturbed, darling. And Mr. Macdonald thought you might be nervous if you saw me go off on a horse that danced on its hind legs. We have just been round the paddocks—I thought we should have been back before you were up. I had been longing for a ride, but of course I wouldn't go at a time when we wanted to be all together."

"I am very glad, dearest—it will do you good," said Margaret, trying to smile. "But it wouldn't have disturbed me if you had come in to speak to me before you went. I was not asleep. I heard you go."

"Oh, if I had only known that!" ejaculated Patty, remorsefully. "But I thought you would be sure to be asleep, so early."

"I am a light sleeper. And I am used to getting up early. And I should have liked to see you on horse-back, dear—mounted as he would mount you. You know how I admired your riding at Warandara."

"I am so sorry! But Mr. Macdonald thought it would frighten you."

"What an extremely odd idea! Is that your habit, Patty?"

"No, Margaret. He lent it to me."

"I suppose you arranged this yesterday, *sub rosa?*"[1]

"Oh, Margaret! there is no *sub rosa* with us three!"

"I did hope not, Patty. Well, go and change your dress, darling; it is later than I think you are aware of."

Patty ran off, feeling decidedly uncomfortable for the moment, and reproaching herself for having broken the club rules, as she now clearly perceived was the case; and Mr. Macdonald, who had turned aside from the foregoing dialogue, came up with a magnificent half blown rose, which he presented to Mrs. Clive.

"If I had known you were awake and going to get up, I should have been here to receive you," he said, with his air of grave sincerity, taking a seat by her side. "I hoped you were having a good rest after your journey."

"Why?" she inquired, laying the rose on her lap, without looking at it. "What makes you think I want more rest than Patty?"

"Mrs. Kinnaird," he dispassionately remarked, "seems as hardy as a little milk maid, if you will forgive the comparison. You are made of more delicate material, and want much more tender care."

Margaret deprecated this opinion with a smile. And she earnestly set herself to conquer the unworthy sense of grievance that she was conscious of harboring, in defiance of all her principles. "I am so glad you did take her," she said cheerfully, tucking the rose into her dress. "I am sure she misses the exercise in Melbourne—people do when they are so used to it. Her husband has brought her up to look on riding as the chief of all accomplishments, and certainly she *does* excel in it, doesn't she?"

"Yes. She has a good seat. I always thought Kinnaird's style a little flash, but of course he understands the whole thing thoroughly. It's about the only thing he *does* understand, between you and me."

"Oh, I know that. He is dreadfully stupid. I often wonder to see how Patty adores him—how she *can*——"

"He adores her, which goes a long way to explain it. And he's a good fellow, though he mayn't be overburdened with brains. You never hear an ill word of Kinnaird from anybody."

"And she's so sweet."

When Patty appeared, her friend put her arm round her, and kissed her, and complimented her on the pretty color her ride had given her; and at breakfast, while dipping strawberries into cream, what time[2] Patty devoured devilled chicken with the appetite of a schoolboy, she spoke of the four-in-hand project and insisted on its being carried out.

"No, indeed," cried Patty. "That *would* be rather too much of a good thing! I have done all I mean to do in that line to-day. I should not have left you now if I had thought you were going to get up; I certainly shall not *think* of leaving you again."

"I *wish* you to go," urged Margaret. "I wish you to do it, to please me."

"But the club meeting, dear?"

"There is plenty of time for both. You can drive after breakfast, and we can have our meeting at 11. And I want to poke through the library—I want to find some passages in Mill that bear on our subject, and that will take a little time. Oh, don't trouble about me; I shall be quite happy in the library till you come back."

Patty looked at her host irresolutely. "What do you say?" she asked him.

"I say that whatever Mrs. Clive orders is to be done," he answered promptly.

So the four bays were put in after breakfast, and Patty, perched on the box seat of the break, took the reins and the great thong in her little hands, and set off in great glory and triumph through the paddocks once more, a groom at her back and her careful host beside her; and Margaret watched them drive away, and then sat down on the verandah in a lonely and deserted fashion and wiped a tear from her eye. "I will *not* be jealous and small minded," she said vehemently to herself; "I am determined I will not." And yet her soul was on fire at the thought that they could leave her alone—leave her out—a second time, even though she had expressly desired them to do so.

(To be continued.)

CHAPTER XIII.
– THE LITTLE RIFT.

" 'There would be no need of legal sanctions, if women were admitted, as on all other grounds they have the clearest title to be, to the same rights of citizenship with men. Let them cease to be confined by custom to one physical function as their means of living and their source of influence, and they would have for the first time an equal voice with men in what concerns that function—and of all the improvements in reserve for mankind which it is now possible to foresee, none might be so fertile as this in almost every kind of moral and social benefit.'[1] Patty, you are not attending."

Patty's pretty mouth was wide open behind her outspread hand, and a long drawn breath was audibly exhaled at the moment when Mrs. Clive ceased speaking. "Oh, I *beg* your pardon," exclaimed the little woman, giving herself a shake. "It is being up so early I suppose that makes me sleepy—and the country air."

"If you feel sleepy," said Margaret, "it is no use going on with this subject." She shut the book on her quotation with a stern demeanor. "We must put it off till another time."

"Oh, no, do go on," prayed Patty eagerly, "I am attending, really, and it is so awfully interesting. And this is the only day we shall be by ourselves to talk about it."

"Yes; that's why I think it was a pity to distract and tire yourself. You could have had the horses to-morrow, or on Sunday, when we could not have a club meeting, and when I should have had my husband to sit with me——"

"But I am not really tired, Margaret. And I would not have gone out to drive if you had not made me. Do—do go on."

Margaret was persuaded to go on. She brought forth, in addition to her marked volumes, a batch of newspaper and magazine cuttings, containing various arguments in favor of the Woman's Suffrage movement, which she read aloud while Mr. Macdonald made notes at a table beside her. She had the whole subject at her finger ends, and the practical object of the discussion was to arrange the plentiful material produced in a systematic form, for Mr. Macdonald's use in the Legislative Assembly[2] when he should get there. She herself was passionately interested, overflowing with ideas and suggestions which she poured out in a molten state; but it was impossible, much as she desired it, to remain blind to the fact that not Patty only, but Mr. Macdonald also, gave but a slack attention to the great cause this morning. His slow eyes continually strayed towards the chief delinquent (luxuriously coiled in a deep arm chair) marking each one of her surreptitious yawns, and when Mrs. Clive, having declaimed a certain glowing paragraph that intoxicated her with enthusiasm, looked up for sympathy, she found her companions stealing secret glances at each other and laughing— laughing while the air about them palpitated with the cry of the oppressed! But she saw in a moment that they had not heard a word of it.

"It is no use," she said, folding up her half read paper with trembling hands. "You are neither of you able to settle down to serious work after all the amusement you have had. We must postpone this sitting."

"Must we?" drawled the host, with caressing gentleness of tone and recovered gravity of face. "*I* am not tired, if Mrs. Kinnaird is. Suppose we put her to bed on a sequestered sofa, and continue the discussion by ourselves?"

"No; a club meeting is a club meeting. And this was such an important one! However, we must see what we can do this afternoon, when Patty is rested."

"I can't help it," poor Patty pleaded. "I hardly slept last night, and those horses *did* take it out of me. My arms feel as if they had been dragged from the sockets. Perhaps, if I have a turn round the verandah for a few minutes, I shall shake it off."

"Take her into the garden," said Margaret to her host, with an air of dignified resignation.

"You are coming too?" he returned, entreatingly.

"No; I want to write to my husband."

"But your husband will be here himself to-morrow."

"Yes. Still I want to write to him."

"Well, you will find everything in the library."

"Thank you. I have everything."

She left the room—it was the late Mrs. Macdonald's boudoir, the extravagant luxury of which had awakened in her the thought that there was something a little vulgar about Yarrock, after all—and retired to her own chamber till lunch time. She even locked the door against her Patty, who, however, made no attempt to invade her friend's apparently desired solitude; and, after spending half an hour in a vain endeavor to compose an irritation of soul that was startlingly acute and obstinate, Mrs. Clive sat down to write to her husband, whom she addressed in these words:—

My own, own Love,

In case you should allow any feeling of laziness or trifle of inconvenience to hinder you from starting by the morning train to-morrow, I write a line to say that you *must* come by that train, and not wait till the evening, because I cannot do without you any longer. My dear Patty is a delightful companion, and Mr. Macdonald is always interesting, and as a kind host unrivalled, but neither of them can enter into all my thoughts and needs as you do. There is no one like one's own husband, and I cannot enjoy even this beautiful place, that is so charming to stay in, unless mine is with me, to share it all. So, dearest one, don't fail to start early. This letter will go by the evening train, and you will get it at breakfast time; and I will tell Mr. Macdonald that you are sure to arrive at noon, and something will be at the station to meet you. It would be a bitter disappointment to me if you did not come till night. I am lonely without you, darling, counting the hours till we meet again.

As she wrote she heard the sound of the piano in the hall—a rich toned instrument, beautifully played—and presently a girlish voice, delicate and fresh and sweet, that she knew was Patty's, singing a plaintive ballad of the day.

"Ah," she thought, lifting her head and listening, "after all, she is not too tired for the things she likes! She can exert herself for *him!*"

With all her passion for music, and her thorough scientific knowledge of it, Margaret could not sing, and she played very little; but her friend, untrained and ignorant, had the soaring notes of a woodland bird and a style of enchanting simplicity. Mr. Macdonald was a born musician—his touch upon the keyboard now was delicious to the cultivated ears that listened to him—and this was his first experience of those vocal resources of which Edward Kinnaird was so ridiculously proud.

"Now, he will make her sing all day—he will want to correct her faults and educate her," thought Margaret, with a new pang, as she set her door ajar to catch the air of Tosti's sentimental ditty—

> Falling leaf and fading tree,
> Lines of white in a sullen sea,
> Shadows rising on you and me.[3]

She was right. The afternoon was one long music lesson, the performers feeling unable to tear themselves from the piano, which became gradually snowed up in bound and unbound scores. Vain as women are said to be, no woman is ever so vain as a man is of proficiency in that particular fine art; it was Mr. Macdonald's hobby, and he was as happy to ride it in the present charming company as Patty had been to ride a hobby of her own beside him at an earlier period of the day. And she, having grown used to the sound of her voice, burned to distinguish herself in the eyes—or, rather, the ears—of such an accomplished critic and generally delightful person, and succeeded in doing so beyond her utmost hopes. And thus the precious hours wore away, and no club meeting took place, and the Franchise was forgotten. Margaret sat in a low chair by the fire, outwardly calm, but inwardly in a seething passion that she would not own meant jealousy, but which made her feel towards Patty as she had never done before. She did not consciously accuse her friend of drawing that other friend from her side, ousting her from the pre-eminent place in which she had seemed so unassailably secure; her regrets were for a wasted day, and that her soul's companion was not keeping up to the mark, as had been expected of her.

Tea time came, and the pair at the piano returned to their lonely comrade, evidently informed by something in her appearance of her inward frame of mind, and suddenly moved to pay her excessive attentions. These, of course, were much harder to bear than neglect, and aggravated the irritation they were intended to pacify. Margaret was horrified to discover in herself an impulse to take her Patty by the arm and shake her when the little woman fawned upon her with propitiatory caresses after ignoring her very existence for the whole afternoon. For she was not so utterly free from "the weaknesses of common women" as Patty had supposed.

It was now too late for the important conference to which this day had been dedicated. Evening was coming on, and while Patty had had a superfluity of air and exercise, Margaret had had none. She was growing conscious of a severe headache, to which she was much subjected, generally as the result of nervous worry, and, though she would not declare it, lest it should seem to reproach them for the noise they had been making, she did hint to her friends that she was not very well, and they took her for a quiet walk round the gardens, which were now very lovely in the mellow evening light. For once she would have preferred to have Mr. Macdonald to herself, as in those old days before the club was constituted; but Patty walked at her side, according to established habit, and somehow the conversation confined itself wholly to commonplace topics. They were all aware this was a change, and it vaguely alarmed them, but not one of them could help it.

The two women dressed for dinner separately; nothing was said about the Greek robe. Patty came forth in bare neck and bustled skirt, and Margaret never looked at her. Margaret herself, heavy eyed and pale, sat down to table in her golden classic raiment, and made an effort to recover the youth and brightness of the night before; but she could not eat and she could not talk. She admitted that her head ached violently, and her companions were overwhelming in their solicitude.

"No, I don't want salts, nor eau-de-cologne, nor anything," she protested, when they hung around her in the drawingroom after dinner, proposing every kind of remedy. "Nothing does a headache of this sort any good, except rest. I shall go to bed."

"And I will come and sit with you, darling," said Patty, tenderly.

"No, thank you," was the prompt response. "I shall be better alone."

"But I am a very good nurse, Margaret; you never hear that I am in the room. And I am sure I could ease you with some cold compresses."

"I don't want nursing—only to lie still."

"If I read to you very quietly, I could read you to sleep in half an hour."

"You are very good, dear; but I'd rather not. You and Mr. Macdonald entertain each other, and don't bother yourselves about me."

"Oh, I am not going to stay up if you are going to bed."

"Why not?"

"It would not be proper," said Patty, with a laugh and a blush.

"How utterly preposterous!" cried Margaret, in scorn. "As if *we* were bound by those absurd conventionalities—*here!*"

"She knows we are not bound by them," Mr. Macdonald interposed, "and she ought to be ashamed to mention them. She *is* ashamed, I can see, by the color of her face. Mrs. Kinnaird, if you have a bad headache too, or are too tired to sit up—if you honestly *want* to go to bed—go, by all means; but if not, don't bring disgrace upon the club by making false pretences."

Patty blushed a deeper blush, but did not look at him nor he at her.

"*Must* you go?" he continued, addressing Mrs. Clive, with

86

a pleading tenderness that lightened her langour for the moment. "Couldn't you lie on a dark sofa, somewhere within hail of us, where at least I could look at you now and then? I can't bear to think of you suffering alone."

"It's no such dreadful suffering," she answered, smiling confidentially into his gravely sympathetic eyes, "and I shall be all right in the morning."

"And you insist on leaving us?"

"Yes. I should only be a wet blanket on you both if I stayed."

"How can you imagine such a thing?"

"Truth, truth—no conventional politeness, please!"— holding up an admonitory finger. "You know it is so. *You* would be a wet blanket on Patty and me if you had a headache."

"I was in hopes not. I thought we were more to each other than that comes to."

She smiled at him, bade good night to Patty, and resolutely walked off. When Patty wanted to attend her, she refused the little woman in a peremptory fashion, that was felt to be positively unkind; yet when the aching head was laid on the pillow, when lights were out, and silent darkness reigned around her, Mrs. Clive had a sense of being forgotten and deserted that brought tears to her eyes—tears that aggravated her headache and induced a feverish restlessness inimical to sleep. It *did* seem hard that she should lie there solitary and in pain, and her two friends pursue the cheerful tenor of their way as if nothing was the matter; perhaps enjoying themselves quite as much without her as with her, and probably— judging from the events of the day—a great deal more. She even wondered how Patty could like to sit up so late in the company of a lone man——!

Patty had her misgivings, as testified by her blushes when the *tête-à-tête* evening was proposed, but they were dispelled very shortly, and she enjoyed the novelty thrust upon her very much indeed. If Mr. Macdonald overstepped that line which she considered necessary to maintain in the case of common persons of his sex, the proceeding was so well disguised by his good manners and his tact that she did not see him do it. They were quite confidential together, and she remained entirely at her ease.

"I am afraid," she said to him, when they returned from escorting the invalid to her bedroom passage, and paused before the fire in the hall; "I am afraid Margaret is vexed with me."

"Never mind," he answered, consolingly; "she is a dear, dear woman, but she does get a little difficult sometimes. When her head is better she will be all right."

"I have not *really* done anything, have I?"

"Of course you haven't. She's a trifle arbitrary, you know, with all her goodness—between you and me."

"Yes. We came here to be free and happy, not to drive at things. There is plenty of time for a club meeting to-morrow."

"Have you felt free and happy since you came here?" he asked, wheeling up a chair to the wide hall fire.

"Yes—until now. To see her hurt and vexed spoils it all."

Patty seated herself in the proffered chair, and he squatted on a stool near her feet, so that he could look up into her charming face as he talked to her.

"Don't let it be spoiled," he entreated with an impressiveness that was all his own. "Why should you and I suffer because she is unreasonable? We'll have the club meeting in the morning, and she'll recover at once. Meanwhile, do let us be free and happy—we don't always get such a chance as this. It is many a year since I have felt as happy as I have been to-day."

But he kept within due bounds, and Patty regarded him as a brother.

CHAPTER XIV.

– THE MUSIC MUTE.

On Saturday morning Patty would not go for a ride, lest Margaret should be offended. Margaret assumed that she certainly would do so—had, in fact, insisted on it before leaving her overnight, and did not herself appear until breakfast was ready. Patty learned from the house maid who brought the early tea that Mrs. Clive was better, and did not go to her friend's room to make personal inquiries; the fact was, she had been brooding upon her own little wrongs, and by this time was inclined to return to Margaret the same kind of treatment that she had received. "After all, one must have some self respect," said the little woman to herself, which was an idea that had never entered her mind before in such a connection.

She presented herself in the hall half an hour before breakfast, and found her host standing there in riding costume, slapping his gaiters with his whip. He looked at her reproachfully, and she looked at him with a pathetic, self pitying smile.

"I would have given *worlds* to go," she said, as he took her hand and held it (for quite a considerable time), "but I thought it better not. You saw how it was yesterday?"

"I am disappointed in you," he answered gravely, and she heard the words with astonishing emotion; they almost made her cry.

"Don't—*don't* say that," she pleaded, "I can't *bear* you to say that."

"You should have thought of me, as well as of her. I have been up since 6. I don't think I was ever so dead set on having a ride before."

"I distinctly said I wouldn't go, last night."

"No. You were a picture of irresolution; and I was sure you would yield, because you knew how much I wanted it."

"I made up my mind that we must keep together, as a club and not as independent individuals, after seeing how Margaret felt about our separating from her yesterday—at least, until her husband comes."

"He will be here to-day—he will be with her to-morrow morning. And she seems rather keen to get him to herself, too. I had no idea they were such a devoted couple."

"Nor I, for I don't think them the least bit suited to each other; but I am glad of it."

"So am I, for I shall get a little more of you. They won't want either of us between 6 and 8 to-morrow morning. Will you ride with me then?"

"Yes," cried Patty, eagerly.

"On your word and honor?"

"On my word and honor I will—with the greatest pleasure in life."

"Done," he said, and resumed possession of her hand under pretence of sealing the solemn covenant. Still holding it, he led her across the hall to the garden door, saying, "Come and look at the exquisite morning you have thrown away"—having a design to take her to a sequestered summer house, and there prosecute the non-club friendship.

But she drew back with a blush. "No, I won't let Margaret come out, and find that I have disappeared into the unknown with you. We will be here to receive her."

"Then come into the conservatory and look at my ferns. We can hear her there."

They passed through wide glass doors into palm roofed, tile paved alleys, and did not talk for some time except to comment on the rare and beautiful plants banked up on either side of them, which to Patty, who had a tiny glass house of her own at Warandara, were objects of enthusiastic admiration and envy. Then he begged her, in the name of honest friendship, to allow him to give her a few odds and ends from his superfluity to add to her collection—things he protested he should be glad to get rid of, though she knew she could not buy them in any market within her reach and means, and she let herself be persuaded to accept them (in the name of honest, as distinguished from conventional, friendship), pouring out her

90

innocent delight and gratitude in a manner that made him forget he was practically an old man.

"Oh," he exclaimed, with an energy that made her jump, "*must* you go away on Monday?"

The look in his eyes checked her exuberance very quickly; her ever ready blush began to rival the hue of the bells of lapageria over her head. "Of course, we must," she lightly answered. "Margaret's children will have been left quite long enough, and her husband too. She has promised we will go back with him."

"But need *you* go? If I ask some people to come on Monday, couldn't you give me a few more days?"

"Oh, no—thank you very much. I am Margaret's guest for the present, and I expect my husband down at any moment."

"*Your* husband, too! I am inclined to think that husbands are a great mistake, do you know."

He had made this remark to a good many married ladies without giving offence, but Teddy's little missus was offended by it, for she divined that he meant it for something more than an idle joke. It was the first time she had seen him forgetful of the line that had to be drawn for common men. "I am not at all of that opinion," she said, straightening her small figure with a gesture that warned him to walk more circumspectly in his intercourse with her. "If all husbands were like Margaret's and mine, there would be no need to make a fuss about the marriage laws."

"Alas, that they are not!" he rejoined, turning aside to gather a bouquet for Mrs. Clive.

"And you must please not class *them* with the—the wretches we are always hearing about."

"Of course I don't. I suppose I was thinking what a great mistake I was myself, as a husband."

"Perhaps that was a good deal your own fault," she retorted.

"No doubt it was," he replied, with an aspect of pained humility that made her feel ready to cut her tongue out for having said a thing so cruel.

"No, no," she hastened to add, with her little hand laid confidingly on his coat sleeve. "I am sure you were the very best of husbands—I *know* you were. And you will be again, some day."

"Never!"

"Oh, yes, you will."

He shook his head with a melancholy dignity that almost brought the tears to her eyes, and then—with her entire concurrence—gently lifted her hand from his arm and kissed it.

Margaret came into the hall from the curtained passage as they returned to it through the conservatory door, and Mr. Macdonald met her in the middle of the great room with an alertness in his measured step, a welcoming look in his impressive eyes, and an offering of his choicest flowers in his hand which combined to bring back to her face the light that had been absent from it when they saw her last. "Oh, how lovely!" she cried, as she took the exquisite bouquet into her hand. "How too, too lovely! Why did you gather them?"

"For a purpose that nothing I have is too good for," he replied gravely.

She smiled, and held them a little away from her, while she embraced Patty with one arm, and exchanged that kiss which seemed exactly like the kisses of the past, but which both felt in a moment to be quite different. "Why have you not had a ride this beautiful morning?" she demanded, like a schoolmistress asking her pupils why they hadn't learned their lessons. "Because we wanted your company," Mr. Macdonald replied, "and you won't go with us. You would insist yesterday on breaking up the club and making us waste our time; but to-day we are not going to allow it."

"*I!*" she exclaimed, indignantly.

"You give me certain orders, and I obey them, as your true knight and devoted servant. But now, instead of obeying, I am going to command—otherwise we shall get nothing done. And I insist on the club meeting at ten o'clock, and that Mrs. Kinnaird does not demoralise us by yawning."

Margaret looked inclined to frown, but smiled again as she took his proffered arm to go in to breakfast. He pressed her hand to his side, without definitely squeezing it, and asked after her health and spirits in a tender undertone that made her believe she had been the exclusive object of his solicitude all the time. And Patty tripped behind them like a mere nobody.

At precisely ten o'clock they assembled in the library, which Margaret preferred to the frivolously luxurious boudoir, and there seemed every prospect of a successful meeting. The papers were produced and sorted, the note book spread out; the president was like a gun freshly charged, ready to go off with full effect when called upon, and the demeanor of her companions was that of intense and concentrated attention. But, alas! that meeting was the deadest of dead failures. There was a semblance of excessive zeal and earnestness, but it rang hollow to them all; there was no heart in it. The horrible suspicion that Mr. Macdonald and Patty were assuming an ardor they did not feel in order to propitiate an exacting task mistress—that they had even conspired together to keep her in a good temper—dawned upon Margaret in a short time, and, of course, a catastrophe ensued. While reading a fine passage from Mill, to which her companions were listening with punctilious respect and attention, she suddenly flung the book upon the table and burst into a passion of tears.

"You don't care about it one bit," she cried, angrily sweeping her handkerchief over her eyes. "It is not real to you, as it is to me—you are only pretending. You are like the rest of the world, after all—both of you!"

"Oh, very well," retorted Patty, walking from the table with great dignity, as if washing her hands of all club affairs for the future. "Pray don't trouble about us any further, if you think that."

"She doesn't think it," Mr. Macdonald gently interposed.

Margaret ran away to her own room, where she remained for half an hour, while the other members of the club discussed the situation and condoled with each other; then, thoroughly ashamed of herself, she returned to beg their pardon. Of course they told her not to mention it, and Mr. Macdonald soothingly explained that it was all due to unstrung nerves and the prostration caused by headache.

"You are not well," he said; "I have seen it for some time. You are not up to the strain of these discussions, feeling things so deeply as you do. Wait till we get back to town, and we will have a series of meetings at our leisure, and while you are in the country just give yourself up to idleness and to taking care of your health. Come, I shall constitute myself your doctor."

He rang a bell and ordered some wine of a particular seal, evidently very choice, to be fetched from the cellar, and administered the same with the tender firmness of a nursing mother disregarding shame-faced protests. Patty offered no assistance, but stood a little apart, with the faintest suspicion of a curl at the corners of her mouth, feeling it hardly fair that all this sympathy should be given on one side, and that the side that was in the wrong. When her host proposed that both ladies should put on their "things,"[1] to drive to the station to meet Mr. Clive, she said she didn't think she would go.

"You will go," Margaret said, solemnly, "unless you *wish* to show resentment for an unfortunate quick word, Patty."

"Oh, my dear, I have no resentment *whatever,*" Patty declared, with a sort of cold cordiality, if there be such a thing. "I should like to go, of course, if you are sure I shall not be *de trop.*"

"*De trop,* Patty!" Margaret's eyes flashed.

"Well, I seem to be looked upon as spoiling things somehow—I am sure I don't know why. You seem to get on better without me than with me." And then Patty flounced off to her room.

"What is she talking of?" cried Mrs. Clive with trembling indignation. "Is it really Patty who is capable of saying a thing so vulgar and childish as that?"

"Never mind her," drawled Mr. Macdonald softly. "She *is* a

93

child in a good many things—not quite like you and me. I have never seen it so plainly as since she came here. But we'll train her in time."

The cloud seemed to have passed over when they mounted into the roomy waggonette, behind a pair of staid brown horses, and fiercely fought for the back seat, which the casting vote assigned to Patty; but in fact that cloud was the precursor of a devastating storm. From this hour they ceased to be friends, though perhaps not quite aware of it, and began positively to dislike each other. That is, Margaret and Patty did so; as for the man who, consciously or unconsciously, had been the destructive agent—as a man mostly is in such cases—it is needless to say that *he* suffered no loss in the affections of either. He became only the more dear and desirable as a confidential friend, to both.

It was a lovely morning for a drive, and the rusty little editor, with his clever, thought-wrinkled face, duly arrived by the morning train, and received a cordial welcome. His wife sat with him in the back seat, holding his hand under the rug, all the way to Yarrock, leaving Patty wholly to her own devices on the box (and Patty enjoyed being left to her own devices very much, and quite recovered from her tantrums). As soon as she got him into the house, hardly allowing time for the initial nip of whisky which sacred custom prescribed, Margaret bustled her husband to her room, and there poured out endearments whose warmth and abundance surprised him.

"Well, this is very nice," he said, with a twinkle in his eye, as he returned her fervent caresses with a sedate but tender kiss. "I had a sort of idea that you would be so well entertained that you wouldn't miss my company at all."

"How could you think so?"

"And I was planning a morning's outing with the girls when I got your letter. What's the matter, Maggie?"

"I didn't say that anything was the matter. I just felt homesick for you."

"I suppose your Patty has been flirting with Macdonald. Three was a bad number, Maggie. There should be four at least."

"No; that was the very charm of it—that we *could* be three."

"Was?"

"Is. I should say."

But the far sighted little man understood the situation perfectly. And withal he was too great a soul to say, "I warned you against being too sanguine, but you would not listen to me."

After a superficially cheerful time in tennis court and arbors, and tea and music in the hall, and a rather brilliantly conversational dinner Mrs. Clive sought her club comrades secretly, and suggested that they should enlarge their number.

"Three are too few," she said; "we can never do any really useful work until there are more of us. Suppose we try to bring more members in? And what do you say to asking Ray to join us, to begin with? You know how liberal he is."

Mr. Macdonald and Patty looked at her dubiously, and then at each other. They did not jump at the proposal.

"That," said Macdonald, "would be making it *a* club instead of *the* club. And I don't think Mr. Clive would care about it a bit."

"I am quite sure he wouldn't," said Patty. "He's far too practical."

"Very well, just as you like," said Margaret, turning away.

And I think that was the last time the club was spoken of between them. Certainly the ballot for Mr. Clive's election was the last piece of business that it transacted.

(To be continued.)

CHAPTER XV.
– "A PURELY INTELLECTUAL FRIENDSHIP."[1]

Before breakfast on Monday morning Macdonald and Patty had a last ride together, and they went a long way, and were not particular about breakfast time. In the glorious sunrising of that most perfect moment of the year they rode up a spur of the ranges[2] behind the house to look at a view—the fertile flats and downs of Yarrock, not yet parched brown, with more blue ranges on the other side; and when the track grew too steep and stony for riding, they dismounted, tied their horses to a tree, and climbed on foot the rest of the way. Reaching the summit, they sat down to rest and look about them. Patty sat on a granite slab, and her companion spread himself on the flowering grass at her feet, amongst dandelion and brown-spotted yellow orchids, and a host of delicate wild blossoms that delighted in the sun. It was a lovely and a lonely spot, miles and miles away from anywhere—so he said. No cattle or sheep grazed there, no cart ever travelled that way, no casual horseman rode along (because they couldn't have done it); the only living creatures to be seen were lizards and spiders and indefatigable ants, and a crow that flapped down on a tree close by and complained of the intrusion of human beings in a grotesquely tragic tone. Other creatures were to be heard—a continuous noise of little insects, buzzing like a comb blown through paper or the whirring of fine-cogged wheels; but these soft sounds, mingling with the rustle of the stiff gum leaves in the wind, only deepened the sense of solitude, while breathing life and music into it as a spirit into flesh. These hills, that from a distance looked as if covered with azure velvet, were a wild jumble of rocks and trees, the rocks swelling out of grassy lawns like dough out of the kneading trough when set to rise before the fire, or piled and strewn in craggy masses down the sides of steep ravines like the ruins of an earthquaked fortress—all tinted and embroidered by the cunning hand of Time, which had had such plentiful material of sun and rain to work with; and saplings of gum and wattle 50 feet high grew out of their split fissures, and veins of thick moss lay in their scooped hollows, and ferns made a dense mat in the dark recesses under them. The whole place was soaked in sunshine. Leaves that were commonly sneered at for being grey were now intensely green; their edges twinkled as they turned in a passing breeze. And anything like the two blues of the distant ranges and the sky it is not within the resources of language to depict.

Patty basked on her warm stone, with her hat tilted back and her hands clasped round her knees, and inhaled the delicious air, scented with eucalyptus and wattle, which was just the ethereal essence of pure life and all natural sweetness.

"Oh," she exclaimed in rapture, "just think of Melbourne now! Figure to yourself the dust, and smoke, and noise, and nastiness, and typhoid fever,[3] and cares, and struggles, and misery, all seething together! Don't you feel as if you were an angel in paradise for a moment, looking down on your poor weltering fellow creatures, as Carlyle calls them,[4] who are not of the elect?"

Mr. Macdonald looked up at her from under his drooped lids.

"If," said he, "I ever *could* feel like an angel in Paradise—not that I know what that is, except negatively, as something transcending mortal conditions—it would be now."

She dropped her eyes to his and blushed. "Don't talk nonsense," she rejoined quickly.

"I never do. I am only saying what you say—that that is just how I feel—a plain answer to a plain question. Nevertheless," he added with decision, "I am not envious of any angel in any paradise whatever. I was never more happy to be my own gross and prosaic self than I am at this moment."

"I don't call you prosaic," said she.

"Compared with my fellows, and not with angels, I don't think I am," he answered. "I often wish I were."

"Oh, don't wish that!"

"No; after all, the poetic temperament—I suppose 'poetic' is the antithesis of 'prosaic'—the poetic temperament, if it lays one open to too much suffering, gives compensation for it. I refuse to believe that the prosaic man *could* enjoy himself as I am doing now."

"It certainly is the most delicious morning to be out in."

"And to be out in it with you—up in this quiet spot, far from the madding crowd[5]—that is enchanting."

"Madding crowds don't inconvenience *us* much, at any time."

"Then I'll say 'far from club meetings.' "

"Oh, no, I can't allow you to say that. We are club members. We must be loyal."

"The first rule of the club, Mrs. Kinnaird, is to be truthful. As a truthful member, I deliberately maintain that I like this better than our official intercourse. And if you tell me you don't, I shan't believe you."

She did not tell him so, but looked intently at the common objects of nature around her, and tried to think of a new topic. As we all know, efforts of that sort seldom succeed in time to be of any use, and a considerable silence ensued. A red-stockinged spider, with a black velvet body, walked by in a stilted fashion on his high jointed, sharp pointed legs. A gauzy dragon fly—nothing but a film, a moving thread of grey shadow—fixed its vague head on a hanging gum leaf and began to vibrate in the sun; like the grin which Alice continued to see when the Cheshire cat had vanished, its swaying quiver was visible when its substance was not to be discerned. And in his company came a sort of brown cockchafer or locust, with two horns, the tips of which spread out when he was not at rest, each like a little fan on a bent handle, and closed when he sat down with a booming buzz and drew his silken wings under their horn coverings. At these creatures Patty gazed intently, and Mr. Macdonald gazed at her.

"I like the club meetings," she said at last, "sometimes——"

"At the proper times—exactly; so do I. But not in season and out of season, whether we are in the frame of mind for them or not." He took his eyes from her too flushed face, and began to tickle the beetle with a blade of grass.

"I certainly didn't like the one we had on Saturday. I suppose we were not in a frame of mind for it, but I never thought Margaret would visit it on us in that way. I was dreadfully disappointed in her."

"Well, you know, you *would* insist on thinking her perfect, though I told you she wasn't. She is a dear woman, of course, but she's decidedly a fanatic."

"It's her intense earnestness."

"Oh, fanatics are always in deadly earnest—that's their 'note,' so to speak. The trouble is that they haven't ballast enough to hold them steady, with such a lot of sail on."

"Well, we won't abuse her behind her back."

"Abuse her—God forbid! I am the last person to do that."

"It vexes me to think about it—it vexes me horribly," said Patty, who was really taking the changed relations between her friend and herself very much to heart; brooding over all the little molehills till she had made mountains out of them (as Margaret was doing also), after the manner of women.

"Then don't think about it," said Macdonald, with his caressing gravity. He had pulled himself into a sitting posture beside her, and as he spoke laid his hand on hers for a moment—only for a moment; he was quite aware that anything beyond that would be a fatal blunder. "Don't let us spoil our last hour together by thinking of anything unpleasant. Let us be able to remember it afterwards as—as what you said just now—as if we had been in Paradise."

"We haven't an hour," said Patty hurriedly, pulling out her watch, "it only wants that to breakfast time. If we don't go at once, we shall be late."

"Oh, there's lots of time—no, don't get up yet! Just five minutes! Look here—you don't know what it has been to me to have you here—to have these quiet talks with you." Patty's color began to come and go in a way that warned him not to be reckless. "So few people understand me, don't you know, and I have no women of my own—only my sister, who is on the other side of the world, and even to her I never talk as I can to you. One *does* want someone that one can be unreserved with sometimes, to whom one can be wholly one's self; and I should like, if I could, if I might, to make a sort of sister of you——"

It was the word to conjure with. Patty's fever of embarrassment cooled down at once. Even though he laid his hand on hers again—for three seconds, at the least—she was not at all frightened. "Anything that I can do to help you," she murmured gently; "anything—at any time——"

"Are you going to stay in town long?"

"I suppose we shall stay till the races are over, at least."

"Then you will let me come and see you—quietly—not always with Mrs. Clive?"

"I think we had better not make any engagements," she said, rising. "And, really, we *must* be getting home."

"Very well; we won't go into details. Only you'll be my little sister—my little *confidante* when I get into trouble—henceforth. Come, take your brother's hand, and let him lead and support you; you'll break your neck if you try to get down this path alone."

It was harder to get down than to get up, and it was breakfast time before they reached the plains. They rode the half-dozen level miles at racing speed, taking all the fences as they came, because there was not time to open gates; and, reaching home in a breathless state, found Margaret pacing the verandah with her husband, on whose arm she leaned, with a look on her face, under the smile of greeting, which said plainly, "This is my last morning, and he has deserted me—for *her*."

The guests left Yarrock after breakfast, and the host, who drove them to the station, bearing that look in mind, allowed the ladies no choice of seats in the waggonette. He took Mrs. Clive by the arm, and gently but firmly propelled her towards the front step. "Your husband can have you at any time," he said quietly; "you must give this last hour to me." She was hoisted with determination into her place beside him, while the other pair gaily arranged themselves behind; and he tucked her up with tender care. Looking at her as he did so, with that pensive gravity which forbade all suspicion of trifling, he said, so that only she could hear him, "I have been looking forward to this."

"To getting rid of me?" she responded, with an attempt at archness. He scorned to smile, or to take any notice of such unworthy flippancy, which, however, plainly indicated that she was quite satisfied of his regret at her departure. He took the reins from the groom, who was to ride ahead to open gates, and gathered his team together.

"Why haven't we four-in-hand this exquisite morning?" cried Patty, "or unicorn,[6] at least."

"Because Mrs. Clive feels more comfortable with a pair," Mr. Macdonald answered over his shoulder. Turning to his companion, he added in a lower tone, "That's one reason. Another is, that I am more free to talk to you. And another is, that I want to make this journey as long as possible, instead of shortening it."

"I suppose you won't let us miss our train?"

"Certainly not. I am perfectly trustworthy in my engagements. But if we had the four bays I must have cut off half an hour at one end or the other. And half an hour means a great deal now."

"You might have had half an hour before breakfast, if you had wanted it."

"Oh, yes, with everybody about! I have a weakness for liking to have you 'neat,' so to speak—undiluted—not mixed with other company."

"And not being able to get me 'neat'—or thinking you were not able, for I was really alone in the garden a good while—poor Raymond has so many short nights that he always takes what he calls a square sleep when he can get it—you took a large draught of Patty neat."

"Patty," said he, "would have broken her heart if I hadn't given her another ride on Redwing, and once she gets in the saddle there's no getting her out of it. She's like a child with a new toy. She kept me jumping fences this morning till I felt as if I had been prize-fighting. You must have noticed our state of breathless exhaustion when we came in."

"I did," said Margaret.

They drove along for some minutes, listening to the cheerful prattle of their companions in the back seat. Mr. Clive had his own ideas about Patty; he did not take her seriously, as Margaret did, but merely as a bright and pleasant little woman, with an inborn gift for perfectly innocent flirtation. He did not draw upon his deep intellect for her entertainment, but drew upon her special genius for his own, refreshing himself in the true holiday manner, as if she had been a novel. She, for her part, thought him quite charming. As she said to Teddy afterwards, she had no idea there was so much in him. The morning was still as beautiful as October morning could be, and it would have been hard not to feel happy in such weather. The cool air was more exhilarating than wine, fresh and delicate beyond expression; and the sunlight, that made earth and sky such a dazzle of pure color, steeped soul and body as in the very essence of life.

"How lovely!" Margaret sighed, out of a silence that seemed to consecrate herself and her companion (not those chattering people behind them) to the priesthood of this divine temple. "Oh, look at that branch of apple blossom against the blue of the sky! Look at that woman's faded red shawl against the soft grey slabs of her house wall! How exquisite! But I have no doubt she is poor and in trouble of some sort—that's the sad note."

"Don't let us have any sad notes," said Mr. Macdonald, "I want you to take away none but happy memories."

"I'm afraid they won't all be happy. But that is not your fault."

"No, it is not my fault, and, as far as you and I are concerned, *we* have no cause for regret or disappointment, have we?"

"Oh, you have been only too good!"

"I have been extremely happy," he slowly and impressively remarked. "To have you under my own roof, to be able to see you all day long, in the quiet intimacy of brother and sister—I can't tell you what it has been. The only drawback was not getting you 'neat'—not 'neat' enough."

"I didn't come here to be taken 'neat.'"

"No, of course. And yet those ante-club days—! After all, you and I understand each other better than other people understand either of us. Don't you think so?"

"Sometimes I think so. But sometimes, when you are laughing with Patty instead of attending to serious things, as I want you to——"

"Oh, but if we had been alone, you know I should have attended. What was the use of attempting that sort of work when you could see it was beyond her? By and bye she may be able to enter into these matters as we do, but at present she is not up to it."

"I really am afraid so."

"I am sure of it. Though, of course, we mustn't let her know we think that."

"Poor child, no!"

"We can say it in confidence, you and I."

"I am not likely to betray confidences."

"I know that. We can trust each other."

"And"—with wistful eagerness—"you are not going to give up the woman's cause?"

"Great heavens, what a question! Of course I am not. I was going to ask you when we could have a talk about it. We must attend to this suffrage business by ourselves. Have you kept your papers?"

"Yes, but, if I hadn't, I know them all by heart."

"Then I must bring my note book some time, when we are sure of not being interrupted, and we'll thresh the whole thing out. How much longer is Mrs. Kinnaird going to stay with you?"

"I don't know. Another week or two, I suppose."

"Bother!"

They reached the little station, and turned out upon the platform to wait for the train. There was no more opportunity for *tête-à-tête;* the four, who were all in good humor, amalgamated, and talked brightly together. When the whiff of smoke that heralded what the stationmaster called "her" was seen, Macdonald sauntered a few steps with Mrs. Clive. "I shall follow you to-morrow," he murmured in an undertone. "I can't stand staying on alone. First or second?" he called aloud, to the again assembled party.

"Second," answered Patty. "We bound ourselves down to it by taking return tickets."

"She" rushed in, and clattered to a brief standstill; Mr. Clive laid hold of his luggage; the ladies took their seats. Patty was the last to enter the carriage, and as she stood on the step, her hand tingling in a parting squeeze that dinted her rings into her fingers, Macdonald whispered in her ear, as if it were a dead secret between themselves, "I shall follow you to-morrow."

CHAPTER XVI.
– BROTHER AND SISTER.

In Margaret's house Patty was as hospitably entertained as heretofore, to all outward appearances, and she made valiant efforts to persuade the family that she enjoyed herself as of old. But the spirit and flavor had gone out of their friendly intercourse; each member of the party was aware of it. Margaret secretly fretted to get rid of her late passionately-desired companion; and Patty longed for liberty and her own husband, as Mrs. Clive had longed for hers at Yarrock, and was similarly spurred to hurry him with a beseeching letter.

In the meantime Mr. Macdonald turned up, according to promise, and called day after day, as had been his wont. But if Margaret chanced to be alone when he was announced, Patty would not go in the drawingroom lest she should interrupt confidences; and if Patty happened to see him first, Margaret assumed herself *de trop* and left them together. Remonstrance on this new departure was neither made nor received in a kindly spirit, and silence concerning it was invariably misunderstood. In short, these truly excellent and high minded women, craving mutual aid to live a noble life, became respectively the prey of that contemptible school girl jealousy and feminine unreasonableness which were the reproach of their sex— the reproach they had solemnly bound themselves to remove. Alas, alas! It seemed but a little matter to the male observer—Seaton Macdonald, for instance, who smiled his superior and tolerating smile—but in reality it was a tragedy of the deepest dye. Let us not dwell further upon the humiliating details. Suffice it to say that before November was out not only had the club burst up, like the land boom,[1] but two of its members had ceased to be on speaking terms, and the third did not dare to communicate with either unless the other could be kept in ignorance of his doing so.

When it was all over, the older of his two friends, who considered she had the first claim on his support and sympathy, poured out to him the story of her grief and wrongs.

"Could you—*could* you," she cried urgently, "continue to care for a woman who was capable of acting in such a way?"

He sighed meditatively, a tacit assent to her implied conviction that it would be impossible to do so; but she wanted to hear him say it in so many words. "Could you?" she repeated. And, having made another attempt to evade her by remarking that it was a disappointing world, he was driven into a corner, and obliged to admit reluctantly that he didn't suppose one could.

"No doubt," said Mrs. Clive, with some sharpness, "she has been giving you her version of the affair—telling you that it was all my fault?"

"I should never," replied Macdonald diplomatically, "listen to anything that was said against you, from anybody."

"But hasn't she been talking to you about it?"

"Not much, and I don't listen to those things. I neither listen nor repeat. It's best not to take any notice."

"How can one help taking notice?" she cried, passionately, dashing away a furtive tear. "It is the most cruel blow, the most horrible disillusionment that I ever had in my life. I thought she was so different——!" and Margaret gave a sudden gulp and hid her face in her handkerchief.

"Oh, bother this woman!" complained the man to himself (he began to feel, for the first time, that perhaps he had had as much pleasure in her society as he was likely to get—that, in this new state of affairs, she promised to become suspicious and tiresome); but aloud he said, as he tenderly laid his hand on her drooping shoulder, "Never mind. You have still got *me*."

"Oh, I hope so—I hope so, indeed," she replied, with a hysterical laugh and sob. "I hope she is not going to rob me of my last remaining friend. I am sure she is trying to." "You and I were friends," he drawled softly, "long before she came upon the scene. She will have no more power to break the bonds between us than she had to make them."

"I hope I can believe that," sighed Margaret, looking at him with red eyes that did not improve her appearance. "I hope I shall find that *you*, at any rate, are true."

He assured her that truth itself was not more true than he was, and, having dried her tears and comforted her heart, went off to administer consolation to Patty.

Poor Patty was in equal need of it, being in the depths of woe. Teddy did what he could for her, by swearing at large in a loud voice, and calling Mrs. Clive a "beast of a woman," a "she devil," and all the bad names he could think of, each new invention more brutally inappropriate than the last; but his efforts did not meet with the success they merited. He was a dear, good fellow, of course, but much too dull and stupid to grasp the bearings of such a delicate and complicated case. Only one person—the "last remaining friend"— knew wherein the bitterness of her disappointment lay. To him she had unburdened herself more than once, and he alone could comfort her.

As he walked down Collins-street from Mrs. Clive's house, he chanced upon Ted at the door of the club, striding in with a country neighbor.

"Hot ain't it?" said Ted.

"Very," Macdonald replied. "Too hot for Mrs. Kinnaird to venture into the Exhibition to-day, I suppose?"

"She was there this morning—I can't keep her away. And now she's nursing a headache, as a natural consequence."

Ted passed into the club, and Macdonald walked a little way down the street, and then stepped into a westward-wending tram, which deposited him at the C.P. in a few minutes. With wonderful sprightliness of movement, he made straight for the lift and the third floor, and took his well known way along the corridor to Patty's sitting room. He tapped at the door, and being bidden to "come in" in a languid voice, entered, and closed it behind him.

Patty was reclining in one of the arm chairs, with her feet on the sofa (the sofa being too short to lie down on). She wore a loose white gown, and her hair was tumbled and her slippers lay on the floor. As soon as she saw who her visitor was she sprang upright, and scrambled for her shoes, and pushed her hairpins into her hair.

"Don't, *don't;* it is only me," he said, with the grammatical inaccuracy that at such moments is common to us all, however highly educated. "Don't disturb yourself when you are not well. I see you are not well."

"It is only a headache," she replied, smiling, as she sat down on the sofa and pulled herself together; but her voice faltered, and her mouth quivered a little. She had been crying over Margaret's perfidy and the sadness of the changed times, and her shaken nerves were too susceptible to his sympathetic look and tone.

He put his hat on a chair, and sat down on the sofa beside

her. "I had a sort of instinct that you were fretting here by yourself," he said, "and I was 'moved,' as the Quakers say, to come and try to comfort you. I wish you wouldn't vex yourself so much about it, poor little woman!"

"She has treated me with such heartless, cold-blooded cruelty—as if I were a stone, that couldn't feel!" wailed Patty, taking out her handkerchief. "I daresay she has told you it was all my fault."

"Now don't, don't," he murmured soothingly. "Come, I won't let you talk about it any more." He took her handkerchief from her, and dabbed her eyes, which were only prettily shining, and not red. "Remember, you have *me*. *I* haven't deserted you. Isn't it any comfort to you to feel that you have me?"

"Oh," she cried impulsively, "if I hadn't you, I don't know *what* I should do!"

It was an emotional moment, and the kind, grave, handsome face was not like the face of a "common man," and she did not sufficiently weigh the meaning of her words. And so the next thing was that she found herself tenderly enfolded in her companion's arms.

I am also sorry to record that for a few seconds she reposed therein, with her tearful face resting on his shoulder, not exactly comprehending what the gentle process of development had brought them to; it was only when he stooped to kiss her, and murmured "My darling!" in the unmistakably "common" fashion, that the shock of sudden enlightenment caused her to rebound from his embrace.

"Oh, what are we doing!" she cried under her breath, while a wave of burning color—the deepest blush she had ever blushed—poured all over her from head to foot. "Oh, don't—don't! It is all my fault, I know—not yours; but I didn't mean that! Oh, you must not—you must not!"

"Are we not brother and sister?" he pleaded, with a persuasive plausibility that Eve's serpent might have envied. But this little delusion had ceased to operate.

"No, no—that's all nonsense! You know we are nothing of the kind—doesn't this prove it? Oh, what do you take me for?" But she could not bear to reproach him. "It was my idiotic conduct—not your fault at all; and in your heart you *know* I never meant that. Please, do go now—don't stop any longer—and let us forget all about it, and be as we were before." She had risen to put him from her, and now he was standing too.

"I hope you will forget it, and forgive me," he answered, with admirable dignity and gravity, "if to remember it would give you the least shadow of pain. But don't be conventional, Patty—not

106

with *me*, dear. You knew I loved you—well, if I mustn't use that word—but I'm not using it in any vulgar sense——."

"Let us say no more about it," she interrupted, in feverish haste and fright, fancying every moment that she heard Teddy's step along the passage. "And please don't stay now—it's better not. *Don't* say any more! We don't know what we are talking about!"

She got him to go; though he had asked her to forgive him he was not in the least repentant, but he was touchingly submissive, and he saw that to go—for the present—was the wise and proper course. "But I shall come again to-morrow," he said as he raised her hand to his lips.

Then he walked back to his club as calmly as usual, smiling a little to himself as he went, leaving her to cry, to pray, to struggle with the newly-revealed wickedness of her heart, in a state of wild and desperate agitation.

We will not dwell too much upon this sad episode in a life otherwise so entirely irreproachable. A few words will tell the tale of the brief month that saw it through.

The first result of her agonised wrestling with temptation was the heroic resolution set forth in the following document:—

"Dear Mr. Macdonald,—

"I write a line to ask you please not to come and see me any more. I know you will understand my reasons, and not think I mean it unkindly.

"Yours sincerely,

"PATRICIA KINNAIRD."

This letter she dashed off breathlessly, with a sputtering pen, and ran down to post just before Teddy came in to dinner. Then she went to bed, and hurt his feelings very much by not allowing him to spend his evening sitting beside her. She said it would worry her, and make her headache worse.

Next day and the day after she was in a constant fever of anxiety lest Mr. Macdonald should not reply to her note, or lest he should answer it by a letter that Teddy would want to know the contents of. She was continually stealing into the hall to look at the glazed rack, hoping and fearing to see her name in the strange handwriting staring the public in the face; but she found nothing. The agony column in the newspaper was equally barren. At last she bethought her of the message book, and, looking in it, she found what she wanted—the unmistakable response, though not addressed to anyone, nor signed by the writer; these three words only— "Whatever you wish."

It was perfectly satisfactory, of course; nothing could have been more so. And yet her heart sank. She began to rack her brains to think why he had taken her at her word so promptly, without a protest or an expression of regret. Could it be that he had gone off to "that woman," and that *she*——! The thought was madness. It impelled her to make inquiries of Teddy as to what he knew of Mr. Macdonald's movements.

"I saw him a day or two ago—I forget when," said Teddy. "He was just going out of town."

"Where to?"

"I don't know. I never asked him."

She drooped more and more. She had no longer any pleasure in the Exhibition, and her head ached every day. She snapped at Teddy, and scorned his common topics of conversation, and upbraided him with his little coarsenesses of speech in a manner to make the dullest man (not hitherto accustomed to it) puzzle himself with conjectures as to what the deuce was up; and this best of husbands did exercise such faculties as he could lay claim to in trying to understand the matter. "It's that beast of a woman," he would say, fuming savagely, "who has upset you and made you ill," which was a statement Patty never attempted to contradict. Perhaps that was really as far as he could see; perhaps it wasn't. There were times when he would sit and look at his wife with a patient wistfulness that made her extremely uncomfortable.

"I'll tell you what it is, old girl—Melbourne doesn't suit you; and if we stay here any longer I shall have you laid up," he said one day, when she declared she hadn't been crying, in face of the clearest evidence to the contrary. "So just pack up, and let us go straight home. You'll be all right when you have your bees and poultry to occupy you, and poor old Jim will be glad of a holiday."

She had a longing for her own *tauri*,[2] as we all have when we are unhappy, and home they went. But that didn't cure her; she drooped still. The bees and poultry remained in Mrs. Murphy's care, and the flowers were left to old Peter, and Mary continued to flirt with Dan and Alec. and otherwise to follow her own devices. Bret Harte neighed to his mistress in vain (it was too hot to ride); the puppies licked her feet and chawed up her gown, and she hardly noticed them; her voice wavered into sobs when she tried to sing Good Bye[3] and Remember Me No More.[4]

"I shall get the doctor to you," said Teddy.

This threat roused her to action for a little while; she set to work to cook, and to strain honey, and to snip dead blossoms from the rose bushes. Then she drooped again, and lost interest in everything except the accounts of the Exhibition concerts in the daily papers. Then she was again roused by her husband telling her he had to go to Sydney to see his father, and asking her if she didn't think it would do her good to go with him.

"Oh, Sydney is unbearable in the height of summer," she said. "Take me as far as Melbourne and leave me there, and call for me on your way back. The Exhibition will soon be over now, Teddy—let me have another peep at it before it is quite gone."

"I'm sure you have had enough of it," he growled.

"No, I haven't. I could never have enough of the music and pictures—never!"

"All right. Of course, if you want to go again, you shall."

Her lightest wish was law.

(To be continued.)

CHAPTER XVII.
– THE "COMMON" END.

On a roasting January day Mr. and Mrs. Kinnaird came to town, and put up at their old quarters in the C.P. The house was full, but they were able to get the little suite they had occupied before, much to the satisfaction of Teddy.

"Well, take care of yourself, old woman, and don't spare money if you want anything," he said, on parting, giving her a hasty hug and kiss. "And do just what you like—just what you like in everything. I can trust you, my dear."

"What do you mean by that?" she returned, quickly. "Did it ever occur to you that you couldn't trust me?"

"Never, never for a moment," he rejoined with strong emphasis; and he put his hand on her shoulder and patted her reassuringly.

One squeeze of the hand, and Ted disappeared; Patty feeling that it was almost a relief to be rid of him for a little while. She began to say to herself, with a sudden eagerness, "Now, what shall I do?"—though she had tacitly given her husband to understand that she would do nothing but rest till bedtime.

She tore off her indoor gown and arrayed herself in walking costume—a costume rather more pronounced in its conventionality than any she wore in the ante-club days. And out into the street she went, regardless of the suffocating heat and dust; trotted across to Bourke-street, hailed a tram, and conveyed herself with all speed to the Exhibition. It was broad daylight still—Teddy had scarcely begun his journey when she reached the end of hers—and she did not stay to consider how she would like returning alone through the crowded city at night. She and Margaret had spent many a happy evening with the pictures or at a concert without any male escort, it being an essential principle of the club that women old enough to take care of themselves should be permitted to do so, and they had rejoiced in their independence. But what a difference there was between being two and being one! She wandered up and down, and hither and thither, like a lost sheep in the wilderness, like a ghost haunting the scene of its earthly joys; and she felt ready to cry for loneliness. "Oh, for the dear club now!" she sighed to herself; "for the days when we sat here together, and talked of high things, and helped each other, and were so happy! Oh, how could—how *could* she do it!"

Margaret, it may be said, had ceased to go to the Exhibition at all. She could not bear the associations of the place—to be reminded at every turn of the cruelty with which her friend had treated her.

When dusk came on, and the electric lights made a new day in the vast building, heated by twelve hours of sun on its zinc roofs to the temperature of an oven, Patty sought the commissioners' room, and ordered a modest dinner of cold fowl and tea. She felt shy of sitting down alone, and glanced furtively at her companioned neighbors, wondering whether they were taking her for an improper person, and wondering also, with a palpitating breast, whether by any chance the one old friend who had remained true to her was there. He was not there. She looked from face to face as she absently ate and drank, and some returned her glance with unwelcome interest, and all were strange. Feeling lonelier than ever, she drifted out again into the noise of the whirring machinery, and, afraid of being taken for a female loafer on the look-out for amatory adventures, hastened through the thronged avenues to the comparative retirement of the picture galleries. There she gazed pensively at the club's old favorites until it drew near concert time, and then took a seat in the gallery, where she was temporarily relieved of her conspicuous solitude and satisfactorily accounted for. The music made her sad and fanciful; a soft passage from "Rosamunda" brought a vision of the Yarrock garden in the moonlight—the stately measure of the "Cornelius" March[1] suggested Margaret's fine severity of enthusiasm; and she left the hall before it was all over, in fear of tram crowds, and went home to bed exhausted and depressed, with a keen sense of disappointment that she did not dare to analyse.

Next morning she went out on her balcony with a parasol,

and, leaning on the parapet, gazed for hours at the bit of Collins-street within her view—the bit of street down which a man would walk or drive who came from a certain Club to see her. "Will he come?" was the dumb cry of her heart. "He *might* come—it would be quite proper for him to come. He may have kept a watch on the list in the hall, and he would certainly come at once if he had an idea that we were here. He would come to see us both, and it is all the same; if I were in my own house alone, I could receive him, or anybody; and this is practically my own house, and he has so often been here before. Oh, I *wish* I could send him a note! But I must not—it would not be right. Teddy trusts me, and I won't do anything that I should not like to tell him of afterwards. But I don't want anything wrong—oh, no! I only want to talk about something better than land syndicates and droughts. And now that he has not Margaret, I *know* I am a comfort to him; he would feel it so dreadfully if he did not see me—if he did not know till I was gone."

She broiled herself on the balcony till nearly noon, and no visitor appeared. Then she dressed, and set forth to lunch and loaf at the Exhibition, which was the place for meeting people. But again she did not happen on the desired person, who naturally avoided the hottest place that could be found on a hot day, and she returned home draggled and dispirited, to fight with mosquitoes through another breathless and weary night.

On the third day, however, she had her heart's desire, and if it brought leanness to her soul that was strictly according to precedent and the way of things in this world. It was a cool, grey, south wind morning that it was a pleasure to be out in, and the Exhibition, whose fever had gone down in the night, was now quite comfortable. She arrived there early, and spent the morning in the picture galleries. Pictures, when no music was going on, were the only things that Mr. Macdonald seemed to care about, and the dull light was very favorable to them. Only a grey sky or the electric lamps enabled one to see them fairly; sunshine was—she had heard both her friends say so—fatal. It was just the morning for connoisseurs to come and look at their favorites, when they would not need to dodge all over the place to get a whole view of them; yet only the commonest of common people were there to take advantage of it. At 1 o'clock she rose with a sigh from a prolonged study of the lovely figure and face—not the dead face, but the young living one—in Leighton's Hercules and Alcestis[2] picture (Mr. Macdonald had pointed out to her how very beautiful it was), and went downstairs to get her lunch, when she saw, coming towards her in the stream of switchback railway customers (but *he* was not going on the switchback surely![3]) the figure she had been vainly seeking for so long.

112

Her heart gave a great jump and seemed to stop beating. At last—at last she would have "somebody to speak to"—someone to take care of her till Teddy came back! She made an involuntary little spring to meet him, her expressive face alight with pleasure; and then she violently checked herself, for she perceived that he was not alone. Two ladies walked beside him, one on either hand; an imposing middle aged woman and a slim fair haired girl, both prettily dressed and carrying themselves like important people. The moment Patty's eyes fell upon that girl, the conviction came to her that she was herself growing old and faded—the first time in her life that such an idea had even faintly suggested itself. And the thought was like a blow, bruising her through and through—a blow from which she would never recover.

The girl was extremely pretty, but it was not her beauty that Patty minded; she knew full well that in spite of her wide mouth and aspiring nose, she could hold her own quite comfortably against any rivalry of that kind; it was the look of youth that staggered her. Eighteen or nineteen, with a skin like the petal of a flower in which the fiercest sunlight could find no flaw, with those delicate, budding contours and that willowy slenderness and flexibility—all the attributes of well bred girlhood—it was this pre-eminent charm, which no art can give or compensate for, which smote Patty to the heart and destroyed her self conceit forever. Not that she hadn't seen plenty of young and pretty girls before. It was seeing one of them in *his* company which made her realise her own disadvantages.

He gave her a friendly look as she passed, and lifted his hat; she returned his salutation with a cold inclination of the head.

Half an hour before concert time she went up to the gallery and took her seat, in order to have a little quiet time to think over her late encounter and to wonder who the pretty girl might be and what she was to Mr. Macdonald; also to get a good place from which she could view the ground floor audience as it came in. "He is sure to come to the concert," she thought, "and those people are not the sort who sit in the gallery. They will take chairs in the middle of the hall and I shall see them, and with my veil on they won't see me."

Thus it fell out. She sat in front of the gallery, in the corner nearest the orchestra, and Mr. Macdonald brought his party to the place she had appointed for them. She had a splendid view of the youthful usurper, and naturally made the most of it. The girl was dressed in white, with a soft white hat and a Liberty silk sash of palest blue—a picture of girlish elegance, there was no denying the fact. And she seemed on the best of terms with her escort. While her chaperon on the other side of him studied the programme with gold rimmed glasses held over her nose, she whispered in his ear, and laughed at things he whispered back, and whispered to him again, till Patty grew positively wild with irritation at the sight.

"I don't call that manners," she said to herself, and thought what a contrast was this giggling creature to the refined and stately Margaret. "And, after all, she's nothing but a child—a mere bread and butter miss. And I'm sure he's not the man to care for a bread and butter miss."

The orchestra came up out of the floor, and took its several seats, and tinkled its instruments into tune. The conductor[4] appeared, was greeted in the usual way, bowed his acknowledgments, and presented his well tailored back to the sympathetic public eye. And in that breathless moment of suspense, between the rattle of the baton on the desk and its first slow sweep through the air, two gentlemen came along the gallery and dropped into two chairs at Patty's side. She threw a casual glance at them, and recognised their faces, but could not at first remember where she had seen them; by and bye, after much effort, she identified them as the men she had seen in the theatre on the memorable night when the club went second class to see The Magistrate; it was they who had looked down on her, stared her out of countenance. In much the same attitude, they leaned their arms on the ledge of the gallery and surveyed the audience below, and between the numbers they "passed remarks" on what they saw as they had done on a former occasion. But they did not notice her now, and talked aloud and freely, as if there was no one within miles of them.

"There's Seaton Macdonald and his new *fiancée*," said one, with a suddenness that made her jump and nearly shocked her into a state of paralysis. "This must be their first public appearance together, for the engagement was only announced last night. Well, she's a fine girl, but hardly so handsome as number one."

"She'll suit him better than number one," said the other.

"What, because she's got money? So she will. He's got the Macdonald nose for money, has Seaton, and the devil's own luck besides. Here's money and beauty, both together—a combination that never occurs in any ordinary fellow's experience. And there's more than that. Miss Joyce plays the violin and writes poetry."

"Great Scott! You don't say so. Then now I begin dimly to see why he put his neck under the yoke—a thing he vowed by all his gods he never would do again. Beauty wouldn't have chained him; money wouldn't have done it—lot of it as there is, and fond of it as he may be. It was the poetry, you may take your oath—or else the violin."

"Both. The capitivating whole."

"Well, if it were my case, I'd rather leave the poetry out.

And as for the violin, I like it in its place—which is on that platform; I'd rather not have my leisure moments disturbed by promiscuous caterwauling at home. I'd like my wife to attend to her children and the pudding making."

"There will be plenty of other people to make the puddings in this case, and to attend to the children too."

"I daresay. But every wife and mother should do it, whatever her class of life. If I were as rich as the Rothschilds, I'd make my wife look after the nursery herself—aye, and the puddings too—because that's her proper sphere and business."

"Happy woman, your wife! Macdonald has more modern views."

"Yes. And how did his modern views answer last time? If he'd made that woman attend to the children and the puddings, she wouldn't have had time to gallivant about and disgrace him."

"Macdonald had a French cook then, who, I am sure, would have tolerated no amateur meddling in his department. And Mrs. Macdonald happened to have no children. Moreover, no husband in the world could have forced *her* into that mould—even you couldn't have done it."

"I'd have made her do her duty, or I'd have packed her off."

"Well, she packed herself off, which comes to the same thing."

"Not at all—not by any means."

"And she was worth all the humdrum pudding makers put together, in spite of the bad end she came to. Perhaps that's why she did come to a bad end." The speaker had the air of a man who knew what he was talking about. "And Macdonald had a lot to answer for—a lot—though, being a man, no one imputed blame to him."

"A man can do what a woman can't."

"So it is generally supposed. I can't see the justice of that theory myself. Anyway, I hope he'll be more careful this time. He has a very fine taste in women—I will say that for him; out of the dozens and dozens that he's carried on with, young and old, married and single, you never knew him to take up with a stupid or vulgar person. She must always have some intellectual charm to recommend her. But that only makes the game more dangerous. This pretty creature, who writes poetry—"

She was leaning back at the moment, with her charming face up lifted, gazing pensively at the conductor's back and the threatening baton; and the man who was speaking of her seemed to regard her almost pitifully—widely envied as she was.

"Well," said his obtuse companion, with a laugh, "it isn't a friendless orphan this time—that'll make a great difference, you'll see. He's got a considerable amount of mother-in-law to reckon with, and if she catches him gallivanting in the way he's been accustomed to, she'll make him sit up—my word!"

"He'll gallivant, in spite of her, to the last hour of his life, in his own secret, subtle, highly cultivated sort of way. Married or single, he's never been able to resist an interesting woman—he goes and makes love to her as inevitably as the sun rises in the morning. He can't help it; I suppose it is in his blood. You might as well try to cure a leopard of his spots. Poor little Miss Joyce! I wish, for her sake, that she made puddings and didn't write poetry."

"For his, you mean."

"O, no. Not for his. As she is now she exactly suits him." The speaker sighed. "All we can hope is that her poetry will be better than the poetry of other women."

The music went on, and Patty sat through it without following another note, like a wooden image. When it was all over she rose in the careful manner of a person who knows himself intoxicated, but is determined not to reveal the fact, and walked stiffly downstairs and out into the street. With the same rigid calmness she conveyed herself home by the familiar tram, ascended mechanically to her private rooms, took off her best bonnet, threw herself down upon her bed, and then went to pieces all in a moment in a tempest of grief and shame.

CHAPTER XVIII.
– RECONCILED.

Early on Monday morning Patty went to the office of the steamship company whose mail boat was to bring her husband back that day, to ask at what hour it was expected. A clerk told her he thought it—or rather she—would arrive in the course of the afternoon, but that if Mrs. Kinnaird would call again presently he might be able to give more definite information. Patty called again, and again, and again; she spent the entire morning calling, patrolling up and down the street in the intervals between each visit. At last she was told that the ship was due at 6 or 7 o'clock; and at once she returned home for lunch and a warm wrap, and then set off to catch the 2 o'clock train to Williamstown,[1] to make sure of being there in time.

All the afternoon she waited on the pier, sitting on the bulwark at the extreme end and gazing seaward until back and eyes were tired, and then relieving herself with a walk between the trucks and rails; all the time sighing with impatience and asking when he thought the steamer would be in of every man who passed her. And her heart leaped when the desired object came into view, dim and formless on the fading horizon, as if she had not seen her husband for a year and had spent every hour of his absence in fretting for him.

Even after a mail ship is in, it takes a long time to prepare itself for the reception of visitors from the shore—half an hour to get round the end of the pier if it goes to a left hand berth, and another half-hour to make fast, roughly speaking; and then the rude and strong crowd up the gangways and choke them, and the weak have to wait and watch their chance for perhaps half an hour more. Ted leaned over the rail, gazing down with much solicitude on the little figure of his wife; and Patty, keeping always under the exact spot where he stood as the vessel moved, looked yearningly up at him.

"What, alone, Pat?" he called to her anxiously. "This is no place for you to be by yourself, at this time o'night."

"I'm all right now you have come," she answered. "Can't I get up to you, Teddy?"

"Keep where you are, clear of the crowd, and I'll be down to you in a minute," he rejoined, and down he came through the mob on the gangway, which had no option but to let him pass, and took his small spouse into the shelter of his powerful person, under which she nestled in perfect safety and content.

"Oh, darling, *darling*," she murmured, with unwonted passion, as she squeezed his great arm between her two little hands, "how *thankful* I am to get you back again. Next time you go away, dearest, you must take me with you."

"I'm always ready to take you with me whenever you want to go," he answered, laying his brown paw over her interlaced fingers. "I'd have taken you now, only you know you said Sydney would be too hot. Been dull without your old man, eh?"

"Dulness is no word for it. I have been simply wretched."

"No old friends turned up to look after you?"

"No, no. I have no friends—I don't want any. I want nobody but you."

Though he was not a very penetrating person, he did begin to see that something must have happened during his absence to make her so very much nicer to him now than she was when he left her, and he came surprisingly near to guessing correctly what it was.

"Feel all right now, Pat?" he queried, as they rattled up to town, sitting very closely together in a corner. "Headache gone? No more nervous feelings, eh?"

"No, love. I am quite well."

"Want to stay on in Melbourne, or to go home?"

"Oh, to go home—to go home! I am sick of Melbourne."

"Well, so am I, to tell the honest truth."

"Then let us go to-morrow, shall we?"

"All right. I have nothing to keep me."

Reaching the I.C.P., they each had a cup of hot coffee, and Patty devoured a sandwich, and carried another upstairs, which she ate as she passed along the corridors, in a vulgar manner.

"And so you are glad to get your poor old husband back again?" said Ted at last, when they reached their rooms, stroking the crown of her head with clumsy tenderness.

She replied by tightening her arm round his neck.

"I used to think—I had a sort of an idea—it just came into my head once or twice," he went on stumblingly, as if ashamed to mention such a thing, "that what's-his-name was going to cut me out."

She clung still closer, and trembled and shivered as if about to cry.

"No, no, I don't mean it seriously—it's only my fun. *I'm* not afraid. Only he's such an awfully clever, fascinating sort of chap, don't you know, while I'm only——"

"While you are the dearest, the truest, the faithfullest, the darlingest——"

This time she did cry outright, sobbing hysterically, while he patted her shoulder to soothe her.

"There, there, there! I'm nothing but a stupid donkey—not half good enough for you. But I do right down love you, my old girl—I'll defy any man to beat me in that." And not another word would he allow on the delicate half-hinted subject, which was never spoken of between them again.

In the morning he went forth with a jubilant air to telegraph to Warandara, and heard the news of Macdonald's engagement in the street. Immediately Mr. Kinnaird proceeded to the club, found the happy man, and congratulated him again and again with many hearty handshakes. "This will be good news for my little wife," he said blusteringly. "Only the other day she was saying how much she would like to see you married." The dear fellow told his simple fib without winking, and imagined it a fine stroke of diplomacy.

"Remember me to her," drawled the bridegroom elect. "I will write myself to tell her all about it."

"Oh, don't trouble—I'll tell her. You'll have no time for writing now—take all your time to attend to your sweetheart. We're just off home for a Darby and Joan[2] summer—no place like home in the hot months! We don't have mosquitoes of a night up our way."

He went back to Patty and did *not* tell her that Macdonald was "hooked at last"—which was his remark to all other people with whom he conversed that day—because he knew quite well that she was aware of the circumstance. He asked her whether she wanted him to order any stores to take up to the station, and she exclaimed, "Oh, by the bye—yes, of course!" and sat down to make a list of groceries, scrubbing brushes and so on, as if her whole soul was wrapped up in such matters. Later, when her commissions were dutifully executed, he said to her cheerily, "Well, old girl, all ready to start?" She answered, "Yes, dearest," with the true honeymoon sweetness in her face and voice, "I am ready whenever you are."

"Come on, then. We'll go home and be jolly, all by ourselves."

They accordingly went home, and they *were* jolly, notwithstanding the fact that poor old Ted had a struggle to make ends meet, instead of rolling in the riches he had confidently expected to enjoy. To be hard up, however, was not the wearing thing to him that it is to most folks; it made no apparent difference in his spirits, or his comfort, or his mode of life. He always assumed it to be but a temporary state of affairs; and, as a matter of fact, good rains and a rise in "Junctions" have since gone far to pull him round.

Patty gave herself wholly to him and the domestic concerns—the bees and flowers, the poultry and dairy, the fruit preserving, the tomato sauce making, the rearing of puppies, the keeping of Mary in her place (which she had been inclined to step out of since the time when her amiable master was the sole mistress of the house); and a most exemplary little Philistine she proved herself, in every respect. Still did she shape her figure to the conventional, and not the classic and artistic, standard, and laced her stays tightly because she thought she was growing stout; and she only ceased to wear a high bonnet when those articles went out of fashion. She gave her lord something besides mutton chops for breakfast every morning, and the best of puddings for his dinner, as a sacred duty; and there was no poor drawingroom "piece" that she wouldn't play, and no silly ballad that she wouldn't sing, if he happened to take a fancy to it. It is needless to tell how he rejoiced in his model woman—how, contrary to the rule of ordinary experience, his uxorious devotion increased day by day. Never will she need to wear a veil, or to sit with her back to windows, in his company. She is ever fair and young, as well as incomparably clever, in his eyes.

*   *   *   *   *   *   *   *

When Mr. Macdonald, having married Miss Joyce within a month of his engagement to her, with the readiest permission of her friends, vanished into outer darkness—that is, went off to England to present his bride at court while the wedding dress was fresh, and to set up a Belgravian household[3] and make himself notorious in the columns of society newspapers—then our two old friends, between whom he had so disastrously interposed, looked across the now empty gap between them and secretly longed to draw the rent together and make another start in life and friendship side by side. But of course they were too proud to sit down and write a letter to say so.

However, the other day Ted wanted to go to town on business, and Patty, of course, went with him. They arrived at night, and next morning he went one way and she another, her way being to Brighton, to see an acquaintance who lived there. She took her first class ticket—in these degenerate days she always took a first class ticket, whether the journey were to be long or short, though much poorer than she used to be—and walked on to the platform just as her train was coming in. Immediately she saw Margaret waiting there, and the sight of the sad, fine face and the severely simple, straight down dress brought the old times back with a rush and a yearning for their restoration that was not be to resisted. Margaret looked thinner and older; she had far more to lose in a comparison with girlhood in its 'teens than Patty, as Patty pitifully recognised in a moment; but *she* wore no veil to disguise the honest work of time. She would scorn to descend to anything so petty. And as Patty continued to look at her with a wildly throbbing heart, wondering if she would turn her head, she stepped into a carriage on the open door of which "Second" was inscribed, and quietly took her seat, and that overwhelmed our little woman altogether.

"*I* have been giving things up," she cried to herself, "but *she* keeps on—she has kept on all the time, with nothing to help and encourage her but her own noble soul. Margaret! Margaret!" She sprang into the second class carriage—fortunately, the compartment only contained themselves—and threw herself upon the bosom of her friend. "Oh, dear Margaret, do forgive me! It was all my fault!"

"My own darling—no, no!" was the prompt and eager answer. "I was the only one to blame."

And so they made it up as easily as they fell out, and are now better friends than they were before. At the present moment they are organising the club afresh, but not quite upon the original basis.

"I think," says Mrs. Clive seriously, "that we had better not take men into it this time. What do *you* think, Patty?"

"I think we'd better not," says Patty, with a sigh.

[THE END.]

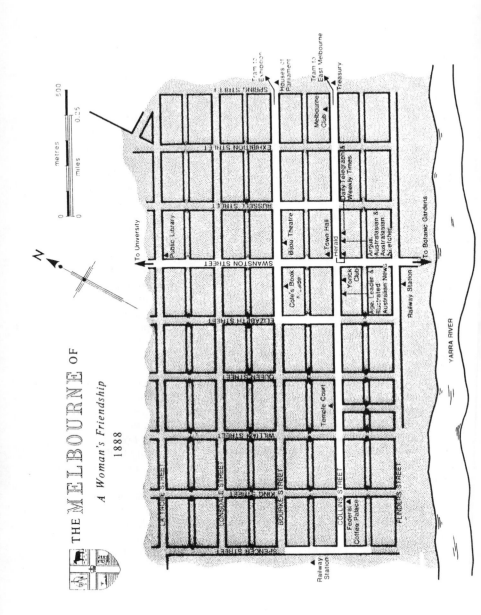

Explanatory Notes

Chapter I

1   (p 5) **the** *Rising Sun* **was a weekly paper.** There is no
exact equivalent amongst contemporary newspapers.
Melbourne, in August 1888 when its Centennial International
Exhibition opened and the story begins, had three weekly
papers which were printed on Wednesday night and issued on
Thursday (though bearing the date of the Saturday following):
the *Australasian*, the *Leader* and the *Weekly Times*. In age, the
fictional newspaper resembles the *Australasian*, which had
been in existence since 1864 and for which Ada Cambridge
began writing in 1873. In espousal of women's suffrage,
however (see note 1 to Chapter III), it is more like the *Sun*, a
small weekly which began in December 1888. There is
probably also an allusion to Louisa Lawson's monthly journal
for women, *Dawn: A Journal for Australian Women* (Sydney
from May 1888), which featured on its masthead an image of
the sun rising above the ocean beyond the Heads of Sydney
Harbour.

2   (p 8) **built upon solid rock, and not upon the sand,**
Matthew vii. 24-6 ['a wise man, which built his house upon a
rock...a foolish man, which built his house upon the sand'].
The Authorised Version is used in these notes.

3   (p 9) **the uniform white terraces of an East Melbourne street.** *Cf* Alexander Sutherland's contemporary description of the residential district to the e. of the city proper: 'one of long terraces; in the main, the houses are of superior class, and the suburb is justified in thinking well of its somewhat aristocratic appearance' (*Victoria and Its Metropolis* McCarron Bird Melbourne 1888 Vol I p 567).

4   (p 9) **the Imperial Coffee Palace,** The 'C.P.', as it is called in the title of Chapter V, is based on the Federal Coffee Palace, a huge ornate building at the w. end of Collins St. It was described in a country newspaper, the *Kowree Ensign*, as a 'gigantic but beautiful pile of buildings', with the comment that 'a number of persons questioned whether the expense of the palace was justifiable, but the Exhibition brought such crowds of people with well-lined pockets that this feeling was not sustained' (20 September 1889). Coffee palaces, to be found throughout the Colony of Victoria in the 1880s, provided accommodation and meals for travellers, but no alcoholic beverages; these institutions were seen as a respectable alternative to the more traditional hostelry, and were established as part of the temperance movement. (For this and subsequent references to places in central Melbourne, see map on p 122.)

5   (p 9) **wherever and whenever they could do so conveniently,** The meeting places mentioned are amongst the landmarks of Melbourne described by Richard Twopeny: 'everyone will agree to admire the classic simplicity of the Public Library, erected some twenty years ago...[it is] absolutely free to everybody, contains over 110,000 volumes, and has accommodation for 600 readers'; 'the Botanic Gardens...are well worth a visit. They have no great scientific pretensions...but are merely pleasure-grounds, decked with all the variety of flowers which this land of Cockaigne [idle luxury] produces in abundance'; 'In connection with the University is an excellent Zoological Museum, which is interesting to more than specialists' ('A Walk Round Melbourne' in *Town Life in Australia* Stock London 1883 pp 1-18). The seaside resort suburb, Brighton, was six miles from the city and reached by suburban railway. The township of Sorrento, near the entrance to Port Phillip Bay, and sixty miles by road from Melbourne, was becoming a favoured watering-place in the late 1880s. The excursion steamer *Ozone* made day trips from Melbourne in the summer months. In 1888 these trips began on Saturday 6 October. (For Brighton, Sorrento and subsequent references to places in Victoria, see map on p xxvi.)

6   (p 9) **the great building in Carlton Gardens;** The vast, domed six-acre building erected for the International Exhibition of 1880 was extended and provided with temporary annexes for the life of the Exhibition of 1888-89. As venue for the former event it features in Cambridge's novels 'Missed in the Crowd' (1881-82), 'A Girl's Ideal' (1881-82) and 'The Three Miss Kings' (1883); for the latter event also in 'Not All in Vain' (1890-91; as book 1892).

7   (p 9) **licensed by Mrs. Grundy** Proverbial custodian of public morals and propriety (after a person mentioned in Thomas Morton's play *Speed the Plough* 1798) and frequently referred to in Cambridge's novels.

8   (p 10) **Cook's Rooms;** Refers to a wax tableau, in the New South Wales Court of the Exhibition, of the landing of Captain James Cook at Botany Bay on 28 April 1770, together with a display of 'many interesting relics of the great navigator' (*Official Record of the Centennial International Exhibition...Melbourne 1888-1889* Sands & McDougall Melbourne 1890 p 213). These latter were 'objects of special study to every visitor' (*Age* 28 August 1888 Exhibition Supplement p 3).

9   (p 10) **Lovers, as a rule, monopolised these retreats,** *Cf* Ada Cambridge *Thirty Years in Australia* Methuen London 1903 (hereafter *Thirty Years*): 'it [the Exhibition] was a very paradise for lovers' (p 187).

10   (p 10) **"gooseberry,"** Chaperone.

Chapter II

1   (p 11) **the British loan pictures were the absorbing interest** In the British Loan Gallery of the Exhibition Buildings were 543 oil paintings, water colours, etchings and engravings brought from England. The *Official Record* notes that this 'magnificent' collection 'contained examples of many of the best painters of the English school during the present century' (p 216) and that the Fine Arts jury expected the works to elevate and purify the public taste (p 217). The pictures included landscapes, seascapes, portraits, historical and religious subjects, and animal life. Cambridge later observed that 'The Art Galleries of the Exhibition were more to us than the Concert Hall, for we were more in them. Amongst the Loan Pictures of one country or another, we met our friends' (*Thirty Years* p 187).

2   (p 11) **a somewhat conspicuous figure** Possibly some likeness is intended to Henrietta Dugdale (1826?-1918), the President of the Victorian Women's Suffrage Society, whose idiosyncratic homemade costume drew much public attention.

3   (p 12) **Leighton's copper-colored Phryne**, Phryne was a famous Athenian courtesan of the 4th century B.C. The *Age* described Sir Frederic (later, Lord) Leighton's painting 'Phryne at Eleusis' , as 'an academy study of a nude figure, of heroic proportions', noting that 'it cannot be alleged against this figure...that it is overdressed' (21 August 1888 Exhibition Supplement p 1). Leighton (1830-96) was the leader of a neoclassical art movement in England.

4   (p 12) **not a picture, but a statue,** May reflect contemporary discussion of the acceptability of the nude in art. Eg 'the prejudice against the nude in painting does not exist to anything like the same extent in respect to sculpture' (*Age* 28 August 1888 Exhibition Supplement p 1).

5   (p 13) **The history of success...John Morley says.** Quotation from *On Compromise* (first published Chapman and Hall London 1874) by John Morley (1838-1923), English journalist, politician and liberal reformer (on p 182 of 2nd edn 1877: 'The history of success, as we can never too often repeat to ourselves, is the history of minorities'). Cambridge used the same statement as prologue to her poem 'Responsibility' published in *Unspoken Thoughts* (1887). 'Responsibility' restates Morley's argument, namely the power of minority opinion to effect beneficent social change and the right of an individual to question authority and custom. In 'A Black Sheep' Richard Delavel and his daughter Sue go to the camp 'to talk over *Mill on Liberty* or *John Morley on compromise* ' (*Age* 5 January 1889 p 14). *On Compromise* was widely read and cited by members of the Victorian Women's Suffrage Society in the 1880s. Cambridge records that a 'dear friend' in Melbourne (an unnamed 'lady') gave her the books of 'Mill, Morley, Thoreau, and the like—that we read together under the trees of her beautiful garden or by a secluded fireside, and which inspired us to the search for that ideal truth which we could not admit was inaccessible' (*Thirty Years* p 286).

6   (p 13) **the Exhibition pictures,** The paintings mentioned here may be identified from the Catalogue in the *Official Record* as 'The Fowler's Crag' by Peter Graham (1836-1921), 'The Poor Man's Friend' by Thomas Faed (1826-1900), 'The Morning of the Battle of Agincourt' by Sir John Gilbert (1817-97), and 'Ripening Sunbeams' by George Vicat Cole (1833-93). This last was said to be 'perhaps the most popular

painting in the collection' (*Official Record* p 19). The painting by William Powell Frith (1819-1909) may be 'Blessing the Little Children', and 'Dying King' the 'Last Days of Edward VI' by Andrew Carrick Gow (1848-1920).

7   (p 14) **Governments...forming national collections** There was discussion at the time of the possible purchase for the National Gallery of Victoria of a number of works of art from the Exhibition, including J M Turner's 'Dunstanborough Castle' (later presented to the Gallery by its owner, the Duke of Westminster). Two other paintings by Turner were also displayed: 'Conway Castle' and 'Mouth of the Thames'.

8   (p 15) **famous Wattses and Holman Hunts..thought them horrid.** The merits of several allegorical paintings by Englishmen G F Watts (1817-1904) and two ('The Shadow of Death' and 'The Scapegoat') by W Holman Hunt (1827-1912) were a topic of controversy in press reports of the Exhibition. After seeing the Dead Sea, which 'The Scapegoat' depicts, Cambridge referred to 'the Holman-Hunty hummocks, salmon-pink' and noted that 'Time was when I sniffed at the colour...but here it was, translated into living light' (*The Retrospect* Stanley Paul London 1912 pp 17-18).

9   (p 15) **the rainbow...Book Arcade,** Cole's Book Arcade, a large and popular bookshop (from 1883 in Bourke St), distinguished by a huge painted rainbow over the entrance.

10   (p 16) **the concert hall,** For the life of the Exhibition, there was an extensive program of over 300 concerts in the hall, which could seat 2,500. Organisers intended the concerts—which provided 'standard classics of the great masters, but also best works of modern composers, interspersed with pieces of light and agreeable character, yet possessing artistic value'—to be both a source of attraction and public education (*Official Record* p 259).

11   (p 16) **"heavy" numbers, a Wagner overture... Beethoven Symphony,** The 'Tannhaüser' and 'Rienzi' overtures by Richard Wagner (1813-83) and the 'Pastoral Symphony' by Ludwig van Beethoven (1770-1827) were amongst the five most popular works performed (*Official Record* p 264). Cambridge later wrote that at the concerts she 'learned to be a Wagnerite, after several unsuccessful attempts' (*Thirty Years* p 186).

12   (p 16) **"Yellow Jasmine" gavotte and "The Last Sleep of the Virgin"** The gavotte, first performed at the concerts on 18 August, was from 'The Language of Flowers', by the musical director and conductor of the orchestra, Frederic

(later, Sir Frederic) Cowen (1852-1935). 'Le Dernier Sommeil de la Vierge' by Jules Massenet (1842-1912) was first performed on 25 August. There is no record of both works having been performed together.

Chapter III

1   (p 18) **paper...on** *The Liberty of Woman.* Articles and editorials discussing women's rights and arguing for extension of the electoral franchise to women were published from time to time in Melbourne newspapers of the 1880s, particularly in the weekly *People's Tribune*, 1883-86 and the weekly *Sun* and the daily *Evening Standard* in 1889. Reference is not being made to any single identifiable item.

2   (p 18) **the Hamlet Club,** Probably refers to the Yorick Club, a literary society established in Melbourne in 1868. The author and journalist Marcus Clarke was one of the founders. In Clarke's satirical description of Collins St in 1874 it is the 'Cassowary Club' in 'Down Camomile [Collins] Street' (*Weekly Times* 17 January 1874, reprinted in *A Colonial City* ed L T Hergenhan U of Queensland Press St Lucia Qld 1972 p 301). By the 1880s its membership included many journalists. In 1888 its premises were adjacent to the offices of the *Age*; at an earlier time its rooms were in the *Melbourne Punch* building next to the *Argus* and *Australasian* offices.

3   (p 19) **the doctor's...Grammar School.** The Melbourne Church of England Grammar School (established in 1858), modelled on English public schools for boys such as Eton and Harrow, and providing education for the wealthy and suitable preparation for university studies. The 'doctor' was Dr John Edward Bromby, headmaster 1858-75, and seen as an enlightened liberal with a considerable influence on colonial society.

4   (p 19) **a Temple barrister,** May refer to the Inns of Court in London or to Temple Court in Collins St, Melbourne where barristers and solicitors had their rooms.

5   (p 19) **inferior to the Exhibition of 1880.** *Cf* the editorial in the *Age* on the closing day of the Centennial Exhibition: 'Although the present exhibition has exceeded that of 1880 in magnitude, it can hardly be contended that it was superior as a display of international industry' (31 January 1889 p 4).

6   (p 19) **Boehm's marble group...under the dome,** The white marble statue 'Young Bull and Herdsman', now in the

National Gallery of Victoria, by Sir Joseph Edgar Boehm (1834-90), Viennese-born sculptor, attracted great attention. At first it was displayed prominently under the dome but, by 18 September, had been removed to the e. nave in order to give this part a more imposing aspect (*Age* Exhibition Supplement p 1).

7   (p 20) **the weak brother,** Person whose beliefs are ill-founded (*cf* 1 Corinthians vii).

8   (p 20) **it is easier for a camel to go through the eye of a needle** '...than for a rich man to enter into the kingdom of God' (Matthew xix. 24).

9   (p 21) **railway journey in a second class carriage** In 'The Reform Club' it is 'an unheard-of thing' (p 153); and *cf The Retrospect*: 'At home [ie Australia] we have no third class, and your own servants do not deign to travel second' (p 257).

10   (p 22) **"Where thou goest, I will go."** Ruth i. 16 ['for whither thou goest, I will go'].

11   (p 22) **The Magistrate** Farce by English playwright Sir Arthur Pinero (1855-1934) which opened at the Bijou Theatre in Bourke St on 18 August 1888 and ran for one month with Melbourne actor-manager, (Lionel) Robert Brough (1857-1906) as Posket. The *Age* of 20 August and the *Australian Journal* (October p 113) confirm the success and popularity of the production.

12   (p 23) **the club** See note 4 to Chapter IV.

Chapter IV

1   (p 26) **great increase of advertisements in the *Sun*,** The land boom and speculative building development of Melbourne which began in the seventies reached its peak in 1888. It gave rise to a huge volume of advertising in the local press; *cf* the first sentence of 'The Reform Club' (p 143).

2   (p 26) **a Norman Shaw house at Bedford Park,** In 1877 English architect Richard Norman Shaw (1831-1912), who had introduced innovations in domestic architecture and built many houses for artists, was commissioned to design and build houses for the first garden suburb in London. These detached houses in their own garden plots at Bedford Park, in the w. of London, were greatly sought after.

3   (p 27) **tram,** Melbourne's cable tram system, inaugurated in 1885, became one of the largest in the world; by 1888 trams ran extensively through the city and inner suburbs.

4   (p 27) **the fashionable club,** Would undoubtedly have been taken by readers in 1889 to be the Melbourne Club; it is named in 'The Reform Club' (p 165). Founded in 1838 it soon became the exclusive preserve of the wealthy establishment. Marcus Clarke lampooned it as the 'Platypus Club' in 1874: 'and the Platypi are very haughty persons' (*A Colonial City* p 301). Sutherland described it in 1888 as the club of 'wealthy squatters...most colonially select' (*Victoria and Its Metropolis* Vol I p 543).

Chapter V

1   (p 30) **like smiling images...Stephenson says.** Unidentified; it is possible that the name has been misspelled and should be (R L) Stevenson (his *The Black Arrow* was advertised in the October 1888 issue of *Mullen's Monthly Circular* [Mullen's was a Melbourne bookshop and circulating library] as a 'New work by Robert Louis Stephenson'). Although there are numerous instances of Stevenson's treating journeys as metaphor, the particular phrase has not been found.

2   (p 32) **prog box** Box containing provisions for a journey or excursion.

3   (p 34) **'cute** Acute, shrewd (also spelled 'cute', as on p 57). *Cf* George Eliot's use: 'Mr Chubb had made up his mind that this 'cute man who kept himself sober was an electioneering agent' (*Felix Holt, The Radical* Blackwood Edinburgh 1895 p 194, First published 1866).

4   (p 35) **clipper.** Woman who outshone her competitors (literally, a fast sailing vessel; American clippers dominated shipping routes to Australia in the middle of the 19th century).

Chapter VI

1   (p 36) **When we get the electoral franchise,** Women did not receive the franchise for Victorian Parliamentary elections until 1908 although they were eligible to vote in Commonwealth elections from Federation in 1901. On the 1889 Women's Suffrage Bill see Editor's Introduction, p xxxiii and note 2 to Chapter VIII.

2   (p 38) **The aesthetic spirit...Liberty silk...Kalizoic muslin...familiar gimcracks.** Margaret Clive is influenced by the aesthetic movement at its height in London in the mid-1880s and imitated in Melbourne: 'If you were rich and "enlightened" or on the fringe of certain artistic circles, you might live in a Norman Shaw house, commission William Morris to design original furniture, and own paintings by Whistler; but if this was not within reach, a fabric from Liberty's, a Japanese screen and an armful of peacock feathers would do just as well and were more easily obtained' (Robin Spencer *The Aesthetic Movement* Studio Vista London 1972 p 7). *Cf* advertisements in the Melbourne press: 'The "Kalizoic" Fancy Goods Warehouse. Messrs Pearce & Co. have opened 55 Collins Street West an emporium for the sale of high class fancy work and goods, presided over by a pupil of the South Kensington School [see note 2 to Chapter XI]' (*Herald* 17 November 1884 [p 4]) 'Russell, Robson and Russell, Direct Silk Importers. Plain Liberty Silks in every shade...Fancy Liberty Silks, newest designs' (*Age* 31 August 1889 p 1). 'Kalizoic' (coined from the Greek 'Kalos', meaning beauty of outward form) is a reference to the Kalizoic Society founded in early 1884 by Melbourne journalists and litterateurs, and having 'the encouragement and cultivation of the beautiful' as its primary aim (*Australasian* 9 February 1884 Supplement p 6). James Smith was President; the *Australasian* editor Henry Gullett and his wife were amongst the members.

3   (p 39) **Thoreau one day, Cotter Morison the next— always an author of revolutionary ideas,** Henry David Thoreau (1817-62), American writer, social critic and naturalist; his *Walden, or Life in the Woods* (1854) is a veiled criticism of industrialism and materialism and an argument for a simple life. *The Service of Man: An Essay Towards the Religion of the Future* (1887), by English author, James Cotter Morison (1832-88) was regarded by his friends as 'an excursion beyond his proper field' (*The Dictionary of National Biography* Ed Sir Leslie Stephen and Sir Sidney Lee Oxford Up London 1967-68 Vol XIII pp 955-6, First published 1885-1901).

4   (p 39) **George Meredith was her king of novel writers,** *Cf Thirty Years* 'there is no luxury in life like a Wagner concert—other music, even other great music, that I am bidden to place higher, seems by comparison what other novels seem beside George Meredith's best (the Meredithian will understand me)' (p 187). For Meredith's influence on Cambridge see Editor's Introduction pp xxxvi-xxxvii.

131

Chapter VII

1   (p 44) *Westminster*...Mona Caird's marriage paper, The article 'Marriage' appeared in the August 1888 issue of the English radical monthly the *Westminster Review* (pp 186-201). Its English author, (Alice) Mona Caird (1855-1932) was a novelist, poet, and proponent of women's rights. Her novel *The Wing of Azraël* (1889), was advertised in the June 1889 issue of *Mullen's Monthly Circular*. The 1888 article explores and deplores the domestic and conjugal subjection of women, and looks forward to 'the day when men and women shall be comrades and fellow-workers as well as lovers and husbands and wives' (p 201). The sentence which Seaton Macdonald reads aloud is on p 186. The 'parable' referred to is the likening of the household captivity of women to the habitual chaining up of a dog on the grounds that he is so accustomed to it that he would, if let loose, run wild. *Cf* the fictional resolution of contentious aspects of the 'marriage question' in Catherine Spence's utopian novel 'A Week in the Future', serialised in the *Centennial Magazine* 1889 (in book form Hale & Iremonger Sydney 1987); Chapter V 'Marriage and the Relations of the Sexes' appeared in the issue for May 1889 pp 731-40.

2   (p 45) **like Una in the way she shines in a shady place".** The 'lovely ladie', the personification of truth, in Edmund Spenser's *The Faerie Queene* (1596) ['Her angels face/ As the great eye of heauen shyned bright,/ And made a sunshine in the shadie place' (Book I Canto iii. 4)].

3   (p 46) **walk by faith...by sight** 2 Corinthians v. 7 ['For we walk by faith, not by sight'].

4   (p 47) **the former on principle, the latter from habit,** Possibly a compositorial error ('former' before 'latter' is the *expected* form) or, if not, an unintended slip of the author's pen. As the clause following clearly refers to the broiled beef steak and not the bottled ale, the intended reading was probably 'the latter from habit, the former on principle' or, possibly, 'the latter on principle, the former from habit'.

5   (p 47) **the Canadian-American question,** Probably refers to contemporary disputes between Canada and the U. S. over fishing rights, and to the question of amendments to the British North America Act which would enable Canada to negotiate commercial treaties with foreign powers.

6   (p 47) **Æolian harp** Wind harp in the form of a box on which strings are stretched and emit musical sounds when a

draught passes through them; from Æolus, god of the winds. *Cf* 'The Three Miss Kings': Patty King 'thrilled like an Æolian harp to the west wind under the spell of those passionate emotions that have no name or shape' (*Australasian* 14 July 1883 Supplement p 2).

7   (p 48) **Mill.** British liberal philosopher John Stuart Mill (1803-73); see note 5 to Chapter II and note 1 to Chapter XIII. *Cf* also 'A Black Sheep', where Richard Delavel reads Mill's *Political Economy* (*Age* 15 September 1888 p 5).

8   (p 48) **"As the climbing...to a quiet man."** Apocrypha Ecclesiasticus xxv.

Chapter VIII

1   (p 50) **Bourke-street crowd.** Bourke St, lined with shops and theatres, was, in contrast to the more exclusive Collins St, for the multitude. In 1888 it was said to provide 'a remarkable vista of life and bustle and activity' and in the evening was 'the metropolitan street, gay and lively' (Sutherland *Victoria and Its Metropolis* Vol 1 p 551).

2   (p 51) **"Get yourself into Parliament...to get us the franchise."** Dr William Maloney, elected to the Legislative Assembly of the Victorian Parliament as member for West Melbourne in March 1889 on behalf of the Workingman's Political League, introduced the Women's Suffrage legislation on 4 September 1889. As a self-made, somewhat bohemian humanitarian reformer, allied with a putative Labour movement, he was the antithesis of Macdonald. He was also short and known as 'the little doctor'.

3   (p 52) **their way to the *Sun* office,** Melbourne readers of 1889 would have imagined the foursome walking w. along Bourke St, turning s. into Swanston St and proceeding to the intersection of Collins St, near which all the metropolitan newspapers then had their offices.

4   (p 53) **the Ladies' Court,** A section in which were displayed craftwork and needlework acquired and executed by the 'ladies' of Victoria, and said to have 'attracted interest among lady visitors' (*Official Record* p 243).

5   (p 53) **German picture gallery,** Exhibited here were 251 works; after the British Loan paintings, the largest single collection. The paintings mentioned are: 'An Autumn Evening' and 'A Winter Evening' by Konrad Alexander Müller-Kurzwelly

(1855-1914); 'After the Storm' by Hans Frederik Gude (1825-1903); and 'Moonlight Night, Dutch Canal' by Louis Douzette (1834-?). The *Official Record* referred to the last two as choice examples of artists of high repute (p 222).

6   (p 54) **the dear fen country in which she was born.**
     Ada Cambridge was born and spent her childhood in such country, in Norfolk. The low lying watery (fen) country of Norfolk and Cambridgeshire is the English setting of many of her novels, most markedly *My Guardian* (1878) and *Path and Goal* (1900).

7   (p 54) **Victorian loan gallery,** Exhibited here were 266 British and European paintings from private collections in the Colony, on loan following the example of the owners of paintings in England (*Official Record* pp 220-1). (The Victorian Artists' Gallery, in which colonial works were displayed—by Louis Buvelot, Charles McCubbin, Tom Roberts and others—is not mentioned in the novel.) The *Age* of 18 September noted that 'After the British Gallery the Victorian loan collection is by far the most interesting in the Exhibition...Commencing with landscape, first in importance is the magnificent work by B W [Benjamin William] Leader [1831-1923] hung in the centre of the north wall of the room, entitled "An April Day" (Exhibition Supplement p 1).

8   (p 54) **Milton and Mary Wollstonecraft on *Marriage and the Rights of Woman.*** Probably refers to John Milton's writings of 1643-45 proposing reform of the marriage laws, in particular his *The Doctrine and Discipline of Divorce* (1643), and to the radical *A Vindication of the Rights of Women* (1792) by English author and feminist, Mary Wollstonecraft (1759-97).

9   (p 54) **Arnold and William Morris** A three volume edition of the poetry of Matthew Arnold (1822-88) was published in 1885 (and a selected poems in 1878). The poetry of William Morris (1834-96) poet, artist, manufacturer and socialist, may be his epic *Sigurd the Volsung and the Fall of the Nibelungs* (1876).

10   (p 55) **the financial prospect was contracting** In 'The Reform Club' Cambridge is more explicit about ominous signs in the financial market (p 149).

11   (p 55) **a week or two before the races,** Refers to the Melbourne spring horse racing carnival, the highlight of which was (and still is) the Melbourne Cup, held on the first Tuesday in November (in 1888, the 6th). A description of Cup Day 1880 occupies a complete chapter of 'The Three Miss

Kings' (*Australasian* 15 September 1883 Supplement p 2 Ch XXI 'The Cup').

Chapter IX

1   (p 57) **Yarrock,** The intended location is in the vicinity of Mt Macedon, 44 miles n.w. of Melbourne: the author was familiar with this country from visits in the early 1880s (see Editor's Introduction p xxvii); and country houses and gardens of the district described in *Thirty Years* would have provided inspiration for Yarrock, in particular one 'pretty house', with a garden 'notoriously one of the loveliest in the land', whose owner had town quarters at the Melbourne Club (p 167). The district is also the setting of Cambridge's *A Platonic Friendship* (1905).

2   (p 58) **Warandara,** While readers could have taken the Kinnaird property, clearly a sheep station, to be anywhere in the sheep country of Victoria, Cambridge probably had in mind the district to the n. of Wangaratta, the town where she lived when she first came to Victoria. The name Warandara may be a concealed reference to Wangaratta, just as Doneraile of 'Missed in the Crowd' (1881-82) is a cryptic one to Coleraine. In *Thirty Years* an actual property, probably in the Wangaratta area, is mentioned: 'I still go, almost yearly, to rest from town life at a station in the neighbourhood of W—,' (p 57). Kinnaird of 'The Reform Club', whose property has the shorter name Wandara, is a 'Murray squatter' (p 143). The Murray River is about 20 miles due n. of Wangaratta.

Chapter X

1   (p 62) **watteau pleat,** A box pleat (see previous paragraph) sweeping down from the shoulders to the hem of the loose back of a gown fitted at the front and sides. In many of the paintings of Antoine Watteau (1684-1721) female figures are depicted wearing this type of gown.

2   (p 62) **'The Relation of Women's Clothes to their Moral and Intellectual Development.' "** Cambridge is borrowing from 'The Three Miss Kings': in Chapter XXV, 'Out in the Cold', journalist Paul Brion is writing on ' "Women's Clothes in Relation to her Moral and Intellectual Development" ' (*Australasian* 15 September 1883 Supplement p 2). Dress reform was widely publicised, and discussed frequently in newspapers, seriously and humorously, stimulated

by the Exhibition of the Rational Dress Association in London in 1883.

3   (p 63) **Spencer-street,** The Spencer Street Railway Station at the w. end of Collins St.

4   (p 65) **the small wayside station** Probably refers to the Macedon Railway Station described in *Thirty Years* as 'the little platform lonely in the scrub' (p 169).

5   (p 65) **brake,** Waggonette; spelled 'break' on p 81.

6   (p 65) **four-in-hand** Vehicle drawn by four horses and driven by one person.

7   (p 65) **felt wide-awake of the country,** Soft wide-brimmed hat—a mark of being Australian and of the country rather than city.

8   (p 67) **a small hamlet on the way** *Cf* 'the little post town' (p 79). Probably Upper Macedon, 3 miles from the railway station; by 1888 it was fast becoming more than a hamlet.

9   (p 68) **the notoriously "beautiful place" of...the colony,** See note 1 to Chapter IX.

Chapter XI

1   (p 70) *portières,* Door curtains (French).

2   (p 71) **South Kensington work,** Fabrics from the circle of artists and craftspersons led by William Morris were first made known through an International Exhibition at South Kensington in 1862; by the early 1880s, the Morris chintz was a household word in England. See also note 2 to Chapter VI.

3   (p 73) **"I helped her** More explicitly in 'The Reform Club', for readers unfamiliar with the corsetry of earlier times: 'I laced her' (p 155).

Chapter XII

1   (p 80) *sub rosa?"* Secretly (Latin).

2   (p 81) **what time** This expression, meaning 'at what [or during which] time' is reproduced in 'The Reform Club' (p 159).

Chapter XIII

1   (p 82) " 'There would...social benefit.' Quotation unidentified, but the views correspond to arguments put forward in Mill's *The Subjection of Women* (1869). Extracts from this work were widely circulated and quoted from by the Victorian Women's Suffrage Society and similar organisations in the Australasian colonies. In 'The Reform Club' the passage is replaced by 'and Margaret, reading Mill' (p 159).

2   (p 83) **Legislative Assembly** Lower House of the Victorian Parliament, and constituted in 1856.

3   (p 85) **Falling leaf...you and me.** Opening lines from the song 'Good Bye' ['Addio'] by Sir (Francesco) Paolo Tosti (1846-1916), Italian composer of songs and ballads who settled in London in 1880. 'Good Bye', amongst the composer's early successes in England, was sung at several Exhibition concerts.

Chapter XIV

1   (p 93) **"things,"** Presumably hats, and possibly gloves. In 'The Reform Club' Patty goes 'to fetch her hat' (p 162).

Chapter XV

1   (p 96) **"A PURELY INTELLECTUAL FRIENDSHIP."** Patty's words in her letter to Ted (p 57).

2   (p 96) **a spur of the ranges** *Cf* 'In the neighbourhood [of Upper Macedon] there are many attractions to the lovers of natural scenery—the falls, hanging rock, Mount Diogenes, & C.' (*The Victorian Municipal Directory and Gazetteer for 1889* Arnall & Jackson Melbourne 1889 p 323). The *Picturesque Atlas of Australasia* records that although the 'mountain' generally means 'the huge abutment that is so prominent an object in the landscape for a distance of fifty miles in a southerly direction, the Mount is in reality a spur thrown out by the Great Dividing Range, which here attains an elevation of three thousand three hundred and twenty-four feet...presenting an endless variety of romantic scenery' (Vol 2

p 283). This was probably written by Cambridge herself—see Editor's Introduction p xxviii.

3   (p 97) **typhoid fever,** *The Victorian Year-Book 1888-9* (Sands & McDougall Melbourne 1890) noted 'the very serious and fatal prevalence of typhoid fever' which accounted for more than 3% of the total deaths from all causes (p 117). As Melbourne's population grew in the 1880s, there was rising public concern with problems of sanitation and refuse disposal, and fear of epidemics.

4   (p 97) **poor weltering fellow creatures, as Carlyle calls them,** Patty is referring to the inhabitants of Melbourne, which is visible from the summit of Mt Macedon. Scottish-born historian and essayist, Thomas Carlyle (1795-1881), profoundly influenced nineteenth century thought and literature. Particular reference is unidentified, but *cf* [of France before the Revolution] 'While the unspeakable confusion is everywhere weltering within...' (*The French Revolution: A History* Chapman & Hall London 1896 Vol 1 p 61; 1st edn 1837). Melbourne readers' interest in Carlyle is indicated by the availability of books about him: eg Mullen's in March 1884 advertised Froude's *Carlyle's Life in London* and, in July 1885, Masson's *Carlyle: Personally and in His Writings.*

5   (p 98) **far from the madding crowd** Title of novel by Thomas Hardy (1840-1928), first published in 1874, originally from the much anthologised 'Elegy in a Country Churchyard' (1751) by Thomas Gray (1716-71) ['Far from the madding crowd's ignoble strife'].

6   (p 100) **unicorn,** Carriage drawn by three horses, two abreast and one in front.

Chapter XVI

1   (p 104) **burst up, like the land boom,** 'On 22 October 1888 the Associated Banks...broke the speculative land boom by agreeing to refuse further overdraft extensions for land purchases and by raising interest rates by 1 per cent' (Geoffrey Serle *The Rush to be Rich* Melbourne UP Melbourne 1971 p 257).

2   (p 108) *tauri,* Territory or hunting-ground (Aboriginal word). *Cf* Cambridge's earlier use: 'they were so glad to be on their own "tauri" tonight' ('The Three Miss Kings' *Australasian* 29 September 1883 Supplement p 2).

3   (p 108) **Good Bye** See note 3 to Chapter XIII.

4   (p 108) **Remember Me No More.** Song, of plaintive
         character, composed by Sir William Robinson (1834-97),
         acting governor of Victoria, March-November 1889. His
         songs, composed during earlier years became popular
         throughout Australia. This one was popularised in Melbourne
         by well-known soprano Rosina Carandini (Mrs Palmer).

Chapter XVII

1   (p 111) **"Rosamunda"..."Cornelius" March** Exhibition
         concert programs included performances of the 'Entr'acte' and
         'Ballet' from 'Rosamunda' by Franz Schubert (1797-
         1828)...Unidentified, though the reference is possibly to
         instrumental music by (Carl August) Peter Cornelius (1824-74),
         German composer of Lieder and opera; none is recorded in the
         programs.

2   (p 112) **Leighton's Hercules and Alcestis** The
         painting, 'Hercules Wrestling with Death for the Body of
         Alcestis' by Leighton (see note 3 to Chapter II), was exhibited
         in the British Loan Gallery. The *Age* saw it as a 'composition
         of great beauty and power' and explained that the ancient Greek
         'story is the vicarious sacrifice by herself of Alcestis for her
         husband, Admetus' and the struggle of the legendary Hercules
         to rescue her from the clutches of Death (28 August 1888
         Exhibition Supplement p 1). The 'young living' face Patty
         gazes at would be that of Hercules.

3   (p 112) **not going on the switchback surely!**
         Originally placed in front of the building but quickly 'relegated
         to the back premises', the switchback railway was seen as
         'unfortunate' by the *Age* of 11 September 1888, which noted
         public objection to its presence anywhere in the Exhibition
         (Exhibition Supplement p 1). The *Official Record* states,
         however, that its success as a 'draw' was marked and that it
         carried in all 339,000 passengers (p 272).

4   (p 114) **The conductor** See note 12 to Chapter II. Cowen is
         named in 'The Reform Club' (p 166).

Chapter XVIII

1   (p 117) **Williamstown,** A seaside suburb w. of the city, a
         9-mile journey by suburban train; in the nineteenth century an
         important shipping port for Melbourne.

2   (p 119) **Darby and Joan** Proverbially devoted, no longer young, married couple.

3   (p 120) **Belgravian household** Belgravia, by the late nineteenth century, was a smart residential district of London with modern stucco-fronted family mansions several stories high.

Appendix I The Reform Club

Note on the Text

This, the first publication of 'The Reform Club', is based on the text in 'The Good Old Times', a 64-page typescript held in the Mitchell Library, Sydney. This typescript, a collection of six short stories, which Ada Cambridge submitted to Angus and Robertson in 1921, was acquired by the Mitchell Library in 1933.

The text has been transcribed from photoprint enlargements of microfilm copy of the typescript. Punctuation, spelling and capitalisation are taken from the typescript; only where the inscriptions are liable to create confusion are they emended. (Most appear to be the result of typewriter miskeyings.) In two cases (154: 32 and 167: 45) the emendation is arrived at by consulting the corresponding reading in 'A Woman's Friendship' (the full List of Editor's Emendations is given on page 177). Cancellations and added readings are not indicated (the great majority of cancelled readings are illegible because of heavy overscoring); the final reading is preferred in every case.

'The Reform Club' is based on 'A Woman's Friendship'. For discussion of the relation between the short story of 1920 and the novel of 1889, see Editor's Introduction, pages xxi-xxii and xxxiv.

The Reform Club.

The Great Exhibition which synchronised with the Great Land Boom brought together three people who formed themselves into what they called a club. If it had had a name the above title would have properly described it. Margaret Clive, happily married to a Melbourne pressman, was its foundress and president; her recently-acquired bosom friend, Patricia Kinnaird, the adored young wife of a Murray squatter (temporarily immersed in the speculative syndicates that were so numerous and fascinating at the time) was next enrolled; the third member was a great landowner, socially more important than either lady—Mr Seaton Macdonald, of Yarrock. Three, all told.

I think it originated in the Exhibition, when the two women stood in the British Loan room of the Picture Galleries, looking at Leighton's copper-coloured Phryne—a much-discussed nude—and Mrs Clive exclaimed in her impassioned way:

"To think of the human body being made like that, and that we should know no better than to distort it so hideously as we do!"

Mrs Clive, by the way, was wearing a gown that had a loose body with a mere apology for a waist, and a skirt without a scrap of bustle, while her bonnet, instead of soaring half a yard into the air as was the fashion at the time, touched its highest point not more than three inches above her head. Mrs Kinnaird was dressed, not extravagantly in the mode, but not in the least outside of it. The back draperies of her skirt hung from the universal cushion, and her smart little jacket "sat" to her charming figure in a manner that necessarily implied stays; her narrow-brimmed hat was tall, with tall bows sticking up in front of it.

"I suppose," said Mrs Kinnaird, "we really do know better, even while we do it."

"That is the worst of it. We know that we are acting like barbarians who think it beautiful to tattoo themselves, and yet we do it all the same. It is a disgrace to us in these days. It justifies the men in sneering at us. They are quite right to despise women."

"But it is a good deal the fault of the men, Margaret. A man can't bear to see a woman going outside the rules, even if she herself has the courage for it. He makes fun of our absurdities in dress, but if we look the least odd he is the first to take fright and to shrink from being seen in the street with us."

"But if enough of us would only make up our minds to be sincere and natural, we should cease to look odd. And the men would side with us as soon as they saw we meant it."

"It is easy to say that! But no talking alters it, Margaret. It is the most absolute bondage in the world. We are tied hand and foot and *can't* escape. One here and there—one like you—refuses to wear a bustle, and feels very uncomfortable because people stare; but it makes no difference. It doesn't affect the mass."

"Oh Patty, *don't* allow yourself to think that way!" Mrs Clive implored, with an earnestness that made her intense eyes glow. "It is the most paralysing thing—it simply kills you. Why, if everybody had that idea—that it was no good for him or her to try, because one can do so little by one's self—what sort of a world would it be? How would *anything* get done? All the great reforms begin with a few people—they begin with *one*—and who knows which one? We never can tell how far our influence goes, but if even it went no further than we can see it, we are still bound to do our best." And so on—at considerable length.

"Ah", sighed Patty in the first pause, "I would give something to be as brave as you are!"

"Don't you think," responded Margaret, "that we were brought together to help each other to be brave?"

A few hours later they left the Concert Hall, in the mood of devotees coming out of church, and proceeding doorwards with the crowd, met the potential third member of the club coming in.

"Looking for *me*!" exclaimed Margaret, hurrying. "You don't know Mr Macdonald, Patty? He wrote that beautiful paper in Saturday's *Sun* on the Liberty of Woman—he is one of the few men who understand us—Good afternoon, Mr Macdonald; let me introduce you to my friend—my great friend—Mrs Kinnaird."

144

Mrs Kinnaird discovered that he was not only her great friend's friend, but that he and her Ted had been Grammar boys together; which made him her friend on the spot. He took them to the Commissioners' Room, where they had tea and talk—not so serious a talk as Mrs Clive could have wished, but very gratifying to her as indicating a mutual pleasure in the encounter.

"Mrs Kinnaird and I," she broke into a light dialogue that did not interest her, "at the moment we met you were planning to go to the theatre tomorrow, as her husband has a dinner at the Club. And to sit in the cheap seats—because we agree that it is both vulgar and cowardly to spend more than we ought to afford merely because we are afraid of losing caste with Mrs Grundy." She enlarged upon the congenial theme.

Their host listened, conscious of Mrs Kinnaird's blush and silence. Then he asked to be allowed to escort them.

"I don't know," was the considered reply. "You are a rich man. It will be no virtue in you. No one who sees *you* in the pit will look down on you for being there. We must make a real thing of it, not a sham."

He turned to the embarrassed younger lady.

"Mrs Clive regards me as a criminal for being what she calls rich," said he, "though I have told her again and again that I can't help it. It's my misfortune, not my fault. I have done all I could to neglect my property, and it will continue to thrive in spite of me. When she drives me to despair with her reproaches, and I offer to give it away to charities, she turns round and abuses me for insulting my betters—says she supposes I want to pose as a pious founder and a candidate for knighthood."

When the ladies arrived at the theatre on the following night it was at the entrance to the pit that he met them.

"It's a free country," said he. "And I've just as much right here as you have."

Mrs Clive vehemently denied it. He was defrauding the Management by not sitting in the dress-circle with his friends.

"Not at all," he maintained. "If I give you the difference in the price of the tickets, for—for the amelioration of the condition of the human race—"

"*Don't* laugh at him, Patty," the indignant lady broke in, resenting the ill-timed pleasantry. And she begged Patty, in a whisper, not to suppose he was always "like this." She said she had never known him so frivolous before. She had already explained the sad and sobering circumstances of his life; how he had married a dreadful woman of the world, with no more intellect than a cunning animal, and how she had run away from him and died abroad; and how he had always had wealth—"that greatest blight and curse on all that is good in people." And yet remained what he was—what *she* knew him to be, and what Patty would find he was when she knew him better.

And as she whispered, he led them into a place where none of them had been before and there were no reserved seats, looking about him with knitted brows.

"You two ladies," he directed them, pausing midway in a narrow aisle, "take the outside. I will— "

"Barricade us against contact with the coat or gown of a shopkeeper," Margaret caught him up. "Thank you, but we prefer you in the middle, so that you can distribute yourself fairly between us." And she pushed her way to the innermost of three chairs, and sat down beside, almost in the pocket of, an overflowing gentleman smelling strongly of leather and onions—odours abominable to her fastidious nose.

"Comfortable?" queried Mr Macdonald, seating himself.

"Perfectly comfortable," she replied, with a dignified smile.

Meanwhile the full-dressed people were sauntering by twos and threes into their circle overhead, arranging themselves leisurely, drawing forth their opera-glasses to survey the house. Seldom are those questing eyes directed downwards, but Patty, glancing up, saw two men in a box near the stage gazing smilingly at their party, while leaning forward on their folded arms and talking with their heads together.

"Is there anyone here you know?" she whispered to her neighbour.

"Two or three," he whispered back.

She was uncomfortable under the eyes of those two men, who presently levelled their glasses at her.

"Please," she whispered again, "talk to both of us."

Then the performance began—the inimitable Brough in *The Magistrate*—and Patty enjoyed herself so much as to disregard all other spectators. She was naturally full of fun, and the star comedian's delicious humour, together with Mr Macdonald's unsmiling comments upon it, so wrought upon her that she giggled like a person who had sat in the pit all her life and knew no better. By the time that the Magistrate was at the end of his troubles with his stepson, she was stifling hysterical peals of laughter, with her handkerchief in her mouth, and sweeping tears from her eyes—to the great entertainment of her confederate, who was himself as grave as a judge.

"Oh, I *am* so ashamed of myself!" she gasped, as she recovered from the crowning paroxysm—brought on by the Magistrate calling his stepson a little beast. "What *will* Mrs Clive think of me?"

"What do you think of her?" he inquired, passing the question on. "Don't you think she disgraces us with this levity?"

Mrs Clive, though surprised at her beloved's conduct, looked round at her with an indulgent smile. She said Patty was always natural, and that it was a pleasure to see her enjoying herself.

They all enjoyed themselves.

They met at the Exhibition next morning, and in the evening attended a Choral Concert together, sitting in the cheap seats. The day after, they went to the Public Library to read Milton and Mary Wollstonecraft on "Marriage and the Rights of Woman." Subsequently they took the train to Brighton Beach, and sat in a group on the steps of the boat-landing below the pier, while Mr Macdonald recited Arnold and William Morris to the accompaniment of the lapping water amongst the barnacled piles behind them. Later, they spent a sunny afternoon discussing the development of socialism in the lake house at the Botanic Gardens; and again they found grateful privacy for talking over their thoughts on friendship in the deserted galleries of the University Museum. Always, it must be understood, with the full knowledge and (tempered) approval of two beloved and much-occupied husbands.

But the great building in Carlton Gardens was the habitual rendezvous, and few private premises licenced by Mrs Grundy could furnish such opportunities for comfortable retirement from observation as were to be found by those who wanted to find them in that apparently public resort. You had but to pass through the turnstile into the fernery, and follow the left-hand path to the end, and there you found a cool green bower all to yourself (or yourselves), with only twittering little birds to spy on you. Or you could go into the Fisheries Court, which was a very deserted place, and sit in a corner on a settee that had springs in both back and seat.

When evening drew on and the seals and the sea-birds had grown sleepy and uninteresting, there would be great peace in a certain alley of the Aquarium, and a darkness in which you could hold your companion's hand as he or she sat beside you, without fear of being discovered by the people passing through. Then there was the Dome. At certain times in the day there were no sightseers up there; you could sit on the steps or lean upon the parapet, and breathe the lofty air, and take your birds' eye view of the far-spreading city, undisturbed by strangers coming suddenly round the corner. In the grounds below there was the Hollow Tree—what tales that tree could have told if it could speak! There was the Bamboo House, with its scent of tobacco and its pleasant cane seats, no one near but the invisible custodian in his little vestibule at the top of the stairs. There were Cook's Rooms; there were chairs behind the big carriages in the Armament Court; in short, the place fairly

147

bristled with invitations to privacy and repose. Lovers were prone to monopolise these retreats, but the unsentimental observer, throwing a furtive glance into them as he passed by, would often notice with amusement that three people had withdrawn themselves instead of two. It was the *Reform Club* holding its little meetings, and not a pair of sweethearts and a "gooseberry", as he would vulgarly suppose. And perhaps there was nothing more curious and interesting in that place of interesting things than these three fairly young persons of kindred spirit and mixed sex, who had no sense of redundancy in their number.

"There are people," Margaret remarked to Patty one day when they were alone together "who say—almost *everybody* says—it is one of those horrible axioms the world takes for granted—that a man and a woman cannot be close friends without danger of becoming more than friends. It does make me so *savage*—that it should be thought we can all be so low, so degraded as that! You know better, don't you? *You* believe, as I do, that a man and a woman—say a man like Mr Macdonald and a woman like me—or like you—can be intellectual, sympathetic, confidential friends, as a man and a man or a woman and a woman are, without thinking, without for a moment dreaming, of *that?*"

"Of course I do," agreed Patty. "But people are always in such a hurry to misjudge."

"It doesn't matter what 'people' say or think."

"No.. But one is always so afraid the man himself might misjudge."

"I am not speaking of common men. Of course they would misjudge, if one gave them the chance, but no woman who respected herself would."

"I have only known common men," Mrs Kinnaird confessed. "Quite good sort of men, that you could like and be nice to; but somehow one can never let one's self go, so to speak. They would make love at once—they would hold one cheap. There is always a line, you know—with common men."

"Of course I know that. But it never ought to have been so, Patty. Men and women have been spoiled, have been simply *ruined*, as companions for each other. That shows it. Oh, to think what it *might* have been but for the horrible ignorance and tyrannies that have corrupted us all—turned innocent human nature into deceit and crime! But things will be different someday. We are at the turning point now. And the few of us who are able for it must lead the way for the others. We must set an example, Patty. You and I, darling, will show them how women may love and be loyal to each other, and he and I—he and both of us—will prove that men and women can be the comrades they were meant to be without forgetting the dignity of either sex."

The remark about women being loyal to each other referred to another subject on which she expressed views not consonant with those of a purblind world—and expressed them strongly and eloquently at Club meetings and elsewhere. Patty fully shared them.

"As if *we* could ever be jealous of each other!"

About the middle of October, when the pursuit of a ready-made fortune had slackened somewhat—the edge of the shadow of the approaching "Bust" beginning to impinge on the dazzling "Boom"—Ted suddenly wanted to go home. He had been in Melbourne since before the shearing, to satisfy Patty's desire for the companionship of her bosom friend, and although he knew that his brother and partner was managing the place all right, he naturally wished to see for himself how things were going on. He proposed to run up—only railway people say down—for a week or two before the races, and expected Patty, as a matter of course, to run up with him.

Patty, to his manifest surprise and secret chagrin, begged off, on the ground that the Exhibition would not last for ever. On the same ground the Clives insisted on his leaving her in town—to stay with them during his absence. The lightest wish of his "little missus" being law to Ted, he went home without her. It was the first time they had been separated in their married lives. The following characteristic letters passed between them during the next few days:

"My dearest, darling old boy,

"I hope you are not very lonely without me, and that Mary attends to you properly and does not put you off with anything that saves her trouble while she spends her time with Dan and Alec which I expect is her chief occupation when there is only Harry to do for. I hope my dear Bret Harte is all right. Tell them nobody is to ride him but you. I hope Mrs Murphy attends to the bees properly and that old Peter remembers to water my flowers. Pat my dear old Rover and all the dogs for me, the darlings. You might bring one of Flo's puppies for the children here. Give my love to Harry and ask him to see they are all fed every day. I can't trust Mary, who is always driving them out of her kitchen as if they were thieves when there is not one of them would meddle with a dish unless she held it to their noses.

"I hope you have had a good clip, darling, and no trouble with the men. The weather has been splendid for shearing, at any rate, and I daresay we shall have rain before long. Mr Macdonald says he has good grass still, though the crops are stunted. He has just done shearing on two of his stations, and is finishing Yarrock, where he lives, but for a cute man of business, as you say he is, he

149

has been taking it very easily, leaving all the work to his managers, which Margaret does not think right of him, and she has been talking to him seriously. However, he is going to Yarrock tomorrow, and he is very anxious for Margaret and me to pay him a week-end visit there. Mr Clive would come after us from Saturday to Monday and take us back, and a little trip into the country does do him so much good after the hard work of the office. There is a lady housekeeper there, and anyway two of us together make it all right. You have no objection, have you, darling? We have got some new books to read together, and we have great plans for the future that we are going to draw up when we are safe from interruption, things Margaret wants Mr Macdonald to do with some of the time and the money that he has so much more of than he wants for himself.

"How I do wish you liked Margaret more, Teddy dear! But you don't know her, else you would. Her house is different from everybody's—beautifully conducted. She calls it a republic, because all work and fare alike. Her husband says it is not economy when she scrubs and cleans instead of the kitchen girl, and in a way she sees that, but she says the more important thing is to reform the present system which puts the servants on one side and the employers on the other, as if they were not all human beings alike—only I can't explain it as well as she does. I'm afraid it would be very difficult for me to do anything of that kind at Wandara, as we are always having people drop in, whereas no one comes here except by invitation. Still I see how right it is and I should like to do something. But what would Dan and Alec think if I waited on them? And if I made an equal of Mary I'm afraid she would be impudent, for she is a little inclined that way already, being so pretty and the men always hanging about her. I have been doing some cooking, and Mr Clive has been paying me no end of compliments. It is a pleasure to see how he enjoys nice things, and sometimes the children do too, but they are very whimsical, for they have never been accustomed to much variety, and Margaret almost lives on milk food, and you know what town milk is. Make Mary give you a fowl for dinner and something besides mutton chops for breakfast. She won't trouble to dress brains and kidneys and things unless you tell her, but there they are, and you may as well have them as not.

"And will you, please darling, look on the top shelf of my wardrobe and find a piece of terra-cotta cashmere, and also my grey hat with the gull's wing, which I want to have done up, and please send them to me the first chance you have. Mary will pack them. And take care of yourself, love, and don't be long, for I miss you dreadfully.

150

"Let me know if you are *sure* you don't mind my going to Yarrock.

"Your lovingest
"Pat."

"Wandara,
"Wednesday.

"My dear old Pat,

"Of course I don't mind. If you and Mrs Clive go together it's all right, and I hope you'll enjoy yourselves. Don't forget to take your songs, and mind you sing if he asks you. It's an awfully pretty place, but I haven't seen it since I was a boy. Don't forget your old husband while you are gadding about. I feel like a fish out of water in the house without you. However, don't fret yourself about Mary; she bustles round in style and gives me all the good things she can think of and takes the best of care of me. She's got her hair done on the top of her head and the most fetching fringe in front. I've had to speak to Dan about being so much in her kitchen of a night.

"Bret Harte is lame, and no one knows how he got so, but I think he'll be all right by the time you come home. Harry has been riding Henry James Junior with a skirt, he's growing a beauty now he's got his spring coat, and will suit you down to the ground when we have tamed him a little more. Old Rover got a poisoned bait, you'll be sorry to hear, but the others are all right and as fat as butter. Mary says she's always stuffing them.

"The garden is awfully pretty, with the roses coming out. Old Peter is watering all the time, but the crops are only about a foot above the ground and they ought to be more than twice as high by now. The wool was got in splendidly and we sent the first drays to the station yesterday. I was there looking after it, and I took the chance to send Mrs Clive a hamper of vegetables, spring stuff, and some young fowls which Mary dressed nicely so as to be no trouble. I hope you won't be gone before they get there.

"I have found the hat and the thingembob cashmere, at least Mary says that's it, and am sending a man to the post with the parcel. I hope you are not going to wear such a beastly colour. Don't you go and let Margaret make a guy of you, there's a dear girl. There's nobody can beat you for taste when you are left to yourself. And as for your doing scrubbing and cleaning and waiting on Dan and Alec, just let me catch you at it. Margaret is a very superior woman, I know, but I think she's decidedly cracked, and I don't want her to make you so too.

"Harry sends his love. They are all asking when you are coming home. I think by the time the Races are over we shall have

151

had enough of Melbourne, what do you think? Anyway it's a comfort to know your new friends haven't entirely put my nose out of joint.

"Send me a line as often as you can to let me know you are all right, and enjoy yourself all you can.

"Your loving husband,

"Edward Kinnaird.

"P.S. Be sure you don't forget to take your songs"

On Thursday morning Mrs Kinnaird and Mrs Clive were in the bedroom of the latter, preparing for their visit to Yarrock. Patty, standing before a long glass, was wearing a strange straight garment of that colour which Ted called beastly, over which Margaret was draping some oriental muslin gleaming with gold thread (it was in fact a window curtain) with an interest betokening a genuine, if passing, sympathy with the ruling passion of her sex.

"There," she said, drawing back for a comprehensive view, "if you could see those lovely folds, Patty, I don't think you would ever endure the hideous, bunched-up, meaningless jumble of a dressmaker's dress again."

Patty took up a hand-mirror, turned her back to the long glass, and surveyed herself intently.

"It is a beautiful piece of stuff," she said, "but doesn't it make me look a little broad across the back?"

"Of course it does. So it ought. Nature never meant us to have backs like the letter V. But I can drape it another way."

She undid the fastenings at the shoulders, and gathered about a yard of the upper edge of the window-curtain into a box-pleat at the back of the neck, pinning it firmly to the top of the shapeless bodice, whence the full width of the muslin fell to the hem of the skirt.

"Now—how does that do?"

Patty thought it did much better. But she wondered what Ted *would* say if he could see her—also what Mr Macdonald would think when she walked into his drawing-room thus fantastically attired.

"Has he ever seen a Greek dress?" she asked timidly.

"Of course he has," answered Margaret. "He has seen me in it. And he said it was lovely. He hates the conventional fashions, as he does all ugly things. When he has done his paper on *Ideals* he is going to write one on *The Relation of Women's Clothes to their Moral and Intellectual Development.*"

This somewhat reconciled Patty to her unfamiliar picturesqueness. When the gold-veined muslin and straight-cut under robe were unbuttoned and unpinned, she folded them like a shawl

152

and carried them off to pack them. One of the advantages of a Greek dress is that, folded, it takes up no space to speak of and can stand any amount of squeezing; so, finding her portmanteau still gaping for more, she put in her best dinner gown—ugly though it might be. "In case of accidents," she said to herself, as she gathered its bulging masses together and with difficulty patted them down.

Towards evening they arrived at the little country station nearest to Yarrock homestead, and saw Mr Macdonald on the platform waiting for them.

"I knew where to look for you," said he, handing them out of their second-class carriage. "I felt sure you would seize this opportunity to demonstrate." (In the early 'eighties it was an unheard-of thing for any but the lowest classes and the despised Chinaman to travel second-class; there was, and still is, no third). "Find it answers? Had a comfortable journey?"

"We don't look for answers in our time," said Margaret, "nor do it for comfort."

"Oh, what a lovely evening!" cried Patty, looking beyond the station sheds and the store and public-house behind them to wooded ranges that were just colouring to the setting sun. "And you have brought a four-in-hand—*how* delicious!"

Whereupon it appeared that Patty behind a team of spanking bays was in her element, and that Margaret, when at full speed they described the letter S through the trees and stumps of a roadless Bush, sat silent and scared, her heart in her mouth; and when, on the metalled highway, the lady on the box seat begged to be allowed to drive them, the cry of panic protest behind her was startling in its unfamiliarity.

"Why, Margaret," Patty remonstrated, "are you such a renegade to your principles as to say that a woman can't do what a man can do?"

"Yes, of course, when it's a matter of physical strength and training, all of which is on one side."

"Not in this case," said Patty.

"I'll have them put in for you tomorrow morning," said Mr Macdonald, forgetting that tomorrow morning was to be devoted to the franchise question.

For the rest of the way the elder lady, the guest of honour, in her seat of honour, pensively gazed over the shadowy country and up at the duck-egg-coloured twilight sky, and listened to the animated dialogue overhead of which she could hear but an odd word now and then— "off shoulder", "fetlock", or some such—and felt just a little isolated. A transient mood, however. Before she could be conscious of it grooms were opening gates, horses sweeping through long avenues of English trees and spacious gardens shedding

153

perfumes of acacia and orange blossom, and her host was lifting her down at a great hall door and welcoming her in words and accents calculated to warm the cockles of any woman's heart.

They had tea in the hall—once the whole area of the Yarrock dwelling-house, now merged like a seed-potato in the buildings that had grown out of it—and the softness of the armchairs, the warmth of the log fire, the pictures on the panelled walls, the rugs on the shining floor, the broad windows with cushioned seats, the cabinets of miscellaneous treasures, transcending even those of the Exhibition, filled her aesthetic soul with joy. It was not for hours that she remembered to think and say how sad and wrong it was that such beauty should not be for all instead of only the idle few.

The housekeeper presently conducted the ladies to their rooms and to further satisfactions. Patty's room was light and gay with chintz and muslin, a Dresden Shepherdess of a room; Margaret's was manifestly the state guest-chamber of the house, heavily magnificent, with "period" furniture and a Romney ancestor over the mantelpiece. She swelled with complacence as she recognised the distinction conferred upon her—and kissed Patty.

"Isn't he a dear?" said she.

"It's the sweetest place I was ever in," said Patty, from the depths of a pink-and-white sofa by her own fireside.

"Too sweet," sighed Margaret. But she smiled, and they were both happy.

Invisible maids had unpacked for them while they were having tea, and Mrs Clive's only evening costume, already exciting interest in the servants' hall, was spread upon the bed. In it she proceeded to array herself, when she had bathed and brushed, and no unprejudiced eye could have seen her when her toilet was completed without acknowledging that the Greek dress was almost as beautiful as she believed it. Her under-robe was of ripe-wheat-tinted satin, her outer drapery gauze of the same colour covered with a conventional pattern of brown and golden sunflowers; and they "went" with her slender height, her fine thin face and classically-coiled dark hair in perfect harmony.

She stood before a mirror which was flanked by two clusters of wax candles, and as a picture—any figure picture in the Exhibition—saw her full-length reflection in that idealising illumination, thrown up against the dim and rich background of the room, and found herself young and beautiful to an extent that astonished her. She gazed until a clock on the chimney-piece struck eight, when she suddenly remembered she had promised to "fix up" Patty, and flew in remorse and haste to her friend's room.

Patty was not there—only a housemaid emptying slops.

154

Mrs Clive inquired, unnecessarily, whether Mrs Kinnaird had gone.

"Yes, madam," said the maid; "just gone."

"Without dressing?"

"No, madam, Mrs Kinnaird is dressed."

"Didn't she want—how did she manage?"

"I laced her, madam."

So Patty had relapsed at the last moment, and then taken flight—but no, that could not be possible!—in order to escape expostulation or reproach. Mrs Clive was conscious of a pang of disappointment, and as consciously ignored it. It was not want of courage or principle on her comrade's part, she was resolutely assured, but simply want of time. She had not gone to Patty's aid, and Patty could not arrange a Greek dress by herself; therefore, seeing the dinner hour drawing on, she had hastily thrust herself into the only gown she was used to—the only thing she *could* do. But why had she brought such a gown, without saying that she had brought it?

"How can I be so foolish?" Margaret thought angrily, as she swept down a long passage to the hall. "As if the dear child may not please herself and wear what she likes!"

The fact was that Patty's courage had failed at the vision of herself in the sack-like under portion of her classic garb—the portion that anybody could put on who could put on a nightgown. She was small and inclined to plumpness, though as yet her figure was one to be proud of as figures went at that day, and she was once for all, and justly, convinced that a Greek dress did not suit her. "I can't carry it off like Margaret—I look podgy and unnatural," she thought, as she turned round and round before the glass while waiting for her friend. "The servants will smile behind my back, and *he* will think I look absurd—I know he will."

There was a tap at the door—not Margaret's—and she wildly tore off the terra-cotta robe before answering it.

"If you please, madam, Mrs Barton sent me to see if I could give you any assistance."

"Oh, thank you—thank you very much!"

Patty seized a skirt of black lace, twinkling with jet ornaments, and tossed it over her head; the band was quickly hooked, the satin bodice laced over it, and the little woman felt herself again.

She rustled into the passage, shaking out her train behind her, and, lifting a curtain, found herself in the hall. There stood the host, his back to the fire, and whatever might have been his passion for classic raiment and his abhorrence of the current mode he certainly regarded her with eyes of admiration as she stepped towards him. She knew the look too well to make any mistake about it, and congratulated herself with fervour on having chosen to be modern

155

after all.

He led her to a chair and put a stool under her feet.

"I quite forgot," she said to him rather hurriedly, "about our club meeting tomorrow morning, when you said I might drive your horses." They called themselves "the club" nowadays, and spoke of their profounder discussions in this official manner.

"So did I", he replied, also speaking quickly. "But I was thinking—can you get up early?"

"Oh, yes. In the country I am used to that."

"I thought perhaps you might like a little ride round the place?"

"I should love it, indeed! But I have no habit with me."

"That's all right. Mrs Barton shall put one in your room."

"Do you keep a supply of habits on the premises?"

"My sister keeps one here to save the trouble of bringing it when she comes to see me. She is in England now," he added, answering a whole string of questions that he saw in Patty's eyes, "and she comprises all my family. She's just about your size. Will you be up—say by six o'clock—if I order the horses? You are a good rider, I know."

"I can ride anything you like to put me on," she declared.

Margaret glided through the curtained archway at the end of the hall, and was half way across the floor before they saw her. She heard their voices, full of interest in the subject, whatever it was, and did not fail to note that they abruptly ceased talking as soon as she appeared.

So at 5.55 next morning Patty was tip-toeing past the door of her friend's room like a cautious burglar. Entering the dim hall, she found her host awaiting her.

"Have you had your tea? That's right. The horses are ready, but I would not have them brought round for fear of waking Mrs Clive. Do you mind coming to the stable yard?"

"No, of course not. I'd love to see the stables. Oh, what a heavenly morning!"

The first rays of the sun were streaming along the level terraces and the vivid lawns that might have been so many bowling greens, and threw the shadow of their two figures before them as they walked. The cold, pure air brought whiffs of fragrance from lilac bushes and English hawthorn hedges and groves of flowering orange and lemon trees. The roses were a dream of beauty. No lovelier morning ever dawned to make mock of a drought-stricken squatter.

And Patty as an expert horsewoman had the time of her life.

In the stable-yard two horses, saddled and bridled, were

being led up and down, arching their necks as they went, and breaking into a sidelong dance at intervals—a huge dappled grey like a field marshall's charger, and a dark chestnut with a black nose that was such a picture of equine shape and elegance as she had never seen before.

"I warn you," said her host as they approached the latter, that that mare takes riding. No vice, of course, but the spirit of fifty race-horses when her blood's up."

Beaming, Patty took the reins and laid her hand on the pommel; upon which the mare began to dance and edge away in a sportive fashion.

"Quick!" called Patty, and in a twinkling she was in her seat, firm and square, with steadfast hands held down, while the quivering animal beneath her pranced about the yard backwards and sidewards, in every direction but the right, like a cat on hot bricks. The little figure was tossed in the air without shifting or bumping or losing its poise for an instant.

"You'll do," said Mr Macdonald, and her bosom swelled with pride at his approval. "But keep her as quiet as you can. She'll be like a bird let out of a cage as soon as she's outside the gates. Don't let her fly away with you."

Said Patty: "I think I had better go first, before you mount, so as not to make a clatter."

She sailed out of the yard, holding the mare in check with one clenched hand and with the other patting the arching neck as she leaned over it; and as soon as she saw space to ride in she broke into a sweeping canter, then into a wild gallop, and was out of sight in two minutes.

Macdonald, who was lengthening a stirrup, jammed the leather into the buckle, and mounted hastily to ride after her.

"Redwing is too fresh," he shouted angrily; "she has not had exercise enough."

"She has, Sir," the old groom bawled in reply. "I've seen to it myself—twice a day regular. But no exercising'll keep her down. You needn't be afeared for the lady, Sir—she knows what she's about."

The great grey pounded out of the yard, and its rider started to race across the paddock, when he saw the chestnut mare returning to meet him, skimming the sunlit plain like a swallow and bearing Patty as lightly as a feather is borne on a high wind. The little woman was wildly happy, her eyes danced, her cheeks were like new-blown roses.

"I couldn't help it," she panted, laughing. "I had to let her out. Oh, she *is* delicious! May I jump her? *May* I? I know she must fly fences like a bird, and she *would* enjoy it so!"

"You would, you mean."

She turned the mare's head towards a rail fence four feet high, and Macdonald was afraid to speak lest he should flurry her, for he saw that she and Redwing were of a mind to do it. They did it to perfection, taking off at the right distance to an inch, sailing over as if on wings, and steadying to a joyous trot as soon as the flying hoofs touched turf again. Patty rode a little way, and, turning, jumped the fence again with the same ease and judgment as before; and then Macdonald called her to him, and they went for their ride.

And Mrs Clive, who knew so much, did not know a thing about horses.

They found her, on their return, sitting on the verandah with a book on her lap, looking as if she also had been up for hours; and her face said as plainly as face could speak, "Why did you not tell me you were going to do this?"

Patty ran up to her and kissed her and poured out her plausible excuses. "We didn't want you to be disturbed, darling. And Mr Macdonald thought you might be nervous if you saw me go off on a horse that danced on its hind legs. We thought we should have been back before you were up. I had been longing for a ride, but of course I wouldn't go at a time when we wanted to be all together."

"I am very glad, dearest—it will do you good," said Margaret, trying to smile. "But it would not have disturbed me if you had come in to speak to me before you went. I was not asleep. I heard you go."

"Oh, *did* you? If I'd only known— "

"Is that your habit, dear?"

"No, Patty blushed, looking at it. "He lent it to me."

"I suppose you arranged it all yesterday? Well, go and change, darling; it is later than I think you are aware of."

Patty ran off, reproaching herself for having broken the club rules, as she now perceived was the case; and Macdonald, who had turned aside from the foregoing dialogue, came up with a magnificent half-blown rose, which he presented to Mrs Clive.

"If I had known you were awake and going to get up, I should have been here to receive you," he said, taking a seat beside her. "I hoped you were having a good rest after your journey."

"Why?" she inquired, laying the rose on her lap without looking at it."What makes you think I want more rest than Patty?"

"Mrs Kinnaird," he dispassionately remarked, "seems as hardy as a little milkmaid, if you will forgive the comparison. You are made of more delicate material."

When Patty reappeared her friend put an arm round her and kissed her, and complimented her on the pretty colour her ride had given her; and at breakfast, while dipping strawberries into cream,

158

what time Patty devoured devilled chicken with the appetite of a schoolboy, she spoke of the four-in-hand project and insisted on its being carried out.

"No, indeed!" cried Patty. "I have done all I mean to do in that line for today. I should not have left you now if I had thought you were going to get up. I shall certainly not *think* of leaving you again."

"Not if I wish it?" urged Margaret. "I do wish you to, Patty—to please me."

"But the club meeting, dear?"

"There is plenty of time for both. You can drive after breakfast, if that suits Mr Macdonald, and we can have our meeting afterwards. I want to poke through the library—I want to find some passages in Mill that bear on our subject—and that will take a little time. Don't trouble about me; I shall be quite happy in the library until you come back." She seemed set on it, really regardless of whether it would be convenient to the host and his stable-yard or not.

Patty looked at him irresolutely. "What do you say?" she asked him.

"I say that whatever Mrs Clive orders is to be done," he answered.

Accordingly the four bays were put in after breakfast (ostensibly to take iron-work to the blacksmith), and Patty, perched on the box seat of the brake, took the heavy reins and the big thong in her little hands and set off in great glory and triumph through the paddocks once more, a groom at her back and her careful host beside her; and Margaret, having watched them drive away, sat down on the verandah and stayed there quite a long time—without a book.

"I will *not* be so small-minded," she said vehemently to herself. And yet her soul was on fire at the thought that they could leave her alone—leave her out—a second time, even though she had expressly desired them to do so.

They took care to be back in time for their club meeting before lunch. And Patty yawned and yawned behind hand and handkerchief, and Margaret, reading Mill, made abrupt stoppages to watch her.

"Oh, I *beg* your pardon," exclaimed the little woman, again and again. "It's the country air."

Margaret shut the book and suggested an adjournment of the meeting. It was impossible to do justice to Mill if you were sleepy, she said.

"Oh, no, do go on," prayed Patty eagerly. "I am attending really, and it is so awfully interesting. And this is the only day we shall be by ourselves to talk about it."

"Yes; that's why I think it was a pity to distract and tire yourself."

"But I am not really tired, Margaret. And I would not have gone for the drive if you had not made me. Do—do go on."

Margaret was persuaded to go on. She brought forth, in addition to her marked volumes, a batch of magazine and newspaper cuttings, containing various arguments in favour of the Woman's Suffrage movement, which she read aloud while Macdonald made notes at a table beside her. She had the whole subject at her finger ends, and the practical object of the discussion was to arrange the material produced in a systematic form for Mr Macdonald's use in the Legislative Assembly—when he should get there. She herself was passionately interested, overflowing with ideas and suggestions which she poured out in a molten state; but it was impossible, much as she desired it, to remain blind to the fact that not Patty only, but Mr Macdonald also, gave but slack attention to the great cause this morning. His slow eyes continually strayed towards the chief delinquent, marking each one of her surreptitious yawns; and when Mrs Clive, having declaimed a certain glowing paragraph that intoxicated her with enthusiasm, looked up for sympathy, she found her companions stealing secret glances at each other and laughing— *laughing* while the air about them palpitated with the cry of the oppressed! She saw in a moment that they had not heard a word of it.

"It is no use," she said, folding up her half-read paper with trembling hands. "You are neither of you able to settle down to serious work after all the amusement you have had."

"Suppose," said the host, "we put her to bed on a sequestered sofa and continue the meeting by ourselves? *I* am not tired."

"No; a club meeting is a club meeting. Never mind"— cheerfully. "Take her into the garden, and we'll see what we can do this afternoon."

She suddenly remembered a letter she wanted to write before the post bag was closed, and retired to her room.

She did write a letter, and this was it:

"My own love,

"I want you *particularly* to come by the morning train tomorrow, and not wait till the evening, as we proposed. You want all the good of the change that you can get, and I feel that I cannot do without you any longer. My dear Patty is a delightful companion, and Mr Macdonald is always interesting and as a kind host unrivalled, but there is no one like one's own, and I cannot enjoy even this beautiful place without you.. So, dearest one, don't fail to start early. This letter will go by the evening train,

160

and you will get it at breakfast time; and I will tell Mr Macdonald that you are to arrive at noon, and something will be at the station to meet you." There was more in the letter, but that was its purport.

As she wrote, she heard the sound of the piano in the hall, and presently a girlish voice that could only be Patty's singing a plaintive ballad of the day.

"Now he will make her sing—he will want to correct her faults and educate her," thought Margaret, with a new pang. For she knew that her host was "musical."

Too true. With Patty's songs, and one thing and another, the afternoon was frittered away, and tea time came and nothing was done. The meeting was put off till next morning.

Next morning Patty would not ride, though Margaret had insisted on it overnight, and both of them were designedly late for breakfast. At 10.30. precisely they assembled in the library.

Papers were produced and sorted. Note-books were spread out. The president was like a gun freshly charged, ready to go off with full effect when called upon. The demeanour of her companions was one of profound earnestness and concentrated attention. But there was something about that excessive zeal that rang hollow to the sensitive ear of Mrs Clive. It did not seem to her to have heart in it. The horrible suspicion that Mr Macdonald and Patty were assuming an ardour they did not feel in order to propitiate an exacting task-mistress—that they had even conspired together to indulge her, to keep her in good temper—grew and grew to certainty, until her dignity, her manners and her principles all gave way before it. While reading a fine passage from Mill, to which they were listening with punctilious respect and silent gravity, her voice suddenly broke, she flung the book on the table and burst into tears.

"You don't care about it one bit," she cried, angrily sweeping her handkerchief over her eyes. "It is not real to you as it is to me—you are only pretending. You are like the rest of the world, after all—both of you!"

She rushed away to her room, where she remained for half an hour, leaving the other members of the club to realise themselves as culprits and consequently to condole with one another; then, thoroughly ashamed of herself, she returned to beg their pardon. They told her not to mention it, and Macdonald explained that it was due to unstrung nerves.

"You are not well," he said. "I have seen it for some time. You are not up to the strain of these discussions. Wait till we get back to town, and while we are in the country just rest and recruit." etc.

Patty stood by, very red in the face, and said nothing. When at noon a double buggy and pair (no more four-in-hands) came round to take them to the station to meet Mr Clive, she was found to have no hat on. Interrogated, she said with an air of surprise that she had not thought of going.

"You will go," Margaret addressed her solemnly, "unless you *wish* to show resentment for an unfortunate quick word, Patty."

"Oh, my dear, I have no resentment *whatever*," Patty declared with a sort of cold cordiality, if there be such a thing. "I should like to go, of course, if you are sure I shall not be *de trop*."

"*De trop*, Patty!" Margaret's stare was tragic.

"Well, I seem to be looked upon as spoiling things somehow—I am sure I don't know why. You seem to get on better without me than with me." She went to fetch her hat.

"What is she talking of?" Mrs Clive appealed to her secretly amused host, and her hands trembled with indignation. "Is it really Patty who is capable of saying a thing so vulgar and childish as that?"

"Oh, well," he soothed her, "she *is* a child in a good many things. But she will outgrow it. We shall train her in time."

So they all went to the station to fetch Mr Clive. Mrs Clive sat with the driver going there, and of course with her husband coming back. She held his hand under the buggy rug, and as soon as she got him into the house, hardly allowing for the initial nip of whiskey which (in the early days) sacred custom prescribed, no matter what the hour of the day, she hustled him to her room, and there poured out endearments whose warmth and abundance surprised him.

"Well, this is very nice," he said, with a twinkle in his eye, as he returned her caresses with a sedate kiss. "I had a sort of an idea that you would be so well entertained that you wouldn't miss my company."

"How *could* you think so?"

"I was planning an outing with the kids when I got your letter. What is the matter, Maggie?"

"Did I say that anything was the matter? Of course not. I just felt homesick for you." And she kissed him again.

"I suppose your Patty has been flirting with Macdonald. Three was a bad number, Maggie. There should be four, at least."

"No. That was the very charm of it—that we *could* be three."

"Was?" he quizzed her.

"Is, I should say."

But the little man understood the situation perfectly, and was too good a little man to say, "I warned you against being too sanguine, and you would not listen to me."

After lunch, tennis and tea, Mrs Clive sought her club comrades secretly and suggested that they should enlarge their number.

"Three are too few," she said; "we can never do any really useful work until there are more of us. Suppose we try to bring more members in? And what do you say to asking Ray to join to begin with? You know how liberal he is."

Macdonald and Patty looked at her dubiously, and then at each other.

"That," said Macdonald, "would be making it *a* club instead of *the* club. And I don't think Clive would care about it a bit."

"I am quite sure he wouldn't," said Patty. "He's far too practical."

"Just as you like," said Margaret, turning away.

And that was the last time the club was spoken of between them. Certainly the ballot for Mr Clive's election was the last piece of business that it transacted. The last time it did anything in its corporate capacity was when it travelled back to Melbourne by the early train on Monday—even then Mr Clive was there, separating Patty from her fellows.

In Margaret's house Patty was as hospitably entertained as heretofore to all outward appearances, and to all outward appearances enjoyed it as she had always done. But it was a hollow pretence on both sides, and they could hardly disguise the fact. The frequent calls of Mr Macdonald—to find only one of them accessible at a time,— made the disguising more and more difficult. If Margaret chanced to be alone when he was announced Patty would not go to the drawing-room lest she should interrupt confidences; if Patty happened to see him first Margaret assumed herself *de trop* and left them together. Remonstrance on this new departure was neither made nor received in a kindly spirit, and silence concerning it was misunderstood. Rapidly the eternal friendship declined to enmity. The friends fretted to be rid of each other. Patty sent a surreptitious letter to Ted, who telegraphed a fake message next day, and came down the day after.

In the freedom of their bedroom at the C.P. she told him her tale, and he comforted her by calling Mrs Clive a "beast", a "she-devil", and such other bad names as he could think of, each more inappropriate than the last; and he summarily took the little lady home, telling her she would be as right as rain once she was "out of this", and had her bees and poultry to look after.

But, strange to say, Home, with all its endearing charms, did not cure her. After the first excitement of her return, she drooped. She was not well—it was evident, although she said she was; no specific ailment was discernible, she was just "not herself"—the old self—the self that had gone so joyously to Melbourne to see the opening of the Exhibition. The signs were unmistakeable: her bees and poultry relapsed into Mrs Murphy's care, the flowers were left to old Peter, Mary continued to flirt with Dan and Alec and generally to follow her own devices; Bret Harte neighed to his mistress in vain (too hot to ride), the dogs licked her feet and she hardly noticed them; her voice wavered into sobs when she tried to sing "Good-bye" and "Remember me no more."

"I shall get the doctor to you," said Teddy.

The threat startled her into action for a little while; she set to work to cook, and to strain honey, and to snip dead blossoms from the rose bushes. Then she drooped again, and lost interest in everything except the accounts of the Exhibition concerts in the daily papers. Then she was again roused by her husband telling her he had to go to Sydney to see his father, and asking her if she didn't think it would do her good to go with him.

"Oh, Sydney is unbearable in the height of summer," she said. "Take me as far as Melbourne and leave me there and call for me on your way back. The Exhibition will soon be over now—let me have another peep at it before it is quite gone."

"I should have thought you'd had enough of that," he growled.

"No, I haven't. I could never have enough of the music and pictures—never!"

"All right. If you want to go again, you shall."

Her lightest wish was law.

So he left her at the C.P., telling her he'd pick her up in a day or two, and she was to take care of herself, and not spare money if she wanted anything, and be sure to lie down for the rest of the day. She saw him off by the slow train, because he wanted to visit a friend on the line at a place the express passed in the middle of the night and then did not stop at, so that the rest of the day was a considerable slice of it; and when he was gone—not because he was gone, of course—she said to herself, "Now what shall I do?" with no intention of spending precious time and opportunity on a hotel sofa with a book.

What she did was to dress in her best and betake herself to the Exhibition, to see pictures and hear music and dine and spend the evening—not considering how she would like returning alone through the crowded city at night, nor what a difference there was between the independence of one and the independence of two (not to say three) in a public place.

She wandered up and down, and hither and thither, in the mighty labyrinth where she and Margaret had spent so many fruitful hours, and felt like a lost sheep in a wilderness, like a ghost haunting the scenes of its earthly joys; and she was ready to cry for

164

loneliness.

"Oh, for the dear club now!" she dumbly lamented; "for the days when we sat here together and talked of high things, and helped each other, and were so happy! Oh, how could—how *could* she do it?"

Margaret, it may be said, had ceased to go to the Exhibition at all. She could not bear the associations of the place—to be reminded at every turn of the cruelty with which her friend had treated her.

When dusk came on and the electric lights made a new day in the vast building, heated by twelve hours of sun on its zinc roofs to the temperature of an oven, Patty sought the Commissioners' room and ordered a modest dinner of cold fowl and tea. She glanced furtively at her neighbours, wondering whether by any chance the one old friend who, she was convinced, had remained true to her was there. He was not there. She looked from face to face as she absently ate and drank, and some returned her glance with unwelcome interest, and all were strange. Feeling lonelier than ever, she drifted out again into the noise of the whirring machinery, and, afraid of being taken for a person on the look-out for amatory adventures, hastened through the thronged avenues to the comparative retirement of the picture galleries. There she gazed pensively at the club's old favourites until it drew near concert time, when she took her seat in the gallery, temporarily relieved of her conspicuous solitude and satisfactorily accounted for. The music made her sad and fanciful, and she left the hall before it was all over in fear of tram crowds, and went to bed exhausted and depressed, with a keen sense of disappointment that she did not dare to analyse.

Next morning she went out on her balcony with a parasol and gazed for hours at the bit of Collins Street down which a man would walk or drive who came from the Melbourne Club to see her—and did not come; then she set forth again to lunch and loaf at the Exhibition, which was the place for meeting people; but still she did not happen upon the desired person, who naturally avoided the hottest place that could be found on a hot day; and she returned draggled and dispirited, to fight with mosquitoes through another breathless and weary night.

On the third day it happened—a cool, grey, south-wind morning, with an ideal light for the pictures. She was drifting into the British Loan room to have another look at the Phryne when she met him drifting out. Her heart gave a great jump.. At last—at last she would have "somebody to speak to"—someone to take care of her till Teddy came back. She made a little involuntary spring towards him, her expressive face alight with pleasure; then violently checked herself, for she perceived that he was not alone. Two ladies walked beside him, one on either side; an imposing middle-aged woman and a slim fair-haired girl, both well-dressed and carrying themselves like important people. The girl was extremely pretty, but it was not her beauty that Patty minded; she knew full well that, in spite of her own wide mouth and aspiring nose, she could hold her own quite comfortably against rivalry of that kind; it was the look of youth that staggered her. Eighteen or nineteen, with a skin like a rose-petal, with those budding contours and that willowy flexibility—all the attributes of well-bred girlhood—it was this pre-eminent charm which nothing can compensate for which smote Patty to the heart and destroyed her self-conceit for ever. Not that she hadn't seen plenty of young and pretty girls before. It was seeing one of them in *his* company which made her realise for the first time that she was thirty-five.

He gave her a friendly look as he passed and lifted his hat; she returned his salutation with a scarlet face and a stiff inclination of the head. And that was all.

Half an hour before concert time she went up to the gallery and took her seat in order to have a good place from which she could view the ground-floor audience as it came in. "He is sure to come to the concert," she thought, "and those people are not the sort who sit in the gallery; they will take chairs in the middle of the hall, and I shall see them, and they won't see me."

Thus it fell out. She sat in front of the gallery, in the corner nearest the orchestra, and Mr Macdonald brought his party to the place she had appointed for them. The girl was dressed in white, with a soft white hat and a sash of palest blue—a picture of girlish elegance; there was no denying the fact. And she seemed on the best of terms with her escort. She whispered in his ear, and laughed at things he whispered back, and whispered to him again, until Patty grew wild with irritation at the sight.

"I don't call that manners," she said to herself, and thought what a contrast was this giggling creature to the refined and stately Margaret. "Nothing but a child, either; a mere bread-and-butter miss. I am sure he is not the man to care for a bread-and-butter miss."

The orchestra came up out of the floor, and took its several seats, and tinkled its instruments into tune. Cowen appeared, was greeted in the usual way, bowed his acknowledgements, presented his well-tailored back to the public eye; and at that moment of suspense between the rattle of the baton on the desk and its first slow sweep through the air two men came along the gallery and dropped into two seats at Patty's side. She threw a casual glance at them and recognised their faces, which after a few seconds' thought she identified as belonging to the men in the theatre who stared her out of countenance on the memorable night when the club went second-class to see *The Magistrate*. In much the same attitude they leaned their arms on the edge of the balcony and surveyed the present audience below, and between the numbers "passed remarks" on what they saw as they had done on the former occasion. But they did not notice her now; they talked aloud and freely, as if they were alone.

"There's Seaton Macdonald and his new fiancée," said one. "This must be their first public appearance, for the engagement was only announced last night. Well, I wonder how *she's* going to stand his promiscuous philanderings."

"Not promiscuous," said the other. "Various, perhaps, but always in good taste. And she's a child, this one—easier to manage than number one."

"That remains to be proved," his companion chuckled. "There's a considerable amount of mother-in-law to reckon with this time. Number One had only her own fists to fight with—poor girl!"

Then they talked about the Land Boom and the Banks.

On the following day Ted returned from Sydney. Of course Patty was at Spencer Street to meet him—he expected her to be there; but what he did not expect was to be received in literally open arms on the crowded platform and kissed in the sight of all men. It did not square with the parting of last week. Not that he objected to the proceeding—far from it—but it surprised him. So did her words of greeting.

"Darling, darling"—and she didn't seem to mind who heard her—"how *thankful* I am to get you back! Next time you go away, dearest, you must take me with you."

"I'm always ready to take you with me, whenever you want to go," he answered, laying his brown paw over her interlaced fingers. "I'd have taken you now, only you know you said Sydney would be too hot. Been dull without your old man, eh?"

"Dulness is no word for it."

"No old friends turned up to look after you?"

"No. I have no friends—at least I don't want any. I only want you."

Although he was not a very penetrating person, he did wonder a little what had happened in his absence to make her so much nicer to him now than she was when he left her, and it was not long before he was able to make a fairly correct guess.

He had had something to eat, washed and changed, and they had gone to their own room that he might rest a little after his night in the train. He lit his pipe and took his wife on his knee, and they sat for some time in contented silence; then he said—stroking the head on his breast with clumsy tenderness:

"And so you are glad to get your poor old husband back again, are you? I used to think—I had a sort of an idea—it just came into my head once or twice—that what's-his-name was going to cut me out."

She clung to him, pressing her face into his waistcoat, and trembled all over as if about to cry.

"No, no, I don't mean it seriously—it's only my fun. *I'm* not afraid. Only he's such an awfully clever, fascinating sort of chap, you know, while I'm only—"

"While you," she burst in, "are the dearest, the truest, the faithfullest, the darlingest—"

This time she did cry outright, sobbing hysterically, while he patted her shoulder to soothe her.

"There, there, there! I'm nothing but a stupid donkey—not half good enough for you. But I do right down love you, my old girl—I'll defy any man to beat me in that." And not another word would he allow on the delicate, half-hinted subject, which was never spoken of between them again.

Afternoon tea was brought up to them; after which he tucked her up on the bed, with a smelling bottle for her headache, and bade her try to get a nap while he did some necessary business; and then he went forth jubilantly to telegraph to Wandara, and heard the news of Macdonald's engagement in the street. Immediately Mr Kinnaird proceeded to the club, found the happy man, and congratulated him again and yet again, with many hearty handshakes.

"This will be good news to my little wife," he said blusteringly. "Only the other day she was saying how much she would like to see you married."

He told his simple fib without winking, and imagined it a fine stroke of diplomacy.

"Remember me to her," drawled the bridegroom elect. "I will write myself to tell her all about it."

"Oh, don't trouble—I'll tell her. You'll have no time for writing now—take all your time to attend to your sweetheart. We're just off home for a Darby and Joan summer—no place like home in the hot months. We don't have mosquitoes of a night up our way."

He went back to Patty and did *not* tell her that Macdonald was "hooked at last"—which was his remark to all other people with whom he conversed that afternoon—because he knew quite well that she was aware of the circumstance. He asked her whether she wanted him to order any stores to take up to the station; and she exclaimed, "O, by the bye—yes, of course!" and sat down to make a list of groceries and what not, as if her whole soul was wrapped up in such matters. Next morning they went home once more—and once for all this time. For the very next thing that happened to Patty was a baby.

Appendix II Bibliographical Note

Bibliographical Note

Although many of Ada Cambridge's works are listed in E. Morris Miller's *Australian Literature: a Bibliography to 1938. Extended to 1950* (edited by Frederick T. Macartney A & R 1956), so many more have since been discovered—essays, poems short fiction and complete novels published in newspapers—that a different sense of her *oeuvre* is emerging.

Macartney's entry for Ada Cambridge (pp 95-9) lists eighteen novels, one collection of short stories, and three volumes of poetry which were published individually in book form. It also notes her two volumes of autobiography, four early 'devotional' works published before the author came to Australia, six novels serialised in the *Australasian*, two contributions to colonial anthologies, and her collaboration on the text of the *Picturesque Atlas of Australasia.*

Penny Smith's thesis 'Voyaging Strange Seas of Thought Alone' (BA Hons; U of Queensland English Dept 1977) includes references to articles in the *Atlantic Monthly*, *Lyceum Annual* and *North American Review.* Raymond Beilby and Cecil Hadgraft in *Ada Cambridge, Tasma and Rosa Praed* (Oxford UP 1979) list another early work: *Little Jenny.* The present editor's 'Newspaper Publication of Novels of Ada Cambridge' in *Australian Literary Studies* (Vol 12 1986 pp 530-1) describes an additional six newspaper serials, four of them 'new' works: for these and fiction discovered since, see table overleaf. Patricia Barton's thesis 'Second Thoughts: The Poetry of Ada Cambridge' (Masters Qualifying; University College Australian Defence Force Academy English Dept 1986) notes several poems published in periodicals and anthologies, additional articles in *Atlantic Monthly* and *Review of Reviews*, and Cambridge's contribution to the *Illustrated Guide to Beechworth and Vicinity.*

The published writings identified to date are readily grouped into four chronological periods:

1 1865-1869 Mostly 'Devotional' Works

The author, in her early twenties and not yet married, lived in Norfolk and Cambridgeshire. Her known publications are two volumes of hymns (one of which, *Hymns on the Holy Communion*, was also published in New York in 1866 by Randolph and Co, a firm specialising in publishing collections of hymns and religious verse), three short (less than 50 pp) moral 'tales', and a secular and passionate poem 'The False Love' in *Once a Week* (Vol 17 19 October 1867 pp 475-7).

2 1871-1889/91 Mostly Novels in Newspapers

Ada Cambridge lived in Victorian country towns. She submitted her fiction for first publication in newspapers or magazines. One novel only was serialised in England; it and two other serials were published in book form during the period. *My Guardian* and *A Mere Chance* were also published at the same time in the U. S. (the former being re-issued there from time to time until the late 1890s). Aside from the fiction, long and short, which is listed in the accompanying table, Cambridge wrote poems for newspapers, the first appearing in the *Sydney Mail* on 18 February 1871, and brought out the collections *The Manor House and Other Poems* (Daldy Isbister London 1875) and *Unspoken Thoughts* (Kegan Paul London 1887). She contributed poems to various periodicals and newspapers and to *The Australian Ladies Annual* (McCarron Bird Melbourne 1878), and descriptive prose to the *Picturesque Atlas of Australasia* (Melbourne 1886 [ie 1888]). Though Cambridge lived remote from Melbourne, she turned to the metropolitan and not the country newspaper press to publish her poetry and fiction. In 1890, however, she began her successful connection with London publishers and after 1891 ceased writing novels for local newspapers.

ADA CAMBRIDGE'S FICTION PUBLISHED 1872—1891

Date	No. of Instalments	Title	Publisher	Comment
31.8.72	1	Bachelor Troubles	Australasian ⎞	Sketches, Loosely
15.2.73	1	The History of Six Hours	Australasian ⎬	linked episodes
28.6.73	1	At Sea	Australasian ⎠	(same characters)
27.3.75—17.7.75	9	Up The Murray	Australasian	Novel
12.76— 6.77	7	My Guardian	Cassell's Family Magazine	Novel. As book Cassell 1878
4.1.79—5.4.79	14	In Two Years' Time	Australasian	Novel. As book Bentley 1879
26.7.79—6.9.79	7	The Captain's Charge	Sydney Mail	Novel
6.12.79—14.2.80	11	Dinah	Australasian	Novel
10.7.80—20.11.80	20	A Mere Chance	Australasian	Novel. As book Bentley 1882
8.10.81—4.3.82	20	Missed In The Crowd	Australasian	Novel
10.12.81—14.1.82	11	A Girl's Ideal	Age	Novel
7.10.82—23.12.82	12	Across the Grain	Australasian	Novel
23.6.83—15.12.83	26	The Three Miss Kings	Australasian	Novel. As book Heinemann 1891
8.3.84—15.3.84	2	Mrs Carlisle's Enemy	Australasian	Short tale
3.5.84—17.5.84	3	A Successful Experiment	Australasian	Short tale
15.11.84—21.2.85	15	Mrs Carnegie's Husband	Australasian	Novel. Rewritten as A Marriage Ceremony Heinemann 1894

Date	No.	Title	Publication	Notes
20.12.84—3.1.85	3	A Honeymoon Adventure	Sydney Mail	Short tale. Rewritten as 'At Midnight' (title story in collection *At Midnight* published by Ward, Lock 1897
27.12.84	1	Under Favourable Circumstances	Australasian	Sketch
17.10.85—5.12.85	8	A Little Minx	Sydney Mail	Novel. As book, Heinemann 1893
28.11.85—23.1.86	8	Against The Rules	Australasian	Novel
3.86	1	The Story Of A Summer	Australian Journal	Sketch
12.87	1	The Perversity Of Human Nature	Illustrated Australian News	Novel-length 'Christmas story',
7.7.88—5.1.89	26	A Black Sheep	Age	Novel. As book *A Marked Man* Heinemann 1890
8.88	1	By The Night Express	Centennial Magazine	Sketch
12.88	1	A Face At The Window	Australian Journal	Sketch
8.89	1	The Unseen Foe	Centennial Magazine	Short tale. Slightly altered part of 'A Little Minx'
31.8.89—26.10.89	9	A Woman's Friendship	Age	Novel. Rewritten as short story 'The Reform Club', first published in the present edition
6.12.90—18.4.91	19	Not All In Vain	Australasian	Novel. As book Heinemann 1892
19.12.91	1	The Charm That Works	Australasian	Novel-length 'Christmas story'. Revised and expanded as *A Humble Enterprise* Ward, Lock 1896

3 1890-1907 Mostly Novels Published Overseas

The author lived in Melbourne from 1893. In this period, fifteen of her novels (some previously serialised), a collection of short stories (*At Midnight* 1897) and her first volume of autobiography (*Thirty Years in Australia* 1903) were published in London. American editions of most titles appeared soon after British release; some works were also published in Australia. For direct Australian publication Cambridge contributed descriptive prose to an *Illustrated Guide to Beechworth* (1892), a short story to the anthology *Childhood in Bird and Blossom: A Souvenir Book of the Children's Hospital Bazaar* (1900), and an article on Ethel Turner for the *Review of Reviews* (20 October 1895 pp 364-7).

4 1909-1924 Miscellany

Cambridge's visit to England in 1908, aged sixty-three, marked the end of concentrated novel-writing and publication. Cambridge went to England again in 1912 on her husband's retirement and then returned to Australia in 1917 after his death. During the final stage of her literary career she produced a second volume of autobiography (*The Retrospect* 1912), a third volume of poetry (*The Hand in the Dark* 1913) her twenty-eighth novel (*The Making of Rachel Rowe* 1914) and numerous literary and reflective essays which appeared in American and English periodicals. Her only known unpublished writings belong to this last period: autobiographical fragments, a playscript and several short stories, including the collection 'The Good Old Times' (which contains the short story 'The Reform Club', based on 'A Woman's Friendship').

From time to time since Ada Cambridge's death her poems have been republished in anthologies of Australian verse; and a new edition of *Unspoken Thoughts* is being prepared by Patricia Barton—to be published by the English Department, University College, Australian Defence Force Academy, Canberra. The author's prose works remained out of print until 1987. At time of writing, the following have been republished:

> *The Three Miss Kings*. Introduction by Audrey Tate Virago London 1987

> *A Marked Man: Some Episodes in His Life*. Introduction by Debra Adelaide Pandora London 1987

'A Sweet Day' in *From the Verandah: Stories of Love and Landscape by Nineteenth Century Australian Women* ed Fiona Giles. McPhee Gribble / Penguin Fitzroy Vic 1987 pp 91-104. First published in *At Midnight and Other Stories* Ward Lock London 1897 pp 253-77.

'The Wind of Destiny' in *Happy Endings: Stories by Australian and New Zealand Women, 1850s-1930s* eds Elizabeth Webby and Lydia Wevers. Allen & Unwin North Sydney NSW 1987 pp 68-91. First published in *Windsor Magazine* Vol IV, July-Nov 1896 pp 49-57; collected in *At Midnight and Other Stories* pp 281-305.

A complete bibliography of the works of Ada Cambridge is being compiled by Elaine Zinkhan and will be published by the Victorian Fiction Research Unit at the University of Queensland.

List of Editor's Emendations

Emended readings, cited by page and line number, appear to the left of the square bracket. The reading in the copy-text appears to the right, with the swung dash indicating a repeated word.

A Woman's Friendship

9:12 Library;] ~:
9:15 rendezvous] ~,
10:3 Cook's] Cooke's
11:22 that she] tha tshe
12:11 dissatisfaction] dissatifaction
12:23 didn't] did'nt
13:10 makes] maks
16:28 mustn't] musn't
17:5 Would] "~
22:33 go."] ~.
26:2 sooner."] ~.
26:10 always] alway
28:16 overmantel] over-/mantel
28:39 hers] her's
30:6 winter.] ~
30:15 suited."] ~.
39:9 Morison] Mor-/rison
40:35 don't] don t
40:39 of—of] ~ ~
45:32 the] th
48:39 timekeeper] time-/keeper
53:6 promptly.] ~
57:2 won't] wont
58:45 won't] won t
60:5 won't] wont
65:29 wide-awake] wide-/awake

66:9 'yes] ~
66:39 "As] '~
70:1 *portières] portiéres*
70:9 "Who] ~
70:11 till] tiil
71:21 won't] wont
71:30 Isn't] Is'nt
73:2 Kinnaird] Kinnard
77:20 gravely, "that] ~," ~
77:30 rapturously, "to] ~," ~
79:24 innkeeper] inn-/keeper
80:16 No,] ~.
83:30 *"I]* ~
83:36 "I] ~
89:19 "but] ~
89:21 you," he] ~, "~
94:40 say."] ~.
95:11 "He's] ~
95:13 "Very] ~
98:8 club] cl ub
104:27 "It] ~
105:22 now she's] now's she
106:14 "if] "~
107:26 KINNAIRD."] ~'
108:23 doesn't] dosen't

176

143:3   people] prople
143:11 Seaton] Seton
145:7   Kinnaird] Clive
145:20 embarrassed] embarassed
145:38 *Don't*] ~,
146:22 gazing] gazingly
146:28 She] "~
147:15 development] developmrnt
147:24 those] rhose
147:44 Cook's] Cooks'
149:15 before] bwfore
150:5   Clive] Clice
150:38 you may] youmay
151:33 before] brfore
153:12 In] in
153:14 second] srcond
153:21 delicious!"] ~!
153:36 Macdonald] macdonald

153:42 fetlock",] ~",,
154:23 pink-and-white] pink and-white
154:32 under-robe] under-/-robe
155:1   Clive] clive
155:12 Patty's] patty's
155:18 Margaret] Magaret
155:31 Margaret's] Magaret's
160:3   Margaret] Magaret
160:20 enthusiasm] enthusiam
162:2   Clive] clive
162:18 well,"] ~," "
162:25 day,] ~
163:5   work] wor
163:12 wouldn't,"] ~,
163:44 discernible] discernable
167:9   philanderings."] ~"
167:45 you? I] ~" "~
168:42 wrapped] wrapprd

In this edition words hyphenated at the end of a line also occur in a hyphenated form in the copy-texts. In each case the hyphen should be retained in quotation.